P9-CDG-790

JONATHAN SWIFT

A Tale of a Tub.

and other satires

Edited with an *Introduction* by

KATHLEEN WILLIAMS

Formerly Professor of English,
University of California, Riverside

London
J. M. Dent & Sons Ltd
New York
E. P. Dutton & Co. Inc.

Printed in Great Britain
by
Biddles Ltd Guildford Surrey
and bound at the
Aldine Press Letchworth Herts
for
J. M. DENT & SONS LTD
Aldine House Albemarle Street London

First published by J. M. Dent in 1909
under the title *A Tale of a Tub, The Battle of the Books and Other Satires.*
New edition, with revised contents, 1975

Published in the U.S.A. by arrangement
with J. M. Dent & Sons Ltd

This book is set in 11 point Garamond roman 156

No. 347 Hardback ISBN 0 460 10347 4
No. 1347 Paperback ISBN 0 460 11347 X

The CONTENTS.

The NOTE ON THE TEXT.

THE text of this edition is reproduced, with the permission of Basil Blackwell and Mott Ltd, Oxford, from the Shakespeare Head Press edition of THE PROSE WORKS OF JONATHAN SWIFT, vols. 1, 2, 4 and 12, edited by Herbert Davis, 1939.

The present editor's notes are printed together at the end of the book, while Swift's own notes from whatever source accompany the text.

The PUBLISHER'S NOTE.

WE should like to thank Clive Probyn, of the Department of English Literature at the University of Lancaster, for providing at short notice a section for the introduction, together with notes, on the *Argument against Abolishing Christianity*. Shortly before Kathleen Williams's death early in 1975, it had been agreed with her that this important work should be included in her selection.

The INTRODUCTION.

JONATHAN SWIFT was born in 1667, in Dublin, but of an English family and one which had traditional ties with the Anglican church. His grandfather, the Vicar of Goodrich in Hereford, was a faithful supporter of Charles I, and devoted his entire fortune to the royalist cause, with the result that his sons had their own way to make. Jonathan's father, the fifth son, and his elder brother Godwin entered the legal profession and went to Ireland, where the elder Jonathan died very young, leaving a wife, a small girl, and a posthumous son, later to become the great Dean. In these difficult circumstances, Swift was educated—at Kilkenny Grammar School and Trinity College—through the help of his uncles; and he then, apparently through further family connections, became secretary to the distinguished former statesman and man of letters Sir William Temple, first at Sheen and then in his house Moor Park, in Surrey. Swift remained with Temple for ten years, except for a period of absence, from 1689. Temple had considerable experience of the world, of politics, and of government, and had rendered good service to his friend William III, but he had left the court to devote himself to the pleasures of an elegant and cultivated retirement. Swift must have learned much, through Temple's familiarity with the places of power, that stood him in good stead when he came himself to enter the complicated politics of the period. But he learned much more still, for he had the resources of Temple's large library available to him, and he read avidly, for hours each day. The result is visible most clearly in the copious learning of *A Tale of a Tub*, but it is there too in the richness and flexibility of his admirable prose style. For other reasons too his time with Temple was important for his future; it was at Moor Park that he contracted Ménière's disease, the alarming and disabling complaint from which he was to suffer recurrently, and with increasing severity, for the rest of his days. More happily, it was here that he met Esther Johnson, the fatherless daughter of Sir William's housekeeper, and a child of eight when Swift joined the household. As Stella, Esther was to grow into the great friend and companion and in some sense (though we do not know in quite what sense) the love of his life.

TEMPLE and Swift appear to have regarded each other with affection and respect, but there are visible also the strains that were almost inevitable given the differences in position and in years. As time went on Swift, very naturally, wanted to be doing something more independent than to live as one of a great man's household, however much he was valued; and equally naturally Temple was reluctant to lose so talented and lively a young secretary. There were difficulties, it seems; and Swift broke away in 1694 when he took orders and in 1695 was presented to the Prebend of Kilroot in the Diocese of Down and Connor. But the following year he returned, though without giving up his Kilroot preferment, at the request of Temple, until the latter's death in 1699. Swift then returned to Ireland as domestic chaplain to the newly appointed Lord Justice, the Earl of Berkeley, and received a cathedral stall in St Patrick's, Dublin—where he was later to become Dean—and the living of Laracor. In 1701 Berkeley was recalled, and Swift returned with him to England; in the same year he published his first political tract, *A Discourse of the Contests and Dissensions between the Nobles and the Commons in Athens and Rome*. Thus by 1701 his life was taking shape. The year sees the real beginnings of his long and complicated relationships of love and anger with both Ireland and England, the comings and goings of the following years, the anxiety to get a permanent settlement in England, the failure to do so, the departure for his exile in Ireland, and the eventual development of his career as one of the greatest in the tradition of great Irish patriots. At the same time, by 1701 he had entered that political world which exercised a continuing fascination over his mind and his feelings until he was too old and ill to respond to it longer.

THE *Contests and Dissensions* is a polished, urbane, and intelligent pamphlet which brought Swift to the attention of the Whig leaders in England, among them Lord Somers, to whom

A Tale of a Tub was later dedicated. At the same time, as a canon of St Patrick's, Swift was coming to be seen as a rising clergyman, and, when the Whigs came to power in 1707, the dignitaries of the Irish Church saw him as the obvious person to be sent to England to petition Queen Anne for remission of the First Fruits, a tax on the Irish clergy. He did not succeed with the Whigs, for Lord Treasurer Godolphin hoped to use the First Fruits as a bargaining point, and to persuade the Irish clergy, in exchange for the remission, to support the removal of the Test Act. This Act, a source of constant manœuvring and acrimony in the politics of the time, was a result of the politico/religious events of the seventeenth century; at the Restoration neither church nor state had forgotten that for years England had been a commonwealth governed by dissenters, and that not only Kings but prelates had been ousted. The Test Act was designed to prevent such a thing happening again by excluding from public office all but Anglican communicants. This effectively limited the exercise of power by either dissenters or Catholics, and the church fought hard to maintain it. They were supported by the Tories, a party traditionally 'for church and King', while the Whigs, who courted the dissenters, were opposed to the Test. Hence Godolphin's manœuvre.

Swift, perhaps, would have had no power to accept Godolphin's terms on behalf of the church, even if he had wished to do so. But however this may be, he deserves all credit for the integrity which remained an outstanding characteristic of his private life. He made no attempt to get agreement from his bishops, although he would certainly have been rewarded by the Whigs, if he could have brought about such an agreement, with a preferment which would have substantially altered his prospects. But the grandson of the gallant Vicar of Goodrich, and the vicar himself of poor Irish parishes where his flock was outnumbered by the dissenting population, was not likely to view with equanimity the repeal of an act which in the opinion of his church prevented the dangers of a new Commonwealth. Swift always believed that the repeal of the Test would go far to destroy his church, and his loyalty to that church never wavered, then or later. He even further destroyed his prospects by writing, at this time, pamphlets expressing opposition to Whig policy from an Anglican point of view. Yet Swift got his remission of the First Fruits after all, through the fall of the Whigs and the accession to power of moderate Tories under Robert Harley, later the first Earl of Oxford. Harley put through the remission in a fortnight, without any bargaining; but he counted on gratitude, and on gaining Swift's now clearly powerful pen for the new government. Swift was indeed grateful, and rightly pleased with his own success. It was done, he wrote to Stella, 'by my personal credit with Mr Harley', though the Irish bishops chose not to recognize his efforts and his achievement.

MUCH that was to prove typical of Swift's career is apparent, then, by 1710, the year of the remission. The implacable hostility to dissent and to the Whigs who supported it; the political stance centred on loyalty to the church; the integrity; and the refusal of those for whom he worked so brilliantly and so passionately, the church and the Tories, to recognize his services or to give him practical demonstration of their recognition. But now for three years he had his period of achievement, exhilaration, masterly ease in the exercise of his powers. Harley made him editor of a new Tory journal *The Examiner*, and he wrote other pamphlets of remarkable brilliance and lasting worth. While some were purely political, the degree to which the churches were then inseparable from politics is shown in the fine and subtle tract *An Argument against Abolishing Christianity* (1711), which in its concern for a strong church of England necessarily deals by implication with the Test Act and the movement for its repeal. In these years Swift became a dominant member of the literary society of London. He had been, and wished to remain, a friend and true admirer of Addison and a benevolent friend of Richard Steele, both Whigs and both, after the manner of eighteenth-century writers, highly political animals. But Addison and Steele, with their friends out of power, were cooling, and Swift became closely associated with others certainly no less brilliant whose loyalty was to the Tories—Pope of course, Gay, Prior, Congreve, and perhaps closest of all Queen Anne's physician, the honest and humane John Arbuthnot. In the enchanting *Journal to Stella*, we can see from day to day how Swift blossomed in this air, delighting in the power of his pen and his personal authority, in the intellectual brilliance of his work, in the sense that he was at the heart of great things and helping to bring them about; in friendship with men whose minds and hearts, he thought, responded to his own. It was a full and vivid life which he never forgot, always looked back to. In a way, his whole life after that could only be exile.

IT did not last. The mutual jealousy of the Tory leaders Oxford and Bolingbroke broke their precarious hold on the government by 1713, although things crawled on until the following year, when the ministry fell and Queen Anne died. The Whigs took over for an extended period of power, Oxford was imprisoned, Bolingbroke fled to the Stuart pretender in France, and Swift was under suspicion. He had managed, with much effort, and delay from the dilatory Oxford, to gain himself a refuge, the Deanery of St Patrick's; but it was by no means commensurate with his services, and more, it meant exile from the friends, the places, the intellectual and literary connections, the whole way of living that he treasured. Swift faced the loss of all his hopes, for the church, the country, his friends, himself, with spirit and dignity. Threatened by the hatred of the now all-powerful Whigs, greeted on his return to Ireland with utter hostility, he settled down to manage the affairs of his cathedral and to look after his people in Dublin. But it was not until 1718 that he was able to recover his interest in public affairs, and to turn to 'the wretched condition of Ireland'.

IRELAND was indeed wretched, exploited as a colony by England and betrayed by the self-interest and the sycophancy of many of its own citizens, and when Swift did turn to the unhappy country he now had to regard as his home for the rest of his life he found a scene which could exercise his powers at a deeper level than his political life in England could do. Here his fierce indignation (the *Saeva Indignatio* of his own epitaph for himself) at injustice and thoughtless cruelty was deeply stirred, to issue in that greatest of all short satires, *A Modest Proposal*, and in other ways in *Gulliver's Travels* and *The Drapier's Letters*. Most moving is the savage, angry pity of works such as these. Swift was a man of the church; and his pastoral position as Dean, which he took very seriously, would have involved him in concern for the distress of the people of Dublin and of the country around it, even if he had not been a man of practical kindness and charity. He gave widely from his own resources to the poor of his deanery and set up schemes of help for them. To fight the vested interests which had reduced them to this plight was only the other side of the same coin. Thus Swift became over the years the Great Dean, the Hibernian Patriot, the Drapier, the trusted champion whom the authorities dared not attack, in Louis Landa's words 'an embodiment of the voice and conscience of Ireland'. The first of the Irish tracts, *A Proposal for the Universal Use of Irish Manufacture* (1720), is typically practical; it not only attacked the tyranny of England but attempted to persuade the Irish themselves to make common cause for their own sakes, to refuse English goods and to rely only on what Ireland could produce. The same practical urgency, the same attention to how things may be remedied as well as to mere declamation against the oppressor, characterize *The Drapier's Letters* of 1724, which was as great a practical success as the influential *Conduct of the Allies* (1711) had been during Swift's period of political activity in England. The *Conduct* helped to turn public opinion against the long war of the Spanish Succession, thus enabling the Tories to put through the peace. The *Letters* so united the people of Ireland, however temporarily, behind the simple but compelling drapier whom all recognized as that formidable dignitary, the Dean of St Patrick's, that the English government was compelled to withdraw the grant made to William Wood (apparently as the result of a bribe to one of the King's mistresses) for the coining of copper coins in Ireland. The grant was infamous in Ireland not only because of its blatantly disreputable nature but because the autonomy of Ireland and the authority of the Irish Parliament had been ignored in order that certain financially powerful persons in England should add to their fortunes in complete disregard of the welfare of a whole country.

DURING these years of exciting and successful action through the power of his pen and the authority of his personal integrity, Swift was also completing his masterpiece (though *A Tale of a Tub* can challenge it) *Gulliver's Travels.* He visited England in 1726 to arrange for its publication and, what to him was at least as important, to see the dear friends who had contributed to the satisfaction of his years in London, Pope, Gay, Arbuthnot the chief among them. In 1727 he made the journey again, for the last time. No account of Swift's life and work should omit his long correspondence with his friends. In their courage and affection, their frankness and trust, their wit and tenderness, they are among the most moving documents to come down to us from that age of great friendships. Particularly touching are those in which he fears, or hears of, the deaths of those he loved: Stella, who after repeated illness died in 1728, John Gay, John Arbuthnot.

THE deaths of these deeply loved friends saddened Swift's later years, as did the defeat of his hopes of improvement in England and Ireland. His success in the *Drapier's Letters* had not held the Irish together, and so had not discouraged English misgovernment, in any permanent way, and the *Modest Proposal* of 1729 is constructed, in part, from his despair that his long years of brave and passionate effort had done so little to inspire men with his own moral courage and his own humanity. It is the last of his many proposals, his last effort to shape his own concern and urgency into a work which could at least show the Irish what their feckless policies of individual, short-term self-interest were leading to for their fellows and ultimately themselves, and could perhaps even shock the faraway English government into seeing the moral and physical horrors which their economic policies did, in terms of real men, women, and children, produce. During the later part of his life Swift went on writing, and some of the finest of his poems (and he is still underrated as a poet) belong to these years. But he grew old, and his long and chronic illness intensified and he was more and more alone, surviving most of those he loved, no longer able to travel to those yet living in England. He did not lack friends or admirers in Ireland, but they were not the men of art and wisdom with whom the great days of his triumphant youth had been passed; and Stella was gone. He was forced to take refuge in the writing of 'la bagatelle', punning poems exchanged with the friends he had in Ireland. And at the very last, even this would no longer serve. He was overtaken by senility and by illness which must often have been agonizing, and in 1742—he was by then, we must remember, seventy-five—he was declared of unsound mind. In October 1745 he died.

THE works of Swift which are brought together in this volume were written at different times in his life, from *A Tale of a Tub* (published in 1710 but finished probably by 1702) to the *Modest Proposal* of 1729. This selection excludes *Gulliver's Travels* (1726), but includes a number of works reprinted less frequently; for example, *A Meditation upon a Broomstick* (which dates at the latest to 1704, probably to a couple of years earlier) and Swift's *Vindication* of Gay's *The Beggar's Opera* (1728). Moreover, the volume provides a representative selection which indicates something of the wide range of Swift's satiric invention and satiric tone, from the teasing humour of the *Tritical Essay*, through the brilliant parodic wit of *A Tale of a Tub*, to the business-like calm of manner which makes the moral outrage and the pity of *A Modest Proposal* so profoundly effective.

THE first of our works to be published was *A Tale of a Tub*, which appeared, along with *The Battle of the Books* and *The Mechanical Operation of the Spirit*, in 1704, although certain materials were added in later editions. Before the *Tale* appeared, Swift had published several poems, and according to his own account in the *Apology* for the *Tale*, which was added to the work for the 5th edition (1710), he had already 'finished the greatest part' of the *Tale* by 1696. It would seem, then, that it was during his time at Kilroot that he conceived the plan of this remarkable work, a work which disputes with *Gulliver's Travels* the title of the greatest satire of our greatest prose satirist.

Swift's parish was poor, and his congregation scanty, for Kilroot was in an area where dissent was strong; and it is not unlikely that this first pastoral experience increased his dislike of dissent and his sense of its potential power, and produced the conditions in which the satire on the 'numerous gross corruptions' in religion took shape in his mind. The *Tale* does present the corruptions in 'religion', that is in all the churches, but it is dissent that bears the brunt of the satire, and the Church of England is seen as at least the best of what there is to choose among. It is thought unlikely that the digressions, which form an integral part of the completed *Tale*, and satirize the parallel abuses and corruptions in learning, were begun so early, and they probably date from 1697. In the meantime, Swift left Kilroot in May 1696 and returned to his work for Temple, who was now finding *his* learning challenged by William Wotton and the classical scholar Richard Bentley. This was the occasion for the writing of *The Battle of the Books*, in which Swift came to the support of true, humane, literary learning, which he found exemplified in Temple, against what to him as to Temple was the pedantry and rudeness of the attackers. The book was begun in 1697, and completed probably after the appearance, also in Temple's support, of the Hon. Charles Boyle's *Examination* of Bentley's *Dissertation on the Epistles of Phalaris* in 1698. In this literary debate, the representatives of a new and more accurate textual scholarship, especially Bentley, were entirely right in matters of fact. Bentley showed conclusively that two of the works cited by Temple in his *Essay on Ancient and Modern Learning* (1690) as examples of the superiority of writers of the ancient world—Aesop's *Fables* and Phalaris's *Epistles*—were actually spurious works of a much later date. Yet his triumph was converted into a partial defeat by the wit and elegance of his opposers, who though their classical learning was comparatively superficial were much more able to employ effectively and engagingly what learning they had. Indeed, the contrast focuses the real issue of the seventeenth-century argument about the respective merits of ancient and modern learning, as Swift shows himself, in the *Battle*, to be thoroughly aware; and it is echoed in the

Battle's conviction that modern learning made its practitioners not less, but more, barbarous, conceited, and inhumane.

THE third work included in Swift's first volume of prose satires, *A Discourse Concerning the Mechanical Operation of the Spirit*, addresses itself to matters similar to those of the religious sections of the *Tale*: it is about the human propensity to confuse its merely physical internal experiences with inspiration from a spiritual source outside itself. The three pieces published together have, therefore, a thematic relationship; all three are about spiritual and/or intellectual errors and abuses which arise from our self-conceit, and like all Swift's finest satire they engage issues which go, in terms of perpetual human relevance, beyond the immediate occasion, beyond the differences of the churches, or the quarrel about the achievements of the ancient and the modern worlds.

The Meditation on a Broomstick was published in a volume called *Miscellanies in Prose and Verse* in 1711. It is there dated August 1704, but if Thomas Sheridan's story of its composition, given in his *Life* of his friend Swift, is correct, this date must be too late. Sheridan tells us that during a visit to the Berkeleys Swift found himself asked by the Countess to read to her daily a passage from the devotional *Meditations* of the Hon. Robert Boyle; and that Swift (who clearly found Boyle's pious work rather simple-minded and cliché-ridden) one day substituted his own short parody of the ruminations of Mr Boyle, reading it with a gravity which wholly deceived her ladyship, who professed herself much instructed. If all this is quite true, then the *Meditation* must have been composed before Sheridan's date, when Swift had already returned to Ireland, perhaps in 1702 when Swift visited Berkeley Castle. But except for the matter of accurate dating, the literal truth of the account matters little. Whether the piece was read aloud or not, or deceived the Countess or not, Sheridan's story captures perfectly Swift's intention—to write a solemn parody which employs the same kind of outworn metaphors and traditional analogies that such meditations of the period—and there were many—exploited. Devotional literature was highly popular, and Boyle (who was also, of course, a distinguished scientist) was much revered. Exaggerated eulogies were in themselves enough to provoke an irreverent response from Swift's active mind.

Closely linked in kind with the *Meditation* is *A Tritical Essay upon the Faculties of the Mind*, also printed in the *Miscellanies* and dated 1707, which again shows Swift's astonishing skill and tact in parodying the ways of thinking and writing of real or invented opponents. Parody is one of his sharpest and most adaptable satiric tools. We do not know in this case of a source as precise as in that of the *Meditation*, although it is quite possible that this too is a parody of a particular work; but any familiarity with the 'many essays and moral discourses', so frequent and so popular in the period, will enable us to recognize the soporific banality, the superficial echoing and re-echoing of hackneyed phrases, which Swift so neatly captures here. The Preface would make clear, even if the *Essay* itself did not, the thing which offends him: 'running into stale topics and threadbare quotations, and not handling their subject fully and closely'. It is part of Swift's unending campaign against the trite, the complacent repetition of notions which, having been neither rethought nor refelt, can only issue in empty banalities that give author and reader alike the comforting illusion of having had a genuine experience. One would be hard put to it to find in Swift's work a phrase, an idea, which was not freshly thought, felt, scrutinized 'fully and closely'. And his scrutiny of the shoddiness of other writers' productions results in a most accurately revealing parody.

The 'Abstract' of Anthony Collins's *Discourse of Free-Thinking*, which belongs to the same period, might also be characterized as a parodic satire, using the term 'parody' in the sense always applicable in Swift's work: a piece of writing that does not simply reproduce another man's style, or even merely exaggerate it to ridiculous effect, but that penetrates to the mental habits which that style embodies. The childishly disjointed manner of his version of Collins's *Discourse* reveals the childishness and illogicality of Deist thinking as it appeared to Swift; the 'Abstract' touches upon a number of important theological issues, but always in the same superficial way.

An Argument against Abolishing Christianity (written in 1708, published in 1711) is much more than another attack on the Deists. Had it been merely this it would not have outlasted the controversy which provoked it. As a work of religious irony it is second only to the brilliant *A Tale of a Tub*. Swift had originally intended a serious counter-argument in his *Remarks upon ... Tindal's Rights of the Christian Church* (1708), and though this rebuttal sometimes uses ridicule and irony it was left unfinished, petering out in annotations. When Swift adopted the ironical mode he shifted the battle onto his own ground and used the weapons of which he was complete master. The *Argument* cuts through all the froth of intellectual speculation to reveal a far more serious threat to the Church of England than that posed by the Deists alone: its oblique and absurdist techniques convey a deep anger provoked by those whose toleration of heterodoxy threatens to topple the state. The tract was a warning to the Whigs to pull back from their policy before it was too late. When Swift left the Whigs for the Tories in 1710 it was because the Whigs had failed in their duty to protect the established church. The Anglican supremacy was, of course, at the very centre of Swift's political and spiritual loyalties. But in the *Argument* only apparently trivial and secular reasons are adduced for its support: it is a prop of the state; it provides a minimal literacy; it serves to distract the dangerous meddling wits and speculators, and so on. The establishment man therefore needs to defend merely nominal allegiance to Anglicanism, since that is all the state insists on: religion is thereby reduced to a socially desirable habit, little more than a Sunday pastime. The crucial irony, of course, is that though the Deists appear to be the threat, it is the complacence and spiritual indifference of the vast majority of Englishmen (the orthodox believers, after all) which are most to blame. A revolutionary challenge from the Deists and freethinkers is as nothing by comparison with Swift's view of the essentially radical view of true Christianity. It is important for us to recognize the distinction which Swift made between upholding the liberty of private conscience and recognizing the political necessity for public order: in 1701 he wrote, 'Every man, as a member of the commonwealth, ought to be content with the possession of his own opinion in private, without perplexing his neighbour or disturbing the public.' The toleration and recognition of freethinking were thus an invitation to anarchy *via* individualism: but if the unorthodox kept their mouths shut, Swift would be the last to make them confess for the sake of political expedience. As individuals they were harmless; collectively and in an organisation they were anathema to him.

IN the *Argument* Swift exemplifies his theory of parody, imitating the style and mode of those whom he means to attack. By contrast, the *Vindication of the Beggar's Opera* is written in Swift's own manner, in which a genuine simplicity and clarity of language is achieved through a disciplined precision of thought, wholly different from the simple-mindedness and vagueness assumed for the purpose of ridiculing Deism. The *Vindication* was originally printed as the third issue of a small weekly paper, the *Intelligencer*, which Swift started in 1728. The paper was short-lived because Swift and his friend Sheridan found themselves doing all the work, without funds to hire the assistance they soon urgently needed. His defence of Gay's *Beggar's Opera* was not wholly a matter of personal friendship, although Gay, like Pope and Arbuthnot, was a close personal and literary associate. The four friends were staunch Tories, who, after the manner of eighteenth-century writers, made no separation between their literary and political activities. Gay's delightful comic opera was a thoroughly engaging and amusing satire of the political morality of the first minister, Walpole, and his Whig government, equated here with the morality of the underworld of highwaymen, thieves, informers, prostitutes; and Swift's mock-ingenuous comment on what have been thought to be political allusions in the work is not meant to be taken at face value. The piece owed its enormous success precisely to the public recognition of its slyly impudent satire.

THE *Hints Towards an Essay on Conversation* probably date from about 1710 to 1712, when Swift published other essays on the importance of preserving the purity of the language, both spoken and written. His own practice is virtually impeccable, but he was much concerned about the deterioration of the language through that affectation of a kind of lazy carelessness which current fashion decreed. This was a lifetime concern. *Polite Conversation* (not included in this selection) took shape early in the eighteenth century but was worked over much later. It is a skilful bringing together, into one conversational situation, of all those ways in which talk can be spun out, by dull and trivial people, without the necessity for first-hand thinking or feeling: proverbial clichés, fashionable words, and all humanity's devices for passing time in a social context. The piece depends, like almost everything Swift wrote, on an extraordinary awareness of the devices by which men—in the eighteenth century as in any other—find ways of avoiding a genuine and strenuous engagement with real meanings, in ourselves, in other people, or in other events. It is amusing and witty (though perhaps a trifle over long for the scope of the jest) but above all it is, characteristically, devastating as well as funny; serious as well as gay.

GAIETY is not what strikes one in the great *Modest Proposal* (1729). Swift is always serious about our unwillingness to face the unpleasant consequences of human actions and here, more especially, of human inaction. In *A Modest Proposal* Swift's ironical surgery on the body politic probes to an altogether deeper and more dangerous level, revealing not only the superficial and the boring but the cruel: the moral indifference which lurks behind a political philosophy (keeping Ireland subjected to punitive and exploitative laws) is fully revealed. Ignorance of the consequences is no excuse, says Swift, for ignorance can be more dangerous than the results of hypocrisy. Swift's insight and extraordinary skill are nowhere seen to more advantage than in this tract, where men's avoidance of the realities of their own motives and the effects of their actions on others is shown to issue in utter misery and degradation for others, in starvation, death, and the lack of humanity which such desperation can bring about. Swift had been for years writing pamphlets on the wretchedness of Ireland and the ways—difficult, indeed, for a country so exploited, but possible—in which the country might help itself despite the cynical indifference of the English government and the sycophantic opportunism of the rack-renting Irish landlords and the struggling Irish tradesmen. Now, in yet another of his many roles, he writes as an economic planner ('projector' he would, scornfully, have said) who can see no way out for Ireland but to fall in with the apparent aims of the English, and of those among the Irish themselves, who seem to regard the whole populace as existing only to be exploited, 'devoured'. There is nothing left but to take this metaphor for the current economic policy to its literal conclusion. Let the Irish poor be slaughtered for food at a tender age, so that they may be as useful, and as well treated while they are being fattened, as any other cattle. The 'proposer', an economic thinker through and through, is merely putting frankly the assumptions that lie, hidden even from themselves, in those who govern; the people are, like beasts, meaningful to government only in terms of the amount per head they contribute—dead or alive, sick or well, happy or despairing—to the economy. The proposer, the most reasonable of men, points out that the slaughter would really be a kindness, to the children themselves as well as to those who either sell or eat their flesh. And most horribly lucid of all is that this is arguably quite true, given the life the Irish poor are presented as living. Of all Swift's satiric attempts to show us how we can blind ourselves to the consequences of what we do, of the evil that we so easily commit by not strenuously attending to people and things, and to our own motives, this is perhaps the most powerful. For all its anger and its compassion, it is wonderfully controlled, precise, and given its desperate assumption (itself a logical deduction from observed facts) a logical creation. This logical imagination, this ferocious fun, this urgent pity for pain and degradation, this hatred of self-deceit: these are the heart of Swift's surpassing greatness.

COMMENT on *A Tale of a Tub* has been left until the close of this introductory essay because, as not only the longest but the most difficult work in this selection, it deserves to be treated at a length which would be inappropriate in a chronological account of Swift's writings. Nor, in the space available, is it possible to do justice to the intellectual and imaginative brilliance of this complex creation, in which for the first time Swift's lively intelligence found itself joyously at work upon a massive body of materials, the accumulated result of his experience in Ireland and England and of his intensive reading, in Trinity and especially in Temple's library. It is a very learned book, steeped in theology and philosophy; but the greatness of the work is not in its learning merely, but in the masterly creation of a satiric structure in which the learning gains a permanent imaginative significance. Some knowledge of the ways of thinking and writing which Swift is satirizing, and to which he points us by his references to writers, philosophers, institutions and the rest, is necessary for a real enjoyment of the *Tale*; and reference to the monumental annotated edition by Guthkelch and Smith, first issued in 1920, and to certain books of scholarly criticism which have appeared more recently, adds immeasurably to one's pleasure. But it must be stressed that the work, while its materials are often of a learned kind, is as high-spirited a piece of learned satire as one could wish to find, in the tradition of other serious scholarly jokers, Erasmus, Rabelais, St Thomas More. A little effort is infinitely rewarding in all these cases, and *A Tale of a Tub* is a wonderfully amusing, charming, and exhilarating thing to read.

YET one must add something to this description. Exhilarating, yes; stimulating, fascinating in its free play of intelligence. Yet it is (perhaps inevitably in that case) upsetting, disturbing; it has always a sense of danger for the reader, and danger, precariously avoided, even for Swift himself. *A Tale of a Tub* only makes more plain a quality that is present in most of Swift's satire, especially in *Gulliver's Travels*, where it is so obscurely disturbing that it has in the past raised an outcry of hatred for, and deliberate (if unconscious) misinterpretation of, the work. Swift can be, and at his greatest always is, devastating because his works are aimed at preventing us from taking things for granted. He allows us little chance to rest upon assumptions; for evasion, complacency, the willingness to avoid whatever threatens our physical or mental comfort, are the things that lead us in the end to the unthinking brutality of *A Modest Proposal*, to the varied evils and absurdities of *Gulliver's Travels*—with the proud misanthropy of Gulliver himself as their culmination—or the mindless activity of *A Tale of a Tub*, what Swift calls 'madness' (for it is the way to all unreason), and which he equates, as was a tendency in his time, with moral error. For reason is still for him not only an intellectual but a moral function, and he would not separate these two aspects.

SWIFT here adopts, as so often, the manner of those whom he wishes to satirize as embodiments of wrong and dangerous ways of thinking: primarily in the areas of religion and of learning, which includes literary creation. To call the *Tale* the result of literary creation on the *mock* author's part would scarcely be appropriate; but the achievement of the *Tale* is that, through parody of a complacent and uncreative fool, Swift does himself achieve literary creation. The tension between the mad and the sane, the shapeless and the meaningfully structured, the weakly silly and the imaginatively powerful, is what gives the *Tale* such extraordinary impact. That impact would be largely lost if the true author, ridiculing complacency and self-deceit, himself betrayed complacency; essential to the effect is Swift's realization of the treacherous depths of his own mind, as a member of the human race in which reason is so precarious and so threatened. Man, as he said in a letter to Pope, is not really *animal rationale*, a rational animal; he is something altogether more tentative and difficult, an animal which has the capability of reason, *animal rationis capax*. And to exercise that capability is an endless struggle. So he is concerned here not only to imitate a man who is, essentially, unable to think, and whose mind whirls in an aimless activity of which he is fatally proud; he is concerned further to challenge and disconcert the reader by continually shifting his ground, so that we can never, in our turn, be complacently sure that we are so superior to the fool who is writing. Most disturbing of all, we are frequently left uncertain about what the author means and what Swift means; there is here no world of certainty, not the 'author's', not the true author's, so necessarily not ours. We are not allowed to settle into anything, any more than Swift seemed to allow himself. All is question, all is danger.

NOWHERE is this more disconcerting than in the most famous of all passages from the *Tale*, from Section IX, the Digression on Madness. Swift's author has been arguing that madness is altogether preferable to sanity, since it enables us to avoid the harshness of reality and live in a world of illusion. Happiness '*is a perpetual Possession of being well Deceived*', and credulity is more peaceful than wisdom, or 'pretended Philosophy', which is always looking beneath the surface. So far, one may persuade oneself that one sees clearly where the satire is going, but after a couple of very complex paragraphs, we come to this:

> He that can with *Epicurus* content his Ideas with the *Films* and *Images* that fly off upon his Senses from the *Superficies* of Things; Such a Man truly wise, creams off Nature, leaving the Sower and the Dregs, for Philosophy and Reason to lap up. This is the sublime and refined Point of Felicity, called, *the Possession of being well Deceived*; the Serene Peaceful State of being a Fool among Knaves.

Suddenly we are faced with something that hardly sounds like the mock author at all. Instead of long, maundering sentences with the clauses barely linked by any connection of ideas, we find calm, well-ordered, logically developed thinking, coolly expressed; instead of complacent optimism, a wholly unillusioned view. Happiness can be achieved, but at the loss of intelligence, of sanity. Is this the mock author or the true? Is this the way that Swift himself sees the alternatives in life? Is this where awareness, avoidance of illusion ends for humanity? Looking back, we see that earlier phrases, such as '*it is a per-perpetual Possession of being well Deceived*', or 'How fading and insipid do all Objects accost us that are not convey'd in the Vehicle of *Delusion*?', have the same cold quietness. This disorienting of the reader is part of the overall strategy of the *Tale*; again, we must not be allowed to settle. But it could not work as it does if it did not suggest to us that our ultimate guide for the duration of the work, the real author, finds the whole discussion disturbing too; that there is no point where any of us can rightly settle. Although there is much to be said about the images, and about the movement of the long passage and its relation to the *Tale* as a whole, it is essentially this pull between the persona and Swift, the modulation into the latter's clarity and precision, that makes for the powerfully disturbing effect.

It is in the digressions, which alternate with the chapters recounting the religious allegory, that Swift's characteristic strategy of disturbance is most evident and most brilliant. The very notion of so many digressions, given the status of separate chapters, is integral to Swift's presentation of the inanity of the self-indulgent 'modern' mind as that is evidenced in its literary and its philosophical writings. 'Modern' here, of course, relates to the famous quarrel of the Ancients and the Moderns of seventeenth-century England and France, and means more than merely 'contemporary'. For Swift it comprehends all those who, since the passing of the great age of classical Rome, have moved away from the standards of integrity, humanity, intelligence, and moral value, which the best of the ancients might be thought to embody in their literature and their philosophy. The mock author, with his loose mental processes evident in his uncontrolled and disconnected style, is visibly moving further away from any kind of reality; the world, both inner and outer, that he projects has no values in it and makes no sense, but he goes on in his solipsistic way, blandly sure that words mean what he wants them to mean, though they continually betray him. The same process is seen in the allegorical story of the development of the Christian churches since primitive times, which the author has to tell and from which he digresses. All the churches have moved away by degrees from the simple reality of the Gospel in which they began. Martin, the Church of England, is the least bad, because he saw, at last, the degeneration of his brothers and himself, and returned as closely as he could to the primitive purity. Peter, the Catholic, remained unregenerate, while the dissenter, Jack, undertook such radical reforms that the very fabric of his inherited coat—Christianity—was damaged. The allegorical story indulges in what seems to us rather knockabout fun, and to some of Swift's contemporaries profanity, in the course of the satire. But Swift is drawing on a well-established tradition of religious polemic familiar to him as a churchman: a tradition shaped in order to ridicule, from an Anglican standpoint, the tendency of the Catholic Church on the one hand to degenerate through a growing worldliness and desire for power, justified by a proliferation of non-biblical doctrines, and the tendency of Dissent on the other to take biblical texts over-literally and apply them indiscriminately, while claiming a direct personal inspiration from God. Swift, like most Anglicans, found this claim almost blasphemously absurd; the dissenters, he thinks, merely mistake their own purely physical impulses for spiritual inspiration, thus degrading the spirit and inflating their own egos. The description of the invented theology and religious practice of the Aeolists beautifully satirizes this confusion in a very physical allegory, for physicality is essential to the point Swift is making. The same tendency is satirized again in the fragment on the *Mechanical Operation of the Spirit*, here from the point of view of a persona who is one of the new scientific virtuosi. The *Tale*'s religious allegory and the digressions together present an inclusive examination of human self-deceit and illusion, by which we contrive to spoil so much that we touch; while the exuberant invention, so precisely calculated to be exactly expressive of our self-interested errors, is dazzling. Swift's particular combination of qualities is never more evident than in this first of his major satires.

The BIBLIOGRAPHY.

I EDITIONS

Prose Works, ed. Herbert Davis (Oxford, 1939–62).

A Tale of a Tub, to which is added The Battle of the Books and The Mechanical Operation of the Spirit, ed. A. C. Guthkelch and D. Nichol Smith (Oxford, 1920; second edition 1958). This is annotated in great detail.

The Poems of Jonathan Swift, ed. Sir Harold Williams, 3 vols (Oxford, 1937; second edition 1958).

The Correspondence of Jonathan Swift, ed. Sir Harold Williams, 5 vols (Oxford, 1963–65).

The Journal to Stella, ed. Sir Harold Williams, 2 vols (Oxford, 1948).

II BIOGRAPHICAL STUDIES

Ehrenpreis, Irvin, *Swift, The Man, His Works, and the Age*. Vol. I, *Mr. Swift and His Contemporaries* (London, 1962). Vol. II, *Doctor Swift* (1967).

— *The Personality of Jonathan Swift* (London, 1958).

Jackson, R. Wyse, *Jonathan Swift, Dean and Pastor* (London, 1939).

Landa, Louis A., *Swift and the Church of Ireland* (Oxford, 1954).

III CRITICAL STUDIES

General

Beaumont, C. A., *Swift's Classical Rhetoric* (Athens, Georgia, 1961).

Bullitt, John M., *Jonathan Swift and the Anatomy of Satire* (Cambridge, Mass., and London, 1953).

Davis, Herbert, *The Satire of Jonathan Swift* (New York, 1947). Essays on the literary, political, and moral satire.

Donoghue, Denis, *Jonathan Swift, A Critical Introduction* (Cambridge, 1969).
Ewald, W. B., *The Masks of Jonathan Swift* (Cambridge, Mass., and Oxford, 1954).
Ferguson, Oliver W., *Jonathan Swift and Ireland* (Urbana, Illinois, 1962).
Jeffares, Alexander Norman (ed.), *Fair Liberty was All His Cry: A tercentenary Tribute to Jonathan Swift, 1667–1745* (London, 1967).
Price, Martin, *Swift's Rhetorical Art* (New Haven, 1953).
Quintana, R., *The Mind and Art of Jonathan Swift* (London and New York, 1936; London, 1953).
— *Swift, An Introduction* (London, 1955). Very useful introductory short study; essays on various aspects of Swift's work, covering his entire career.
Rawson, C. J., *Gulliver and the Gentle* Reader. *Studies in Swift and our Time* (London and Boston, 1973).
Rosenheim, Edward R., *Swift and the Satirist's Art* (Chicago, 1965).
Tuveson, Ernest (ed.), *Swift: A Collection of Critical Essays*, Twentieth Century Views (Englewood Cliffs, New Jersey, 1964).
Vickers, Brian, *The World of Jonathan Swift* (Cambridge, Mass., 1968).
Voigt, Milton, *Swift and the Twentieth Century* (Detroit, 1964).
Williams, Kathleen, *Jonathan Swift and the Age of Compromise* (Lawrence, Kansas, 1958; London, 1959).
— *Swift: The Critical Heritage* (London, 1970).

The Battle of the Books
Jones, Richard Foster, *Ancients and Moderns, a Study of the Background of the Battle of the Books* (St Louis, Missouri, 1936).

A Tale of a Tub
Harth, Phillip, *Swift and Anglican Rationalism. The Religious Background of A Tale of a Tub* (Chicago, 1961).
Paulson, Ronald, *Theme and Structure in Swift's Tale of a Tub* (New Haven, 1960).

Starkman, Miriam K., *Swift's Satire on Learning in A Tale of a Tub* (Princeton, 1950).

Gulliver's Travels

Case, Arthur E., *Four Essays on Gulliver's Travels* (Princeton, 1945).

Eddy, William A., *Gulliver's Travels, A Critical Study* (Princeton, 1923).

Nicholson, Marjorie, and Mohler, Nora M., 'The Scientific Background of Swift's voyage to Laputa', *Annals of Science*, ii (1937); reprinted in M. Nicholson, *Science and Imagination* (Ithaca, New York and London, 1956).

Williams, Harold, *The Text of Gulliver's Travels* (Cambridge, 1952).

A

TALE

OF A

TUB.

Written for the Universal Improvement of Mankind.

Diu multumque desideratum.

To which is added,

An ACCOUNT of a

BATTEL

BETWEEN THE

Antient and Modern BOOKS in St. *James's* Library.

Basima eacabasa eanaa irraurista. diarba da caeotaba fobor camelanthi. *Iren. Lib.* 1. C. 18.

——*Juvatque novos decerpere flores,*
Insignemque meo capiti petere inde coronam,
Unde prius nulli velarunt tempora Musæ. Lucret.

The Fifth EDITION: With the Author's Apology and Explanatory Notes. By *W. W--tt--n*, B. D. and others.

LONDON: Printed for *John Nutt*, near *Stationers-Hall*. MDCCX.

Treatises wrote by the same Author, most of them mentioned in the following Discourses; which will be speedily published.

A Character of the present Set of Wits *in this Island.*

A Panegyrical Essay upon the Number THREE.

A Dissertation upon the principal Productions of Grub-street.

Lectures upon a Dissection of Human Nature.

A Panegyrick upon the World.

An Analytical Discourse upon Zeal, Histori-theo-physi-logically *considered.*

A general History of Ears.

A modest Defence of the Proceedings of the Rabble *in all Ages.*

A Description of the Kingdom of Absurdities.

A Voyage into England, *by a Person of Quality in* Terra Australis incognita, *translated from the Original.*

A Critical Essay upon the Art of Canting, *Philosophically, Physically, and Musically considered.*

AN

APOLOGY

For the, &c.

*I*F *good and ill Nature equally operated upon Mankind, I might have saved my self the Trouble of this Apology; for it is manifest by the Reception the following Discourse hath met with, that those who approve it, are a great Majority among the Men of Tast; yet there have been two or three Treatises written expresly against it, besides many others that have flirted at it occasionally, without one Syllable having been ever published in its Defence, or even Quotation to its Advantage, that I can remember, except by the Polite Author of a late Discourse between a Deist and a Socinian.*

Therefore, since the Book seems calculated to live at least as long as our Language, and our Tast admit no great Alterations, I am content to convey some Apology along with it.

The greatest Part of that Book was finished above thirteen Years since, 1696, *which is eight Years before it was published. The Author was then young, his Invention at the Height, and his Reading fresh in his Head. By the Assistance of some Thinking, and much Conversation, he had endeavour'd to Strip himself of as many real Prejudices as he could; I say real ones, because under the Notion of Prejudices, he knew to what dangerous Heights some Men have proceeded. Thus prepared, he thought the numerous and gross Corruptions in Religion and Learning might furnish Matter for a Satyr, that would be useful and diverting: He resolved to proceed in a manner, that should be altogether new, the World having been already too long nauseated with endless Repetitions upon every Subject. The Abuses in Religion he proposed to set forth in the Allegory of the Coats, and the three Brothers, which was to make up the Body of the Discourse. Those in Learning he chose to introduce by way of Digressions. He was then a young Gentleman much in the World, and wrote to the Tast of those who were like himself; therefore in order to allure them, he gave a Liberty to his Pen, which might not suit with ma-*

turer Years, or graver Characters, and which he could have easily corrected with a very few Blots, had he been Master of his Papers for a Year or two before their Publication.

Not that he would hcve governed his Judgment by the ill-placed Cavils of the Sour, the Envious, the Stupid, and the Tastless, which he mentions with disdain. He acknowledges there are several youthful Sallies, which from the Grave and the Wise may deserve a Rebuke. *But he desires to be answerable no farther than he is guilty, and that his Faults may not be multiply'd by the ignorant, the unnatural, and uncharitable Applications of those who have neither Candor to suppose good Meanings, nor Palate to distinguish true Ones. After which, he will forfeit his Life, if any one Opinion can be fairly deduced from that Book, which is contrary to* Religion *or Morality.*

Why should any Clergyman of our Church be angry to see the Follies of Fanaticism and Superstition exposed, tho' in the most ridiculous Manner? since that is perhaps the most probable way to cure them, or at least to hinder them from farther spreading. Besides, tho' it was not intended for their Perusal; it raillies nothing but what they preach against. It contains nothing to provoke them by the least Scurillity upon their Persons or their Functions. It Celebrates the Church of England *as the most perfect of all others in Discipline and Doctrine, it advances no Opinion they reject, nor condemns any they receive. If the Clergy's* Resentments *lay upon their Hands, in my humble Opinion, they might have found more proper Objects to employ them on:* Nondum tibi defuit Hostis; *I mean those heavy, illiterate Scriblers, prostitute in their* Reputations, *vicious in their Lives, and ruin'd in their Fortunes, who to the shame of good Sense as well as Piety, are greedily read, meerly upon the Strength of bold, false, impious Assertions, mixt with unmannerly* Reflections *upon the Priesthood, and openly intended against all* Religion; *in short, full of such Principles as are kindly received, because they are levell'd to remove those Terrors that* Religion *tells Men will be the Consequence of immoral Lives. Nothing like which is to be met with in this Discourse, tho' some of them are pleased so freely to censure it. And I wish, there were no other Instance of what I have too frequently observed, that many of that* Reverend *Body are not always very nice in distinguishing between their Enemies and their Friends.*

Had the Author's Intentions met with a more candid Interpretation from some whom out of Respect *he forbears to name, he might have been encouraged to an Examination of Books written by some of those Authors above-described, whose Errors, Ignorance, Dullness and Villany, he thinks he could have detected and exposed in such a Manner, that the Persons who are most conceived to be infected by them, would soon lay them aside and be ashamed: But he has now given over those Thoughts, since the* weightiest *Men in the* weightiest *Stations are pleased to think it a more dangerous Point to laugh at those Corruptions in* Re-*ligion, which they themselves must disapprove, than to endeavour pulling up those very Foundations, wherein all Christians have agreed.*

He thinks it no fair Proceeding, that any Person should offer determinately to fix a name upon the Author of this Discourse, who hath all along concealed himself from most of his nearest Friends: Yet several have gone a farther Step, and pronounced another Book to have been the Work of the same Hand with this; which the Author directly affirms to be a thorough mistake; he having yet never so much as read that Discourse, a plain Instance how little Truth, there often is in general Surmises, or in Conjectures drawn from a Similitude of Style, or way of thinking.

Letter of Enthusiasm.

Had the Author writ a Book to expose the Abuses in Law, or in Physick, he believes the Learned Professors in either Faculty, would have been so far from resenting it, as to have given him Thanks for his Pains, especially if he had made an honourable Reservation *for the true Practice of either Science: But* Religion *they tell us ought not to be ridiculed, and they tell us Truth, yet surely the Corruptions in it may; for we are taught by the tritest Maxim in the World, that* Religion *being the best of Things, its Corruptions are likely to be the worst.*

There is one Thing which the judicious Reader *cannot but have observed, that some of those Passages in this Discourse, which appear most liable to Objection are what they call Parodies, where the Author personates the Style and Manner of other Writers, whom he has a mind to expose. I shall produce one Instance, it is in the* [42nd] Page. Dryden, L'Estrange, *and some others I shall not name, are here levelled at, who having spent their Lives in Faction, and Apostacies, and all manner of Vice, pretended to be Sufferers for Loyalty and* Religion. *So* Dryden *tells us in one of his Prefaces of his Merits and Suffering, thanks God that he* possesses his Soul in Patience: *In other Places he talks at the same* Rate, *and* L'Estrange *often uses the like Style, and I believe the* Reaaer *may find more Persons to give that Passage an Application: But this is enough to direct those who may have over-look'd the Authors Intention.*

There are three or four other Passages which prejudiced or ignorant Readers *have drawn by great* Force *to hint at ill Meanings; as if they glanced at some* Tenets *in* Religion, *in answer to all which, the Author solemnly protests he is entirely Innocent, and never had it once in his Thoughts that any thing he said would in the least be capable of such Interpretations, which he will engage to deduce full as fairly from the most innocent Book in the World. And it will be obvious to every* Reader, *that this was not any part of his Scheme or Design, the Abuses he notes being such as all Church of* England *Men agree in, nor was it proper for his Subject to meddle with other Points, than such as have been perpetually controverted since the* Reformation.

To instance only in that Passage about the three wooden Machines mentioned in the Introduction: In the Original Manuscript there was a description of a Fourth, *which those who had the Papers in their Power, blotted out, as having something in it of Satyr, that I suppose they thought was too particular, and therefore they were forced to change it to the Number* Three, *from whence some have endeavour'd to squeeze out a dangerous Meaning that was never thought on. And indeed the Conceit was half spoiled by changing the Numbers; that of* Four *being much more Cabalistick, and therefore better exposing the pretended Virtue of Numbers, a Superstitition there intended to be ridicul'd.*

Another Thing to be observed is, that there generally runs an Irony through the Thread of the whole Book, which the Men of Tast *will observe and distinguish, and which will render some Objections that have been made, very weak and insignificant.*

This Apology being chiefly intended for the Satisfaction of future Readers, *it may be thought unnecessary to take any notice of such* Treatises *as have been writ against this ensuing Discourse, which are already sunk into waste Paper and Oblivion; after the usual* Fate *of common Answerers to Books, which are allowed to have any Merit: They are indeed like Annuals that grow about a young* Tree, *and seem to vye with it for a Summer, but fall and die with the* Leaves *in Autumn, and are never heard of any more. When Dr.* Eachard *writ his Book about the Contempt of the Clergy, numbers of those Answerers immediately started up, whose Memory if he had not kept alive by his* Replies, *it would now be utterly unknown that he were ever answered at all. There is indeed an*

Exception, when any great Genius thinks it worth his while to expose a foolish Piece; so we still read Marvel's Answer to Parker with Pleasure, tho' the Book it answers be sunk long ago; so the Earl of Orrery's Remarks will be read with Delight, when the Dissertation he exposes will neither be sought nor found; but these are no Enterprises for common Hands, nor to be hoped for above once or twice in an Age. Men would be more cautious of losing their Time in such an Undertaking, if they did but consider, that to answer a Book effectually, requires more Pains and Skill, more Wit, Learning, and Judgment than were employ'd in the Writing it. And the Author assures those Gentlemen who have given themselves that Trouble with him, that his Discourse is the Product of the Study, the Observation, and the Invention of several Years, that he often blotted out much more than he left, and if his Papers had not been a long time out of his Possession, they must have still undergone more severe Corrections; and do they think such a Building is to be battered with Dirt-Pellets however envenom'd the Mouths may be that discharge them. He hath seen the Productions but of two Answerers, One of which first appear'd as from an unknown hand, but since avowed by a Person, who upon some Occasions hath discover'd no ill Vein of Humor. 'Tis a Pity any Occasions should put him under a necessity of being so hasty in his Productions, which otherwise might often be entertaining. But there were other Reasons obvious enough for his Miscarriage in this; he writ against the Conviction of his Talent, and enter'd upon one of the wrongest Attempts in Nature, to turn into ridicule by a Weeks Labour, a Work which had cost so much time, and met with so much Success in ridiculing others, the manner how he has handled his Subject, I have now forgot, having just look'd it over when it first came out, as others did, meerly for the sake of the Title.

The other Answer is from a Person of a graver Character, and is made up of half Invective, and half Annotation. In the latter of which he hath generally succeeded well enough. And the Project at that time was not amiss, to draw in Readers to his Pamphlet, several having appear'd desirous that there might be some Explication of the more difficult Passages. Neither can he be altogether blamed for offering at the Invective Part, because it is agreed on all hands that the Author had given him sufficient Provocation. The great Objection is against his manner of treating it, very unsuitable to one of his Function. It was determined by a fair Majority, that this Answerer had in a way not to be pardon'd, *drawn his Pen against a certain great Man then alive, and universally reverenced for every good Quality that could possibly enter into the Composition of the most accomplish'd Person; it was observed, how he was pleased and affected to have that noble Writer call'd his Adversary, and it was a Point of Satyr well directed, for I have been told, Sir* W. T. *was sufficiently mortify'd at the Term. All the Men of Wit and Politeness were immediately up in Arms, through Indignation, which prevailed over their Contempt, by the Consequences they apprehended from such an Example, and it grew to be* Porsenna'*s Case;* Idem trecenti juravimus. *In short, things were ripe for a general Insurrection, till my Lord* Orrery *had a little laid the Spirit, and settled the Ferment. But his Lordship being principally engaged with another Antagonist, it was thought necessary in order to quiet the Minds of Men, that this Opposer should receive a* Reprimand, *which partly occasioned that Discourse of the Battle of the Books, and the Author was farther at the Pains to insert one or two* Remarks *on him in the Body of the Book.*

This Answerer has been pleased to find Fault with about a dozen Passages, which the Author will not be at the Trouble of defending, farther than by assuring the Reader, *that for the greater Part the* Reflecter *is entirely mistaken, and forces Interpretations which never once entered into the Writer's Head, nor will he is sure into that of any* Reader *of Tast and Candor; he allows two or three at most there produced to have been deliver'd unwarily, for which he desires to plead the Excuse offered already, of his Youth, and Franckness of Speech, and his Papers being out of his Power at the Time they were published.*

But this Answerer insists, and says, what he chiefly dislikes, is the Design; *what that was I have already told, and I believe there is not a Person in* England *who can understand that Book, that ever imagined it to have been any thing else, but to expose the Abuses and Corruptions in* Learning *and* Religion.

But it would be good to know what Design *this* Reflecter *was serving, when he concludes his Pamphlet with a Caution to* Readers, *to beware of thinking the Authors Wit was entirely his own, surely this must have had some Allay of Personal Animosity, at least mixt with the* Design *of serving the Publick by so useful a Discovery; and it indeed touches the Author in a very tender Point, who insists upon it, that through the whole Book he has not borrowed one single Hint from any Writer in the World; and he thought, of all Criticisms, that would never have been one,*

He conceived it was never disputed to be an Original, whatever Faults it might have. However this Answerer produces three Instances to prove this Author's Wit is not his own in many Places. *The first is, that the Names of* Peter, Martin *and* Jack *are borrowed from a Letter of the late Duke of* Buckingham. *Whatever Wit is contained in those three Names, the Author is content to give it up, and desires his* Readers *will substract as much as they placed upon that Account; at the same time protesting solemnly that he never once heard of that Letter, except in this Passage of the Answerer: So that the Names were not borrowed as he affirms, tho' they should happen to be the same; which however is odd enough, and what he hardly believes; that of* Jack, *being not quite so obvious as the other two. The second Instance to shew* the Author's Wit is not his own, *is* Peter'*s* Banter (*as he calls it in his* Alsatia *Phrase) upon Transubstantiation, which is taken from the same Duke's Conference with an* Irish *Priest, where a Cork is turned into a Horse. This the Author confesses to have seen, about ten Years after his Book was writ, and a Year or two after it was published. Nay, the Answerer overthrows this himself; for he allows the Tale was writ in* 1697; *and I think that Pamphlet was not printed in many Years after. It was necessary, that Corruption should have some Allegory as well as the rest; and the Author invented the properest he could, without enquiring what other People had writ, and the commonest* Reader *will find, there is not the least* Resemblance *between the two Stories. The third Instance is in these Words:* I have been assured, that the Battle in St. *James*'s Library, is *mutatis mutandis*, taken out of a *French* Book, entituled, *Combat des livres*, if I misremember not. *In which Passage there are two Clauses observable:* I have been assured; *and*, if I misremember not. *I desire first to know, whether if that Conjecture proves an utter falshood, those two Clauses will be a sufficient Excuse for this worthy Critick. The Matter is a Trifle; but, would he venture to pronounce at this* Rate *upon one of greater Moment? I know nothing more contemptible in a Writer than the Character of a Plagiary; which he here fixes at a venture, and this, not for a Passage, but a whole Discourse, taken out from another Book only* mutatis mutandis. *The Author is as much in the dark about this as the Answerer; and will imitate him by an Affirmation at* Random; *that if there be a word of Truth in this* Reflec*tion, he is a paultry, imitating Pedant, and the Answerer is a Person of Wit, Manners and Truth. He takes his Boldness, from never having* *seen any such Treatise in his Life nor heard of it before; and he is sure it is impossible for two Writers of different Times and Countries to agree in their Thoughts after such a Manner, that two continued Discourses shall be the same only* mutatis mutandis. *Neither will he insist upon the mistake of the Title, but let the Answerer and his Friend produce any Book they please, he defies them to shew one single Particular, where the judicious Reader will affirm he has been obliged for the smallest Hint; giving only Allowance for the accidental encountring of a single Thought, which he knows may sometimes happen; tho' he has never yet found it in that Discourse, nor has heard it objected by any body else.*

So that if ever any design was unfortunately executed, it must be that of this Answerer, who when he would have it observed that the Author's Wit is not his own, is able to produce but three Instances, two of them meer Trifles, and all three manifestly false. If this be the way these Gentlemen deal with the World in those Criticisms, where we have not Leisure to defeat them, their Readers had need be cautious how they rely upon their Credit; and whether this Proceeding can be reconciled to Humanity or Truth, let those who think it worth their while, determine.

It is agreed, this Answerer would have succeeded much better, if he had stuck wholly to his Business as a Commentator upon the Tale of a Tub, *wherein it cannot be deny'd that he hath been of some Service to the Publick, and has given very fair Conjectures towards clearing up some difficult Passages; but, it is the frequent Error of those Men (otherwise very commendable for their Labors) to make Excursions beyond their Talent and their Office, by pretending to point out the Beauties and the Faults; which is no part of their Trade, which they always fail in, which the World never expected from them, nor gave them any thanks for endeavouring at. The Part of* Min-ellius, *or* Farnaby *would have fallen in with his Genius, and might have been serviceable to many Readers who cannot enter into the abstruser Parts of that Discourse; but* Optat ephippia bos piger. *The dull, unwieldy, ill-shaped Ox would needs put on the Furniture of a Horse, not considering he was born to Labour, to plow the Ground for the Sake of superior Beings, and that he has neither the Shape, Mettle nor Speed of that nobler Animal he would affect to personate.*

It is another Pattern of this Answerer's fair dealing, to give us Hints that the Author is dead, and yet to lay the Suspicion upon somebody, I know not who, in the Country; to which can be only returned, that he is absolutely mistaken in all his Conjectures; and surely Conjectures are at best too light a Pretence to allow a Man to assign a Name in Publick. He condemns a Book, and consequently the Author, of whom he is utterly ignorant, yet at the same time fixes in Print, what he thinks a disadvantageous Character upon those who never deserved it. A Man who receives a Buffet in the Dark may be allowed to be vexed; but it is an odd kind of Revenge *to go to Cuffs in broad day with the first he meets with, and lay the last* Nights *Injury at his Door. And thus much for this* discreet, candid, pious, *and* ingenious *Answerer.*

How the Author came to be without his Papers, is a Story not proper to be told, and of very little use, being a private Fact of which the Reader *would believe as little or as much as he thought good. He had however a blotted Copy by him, which he intended to have writ over, with many Alterations, and this the Publishers were well aware of, having put it into the Booksellers Preface, that they* apprehended a surreptitious Copy, which was to be altered, *&c. This though not regarded by* Readers, *was a real* Truth, *only the surreptitious Copy was rather that which was printed, and they made all hast they could, which indeed was needless; the Author not being at all prepared; but he has been told, the Bookseller was in much Pain, having given a good Sum of Money for the Copy.*

In the Authors Original Copy there were not so many Chasms as appear in the Book; and why some of them were left he knows not; had the Publication been trusted to him, he should have made several Corrections of Passages against which nothing hath been ever objected. He should likewise have altered a few of those that seem with any Reason *to be excepted against, but to deal freely, the greatest* Number *he should have left untouch'd, as never suspecting it possible any wrong Interpretations could be made of them.*

The Author observes, at the End of the Book there is a Discourse called A Fragment; *which he more wondered to see in Print than all the rest. Having been a most imperfect Sketch with the Addition of a few loose Hints, which he once lent a Gentleman who had designed a Discourse of somewhat the same Subject; he never thought of it afterwards, and it was a sufficient Surprize to see it pieced up together, wholly out of the Method and Scheme he had intended, for it was the Ground-work of a much larger Discourse, and he was sorry to observe the Materials so foolishly employ'd.*

There is one farther Objection made by those who have answered this Book, as well as by some others, that Peter *is frequently made to repeat Oaths and Curses. Every* Reader *observes it was necessary to know that* Peter *did Swear and Curse. The Oaths are not printed out, but only supposed, and the Idea of an Oath is not immoral, like the Idea of a Prophane or Immodest Speech. A Man may laugh at the Popish Folly of cursing People to Hell, and imagine them swearing, without any crime; but lewd Words, or dangerous Opinions though printed by halves, fill the Readers Mind with ill Idea's; and of these the Author cannot be accused. For the judicious* Reader *will find that the severest Stroaks of Satyr in his Book are levelled against the modern Custom of Employing Wit upon those Topicks, of which there is a remarkable Instance in the* [92nd] Page, *as well as in several others, tho' perhaps once or twice exprest in too free a manner, excusable only for the* Reasons *already alledged. Some Overtures have been made by a third Hand to the Bookseller for the Author's altering those Passages which he thought might require it. But it seems the Bookseller will not hear of any such Thing, being apprehensive it might spoil the Sale of the Book.*

The Author cannot conclude this Apology, without making this one Reflection; that, as Wit is the noblest and most useful Gift of humane Nature, so Humor is the most agreeable, and where these two enter far into the Composition of any Work, they will render it always acceptable to the World. Now, the great Part of those who have no Share or Tast of either, but by their Pride, Pedantry and Ill Manners, lay themselves bare to the Lashes of Both, think the Blow is weak, because they are insensible, and where Wit hath any mixture of Raillery; 'Tis but calling it Banter, *and the work is done. This Polite Word of theirs was first borrowed from the Bullies in* White-Fryars, *then fell among the Footmen, and at last retired to the Pedants, by whom it is applied as properly to the Productions of Wit, as if I should apply it to Sir* Isaac Newton'*s Mathematicks, but, if this* Bantring *as they call it, be so despisable a Thing, whence comes it to pass they have such a perpetual Itch towards it themselves? To instance only in the Answerer already mentioned; it is grievous to see him in some of his Writings at every turn going out of his way to be waggish, to tell us of a* Cow that prickt up her Tail, *and in his answer to this Discourse, he says* it is all a Farce and a Ladle; *With other Passages equally shining. One may say of these* Impedimenta Literarum, *that Wit ows them a Shame; and they cannot take wiser*

Counsel than to keep out of harms way, or at least not to come till they are sure they are called.

To conclude; with those Allowances above-required, this Book should be read, after which the Author conceives, few things will remain which may not be excused in a young Writer. He wrote only to the Men of Wit and Tast, and he thinks he is not mistaken in his Accounts, when he says they have been all of his side, enough to give him the vanity of telling his Name, wherein the World with all its wise Conjectures, is yet very much in the dark, which Circumstance is no disagreeable Amusement either to the Publick or himself.

The Author is informed, that the Bookseller has prevailed on several Gentlemen, to write some explanatory Notes, for the goodness of which he is not to answer, having never seen any of them, nor intends it, till they appear in Print, when it is not unlikely he may have the Pleasure to find twenty Meanings, which never enter'd into his Imagination.

June 3. 1709.

POSTSCRIPT.

S*Ince the writing of this which was about a Year ago; a Prostitute Bookseller hath publish'd a foolish Paper, under the Name of Notes on the* Tale of a Tub, *with some Account of the Author, and with an Insolence which I suppose is punishable by Law, hath presumed to assign certain Names. It will be enough for the Author to assure the World, that the Writer of that Paper is utterly wrong in all his Conjectures upon that Affair. The Author farther asserts that the whole Work is entirely of one Hand, which every Reader of Judgment will easily discover. The Gentleman who gave the Copy to the Bookseller, being a Friend of the Author, and using no other Liberties besides that of expunging certain Passages where now the Chasms appear under the Name of* Desiderata. *But if any Person will prove his Claim to three Lines in the whole Book, let him step forth and tell his Name and Titles, upon which the Bookseller shall have Orders to prefix them to the next Edition, and the Claimant shall from henceforward be acknowledged the undisputed Author.*

TO

The Right Honourable,

JOHN

Lord SOMMERS.

My LORD,

THO' the Author has written a large Dedication, yet That being address'd to a Prince, whom I am never likely to have the Honor of being known to; A Person, besides, as far as I can observe, not at all regarded, or thought on by any of our present Writers; And, being wholly free from that Slavery, which Booksellers usually lie under, to the Caprices of Authors; I think it a wise Piece of Presumption, to inscribe these Papers to your Lordship, and to implore your Lordship's Protection of them. God and your Lordship know their Faults, and their Merits; for as to my own Particular, I am altogether a Stranger to the Matter; And, tho' every Body else should be equally ignorant, I do not fear the Sale of the Book, at all the worse, upon that Score. Your Lordship's Name on the Front, in Capital Letters, will at any time get off one Edition: Neither would I desire any other Help, to grow an Alderman, than a Patent for the sole Priviledge of Dedicating to your Lordship.

I should now, in right of a Dedicator, give your Lordship a List of your own Virtues, and at the same time, be very unwilling to offend your Modesty; But, chiefly, I should celebrate your Liberality towards Men of great Parts and small Fortunes, and give you broad Hints, that I mean my self. And, I was just going on in the usual Method, to peruse a hundred or two of Dedications, and transcribe an Abstract, to be applied to your Lordship; But, I was diverted by a certain Accident. For, upon the

Covers of these Papers, I casually observed written in large Letters, the two following Words, *DETUR DIGNISSIMO;* which, for ought I knew, might contain some important Meaning. But, it unluckily fell out, that none of the Authors I employ, understood *Latin* (tho' I have them often in pay, to translate out of that Language) I was therefore compelled to have recourse to the Curate of our Parish, who Englished it thus, *Let it be given to the Worthiest;* And his Comment was, that the Author meant, his Work should be dedicated to the sublimest Genius of the Age, for Wit, Learning, Judgment, Eloquence and Wisdom. I call'd at a Poet's Chamber (who works for my Shop) in an Alley hard by, shewed him the Translation, and desired his Opinion, who it was that the Author could mean; He told me, after some Consideration, that Vanity was a Thing he abhorr'd; but by the Description, he thought Himself to be the Person aimed at; And, at the same time, he very kindly offer'd his own Assistance *gratis*, towards penning a Dedication to Himself. I desired him, however, to give a second Guess; Why then, said he, It must be I, or my Lord *Sommers*. From thence I went to several other Wits of my Acquaintance, with no small Hazard and Weariness to my Person, from a prodigious Number of dark, winding Stairs; But found them all in the same Story, both of your Lordship and themselves. Now, your Lordship is to understand, that this Proceeding was not of my own Invention; For, I have somewhere heard, it is a Maxim, that those, to whom every Body allows the second Place, have an undoubted Title to the First.

THIS infallibly convinced me, that your Lordship was the Person intended by the Author. But, being very unacquainted in the Style and Form of Dedications, I employ'd those Wits aforesaid, to furnish me with Hints and Materials, towards a Panegyrick upon your Lordship's Virtues.

IN two Days, they brought me ten Sheets of Paper, fill'd up on every Side. They swore to me, that they had ransack'd whatever could be found in the Characters of *Socrates*, *Aristides*, *Epaminondas*, *Cato*, *Tully*, *Atticus*, and other hard Names, which I cannot now recollect. However, I have Reason to believe, they imposed upon my Ignorance, because, when I came to read over their Collections, there was not a Syllable there, but what I and every body else knew as well as themselves: Therefore, I grievously suspect a Cheat; and, that these Authors of mine, stole and transcribed every Word, from the universal Report of Mankind. So that I look upon my self, as fifty Shillings out of Pocket, to no manner of Purpose.

If, by altering the Title, I could make the same Materials serve for another Dedication (as my Betters have done) it would help to make up my Loss: But, I have made several Persons, dip here and there in those Papers, and before they read three Lines, they have all assured me, plainly, that they cannot possibly be applied to any Person besides your Lordship.

I expected, indeed, to have heard of your Lordship's Bravery, at the Head of an Army; Of your undaunted Courage, in mounting a Breach, or scaling a Wall; Or, to have had your Pedigree trac'd in a Lineal Descent from the House of *Austria*; Or, of your wonderful Talent at Dress and Dancing; Or, your Profound Knowledge in *Algebra*, *Metaphysicks*, and the Oriental Tongues. But to ply the World with an old beaten Story of your Wit, and Eloquence, and Learning, and Wisdom, and Justice, and Politeness, and Candor, and Evenness of Temper in all Scenes of Life; Of that great Discernment in Discovering, and Readiness in Favouring deserving Men; with forty other common Topicks: I confess, I have neither Conscience, nor Countenance to do it. Because, there is no Virtue, either of a Publick or Private Life, which some Circumstances of your own, have not often produced upon the Stage of the World; And those few, which for want of Occasions to exert them, might otherwise have pass'd unseen or unobserved by your *Friends*, your *Enemies* have at length brought to Light.

'Tis true, I should be very loth, the Bright Example of your Lordship's Virtues should be lost to After-Ages, both for their sake and your own; but chiefly, because they will be so very necessary to adorn the History of a *late Reign*; And That is another Reason, why I would forbear to make a Recital of them here; Because, I have been told by Wise Men, that as Dedications have run for some Years past, a good Historian will not be apt to have Recourse thither, in search of Characters.

There is one Point, wherein I think we Dedicators would do

well to change our Measures; I mean, instead of running on so far, upon the Praise of our Patrons *Liberality*, to spend a Word or two, in admiring their *Patience*. I can put no greater Compliment on your Lordship's, than by giving you so ample an Occasion to exercise it at present. Tho', perhaps, I shall not be apt to reckon much Merit to your Lordship upon that Score, who having been formerly used to tedious Harangues, and sometimes to as little Purpose, will be the readier to pardon this, especially, when it is offered by one, who is with all Respect and Veneration,

My LORD,

Your Lordship's most Obedient,

and most Faithful Servant,

The Bookseller.

THE BOOKSELLER TO THE READER.

IT *is now Six Years since these Papers came first to my Hands, which seems to have been about a Twelvemonth after they were writ: For, the Author tells us in his Preface to the first Treatise, that he hath calculated it for the Year* 1697, *and in several Passages of that Discourse, as well as the second, it appears, they were written about that Time.*

As to the Author, I can give no manner of Satisfaction; However, I am credibly informed that this Publication is without his Knowledge; for he concludes the Copy is lost, having lent it to a Person, since dead, and being never in Possession of it after: So that, whether the Work received his last Hand, or, whether he intended to fill up the defective Places, is like to remain a Secret.

If I should go about to tell the Reader, *by what Accident, I became Master of these Papers, it would, in this unbelieving Age, pass for little more than the Cant, or Jargon of the Trade. I, therefore, gladly spare both him and my self so unnecessary a Trouble. There yet remains a difficult Question, why I publish'd them no sooner. I forbore upon two Accounts: First, because I thought I had better Work upon my Hands; and Secondly, because, I was not without some Hope of hearing from the Author, and receiving his Directions. But, I have been lately alarm'd with Intelligence of a surreptitious Copy, which a certain great Wit had new polish'd and refin'd, or as our present Writers express themselves,* fitted to the Humor of the Age; *as they have already done, with great Felicity, to* Don Quixot, Boccalini, la Bruyere *and other Authors. However, I thought it fairer Dealing, to offer the whole Work in its Naturals. If any Gentleman will please to furnish me with a Key, in order to explain the more difficult Parts, I shall very gratefully acknowledge the Favour, and print it by it self.*

THE

Epistle Dedicatory,

TO

His Royal Highness

PRINCE POSTERITY.

SIR,

I HERE present *Your Highness* with the Fruits of a very few leisure Hours, stollen from the short Intervals of a World of Business, and of an Employment quite alien from such Amusements as this: The poor Production of that Refuse of Time which has lain heavy upon my Hands, during a long Prorogation of Parliament, a great Dearth of Forein News, and a tedious Fit of rainy Weather: For which, and other Reasons, it cannot chuse extreamly to deserve such a Patronage as that of *Your Highness*, whose numberless Virtues in so few Years, make the World look upon You as the future Example to all Princes: For altho' *Your Highness* is hardly got clear of Infancy, yet has the universal learned World already resolv'd upon appealing to Your future Dictates with the lowest and most resigned Sub-

The Citation out of Irenæus *in the* Title-Page, *which seems to be all* Gibberish, *is a Form of Initiation used antiently by the* Marcosian Hereticks. W. Wotton.

It is the usual Style of decry'd Writers to appeal to Posterity, *who is here represented as a Prince in his Nonage, and* Time *as his Governour, and the Author begins in a way very frequent with him, by personating other Writers, who sometimes offer such Reasons and Excuses for publishing their Works as they ought chiefly to conceal and be asham'd of.*

mission: Fate having decreed You sole Arbiter of the Productions of human Wit, in this polite and most accomplish'd Age. Methinks, the Number of Appellants were enough to shock and startle any Judge of a Genius less unlimited than Yours: But in order to prevent such glorious Tryals, the *Person* (it seems) to whose Care the Education of *Your Highness* is committed, has resolved (as I am told) to keep you in almost an universal Ignorance of our Studies, which it is Your inherent Birth-right to inspect.

It is amazing to me, that this *Person* should have Assurance in the face of the Sun, to go about persuading *Your Highness*, that our Age is almost wholly illiterate, and has hardly produc'd one Writer upon any Subject. I know very well, that when *Your Highness* shall come to riper Years, and have gone through the Learning of Antiquity, you will be too curious to neglect inquiring into the Authors of the very age before You: And to think that this *Insolent*, in the Account he is preparing for Your View, designs to reduce them to a Number so insignificant as I am asham'd to mention; it moves my Zeal and my Spleen for the Honor and Interest of our vast flourishing Body, as well as of my self, for whom I know by long Experience, he has profess'd, and still continues a peculiar Malice.

'Tis not unlikely, that when *Your Highness* will one day peruse what I am now writing, You may be ready to expostulate with Your *Governour* upon the Credit of what I here affirm, and command Him to shew You some of our Productions. To which he will answer, (for I am well informed of his Designs) by asking *Your Highness*, where they are? and what is become of them? and pretend it a Demonstration that there never were any, because they are not then to be found: Not to be found! Who has mislaid them? Are they sunk in the Abyss of Things? 'Tis certain, that in their own Nature they were *light* enough to swim upon the Surface for all Eternity. Therefore the Fault is in Him, who tied Weights so heavy to their Heels, as to depress them to the Center. Is their very Essence destroyed? Who has annihilated them? Were they drowned by *Purges* or martyred by *Pipes?* Who administred them to the Posteriors of ——? But that it may no longer be a Doubt with *Your Highness*, who is to be the Author of this universal Ruin; I beseech You to observe that large and terrible *Scythe* which your *Governour* affects to bear continually about him. Be pleased to remark the Length and Strength, the Sharpness and Hardness of his *Nails* and *Teeth*: Consider his baneful abominable *Breath*, Enemy to Life and Matter, infectious and corrupting: And then reflect whether it be possible for any mortal Ink and Paper of this Generation to make a suitable Resistance. Oh, that *Your Highness* would one day resolve to disarm this Usurping * *Maitre du Palais*, of his furious Engins, and bring Your Empire † *hors de Page*.

It were endless to recount the several Methods of Tyranny and Destruction, which Your *Governour* is pleased to practise upon this Occasion. His inveterate Malice is such to the Writings of our Age, that of several Thousands produced yearly from this renowned City, before the next Revolution of the Sun, there is not one to be heard of: Unhappy Infants, many of them barbarously destroyed, before they have so much as learnt their *Mother-Tongue* to beg for Pity. Some he stifles in their Cradles, others he frights into Convulsions, whereof they suddenly die; Some he flays alive, others he tears Limb from Limb: Great Numbers are offered to *Moloch*, and the rest tainted by his Breath, die of a languishing Consumption.

But the Concern I have most at Heart, is for our Corporation of *Poets*, from whom I am preparing a Petition to *Your Highness*, to be subscribed with the Names of one hundred thirty six of the first Rate, but whose immortal Productions are never likely to reach your Eyes, tho' each of them is now an humble and an earnest Appellant for the Laurel, and has large comely Volumes ready to shew for a Support to his Pretensions. The *never-dying* Works of these illustrious Persons, Your *Governour*, Sir, has devoted to unavoidable Death, and *Your Highness* is to be made believe, that our Age has never arrived at the Honor to produce one single Poet.

We confess *Immortality* to be a great and powerful Goddess, but in vain we offer up to her our Devotions and our Sacrifices, if *Your Highness*'s *Governour*, who has usurped the *Priesthood*,

* *Comptroller*. † *Out of Guardianship*.

must by an unparallel'd Ambition and Avarice, wholly intercept and devour them.

To affirm that our Age is altogether Unlearned, and devoid of Writers in any kind, seems to be an Assertion so bold and so false, that I have been sometime thinking, the contrary may almost be proved by uncontroulable Demonstration. 'Tis true indeed, that altho' their Numbers be vast, and their Productions numerous in proportion, yet are they hurryed so hastily off the Scene, that they escape our Memory, and delude our Sight. When I first thought of this Address, I had prepared a copious List of *Titles* to present *Your Highness* as an undisputed Argument for what I affirm. The Originals were posted fresh upon all Gates and Corners of Streets; but returning in a very few Hours to take a Review, they were all torn down, and fresh ones in their Places: I enquired after them among Readers and Booksellers, but I enquired in vain, the *Memorial of them was lost among Men, their Place was no more to be found*: and I was laughed to scorn, for a *Clown* and a *Pedant*, without all Taste and Refinement, little versed in the Course of *present* Affairs, and that knew nothing of what had pass'd in the best Companies of Court and Town. So that I can only avow in general to *Your Highness*, that we do abound in Learning and Wit; but to fix upon Particulars, is a Task too slippery for my slender Abilities. If I should venture in a windy Day, to affirm to *Your Highness*, that there is a huge Cloud near the *Horizon* in the Form of a *Bear*, another in the *Zenith* with the Head of an *Ass*, a third to the Westward with Claws like a *Dragon*; and *Your Highness* should in a few Minutes think fit to examine the Truth; 'tis certain, they would all be changed in Figure and Position, new ones would arise, and all we could agree upon would be, that Clouds there were, but that I was grosly mistaken in the *Zoography* and *Topography* of them.

But Your *Governour*, perhaps, may still insist, and put the Question: What is then become of those immense Bales of Paper, which must needs have been employ'd in such Numbers of Books? Can these also be wholly annihilate, and so of a sudden as I pretend? What shall I say in return of so invidious an Objection? It ill befits the Distance between *Your Highness* and Me, to send You for ocular Conviction to a *Jakes*, or an *Oven*; to the

Windows of a *Bawdy-house*, or to a sordid *Lanthorn*. Books, like Men their Authors, have no more than one Way of coming into the World, but there are ten Thousand to go out of it, and return no more.

I profess to *Your Highness*, in the Integrity of my Heart, that what I am going to say is literally true this Minute I am writing: What Revolutions may happen before it shall be ready for your Perusal, I can by no means warrant: However I beg You to accept it as a Specimen of our Learning, our Politeness and our Wit. I do therefore affirm upon the Word of a sincere Man, that there is now actually in being, a certain Poet called *John Dryden*, whose Translation of *Virgil* was lately printed in a large Folio, well bound, and if diligent search were made, for ought I know, is yet to be seen. There is another call'd *Nahum Tate*, who is ready to make Oath that he has caused many Rheams of Verse to be published, whereof both himself and his Bookseller (if lawfully required) can still produce authentick Copies, and therefore wonders why the World is pleased to make such a Secret of it. There is a Third, known by the Name of *Tom Durfey*, a Poet of a vast Comprehension, an universal Genius, and most profound Learning. There are also one Mr. *Rymer*, and one Mr. *Dennis*, most profound Criticks. There is a Person styl'd Dr. *Bentley*, who has written near a thousand Pages of immense Erudition, *giving a full and true Account* of a certain *Squable* of wonderful Importance between himself and a Bookseller: He is a Writer of infinite Wit and Humour; no Man raillyes with a better Grace, and in more sprightly Turns. Farther, I avow to *Your Highness*, that with these Eyes I have beheld the Person of *William Wotton*, B.D. who has written a good sizeable Volume against a *Friend of Your Governor* (from whom, alas! he must therefore look for little Favour) in a most gentlemanly Style, adorned with utmost Politeness and Civility; replete with Discoveries equally valuable for their Novelty and Use: and embellish'd with *Traits* of Wit so poignant and so apposite, that he is a worthy Yokemate to his foremention'd *Friend*.

WHY should I go upon farther Particulars, which might fill a Volume with the just Elogies of my cotemporary Brethren? I shall bequeath this Piece of Justice to a larger Work: wherein I intend to write a Character of the present Set of *Wits* in our Nation: Their Persons I shall describe particularly, and at Length, their Genius and Understandings in *Mignature*.

IN the mean time, I do here make bold to present *Your Highness* with a faithful Abstract drawn from the Universal Body of all Arts and Sciences, intended wholly for your Service and Instruction: Nor do I doubt in the least, but *Your Highness* will peruse it as carefully, and make as considerable Improvements, as *other* young *Princes* have already done by the many Volumes of late Years written for a Help to their Studies.

THAT *Your Highness* may advance in Wisdom and Virtue, as well as Years, and at last out-shine all Your Royal Ancestors, shall be the daily Prayer of,

SIR,

Decemb.
1697.

Your Highness's

Most devoted, &c.

THE
PREFACE.

THE Wits of the present Age being so very numerous and penetrating, it seems, the Grandees of *Church* and *State* begin to fall under horrible Apprehensions, lest these Gentlemen, during the intervals of a long Peace, should find leisure to pick Holes in the weak sides of Religion and Government. To prevent which, there has been much Thought employ'd of late upon certain Projects for taking off the Force, and Edge of those formidable Enquirers, from canvasing and reasoning upon such delicate Points. They have at length fixed upon one, which will require some Time as well as Cost, to perfect. Mean while the Danger hourly increasing, by new Levies of Wits all appointed (as there is Reason to fear) with Pen, Ink, and Paper which may at an hours Warning be drawn out into Pamphlets, and other Offensive Weapons, ready for immediate Execution: It was judged of absolute necessity, that some present Expedient be thought on, till the main Design can be brought to Maturity. To this End, at a Grand Committee, some Days ago, this important Discovery was made by a certain curious and refined Observer; That Sea-men have a Custom when they meet a *Whale*, to fling him out an empty *Tub*, by way of Amusement, to divert him from laying violent Hands upon the Ship. This Parable was immediately mythologiz'd: The *Whale* was interpreted to be *Hobbes*'s *Leviathan*, which tosses and plays with all other Schemes of Religion and Government, whereof a great many are hollow, and dry, and empty, and noisy, and wooden, and given to Rotation. This is the *Leviathan* from whence the terrible Wits of our Age are said to borrow their Weapons. The *Ship* in danger, is easily understood to be its old Antitype the *Commonwealth*. But, how to analyze the *Tub*, was a Matter of difficulty; when after long Enquiry and Debate, the literal Meaning was preserved: And it was decreed, that in order to prevent these *Leviathans* from tossing and sporting with the *Commonwealth*, (which of it self is too apt to *fluctuate*) they should be diverted from that Game by a *Tale of a Tub*. And my Genius being conceived to lye not unhappily that way, I had the Honor done me to be engaged in the Performance.

THIS is the sole Design in publishing the following Treatise, which I hope will serve for an *Interim* of some Months to employ those unquiet Spirits, till the perfecting of that great Work: into the Secret of which, it is reasonable the courteous Reader should have some little Light.

IT is intended that a large Academy be erected, capable of containing nine thousand seven hundred forty and three Persons; which by modest Computation is reckoned to be pretty near the current Number of *Wits* in this Island. These are to be disposed into the several Schools of this Academy, and there pursue those Studies to which their Genius most inclines them. The Undertaker himself will publish his Proposals with all convenient speed, to which I shall refer the curious Reader for a more particular Account, mentioning at present only a few of the Principal Schools. There is first, a large *Pederastick* School, with *French* and *Italian* Masters. There is also, the *Spelling* School, *a very spacious Building*: the School of *Looking Glasses*: The School of *Swearing*: the School of *Criticks*: the School of *Salivation*: The School of *Hobby-Horses*: The School of *Poetry*: * The School of *Tops*: the School of *Spleen*: The School of *Gaming*: with many others too tedious to recount. No Person to be admitted Member into any of these Schools, without an Attestation under two sufficient Persons Hands, certifying him to be a *Wit*.

BUT, to return. I am sufficiently instructed in the Principal Duty of a Preface, if my Genius were capable of arriving at it. Thrice have I forced my Imagination to make the *Tour* of my Invention, and thrice it has returned empty; the latter having been wholly drained by the following Treatise. Not so, my more successful Brethren the *Moderns*, who will by no means let slip a

* *This I think the Author should have omitted, it being of the very same Nature with the* School of Hobby-Horses, *if one may venture to censure one who is so severe a Censurer of others, perhaps with too little Distinction.*

Preface or Dedication, without some notable distinguishing Stroke, to surprize the Reader at the Entry, and kindle a Wonderful Expectation of what is to ensue. Such was that of a most ingenious Poet, who solliciting his Brain for something new, compared himself to the *Hangman*, and his Patron to the *Patient*: This was * *Insigne*, *recens*, *indictum ore alio*. When I went thro' That necessary and noble † Course of Study, I had the happiness to observe many such egregious Touches, which I shall not injure the Authors by transplanting: Because I have remarked, that nothing is so very tender as a *Modern* Piece of Wit, and which is apt to suffer so much in the Carriage. Some things are extreamly witty *to day*, or *fasting*, or *in this place*, or *at eight a clock*, or *over a Bottle*, or *spoke by Mr*. What d'y'call'm, or *in a Summer's Morning*: Any of which, by the smallest Transposal or Misapplication, is utterly annihilate. Thus, *Wit* has its Walks and Purlieus, out of which it may not stray the breadth of an Hair, upon peril of being lost. The *Moderns* have artfully fixed this *Mercury*, and reduced it to the Circumstances of Time, Place and Person. Such a Jest there is, that will not pass out of *Covent-Garden*; and such a one, that is no where intelligible but at *Hide-Park* Corner. Now, tho' it sometimes tenderly affects me to consider, that all the towardly Passages I shall deliver in the following Treatise, will grow quite out of date and relish with the first shifting of the present Scene: yet I must need subscribe to the Justice of this Proceeding: because, I cannot imagine why we should be at Expence to furnish Wit for succeeding Ages, when the former have made no sort of Provision for ours; wherein I speak the Sentiment of the very newest, and consequently the most Orthodox Refiners, as well as my own. However, being extreamly sollicitous, that every accomplished Person who has got into the Taste of Wit, calculated for this present Month of *August*, 1697, should descend to the very *bottom* of all the *Sublime* throughout this Treatise; I hold fit to lay down this general Maxim. Whatever Reader desires to have a thorow Comprehension of an Author's Thoughts, cannot take a better Method, than

* *Hor.*

† *Reading Prefaces*, &c.

* *Something extraordinary, new and never hit upon before.*

by putting himself into the Circumstances and Postures of Life, that the Writer was in, upon every important Passage as it flow'd from his Pen; For this will introduce a Parity and strict Correspondence of Idea's between the Reader and the Author. Now, to assist the diligent Reader in so delicate an Affair, as far as brevity will permit, I have recollected, that the shrewdest Pieces of this Treatise, were conceived in Bed, in a Garret: At other times (for a Reason best known to my self) I thought fit to sharpen my Invention with Hunger; and in general, the whole Work was begun, continued, and ended, under a long Course of Physick, and a great want of Money. Now, I do affirm, it will be absolutely impossible for the candid Peruser to go along with me in a great many bright Passages, unless upon the several Difficulties emergent, he will please to capacitate and prepare himself by these Directions. And this I lay down as my principal *Postulatum*.

BECAUSE I have profess'd to be a most devoted Servant of all *Modern* Forms: I apprehend some curious *Wit* may object against me, for proceeding thus far in a Preface, without declaiming, according to the Custom, against the Multitude of Writers whereof the whole Multitude of Writers most reasonably complains. I am just come from perusing some hundreds of Prefaces, wherein the Authors do at the very beginning address the gentle Reader concerning this enormous Grievance. Of these I have preserved a few Examples, and shall set them down as near as my Memory has been able to retain them.

One begins thus;

For a Man to set up for a Writer, when the Press swarms with, &c.

Another;

The Tax upon Paper does not lessen the Number of Scriblers, who daily pester, &c.

Another;

When every little Would-be-wit takes Pen in hand, 'tis in vain to enter the Lists, &c.

Another;

To observe what Trash the Press swarms with, &c.

Another;

SIR, *It is meerly in Obedience to your Commands that I venture into the Publick; for who upon a less Consideration would be of a Party with such a Rabble of Scriblers,* &c.

Now, I have two Words in my own Defence, against this Objection. First: I am far from granting the Number of Writers, a Nuisance to our Nation, having strenuously maintained the contrary in several Parts of the following Discourse. Secondly: I do not well understand the Justice of this Proceeding, because I observe many of these polite Prefaces, to be not only from the same Hand, but from those who are most voluminous in their several Productions. Upon which I shall tell the Reader a short Tale.

A Mountebank in Leicester-Fields, *had drawn a huge Assembly about him. Among the rest, a fat unweildy Fellow, half stifled in the Press, would be every fit crying out, Lord! what a filthy Crowd is here? Pray, good People, give way a little, Bless me! what a Devil has rak'd this Rabble together: Z——ds, what squeezing is this! Honest Friend, remove your Elbow. At last, a* Weaver *that stood next him could hold no longer: A Plague confound you* (said he) *for an over-grown Sloven; and who (in the Devil's Name) I wonder, helps to make up the Crowd half so much as your self? Don't you consider (with a Pox) that you take up more room with that Carkass than any five here? Is not the Place as free for us as for you? Bring your own Guts to a reasonable Compass (and be d——n'd) and then I'll engage we shall have room enough for us all.*

There are certain common Privileges of a Writer, the Benefit whereof, I hope, there will be no Reason to doubt; Particularly, that where I am not understood, it shall be concluded, that something very useful and profound is coucht underneath: And again, that whatever word or Sentence is Printed in a different Character, shall be judged to contain something extraordinary either of *Wit* or *Sublime.*

As for the Liberty I have thought fit to take of praising my self, upon some Occasions or none; I am sure it will need no Excuse, if a Multitude of great Examples be allowed sufficient Authority: For it is here to be noted, that *Praise* was originally a Pension paid by the World: but the *Moderns* finding the Trouble and Charge too great in collecting it, have lately bought out the *Fee-Simple*; since which time, the Right of Presentation is wholly in our selves. For this Reason it is, that when an Author makes his own Elogy, he uses a certain form to declare and insist upon his Title, which is commonly in these or the like words, *I speak without Vanity*; which I think plainly shews it to be a Matter of Right and Justice. Now, I do here once for all declare, that in every Encounter of this Nature, thro' the following Treatise, the Form aforesaid is imply'd; which I mention, to save the Trouble of repeating it on so many Occasions.

'Tis a great Ease to my Conscience that I have writ so elaborate and useful a Discourse without one grain of Satyr intermixt; which is the sole point wherein I have taken leave to dissent from the famous Originals of our Age and Country. I have observ'd some Satyrists to use the Publick much at the Rate that Pedants do a naughty Boy ready Hors'd for Discipline: First expostulate the Case, then plead the Necessity of the Rod, from great Provocations, and conclude every Period with a Lash. Now, if I know any thing of Mankind, these Gentlemen might very well spare their Reproof and Correction: For there is not, through all Nature, another so callous and insensible a Member as the *World's Posteriors*, whether you apply to it the *Toe* or the *Birch*. Besides, most of our late Satyrists seem to lye under a sort of Mistake, that because *Nettles* have the Prerogative to Sting, therefore all *other Weeds* must do so too. I make not this Comparison out of the least Design to detract from these worthy Writers: For it is well known among *Mythologists*, that *Weeds* have the Preeminence over all other Vegetables; and therefore the first *Monarch* of this Island, whose Taste and Judgment were so acute and refined, did very wisely root out the *Roses* from the Collar of the *Order*, and plant the *Thistles* in their stead as the nobler Flower of the two. For which Reason it is conjectured by profounder Antiquaries, that the Satyrical Itch, so prevalent in this part of our Island, was first brought among us from beyond the *Tweed*. Here may it long flourish and abound; May it survive and neglect the Scorn of the World, with as much Ease and Contempt as the World is insensible to the Lashes of it. May their own Dullness, or that of their Party, be no Discouragement for the Authors to proceed; but let them remember, it is with *Wits* as with *Razors*, which are never so apt to *cut* those they are employ'd on, as when they have *lost their Edge*. Besides, those whose

Teeth are too rotten to bite, are best of all others, qualified to revenge that Defect with their Breath.

I am not like other Men, to envy or undervalue the Talents I cannot reach; for which Reason I must needs bear a true Honour to this large eminent Sect of our *British* Writers. And I hope, this little Panegyrick will not be offensive to their Ears, since it has the Advantage of being only designed for themselves. Indeed, Nature her self has taken order, that Fame and Honour should be purchased at a better Pennyworth by Satyr, than by any other Productions of the Brain; the World being soonest provoked to *Praise* by *Lashes*, as Men are to *Love*. There is a Problem in an ancient Author, why Dedications, and other Bundles of Flattery run all upon stale musty Topicks, without the smallest Tincture of any thing New; not only to the torment and nauseating of the *Christian* Reader, but (if not suddenly prevented) to the universal spreading of that pestilent Disease, the Lethargy, in this Island: whereas, there is very little Satyr which has not something in it untouch'd before. The Defects of the former are usually imputed to the want of Invention among those who are Dealers in that kind: But, I think, with a great deal of Injustice; the Solution being easy and natural. For, the Materials of Panegyrick being very few in Number, have been long since exhausted: For, as Health is but one Thing, and has been always the same, whereas Diseases are by thousands, besides new and daily Additions; So, all the Virtues that have been ever in Mankind, are to be counted upon a few Fingers, but his Follies and Vices are innumerable, and Time adds hourly to the Heap. Now, the utmost a poor Poet can do, is to get by heart a List of the Cardinal Virtues, and deal them with his utmost Liberality to his Hero or his Patron: He may ring the Changes as far as it will go, and vary his Phrase till he has talk'd round; but the Reader quickly finds, it is all * *Pork*, with a little variety of Sawce: For there is no inventing Terms of Art beyond our Idea's; and when Idea's are exhausted, Terms of Art must be so too.

* *Plutarch.*

BUT, tho' the Matter for Panegyrick were as fruitful as the Topicks of Satyr, yet would it not be hard to find out a sufficient Reason, why the latter will be always better received than the first. For, this being bestowed only upon one or a few Persons at a time, is sure to raise Envy, and consequently ill words from the rest, who have no share in the Blessing: But Satyr being levelled at all, is never resented for an offence by any, since every individual Person makes bold to understand it of others, and very wisely removes his particular Part of the Burthen upon the shoulders of the World, which are broad enough, and able to bear it. To this purpose, I have sometimes reflected upon the Difference between *Athens* and *England*, with respect to the Point before us. In the *Attick* * Commonwealth, it was the Privilege and Birth-right of every Citizen and Poet, to rail aloud and in publick, or to expose upon the Stage by Name, any Person they pleased, tho' of the greatest Figure, whether a *Creon*, an *Hyperbolus*, an *Alcibiades*, or a *Demosthenes*: But on the other side, the least reflecting word let fall against the *People* in general, was immediately caught up, and revenged upon the Authors, however considerable for their Quality or their Merits. Whereas, in *England* it is just the Reverse of all this. Here, you may securely display your utmost *Rhetorick* against Mankind, in the Face of the World; tell them, "*That all are* "*gone astray; That there is none that doth good, no not one; That we live* "*in the very Dregs of Time; That Knavery and Atheism are Epidemick* "*as the Pox; That Honesty is fled with Astræa*; with any other Common places *equally* new and eloquent, which are furnished by the * *Splendida bilis*. And when you have done, the whole Audience, far from being offended, shall return you thanks as a Deliverer of precious and useful Truths. Nay farther; It is but to venture your Lungs, and you may preach in *Covent-Garden* against Foppery and Fornication, and *something else*: Against Pride, and Dissimulation, and Bribery, at *White Hall*: You may expose Rapine and Injustice in the *Inns* of *Court* Chappel: And in a *City* Pulpit be as fierce as you please, against Avarice, Hypocrisie and Extortion. 'Tis but a *Ball* bandied to and fro, and every Man carries a *Racket* about Him to strike it from himself among the rest of the Company. But on the other side, whoever should mistake the Nature of things so far, as to drop but a single Hint in publick, How *such a one*, starved half

* *Vid. Xenoph.*

* *Hor.*

* *Spleen.*

the Fleet, and half-poison'd the rest: How *such a one*, from a true Principle of *Love* and *Honour*, pays no Debts but for *Wenches* and *Play*: How *such a one* has got a Clap and runs out of his Estate: * How *Paris* bribed by *Juno* and *Venus*, loath to offend either Party, slept out the whole Cause on the Bench: Or, how *such an Orator* makes long Speeches in the Senate with much Thought, little Sense, and to no Purpose; whoever, I say, should venture to be thus particular, must expect to be imprisoned for *Scandalum Magnatum*: to have *Challenges* sent him; to be sued for *Defamation*; and to be *brought before the Bar of the House*.

BUT I forget that I am expatiating on a Subject, wherein I have no concern, having neither a Talent nor an Inclination for Satyr; On the other side, I am so entirely satisfied with the whole present Procedure of human Things, that I have been for some Years preparing Materials towards *A Panegyrick upon the World*; to which I intended to add a Second Part, entituled, *A Modest Defence of the Proceedings of the Rabble in all Ages*. Both these I had Thoughts to publish by way of Appendix to the following Treatise; but finding my Common-Place-Book fill much slower than I had reason to expect, I have chosen to defer them to another Occasion. Besides, I have been unhappily prevented in that Design, by a certain Domestick Misfortune, in the Particulars whereof, tho' it would be very seasonable, and much in the *Modern* way, to inform the *gentle Reader*, and would also be of great Assistance towards extending this Preface into the Size now in Vogue, which by Rule ought to be *large* in proportion as the subsequent Volume is *small*; Yet I shall now dismiss our impatient Reader from any farther Attendance at the *Porch*; and having duly prepared his Mind by a preliminary Discourse, shall gladly introduce him to the sublime Mysteries that ensue.

---

* Juno *and* Venus *are Money and a Mistress, very powerful Bribes to a Judge, if Scandal says true. I remember such Reflexions were cast about that time, but I cannot fix the Person intended here.*

A TALE
OF A
TUB, &c.

SECT. I.

The INTRODUCTION.

WHOEVER hath an Ambition to be heard in a Crowd, must press, and squeeze, and thrust, and climb with indefatigable Pains, till he has exalted himself to a certain Degree of Altitude above them. Now, in all Assemblies, tho' you wedge them ever so close, we may observe this peculiar Property; that, over their Heads there is Room enough; but how to reach it, is the difficult Point; It being as hard to get quit of *Number* as of *Hell*;

> *——— *Evadere ad auras,*
> *Hoc opus, hic labor est.*

To this End, the Philosopher's Way in all Ages has been by erecting certain *Edifices in the Air*; But, whatever Practice and Reputation these kind of Structures have formerly possessed, or may still continue in, not excepting even that of *Socrates*, when he was suspended in a Basket to help Contemplation; I think, with due Submission, they seem to labour under two In-

---

* *But to return, and view the cheerful Skies;*
In this the Task and mighty Labour lies.

conveniences. *First*, That the Foundations being laid too high, they have been often out of *Sight*, and ever out of *Hearing*. *Secondly*, That the Materials, being very transitory, have suffer'd much from Inclemencies of Air, especially in these North-West Regions.

THEREFORE, towards the just Performance of this great Work, there remain but three Methods that I can think on; Whereof the Wisdom of our Ancestors being highly sensible, has, to encourage all aspiring Adventurers, thought fit to erect three wooden Machines, for the Use of those Orators who desire to talk much without Interruption. These are, the *Pulpit*, the *Ladder*, and the *Stage-Itinerant*. For, as to the *Bar*, tho' it be compounded of the same Matter, and designed for the same Use, it cannot however be well allowed the Honor of a fourth, by reason of its level or inferior Situation, exposing it to perpetual Interruption from Collaterals. Neither can the *Bench* it self, tho raised to a proper Eminency, put in a better Claim, whatever its Advocates insist on. For if they please to look into the original Design of its Erection, and the Circumstances or Adjuncts subservient to that Design, they will soon acknowledge the present Practice exactly correspondent to the Primitive Institution, and both to answer the Etymology of the Name, which in the *Phœnician* Tongue is a Word of great Signification, importing, if literally interpreted, *The Place of Sleep*; but in common Acceptation, *A Seat well bolster'd and cushion'd, for the Repose of old and gouty Limbs: Senes ut in otia tuta recedant*. Fortune being indebted to them this Part of Retaliation, that, as formerly, they have long *Talkt*, whilst others *Slept*, so now they may *Sleep* as long whilst others *Talk*.

BUT if no other Argument could occur to exclude the *Bench* and the *Bar* from the List of Oratorial Machines, it were sufficient, that the Admission of them would overthrow a Number which I was resolved to establish, whatever Argument it might cost me; in imitation of that prudent Method observed by many other Philosophers and great Clerks, whose chief Art in Division has been, to grow fond of some proper mystical Number, which their Imaginations have rendred Sacred, to a Degree, that they force common Reason to find room for it in every part of Nature;

reducing, including, and adjusting every *Genus* and *Species* within that Compass, by coupling some against their Wills, and banishing others at any Rate. Now among all the rest, the profound Number *THREE* is that which hath most employ'd my sublimest Speculations, nor ever without wonderful Delight. There is now in the Press, (and will be publish'd next Term) a Panegyrical Essay of mine upon this Number, wherein I have by most convincing Proofs, not only reduced the *Senses* and the *Elements* under its Banner, but brought over several Deserters from its two great Rivals *SEVEN* and *NINE*.

Now, the first of these Oratorial Machines in Place as well as Dignity, is the *Pulpit*. Of *Pulpits* there are in this Island several sorts; but I esteem only That made of Timber from the *Sylva Caledonia*, which agrees very well with our Climate. If it be upon its Decay, 'tis the better, both for Conveyance of Sound, and for other Reasons to be mentioned by and by. The Degree of Perfection in Shape and Size, I take to consist, in being extreamly narrow, with little Ornament, and best of all without a Cover; (for by antient Rule, it ought to be the only uncover'd *Vessel* in every Assembly where it is rightfully used) by which means, from its near Resemblance to a Pillory, it will ever have a mighty Influence on human Ears.

Of *Ladders* I need say nothing: 'Tis observed by Foreigners themselves, to the Honor of our Country, that we excel all Nations in our Practice and Understanding of this Machine. The ascending Orators do not only oblige their Audience in the agreeable Delivery, but the whole World in their *early* Publication of these Speeches; which I look upon as the choicest Treasury of our *British* Eloquence, and whereof I am informed, that worthy Citizen and Bookseller, Mr. *John Dunton*, hath made a faithful and a painful Collection, which he shortly designs to publish in Twelve Volumes in Folio, illustrated with Copper-Plates. A Work highly useful and curious, and altogether worthy of such a Hand.

The last Engine of Orators, is the * *Stage Itinerant*, erected

* *Is the* Mountebank's Stage, *whose Orators the Author determines either to the* Gallows *or a* Conventicle.

with much Sagacity, † *sub Jove pluvio, in triviis & quadriviis*. It is the great Seminary of the two former, and its Orators are sometimes preferred to the One, and sometimes to the Other, in proportion to their Deservings, there being a strict and perpetual Intercourse between all three.

FROM this accurate Deduction it is manifest, that for obtaining Attention in Publick, there is of necessity required a *superiour Position of Place*. But, altho' this Point be generally granted, yet the Cause is little agreed in; and it seems to me, that very few Philosophers have fallen into a true, natural Solution of this *Phænomenon*. The deepest Account, and the most fairly digested of any I have yet met with, is this, That Air being a heavy Body, and therefore (according to the System of * *Epicurus*) continually descending, must needs be more so, when loaden and press'd down by Words; which are also Bodies of much Weight and Gravity, as it is manifest from those deep *Impressions* they make and leave upon us; and therefore must be delivered from a due Altitude, or else they will neither carry a good Aim, nor fall down with a sufficient Force.

*Lucret. Lib. 2.

* *Corpoream quoque enim vocem constare fatendum est,*
Et sonitum, quoniam possunt impellere Sensus. Lucr. *Lib.* 4.

AND I am the readier to favour this Conjecture, from a common Observation; that in the several Assemblies of these Orators, Nature it self hath instructed the Hearers, to stand with their Mouths open, and erected parallel to the Horizon, so as they may be intersected by a perpendicular Line from the Zenith to the Center of the Earth. In which Position, if the Audience be well compact, every one carries home a Share, and little or nothing is lost.

I confess, there is something yet more refined in the Contrivance and Structure of our Modern Theatres. For, First; the Pit is sunk below the Stage with due regard to the Institution above-deduced; that whatever *weighty* Matter shall be delivered thence (whether it be *Lead* or *Gold*) may fall plum into the Jaws of cer-

† *In the Open Air, and in Streets where the greatest Resort is.*
* *'Tis certain then, that* Voice *that thus can wound*
Is all Material; Body *every* Sound.

tain *Criticks* (as I think they are called) which stand ready open to devour them. Then, the Boxes are built round, and raised to a Level with the Scene, in deference to the Ladies, because, That large Portion of Wit laid out in raising Pruriences and Protuberances, is observ'd to run much upon a Line, and ever in a Circle. The whining Passions and little starved Conceits, are gently wafted up by their own extreme Levity, to the middle Region, and there fix and are frozen by the frigid Understandings of the Inhabitants. Bombast and Buffoonry, by Nature lofty and light, soar highest of all, and would be lost in the Roof, if the prudent Architect had not with much Foresight contrived for them a fourth Place, called *the Twelve-Peny Gallery*, and there planted a suitable Colony, who greedily intercept them in their Passage.

Now this Physico-logical Scheme of Oratorial Receptacles or Machines, contains a great Mystery, being a Type, a Sign, an Emblem, a Shadow, a Symbol, bearing Analogy to the spacious Commonwealth of Writers, and to those Methods by which they must exalt themselves to a certain Eminency above the inferiour World. By the *Pulpit* are adumbrated the Writings of our *Modern Saints* in *Great Britain*, as they have spiritualized and refined them from the Dross and Grossness of *Sense* and *Human Reason*. The Matter, as we have said, is of rotten Wood, and that upon two Considerations; Because it is the Quality of rotten Wood to give *Light* in the Dark: And secondly, Because its Cavities are full of Worms: which is a * Type with a Pair of Handles, having a Respect to the two principal Qualifications of the Orator, and the two different Fates attending upon his Works.

The *Ladder* is an adequate Symbol of *Faction* and of *Poetry*, to both of which so noble a Number of Authors are indebted for their Fame. † Of *Faction*, because * * * * *

* *The Two Principal Qualifications of a Phanatick Preacher are, his Inward Light, and his Head full of Maggots, and the Two different Fates of his Writings are, to be burnt or Worm eaten.*

† *Here is pretended a Defect in the Manuscript, and this is very frequent with our Author, either when he thinks he cannot say any thing worth* Read*ing, or when he has no mind to enter on the Subject, or when it is a Matter of little Moment, or perhaps to amuse his* Reader *(whereof he is frequently very fond) or lastly, with some Satyrical Intention.*

Hiatus in MS.

* * * * * * * * *
* * * * * * * * *
* * * * * * * * *

* * * * Of *Poetry*, because its Orators do *perorare* with a Song; and because climbing up by slow Degrees, Fate is sure to turn them off before they can reach within many Steps of the Top: And because it is a Preferment attained by transferring of Propriety, and a confounding of *Meum* and *Tuum*.

UNDER the *Stage-Itinerant* are couched those Productions designed for the Pleasure and Delight of Mortal Man; such as, *Six-peny-worth of Wit*, Westminster *Drolleries*, *Delightful Tales*, *Compleat Jesters*, and the like; by which the Writers of and for *GRUB-STREET*, have in these latter Ages so nobly triumph'd over *Time*; have clipt his Wings, pared his Nails, filed his Teeth, turn'd back his Hour-Glass, blunted his Scythe, and drawn the Hob-Nails out of his Shoes. It is under this Classis, I have presumed to list my present Treatise, being just come from having the Honor conferred upon me, to be adopted a Member of that Illustrious Fraternity.

Now, I am not unaware, how the Productions of the *Grub-street* Brotherhood, have of late Years fallen under many Prejudices, nor how it has been the perpetual Employment of two *Junior* start-up Societies, to ridicule them and their Authors, as unworthy their established Post in the Commonwealth of Wit and Learning. Their own Consciences will easily inform them, whom I mean; Nor has the World been so negligent a Looker on, as not to observe the continual Efforts made by the Societies of *Gresham* and of * *Will*'s to edify a Name and Reputation upon the Ruin of OURS. And this is yet a more feeling Grief to Us upon the Regards of Tenderness as well as of Justice, when we reflect on their Proceedings, not only as unjust, but as ungrateful, undutiful, and unnatural. For, how can it be forgot by the

* Will's Coffee-House, *was formerly the Place where the Poets usually met, which tho it be yet fresh in memory, yet in some Years may be forgot, and want this Explanation.*

World or themselves, (to say nothing of our own Records, which are full and clear in the Point) that they both are Seminaries, not only of our *Planting*, but our *Watering* too? I am informed, Our two *Rivals* have lately made an Offer to enter into the Lists with united Forces, and Challenge us to a Comparison of Books, both as to *Weight* and *Number*. In Return to which, (with Licence from our *President*) I humbly offer two Answers: First, We say, the proposal is like that which *Archimedes* made upon a * *smaller* Affair, including an impossibility in the Practice; For, where can they find Scales of *Capacity* enough for the first, or an Arithmetician of *Capacity* enough for the Second. Secondly, We are ready to accept the Challenge, but with this Condition, that a third indifferent Person be assigned, to whose impartial Judgment it shall be left to decide, which Society each Book, Treatise or Pamphlet do most properly belong to. This Point, God knows, is very far from being fixed at present; For, We are ready to produce a Catalogue of some Thousands, which in all common Justice ought to be entitled to Our Fraternity, but by the revolted and new-fangled Writers, most perfidiously ascribed to the others. Upon all which, we think it very unbecoming our Prudence, that the Determination should be remitted to the Authors themselves; when our Adversaries by Briguing and Caballing, have caused so universal a Defection from us, that the greatest Part of our Society hath already deserted to them, and our nearest Friends begin to stand aloof, as if they were half-ashamed to own Us.

*Viz. *About moving the Earth.*

THIS is the utmost I am authorized to say upon so ungrateful and melancholy a Subject; because We are extreme unwilling to inflame a Controversy, whose Continuance may be so fatal to the Interests of Us All, desiring much rather that Things be amicably composed; and We shall so far advance on our Side, as to be ready to receive the two *Prodigals* with open Arms, whenever they shall think fit to return from their *Husks* and their *Harlots*; which I think from the * present Course of their Studies they most properly may be said to be engaged in; and like an indulgent Parent, continue to them our Affection and our Blessing.

* *Virtuoso Experiments, and Modern Comedies.*

But the greatest Maim given to that general Reception, which the Writings of our Society have formerly received, (next to the transitory State of all sublunary Things,) hath been a superficial Vein among many Readers of the present Age, who will by no means be persuaded to inspect beyond the Surface and the Rind of Things; whereas, *Wisdom* is a *Fox*, who after long hunting, will at last cost you the Pains to dig out: 'Tis a *Cheese*, which by how much the richer, has the thicker, the homelier, and the courser Coat; and whereof to a judicious Palate, the *Maggots* are the best. 'Tis a *Sack-Posset*, wherein the deeper you go, you will find it the sweeter. *Wisdom* is a *Hen*, whose *Cackling* we must value and consider, because it is attended with an *Egg*; But then, lastly, 'tis a *Nut*, which unless you chuse with Judgment, may cost you a Tooth, and pay you with nothing but a *Worm*. In consequence of these momentous Truths, the *Grubæan* Sages have always chosen to convey their Precepts and their Arts, shut up within the Vehicles of Types and Fables, which having been perhaps more careful and curious in adorning, than was altogether necessary, it has fared with these Vehicles after the usual Fate of Coaches over-finely painted and gilt; that the transitory Gazers have so dazzled their Eyes, and fill'd their Imaginations with the outward Lustre, as neither to regard or consider, the Person or the Parts of the Owner within. A Misfortune we undergo with somewhat less Reluctancy, because it has been common to us with *Pythagoras*, *Æsop*, *Socrates*, and other of our Predecessors.

However, that neither the World nor our selves may any longer suffer by such misunderstandings, I have been prevailed on, after much importunity from my Friends, to travel in a compleat and laborious Dissertation upon the prime Productions of our Society, which besides their beautiful Externals for the Gratification of superficial Readers, have darkly and deeply couched under them, the most finished and refined Systems of all Sciences and Arts; as I do not doubt to lay open by Untwisting or Unwinding, and either to draw up by Exantlation, or display by Incision.

This great Work was entred upon some Years ago, by one of our most eminent Members: He began with the History of

† *Reynard* the *Fox*, but neither lived to publish his Essay, nor to proceed farther in so useful an Attempt which is very much to be lamented, because the Discovery he made, and communicated with his Friends, is now universally received; nor, do I think, any of the Learned will dispute, that famous Treatise to be a compleat Body of Civil Knowledge, and the *Revelation*, or rather the *Apocalyps* of all State-*Arcana*. But the Progress I have made is much greater, having already finished my Annotations upon several Dozens; From some of which, I shall impart a few Hints to the candid Reader, as far as will be necessary to the Conclusion at which I aim.

THE first Piece I have handled is that of *Tom Thumb*, whose Author was a *Pythagorean* Philosopher. This dark Treatise contains the whole Scheme of the *Metempsychosis*, deducing the Progress of the Soul thro' all her Stages.

THE next is Dr. *Faustus*, penn'd by *Artephius*, an Author *bonæ notæ*, and an *Adeptus*; He published it in the * nine hundred eighty fourth Year of his Age; this Writer proceeds wholly by *Reincrudation*, or in the *via humida*: And the Marriage between *Faustus* and *Helen*, does most conspicuously dilucidate the fermenting of the *Male* and *Female Dragon*.

* *He lived a thousand.*

WHITTINGTON *and his Cat*, is the Work of that Mysterious *Rabbi*, *Jehuda Hannasi*, containing a Defence of the *Gemara* of the *Jerusalem Misna*, and its just preference to that of *Babylon*, contrary to the vulgar Opinion.

THE *Hind and Panther*. This is the Master-piece of a famous Writer || now living, intended for a compleat Abstract of sixteen thousand Schoolmen from *Scotus* to *Bellarmin*.

|| Viz *in the Year* 1698.

TOMMY POTTS. Another Piece supposed by the same Hand, by way of Supplement to the former.

THE *Wise Men of* Goatham, *cum Appendice*. This is a Treatise of immense Erudition, being the great Original and Fountain of

† *The Author seems here to be mistaken, for I have seen a Latin Edition of* Reynard *the Fox, above an hundred Years old, which I take to be the Original; for the rest it has been thought by many People to contain some Satyrical Design in it.*

those Arguments, bandied about both in *France* and *England*, for a just Defence of the *Modern* Learning and Wit, against the Presumption, the Pride, and the Ignorance of the *Antients*. This unknown Author hath so exhausted the Subject, that a penetrating Reader will easily discover, whatever hath been written since upon that Dispute, to be little more than Repetition. * An Abstract of this Treatise hath been lately published by a *worthy Member* of our Society.

THESE Notices may serve to give the Learned Reader an Idea as well as a Taste of what the whole Work is likely to produce: wherein I have now altogether circumscribed my Thoughts and my Studies; and if I can bring it to a Perfection before I die, shall reckon I have well employ'd the † poor Remains of an unfortunate Life. This indeed is more than I can justly expect from a Quill worn to the Pith in the Service of the State, in *Pro's* and *Con's* upon *Popish Plots*, and || *Meal-Tubs*, and *Exclusion Bills*, and *Passive Obedience*, and *Addresses of Lives and Fortunes*; and *Prerogative*, and *Property*, and *Liberty of Conscience*, and *Letters to a Friend*: From an Understanding and a Conscience, threadbare and ragged with perpetual turning; From a Head broken in a hundred places, by the Malignants of the opposite Factions, and from a Body spent with Poxes ill cured, by trusting to Bawds and Surgeons, who, (as it afterwards appeared) were profess'd Enemies to Me and the Government, and revenged their Party's Quarrel upon my Nose and Shins. Four-score and eleven Pamphlets have I writ under three Reigns, and for the Service of six and thirty Factions. But finding the State has no farther Occasion for Me and my Ink, I retire willingly to draw it out into Speculations more becoming a Philosopher, having, to my unspeakable Comfort, passed a long Life, with a Conscience void of Offence.

---

* *This I suppose to be understood of Mr.* Wottons *Discourse of Antient and Modern Learning.*

† *Here the Author seems to personate* L'estrange, Dryden, *and some others, who after having past their Lives in Vices, Faction and Falshood, have the Impudence to talk of Merit and Innocence and Sufferings.*

|| *In King* Charles *the* II. *Time, there was an Account of a* Presbyterian *Plot, found in a Tub, which then made much Noise.*

But to return. I am assured from the Reader's Candor, that the brief Specimen I have given, will easily clear all the rest of our Society's Productions from an Aspersion grown, as it is manifest, out of Envy and Ignorance: That they are of little farther Use or Value to Mankind, beyond the common Entertainments of their Wit and their Style: For these I am sure have never yet been disputed by our keenest Adversaries: In both which, as well as the more profound and mystical Part, I have throughout this Treatise closely followed the most applauded Originals. And to render all compleat, I have with much Thought and Application of Mind, so ordered, that the chief Title prefixed to it, (I mean, That under which I design it shall pass in the common Conversations of Court and Town) is modelled exactly after the Manner peculiar to *Our* Society.

I confess to have been somewhat liberal in the Business of * Titles, having observed the Humor of multiplying them, to bear great Vogue among certain Writers, whom I exceedingly Reverence. And indeed, it seems not unreasonable, that Books, the Children of the Brain, should have the Honor to be Christned with variety of Names, as well as other Infants of Quality. Our famous *Dryden* has ventured to proceed a Point farther, endeavouring to introduce also a Multiplicity of * *God-fathers*; which is an Improvement of much more Advantage, upon a very obvious Account. 'Tis a Pity this admirable Invention has not been better cultivated, so as to grow by this time into general Imitation, when such an Authority serves it for a Precedent. Nor have my Endeavours been wanting to second so useful an Example: But it seems, there is an unhappy Expence usually annexed to the Calling of a God-Father, which was clearly out of my Head, as it is very reasonable to believe. Where the Pinch lay, I cannot certainly affirm; but having employ'd a World of Thoughts and Pains, to split my Treatise into forty Sections, and having entreated forty Lords of my Acquaintance, that they would do me the Honor to stand, they all made it a Matter of Conscience, and sent me their Excuses.

* *The Title Page in the Original was so torn, that it was not possible to recover several Titles which the Author here speaks of.*

* *See* Virgil *translated,* &c.

SECTION II.

ONCE upon a Time, there was a Man who had Three *Sons by one Wife, and all at a Birth, neither could the Mid-Wife tell certainly which was the Eldest. Their Father died while they were young, and upon his Death-Bed, calling the Lads to him, spoke thus,

SONS; *because I have purchased no Estate, nor was born to any, I have long considered of some good Legacies to bequeath You; And at last, with much Care as well as Expence, have provided each of you* (here they are) *a new* † *Coat. Now, you are to understand, that these Coats have two Virtues contained in them: One is, that with good wearing, they will last you fresh and sound as long as you live: The other is, that they will grow in the same proportion with your Bodies, lengthning and widening of themselves, so as to be always fit. Here, let me see them on you before I die. So, very well; Pray Children, wear them clean, and brush them often. You will find in my* ‖ *Will* (here it is) *full Instructions in every particular concerning the Wearing and Management of your Coats; wherein you must be very exact, to avoid the Penalties I have appointed for every Transgression or Neglect, upon which your future Fortunes will entirely depend. I have also commanded in my Will, that you should live together in one House like Brethren and Friends, for then you will be sure to thrive, and not otherwise.*

HERE the Story says, this good Father died, and the three Sons went all together to seek their Fortunes.

I shall not trouble you with recounting what Adventures they met for the first seven Years, any farther than by taking notice, that they carefully observed their Father's Will, and kept their Coats in very good Order; That they travelled thro'

* *By these three Sons,* Peter, Martyn *and* Jack; Popery, *the* Church *of* England, *and our Protestant* Dissenters *are designed.* W. Wotton.

† *By his Coats which he gave his Sons, the Garments of the* Israelites. W. Wotton.

An Error (with Submission) of the learned Commentator; for by the Coats are meant the Doctrine and Faith of Christianity, *by the Wisdom of the Divine Founder fitted to all Times, Places and Circumstances.* Lambin.

‖ *The New Testament.*

several Countries, encountred a reasonable Quantity of Gyants and slew certain Dragons.

BEING now arrived at the proper Age for producing themselves, they came up to Town, and fell in love with the Ladies, but especially three, who about that time were in chief Reputation: The * Dutchess *d' Argent*, *Madame de Grands Titres*, and the Countess *d' Orgueil*. On their first Appearance, our three Adventurers met with a very bad Reception; and soon with great Sagacity guessing out the Reason, they quickly began to improve in the good Qualities of the Town: They Writ, and Raillyed, and Rhymed, and Sung, and Said, and said Nothing; They Drank, and Fought, and Whor'd, and Slept, and Swore, and took Snuff: They went to new Plays on the first Night, haunted the *Chocolate*-Houses, beat the Watch, lay on Bulks, and got Claps: They bilkt Hackney-Coachmen, ran in Debt with Shop-keepers, and lay with their Wives: They kill'd Bayliffs, kick'd Fidlers down Stairs, eat at *Locket*'s, loytered at *Will*'s: They talk'd of the Drawing-Room and never came there, Dined with Lords they never saw; Whisper'd a Dutchess, and spoke never a Word; exposed the Scrawls of their Laundress for Billets-doux of Quality: came ever just from Court and were never seen in it; attended the Levee *sub dio*; Got a list of Peers by heart in one Company, and with great Familiarity retailed them in another. Above all, they constantly attended those Committees of Senators who are silent in the *House*, and loud in the *Coffee-House*, where they nightly adjourn to chew the Cud of Politicks, and are encompass'd with a Ring of Disciples, who lye in wait to catch up their Droppings. The three Brothers had acquired forty other Qualifications of the like Stamp, too tedious to recount, and by consequence, were justly reckoned the most accomplish'd Persons in Town: But all would not suffice, and the Ladies aforesaid continued still inflexible: To clear up which Difficulty, I must with the

* *Their Mistresses are the* Dutchess d'Argent, Madamoiselle de Grands Titres, *and the* Countess d'Orgueil, *i. e.* Covetousness, Ambition *and* Pride, *which were the three great Vices that the ancient Fathers inveighed against as the first Corruptions of Christianity*. W. Wotton.

Reader's good Leave and Patience, have recourse to some Points of Weight, which the Authors of that Age have not sufficiently illustrated.

For, * about this Time it happened a Sect arose, whose Tenents obtained and spread very far, especially in the *Grand Monde*, and among every Body of good Fashion. They worshipped a sort of *Idol*, who, as their Doctrine delivered, did daily create Men, by a kind of Manufactory Operation. This † *Idol* they placed in the highest Parts of the House, on an Altar erected about three Foot: He was shewn in the Posture of a *Persian* Emperor, sitting on a *Superficies*, with his Legs interwoven under him. This God had a *Goose* for his Ensign; whence it is, that some Learned Men pretend to deduce his Original from *Jupiter Capitolinus*. At his left Hand, beneath the Altar, *Hell* seemed to open, and catch at the Animals the *Idol* was creating; to prevent which, certain of his Priests hourly flung in Pieces of the uninformed Mass, or Substance, and sometimes whole Limbs already enlivened, which that horrid Gulph insatiably swallowed, terrible to behold. The *Goose* was also held a subaltern Divinity, or *Deus minorum Gentium*, before whose Shrine was sacrificed that Creature, whose hourly Food is humane Gore, and who is in so great Renown abroad, for being the Delight and Favourite of the || *Ægyptian Cercopithecus*. Millions of these Animals were cruelly slaughtered every Day, to appease the Hunger of that consuming Deity. The chief *Idol* was also worshipped as the Inventor of the *Yard* and the *Needle*, whether as the God of Seamen, or on Account of certain other mystical Attributes, hath not been sufficiently cleared.

The Worshippers of this Deity had also a System of their Belief, which seemed to turn upon the following Fundamental. They held the Universe to be a large *Suit of Cloaths*, which *invests* every Thing: That the Earth is *invested* by the Air; The Air is

* *This is an Occasional Satyr upon Dress and Fashion, in order to introduce what follows.*

† *By this* Idol *is meant a Taylor.*

|| *The* Ægyptians *worship'd a Monkey, which Animal is very fond of eating Lice, styled here Creatures that feed on Human Gore.*

invested by the Stars; and the Stars are *invested* by the *Primum Mobile*. Look on this Globe of Earth, you will find it to be a very compleat and fashionable *Dress*. What is that which some call *Land*, but a fine Coat faced with Green? or the Sea, but a Wast-coat of Water-Tabby? Proceed to the particular Works of the Creation, you will find how curious *Journey-man* Nature hath been, to trim up the *vegetable* Beaux: Observe how sparkish a Perewig adorns the Head of a *Beech*, and what a fine Doublet of white Satin is worn by the *Birch*. To conclude from all, what is Man himself but a * *Micro-Coat*, or rather a compleat Suit of Cloaths with all its Trimmings? As to his Body, there can be no dispute; but examine even the Acquirements of his Mind, you will find them all contribute in their Order, towards furnishing out an exact Dress: To instance no more; Is not Religion a *Cloak*, Honesty a *Pair of Shoes*, worn out in the Dirt, Self-love a *Surtout*, Vanity a *Shirt*, and Conscience a *Pair of Breeches*, which, tho' a Cover for Lewdness as well as Nastiness, is easily slipt down for the Service of both.

THESE *Postulata* being admitted, it will follow in due Course of Reasoning, that those Beings which the World calls improperly *Suits of Cloaths*, are in Reality the most refined Species of Animals, or to proceed higher, that they are Rational Creatures, or Men. For, is it not manifest, that They live, and move, and talk, and perform all other Offices of Human Life? Are not Beauty, and Wit, and Mien, and Breeding, their inseparable Proprieties? In short, we see nothing but them, hear nothing but them. Is it not they who walk the Streets, fill up *Parliament*——, *Coffee*—, *Play*—, *Bawdy-Houses*? 'Tis true indeed, that these Animals, which are vulgarly called *Suits of Cloaths*, or *Dresses*, do according to certain Compositions receive different Appellations. If one of them be trimm'd up with a Gold Chain, and a red Gown, and a white Rod, and a great Horse, it is called a *Lord-Mayor*; If certain Ermins and Furs be placed in a certain Position, we stile them a *Judge*, and so, an apt Conjunction of Lawn and black Sattin, we intitle a *Bishop*.

* *Alluding to the Word* Microcosm, *or a little World, as Man hath been called by Philosophers.*

Others of these Professors, though agreeing in the main System, were yet more refined upon certain Branches of it; and held that Man was an Animal compounded of two *Dresses*, the *Natural* and the *Celestial Suit*, which were the Body and the Soul: That the Soul was the outward, and the Body the inward Cloathing; that the latter was *ex traduce*; but the former of daily Creation and Circumfusion. This last they proved by *Scripture*, because, *in Them we Live, and Move, and have our Being*: As likewise by Philosophy, because they are *All in All, and All in every Part*. Besides, said they, separate these two, and you will find the Body to be only a sensless unsavory Carcass. By all which it is manifest, that the outward Dress must needs be the Soul.

To this System of Religion were tagged several subaltern Doctrines, which were entertained with great Vogue: as particularly, the Faculties of the Mind were deduced by the Learned among them in this manner: *Embroidery*, was *Sheer wit; Gold Fringe* was *agreeable Conversation*, *Gold Lace* was *Repartee*, a huge long *Periwig* was *Humor*, and a *Coat full of Powder* was very good *Raillery*: All which required abundance of *Finesse* and *Delicatesse* to manage with Advantage, as well as a strict Observance after Times and Fashions.

I have with much Pains and Reading, collected out of antient Authors, this short Summary of a Body of Philosophy and Divinity, which seems to have been composed by a Vein and Race of Thinking, very different from any other Systems, either *Antient* or *Modern*. And it was not meerly to entertain or satisfy the Reader's Curiosity, but rather to give him Light into several Circumstances of the following Story: that knowing the State of Dispositions and Opinions in an Age so remote, he may better comprehend those great Events which were the issue of them. I advise therefore the courteous Reader, to peruse with a world of Application, again and again, whatever I have written upon this Matter. And so leaving these broken Ends, I carefully gather up the chief Thread of my Story, and proceed.

These Opinions therefore were so universal, as well as the Practices of them, among the refined Part of Court and Town, that our three Brother-Adventurers, as their Circumstances then stood, were strangely at a loss. For, on the one side, the three Ladies they address'd themselves to, (whom we have named already) were ever at the very Top of the Fashion, and abhorred all that were below it, but the breadth of a Hair. On the other side, their Father's Will was very precise, and it was the main Precept in it, with the greatest Penalties annexed, not to add to, or diminish from their Coats, one Thread, without a positive Command in the Will. Now, the Coats their Father had left them were, 'tis true, of very good Cloth, and besides, so neatly sown, you would swear they were all of a Piece, but at the same time, very plain, and with little or no Ornament; And it happened, that before they were a Month in Town, great * *Shoulder-knots* came up; Strait, all the World was *Shoulder-knots*; no approaching the Ladies *Ruelles* without the *Quota* of *Shoulder-knots: That Fellow*, cries one, *has no Soul; where is his Shoulder-knot?* Our three Brethren soon discovered their Want by sad Experience, meeting in their Walks with forty Mortifications and Indignities. If they went to the *Play-house*, the Door-keeper shewed them into the Twelve-peny Gallery. If they called a Boat, says a Water-man, *I am first Sculler*: If they stept to the *Rose* to take a Bottle, the Drawer would cry, *Friend, we sell no Ale*. If they went to visit a Lady, a Footman met them at the Door with, *Pray send up your Message*. In this unhappy Case, they

---

The first part of the Tale *is the History of* Peter; *thereby* Popery *is exposed, every Body knows the* Papists *have made great Additions to Christianity, that indeed is the great Exception which the* Church of England *makes against them, accordingly* Peter *begins his Pranks, with adding a* Shoulder-knot *to his Coat*. W. Wotton.

His Description of the Cloth of which the Coat was made, has a farther meaning than the Words may seem to import, "The Coats their Father had left them, were of very good Cloth, and besides so neatly Sown, you would swear it had been all of a Piece, but at the same time very plain with little or no Ornament." *This is the distinguishing Character of the Christian* Religion. Christiana Religio absoluta & simplex, *was* Ammianus Marcellinus's *Description of it, who was himself a Heathen*. W. Wotton.

* *By this is understood the first introducing of* Pageantry, *and unnecessary Ornaments in the Church, such as were neither for Convenience nor Edification, as a* Shoulder-knot, *in which there is neither Symmetry nor Use*.

went immediately to consult their Father's Will, read it over and over, but not a Word of the *Shoulder-knot*. What should they do? What Temper should they find? Obedience was absolutely necessary, and yet *Shoulder-knots* appeared extreamly requisite. After much Thought, one of the Brothers who happened to be more *Book-learned* than the other two, said he had found an Expedient. *'Tis true*, said he, *there is nothing here in this Will*, * totidem verbis, *making mention of* Shoulder-knots, *but I dare conjecture, we may find them* inclusivè, *or* totidem syllabis. This Distinction was immediately approved by all; and so they fell again to examine the Will. But their evil Star had so directed the Matter, that the first Syllable was not to be found in the whole Writing. Upon which Disappointment, he, who found the former Evasion, took heart, and said, *Brothers, there is yet Hopes; for tho' we cannot find them* totidem verbis, *nor* totidem syllabis, *I dare engage we shall make them out* tertio modo, *or* totidem literis. This Discovery was also highly commended, upon which they fell once more to the Scrutiny, and soon picked out *S*, *H*, *O*, *U*, *L*, *D*, *E*, *R*; when the same Planet, Enemy to their Repose, had wonderfully contrived, that a *K* was not to be found. Here was a weighty Difficulty! But the distinguishing Brother (for whom we shall hereafter find a Name) now his Hand was in, proved by a very good Argument, that *K* was a modern illegitimate Letter, unknown to the Learned Ages, nor any where to be found in antient Manuscripts. 'Tis true, said he, the Word *Calendæ* hath in † *Q.V.C.* been sometimes writ with a *K*, but erroneously, for in the best Copies it is ever spelt with a *C*. And by consequence it was a gross Mistake in our Language to spell *Knot* with a *K*, but that from henceforward, he would take care it should be writ with a *C*. Upon this, all farther Difficulty vanished; *Shoulder-Knots* were

† *Quibusdam Veteribus Codicibus.*

* *When the Papists cannot find any thing which they want in Scripture, they go to* Oral Tradition: *Thus* Peter *is introduced satisfy'd with the Tedious way of looking for all the Letters of any Word, which he has occasion for in the* Will, *when neither the constituent Syllables, nor much less the whole Word, were there* in Terminis. W. Wotton.

† *Some antient Manuscripts.*

made clearly out, to be *Jure Paterno*, and our three Gentlemen swaggered with as large and as flanting ones as the best.

But, as human Happiness is of a very short Duration, so in those Days were human Fashions, upon which it entirely depends. *Shoulder-Knots* had their Time, and we must now imagine them in their Decline; for a certain Lord came just from *Paris*, with fifty Yards of *Gold Lace* upon his Coat, exactly trimm'd after the Court-Fashion of that *Month*. In two Days, all Mankind appear'd closed up in Bars of * *Gold Lace*: whoever durst peep abroad without his Complement of *Gold Lace*, was as scandalous as a ——, and as ill received among the Women. What should our three Knights do in this momentous Affair? They had sufficiently strained a Point already, in the Affair of *Shoulder-Knots*: Upon Recourse to the Will, nothing appeared there but *altum silentium*. That of the *Shoulder-Knots* was a loose, flying, circumstantial Point; but this of *Gold Lace*, seemed too considerable an Alteration without better Warrant; it did *aliquo modo essentiæ adhærere*, and therefore required a positive Precept. But about this time it fell out, that the Learned Brother aforesaid, had read *Aristotelis Dialectica*, and especially that wonderful Piece *de Interpretatione*, which has the Faculty of teaching its Readers to find out a Meaning in every Thing but it self; like Commentators on the *Revelations*, who proceed Prophets without understanding a Syllable of the Text. *Brothers*, said he, † *You are to be informed, that, of Wills*, duo sunt genera, || *Nuncupatory and scriptory: that in the Scriptory Will here before us, there is no Precept or Mention about Gold Lace*, conceditur: *But*, si idem affirmetur de nuncupatorio, negatur, *For Brothers, if you remember, we heard a Fellow say when we were Boys, that he heard my Father's Man say, that*

* *I cannot tell whether the Author means any new Innovation by this Word, or whether it be only to introduce the new Methods of forcing and perverting Scripture.*

† *The next Subject of our Author's Wit, is the Glosses and Interpretations of Scripture, very many absurd ones of which are allow'd in the most Authentick Books of the* Church of Rome. W. Wotton.

|| *By this is meant* Tradition, *allowed to have equal Authority with the Scripture, or rather greater.*

he heard my Father *say, that he would advise his Sons to get* Gold Lace *on their Coats, as soon as ever they could procure Money to buy it. By G---- that is very true,* cries the other; *I remember it perfectly well,* said the third. And so without more ado they got the largest *Gold Lace* in the Parish, and walk'd about as fine as Lords.

A while after, there came up *all in Fashion,* a pretty sort of * *flame Coloured Sattin* for Linings, and the *Mercer* brought a Pattern of it immediately to our three Gentlemen, *An please your Worships* (said he) † *My Lord C--, and Sir* J. W. *had Linings out of this very Piece last Night; it takes wonderfully, and I shall not have a Remnant left, enough to make my Wife a Pin-cushion by to morrow Morning at ten a Clock.* Upon this, they fell again to romage the Will, because the present Case also required a positive Precept, the Lining being held by Orthodox Writers to be of the Essence of the Coat. After long search, they could fix upon nothing to the Matter in hand, except a short Advice of their Fathers in the Will, || to take care of *Fire,* and put out their *Candles* before they went to Sleep. This tho' a good deal for the Purpose, and helping very far towards Self-Conviction, yet not seeming wholly of Force to establish a Command; and being resolved to avoid farther Scruple, as well as future Occasion for Scandal, says He

---

* *This is Purgatory, whereof he speaks more particularly hereafter, but here only to shew how Scripture was perverted to prove it, which was done by giving equal Authority with the* Canon *to* Apocrypha, *called here a* Codicil annex'd.

It is likely the Author, in every one of these Changes in the Brother's Dresses, referrs to some particular Error in the Church of Rome; *tho' it is not easy I think to apply them all, but by this of* Flame Colour'd Satin *is manifestly intended* Purgatory; *by* Gold Lace *may perhaps be understood, the lofty Ornaments and Plate in the Churches. The* Shoulder-Knots *and* Silver Fringe, *are not so obvious, at least to me; but the* Indian *Figures of Men, Women and Children plainly relate to the Pictures in the Romish Churches, of God like an old Man, of the Virgin* Mary *and our Saviour as a Child.*

† *This shews the Time the Author writ, it being about fourteen Years since those two Persons were reckoned the fine Gentlemen of the Town.*

|| *That is, to take care of* Hell, *and, in order to do that, to subdue and extinguish their Lusts.*

that was the Scholar; *I remember to have read in Wills, of a Codicil annexed, which is indeed a Part of the Will, and what it contains hath equal authority with the rest. Now, I have been considering of this same Will here before us, and I cannot reckon it to be compleat for want of such a Codicil. I will therefore fasten one in its proper Place very dexterously; I have had it by me some Time, it was written by a * Dog-keeper of my Grand-father's, and talks a great deal (as good Luck would have it) of this very flame-colour'd Sattin.* The Project was immediately approved by the other two; an old Parchment Scrowl was tagged on according to Art, in the Form of a *Codicil annext*, and the *Sattin* bought and worn.

NEXT Winter, a *Player*, hired for the Purpose by the Corporation of *Fringe-makers*, acted his Part in a new Comedy, all covered with † *Silver Fringe*, and according to the laudable Custom gave Rise to that Fashion. Upon which, the Brothers consulting their Father's Will, to their great Astonishment found these Words; Item, *I charge and command my said three Sons, to wear no sort of* Silver Fringe *upon or about their said Coats*, &c. with a Penalty in case of Disobedience, too long here to insert. However, after some Pause the Brother so often mentioned for his Erudition, who was well Skill'd in Criticisms, had found in a certain Author, which he said should be nameless, that the same Word which in the Will is called *Fringe*, does also signifie a *Broom-stick*; and doubtless ought to have the same Interpretation in this Paragraph. This, another of the Brothers disliked, because of that Epithet, *Silver*, which could not, he humbly conceived, in Propriety of Speech be reasonably applied to a *Broom-stick*: but it was replied upon him, that this Epithet was understood in a *Mythological*, and *Allegorical* Sense. However, he objected again, why their Father should forbid them to wear a *Broom-stick* on their Coats, a Caution that seemed unnatural and impertinent; upon which he was taken up short, as one that spoke irreverently of a *Mystery*, which doubtless was very useful and significant,

* *I believe this refers to that part of the* Apocrypha *where mention is made of* Tobit *and his* Dog.

† *This is certainly the farther introducing the Pomps of Habit and Ornament.*

but ought not to be over-curiously pryed into, or nicely reasoned upon. And in short, their Father's Authority being now considerably sunk, this Expedient was allowed to serve as a lawful Dispensation, for wearing their full Proportion of *Silver Fringe*.

A while after, was revived an old Fashion, long antiquated, of *Embroidery* with * *Indian Figures* of Men, Women and Children. Here they had no Occasion to examine the Will. They remembred but too well, how their Father had always abhorred this Fashion; that he made several Paragraphs on purpose, importing his utter Detestation of it, and bestowing his everlasting Curse to his Sons whenever they should wear it. For all this, in a few Days, they appeared higher in the Fashion than any Body else in the Town. But they solved the Matter by saying, that these Figures were not at all the *same* with those that were formerly worn, and were meant in the Will. Besides, they did not wear them in that Sense, as forbidden by their Father, but as they were a commendable Custom, and of great Use to the Publick. That these rigorous Clauses in the Will did therefore require some *Allowance*, and a favourable Interpretation, and ought to be understood *cum grano Salis*.

But, Fashions perpetually altering in that Age, the Scholastick Brother grew weary of searching farther Evasions, and solving everlasting Contradictions. Resolved therefore at all Hazards, to comply with the Modes of the World, they concerted Matters together, and agreed unanimously, to † lock up their Father's Will in a *Strong-Box*, brought out of *Greece* or *Italy*, (I have forgot which) and trouble themselves no farther to examine it, but only refer to its Authority whenever they thought fit. In consequence whereof, a while after, it grew a general Mode

* *The Images of Saints, the Blessed Virgin, and our Saviour an Infant.*
Ibid. *Images in the* Church of Rome *give him but too fair a Handle.* The Brothers remembred,*&c. The Allegory here is direct.* W. Wotton.

† *The Papists formerly forbad the People the Use of Scripture in a Vulgar Tongue,* Peter *therefore* locks up his Father's Will in a Strong Box, brought out of *Greece* or *Italy. Those Countries are named because the* New Testament *is written in* Greek; *and the* Vulgar Latin, *which is the Authentick Edition of the* Bible *in the Church of* Rome, *is in the Language of old* Italy. W. Wotton.

to wear an infinite Number of *Points*, most of them *tagg'd with Silver*: Upon which the Scholar pronounced * *ex Cathedra*, that *Points* were absolutely *Jure Paterno*, as they might very well remember. 'Tis true indeed, the Fashion prescribed somewhat more than were directly named in the Will; However, that they, as Heirs general of their Father, had power to make and add certain Clauses for publick Emolument, though not deducible, *totidem verbis*, from the Letter of the Will, or else, *Multa absurda sequerentur*. This was understood for *Canonical*, and therefore on the following *Sunday* they came to Church all covered with *Points*.

THE Learned Brother so often mentioned, was reckon'd the best Scholar in all that or the next Street to it; insomuch, as having run something behind-hand with the World, he obtained the Favour from a † *certain Lord*, to receive him into his House, and to teach his Children. A while after, the *Lord* died, and he by long Practice upon his Father's Will, found the way of contriving a *Deed of Conveyance* of that House to Himself and his Heirs: Upon which he took Possession, turned the young Squires out, and received his Brothers in their stead.

* *The* Popes *in their Decretals and Bulls, have given their Sanction to very many gainful Doctrines which are now received in the* Church of Rome *that are not mention'd in Scripture, and are unknown to the Primitive Church.* Peter *accordingly pronounces* ex Cathedra, *That* Points tagged with Silver were absolutely *Jure Paterno, and so they wore them in great Numbers.* W. Wotton.

† *This was* Constantine the Great, *from whom the* Popes *pretend a Donation of St.* Peter'*s Patrimony, which they have been never able to produce.*

Ibid. *The Bishops of* Rome *enjoyed their Priviledges in* Rome *at first by the favour of Emperors, whom at last they shut out of their own Capital City, and then forged a Donation from* Constantine the Great, *the better to justifie what they did. In Imitation of this,* Peter having run something behind hand in the World, obtained Leave of a certain Lord, *&c.* W. Wotton.

SECT. III.

A Digression concerning Criticks.

THO' I have been hitherto as cautious as I could, upon all Occasions, most nicely to follow the Rules and Methods of Writing, laid down by the Example of our illustrious *Moderns*; yet has the unhappy shortness of my Memory led me into an Error, from which I must immediately extricate my self, before I can decently pursue my Principal Subject. I confess with Shame, it was an unpardonable Omission to proceed so far as I have already done, before I had performed the due Discourses, Expostulatory, Supplicatory, or Deprecatory with my *good Lords* the *Criticks*. Towards some Atonement for this grievous Neglect, I do here make humbly bold to present them with a short Account of themselves and their *Art*, by looking into the Original and Pedigree of the Word, as it is generally understood among us, and very briefly considering the antient and present State thereof.

BY the Word, *Critick*, at this Day so frequent in all Conversations, there have sometimes been distinguished three very different Species of Mortal Men, according as I have read in *Antient Books and Pamphlets*. For first, by this Term were understood such Persons as invented or drew up Rules for themselves and the World, by observing which, a careful Reader might be able to pronounce upon the productions of the *Learned*, form his Taste to a true Relish of the *Sublime* and the *Admirable*, and divide every Beauty of Matter or of Style from the Corruption that Apes it: In their common perusal of Books, singling out the Errors and Defects, the Nauseous, the Fulsome, the Dull, and the Impertinent, with the Caution of a Man that walks thro' *Edenborough* Streets in a Morning, who is indeed as careful as he can, to watch diligently, and spy out the Filth in his Way, not that he is curious to observe the Colour and Complexion of the Ordure, or take its Dimensions, much less to be padling in, or tasting it: but only with a Design to come out as cleanly as he may. These men seem, tho' very erroneously, to have understood the Appellation of, *Critick* in a literal Sence; That one principal part of his Office was to Praise and Acquit; and, that a *Critick*, who sets up to Read, only for an Occasion of Censure and Reproof, is a Creature as barbarous as a *Judge*, who should take up a Resolution to hang all Men that came before him upon a Tryal.

AGAIN; by the Word *Critick*, have been meant, the Restorers of Antient Learning from the Worms, and Graves, and Dust of Manuscripts.

Now, the Races of these two have been for some Ages utterly extinct; and besides, to discourse any farther of them would not be at all to my purpose.

THE Third, and Noblest Sort, is that of the *TRUE CRITICK*, whose Original is the most Antient of all. Every *True Critick* is a Hero born, descending in a direct Line from a Celestial Stem, by *Momus* and *Hybris*, who begat *Zoilus*, who begat *Tigellius*, who begat *Etcætera* the Elder, who begat *Bently*, and *Rymer*, and *Wotton*, and *Perrault*, and *Dennis*, who begat *Etcætera* the Younger.

AND these are the *Criticks* from whom the Commonwealth of Learning has in all Ages received such immense benefits, that the Gratitude of their Admirers placed their Origine in Heaven, among those of *Hercules*, *Theseus*, *Perseus*, and other great Deservers of Mankind. But Heroick Virtue it self hath not been exempt from the Obloquy of Evil Tongues. For it hath been objected, that those Antient Heroes, famous for their Combating so many Giants, and Dragons, and Robbers, were in their own Persons a greater Nuisance to Mankind, than any of those Monsters they subdued; and therefore, to render their Obligations more Compleat, when all *other* Vermin were destroy'd, should in Conscience have concluded with the same Justice upon themselves: as *Hercules* most generously did, and hath upon that Score, procured to himself more Temples and Votaries than the best of his Fellows. For these Reasons, I suppose it is, why some have conceived, it would be very expedient for the Publick Good of Learning, that every *True Critick*, as soon as he had finished his Task assigned, should immediately deliver himself up to Ratsbane, or Hemp, or from some convenient *Altitude*, and that no Man's Pretensions to so illustrious a Character, should by any means be received, before That Operation were performed.

Now, from this Heavenly Descent of *Criticism*, and the close Analogy it bears to *Heroick Virtue*, 'tis easie to Assign the proper Employment of a *True Antient Genuine Critick*; which is, to travel thro' this vast World of Writings: to pursue and hunt those Monstrous Faults bred within them: to drag out the lurking Errors like *Cacus* from his Den; to multiply them like *Hydra*'s Heads; and rake them together like *Augeas*'s Dung. Or else to drive away a sort of *Dangerous Fowl*, who have a perverse Inclination to plunder the best Branches of the *Tree of Knowledge*, like those *Stymphalian* Birds that eat up the Fruit.

THESE Reasonings will furnish us with an adequate Definition of a *True Critick*; that, He is *a Discoverer and Collector of Writers Faults*. Which may be farther put beyond Dispute by the following Demonstration: That whoever will examine the Writings in all kinds, wherewith this antient Sect has honour'd the World, shall immediately find, from the whole Thread and Tenour of them, that the Idea's of the Authors have been altogether conversant, and taken up with the Faults and Blemishes, and Oversights, and Mistakes of other Writers; and let the Subject treated on be whatever it will, their Imaginations are so entirely possess'd and replete with the Defects of other Pens, that the very Quintessence of what is bad, does of necessity distill into their own: by which means the Whole appears to be nothing else but an *Abstract* of the *Criticisms* themselves have made.

HAVING thus briefly consider'd the Original and Office of a *Critick*, as the Word is understood in its most noble and universal Acceptation, I proceed to refute the Objections of those who argue from the Silence and Pretermission of Authors; by which they pretend to prove, that the very Art of *Criticism*, as now exercised, and by me explained, is wholly *Modern*; and consequently, that the *Criticks* of *Great Britain* and *France*, have no Title to an Original so Antient and Illustrious as I have deduced. Now, If I can clearly make out on the contrary, that the most Antient Writers have particularly described, both the Person and the Office of a *True Critick*, agreeable to the Definition laid down by me; their Grand Objection, from the Silence of Authors, will fall to the Ground.

I confess to have for a long time born a part in this general

Error; from which I should never have acquitted my self, but thro' the Assistance of our Noble *Moderns*; whose most edifying Volumes I turn indefatigably over Night and Day, for the Improvement of my Mind, and the good of my Country: These have with unwearied Pains made many useful Searches into the weak sides of the *Antients*, and given us a comprehensive List of them. * Besides, they have proved beyond contradiction, that the very finest Things delivered of old, have been long since invented, and brought to Light by much later Pens, and that the noblest Discoveries those *Antients* ever made, of Art or of Nature, have all been produced by the transcending Genius of the present Age. Which clearly shews, how little Merit those *Ancients* can justly pretend to; and takes off that blind Admiration paid them by Men in a Corner, who have the Unhappiness of conversing too little with *present Things*. Reflecting maturely upon all this, and taking in the whole Compass of Human Nature, I easily concluded, that these *Antients*, highly sensible of their many Imperfections, must needs have endeavoured from some Passages in their Works, to obviate, soften, or divert the Censorious Reader, by *Satyr*, or *Panegyrick* upon the *True Criticks*, in Imitation of their *Masters* the *Moderns*. Now, in the *Common-Places* of * both these, I was plentifully instructed, by a long Course of useful Study in *Prefaces* and *Prologues*; and therefore immediately resolved to try what I could discover of either, by a diligent Perusal of the most Antient Writers, and especially those who treated of the earliest Times. Here I found to my great Surprize, that although they all entred, upon Occasion, into particular Descriptions of the *True Critick*, according as they were governed by their Fears or their Hopes: yet whatever they touch'd of that kind, was with abundance of Caution, adventuring no farther than *Mythology* and *Hieroglyphick*. This, I suppose, gave ground to superficial Readers, for urging the Silence of Authors, against the Antiquity of the *True Critick*; tho' the *Types* are so apposite, and the Applications so necessary and natural, that it is not easy to conceive, how any Reader of a *Modern Eye* and *Taste* could over-look them. I shall venture from a great Number

* *See* Wotton *of Antient and Modern Learning.*

* *Satyr, and Panegyrick upon Criticks.*

to produce a few, which I am very confident, will put this Question beyond Dispute.

It well deserves considering, that these *Antient Writers* in treating Enigmatically upon the Subject, have generally fixed upon the very *same Hieroglyph*, varying only the Story according to their Affections or their Wit. For first; *Pausanias* is of Opinion, that the Perfection of Writing correct was entirely owing to the Institution of *Criticks*; and, that he can possibly mean no other than the *True Critick*, is, I think, manifest enough from the following Description. He says, *They were a Race of Men, who delighted to nibble at the Superfluities, and Excrescencies of Books; which the Learned at length observing, took Warning of their own Accord, to lop* the *Luxuriant*, the *Rotten*, the *Dead*, the *Sapless*, and the *Overgrown Branches from their Works*. But now, all this he cunningly shades under the following Allegory; *that the* * Nauplians *in* Argia, *learned the Art of pruning their Vines, by observing, that when an* ASS *had browsed upon one of them, it thrived the better, and bore fairer Fruit*. But † *Herodotus* holding the very same *Hieroglyph*, speaks much plainer, and almost *in terminis*. He hath been so bold as to tax the *True Criticks*, of Ignorance and Malice; telling us openly, for I think nothing can be plainer, that *in the Western Part of* Libya, *there were* ASSES *with* HORNS: Upon which Relation || *Ctesias* yet refines, mentioning the very same animal about *India*, adding, *That whereas all other* ASSES *wanted a* Gall, *these horned ones were so redundant in that Part, that their Flesh was not to be eaten because of its extream* Bitterness.

* *Lib*——

† *Lib*. 4.

|| Vide *excerpta ex eo apud* Photium.

Now, the Reason why those Antient Writers treated this Subject only by Types and Figures, was, because they durst not make open Attacks against a Party so Potent and so Terrible, as the *Criticks* of those Ages were: whose very Voice was so Dreadful, that a Legion of Authors would tremble, and drop their Pens at the Sound; For so * *Herodotus* tells us expresly in another Place, how *a vast Army of* Scythians *was put to flight in a Panick Terror, by the Braying of an* ASS. From hence it is conjectured by certain profound *Philologers*, that the great Awe and Reverence paid to a *True Critick*, by the

* *Lib*. 4.

Writers of *Britain*, have been derived to Us, from those our *Scythian* Ancestors. In short, this Dread was so universal, that in process of Time, those Authors who had a mind to publish their Sentiments more freely, in describing the *True Criticks* of their several Ages, were forced to leave off the use of the former *Hieroglyph*, as too nearly approaching the *Prototype*, and invented other Terms instead thereof that were more cautious and mystical; so † *Diodorus* speaking to the same purpose, ventures no farther than to say, That *in the Mountains of* Helicon *there grows a certain* Weed, *which bears a Flower of so damned a Scent, as to poison those who offer to smell it. Lucretius* gives exactly the Same Relation,

† *Lib.*

> || *Est etiam in magnis Heliconis montibus arbos,*
> *Floris odore hominem tetro consueta necare.* Lib. 6.

But *Ctesias*, whom we lately quoted, hath been a great deal bolder; He had been used with much severity by the *True Criticks* of his own Age, and therefore could not forbear to leave behind him, at least one deep Mark of his Vengeance against the whole Tribe. His Meaning is so near the Surface, that I wonder how it possibly came to be overlook'd by those who deny the Antiquity of the *True Criticks*. For pretending to make a Description of many strange Animals about *India*, he hath set down these remarkable Words. *Amongst the rest*, says he, *there is a* Serpent *that wants* Teeth, *and consequently cannot bite, but if its* Vomit (*to which it is much addicted*) *happens to fall upon any Thing, a certain Rottenness or Corruption ensues: These* Serpents *are generally found among the Mountains where* Jewels *grow, and they frequently emit a* poisonous Juice *whereof, whoever drinks, that Person's* Brains *flie out of his Nostrils.*

There was also among the *Antients* a sort of *Critick*, not distinguisht in *Specie* from the Former, but in Growth or Degree, who seem to have been only the *Tyro's* or *junior* Scholars; yet, because of their differing Employments, they are frequently mentioned as a Sect by themselves. The usual exercise of these

|| *Near Helicon, and round the Learned Hill,*
Grow Trees, whose Blossoms with their Odour kill.

younger Students, was to attend constantly at Theatres, and learn to Spy out the *worst Parts* of the Play, whereof they were obliged carefully to take Note, and render a rational Account, to their Tutors. Flesht at these smaller Sports, like young Wolves, they grew up in Time, to be nimble and strong enough for hunting down large Game. For it hath been observed both among Antients and Moderns, that a *True Critick* hath one Quality in common with a *Whore* and an *Alderman*, never to change his Title or his Nature; that a *Grey Critick* has been certainly a *Green* one, the Perfections and Acquirements of his Age bëing only the improved Talents of his Youth; like *Hemp*, which some Naturalists inform us, is bad for *Suffocations*, tho' taken but in the Seed. I esteem the Invention, or at least the Refinement of *Prologues*, to have been owing to these younger Proficients, of whom *Terence* makes frequent and honourable mention, under the Name of *Malevoli*.

Now, 'tis certain, the Institution of the *True Criticks*, was of absolute Necessity to the Commonwealth of Learning. For all Human Actions seem to be divided like *Themistocles* and his Company; One Man can *Fiddle*, and another can make *a small Town a great City*, and he that cannot do either one or the other, deserves to be kick'd out of the Creation. The avoiding of which Penalty, has doubtless given the first Birth to the Nation of *Criticks*, and withal, an Occasion for their secret Detractors to report; that a *True Critick* is a sort of Mechanick, set up with a Stock and Tools for his Trade, at as little Expence as a *Taylor*; and that there is much Analogy between the Utensils and Abilities of both: That the *Taylor's Hell* is the Type of a Critick's *Common-Place-Book*, and his Wit and Learning held forth by the *Goose*: That it requires at least as many of these, to the making up of one Scholar, as of the others to the Composition of a Man: That the Valour of both is equal, and their *Weapons* near of a Size. Much may be said in answer to these invidious Reflections; and I can positively affirm the first to be a Falshood: For, on the contrary, nothing is more certain, than that it requires greater Layings out, to be free of the *Critick's* Company, than of any other you can name. For, as to be a *true Beggar*, it will cost the richest Candidate every Groat he is worth; so, before one can commence a *True Critick*, it will cost a man all the good Qualities of his Mind; which, perhaps, for a less Purchase, would be thought but an indifferent Bargain.

HAVING thus amply proved the Antiquity of *Criticism*, and described the Primitive State of it; I shall now examine the present Condition of this Empire, and shew how well it agrees with its antient self. * A certain Author, whose Works have many Ages since been entirely lost, does in his fifth Book and eighth Chapter, say of *Criticks*, that *their Writings are the Mirrors of Learning*. This I understand in a literal Sense, and suppose our Author must mean, that whoever designs to be a perfect Writer, must inspect into the Books of *Criticks*, and correct his Invention there as in a Mirror. Now, whoever considers, that the *Mirrors* of the Antients were made of *Brass*, and *sine Mercurio*, may presently apply the two Principal Qualifications of a *True Modern Critick*, and consequently, must needs conclude, that these have always been, and must be for ever the same. For, *Brass* is an Emblem of Duration, and when it is skilfully burnished, will cast *Reflections* from its own *Superficies*, without any Assistance of *Mercury* from behind. All the other Talents of a *Critick* will not require a particular Mention, being included, or easily deducible to these. However, I shall conclude with three Maxims, which may serve both as Characteristicks to distinguish a *True Modern Critick* from a Pretender, and will be also of admirable Use to those worthy Spirits, who engage in so useful and honourable an Art.

* *A Quotation after the manner of a great Author. Vide* Bently's *Dissertation, &c.*

THE first is, That *Criticism*, contrary to all other Faculties of the Intellect, is ever held the truest and best, when it is the very *first* Result of the *Critick*'s Mind: As Fowlers reckon the first aim for the surest, and seldom fail of missing the Mark, if they stay for a Second.

SECONDLY; The *True Criticks* are known by their Talent of swarming about the noblest Writers, to which they are carried meerly by Instinct, as a Rat to the best Cheese, or a Wasp to the fairest Fruit. So, when the *King* is a Horse-back, he is sure to be the *dirtiest* Person of the Company, and they that make their Court best, are such as *bespatter* him most.

Lastly; A *True Critick*, in the Perusal of a Book, is like a *Dog* at a Feast, whose Thoughts and Stomach are wholly set upon what the Guests *fling away*, and consequently, is apt to *Snarl* most, when there are the fewest *Bones*.

Thus much, I think, is sufficient to serve by way of Address to my Patrons, the *True Modern Criticks*, and may very well atone for my past Silence, as well as That which I am like to observe for the future. I hope I have deserved so well of their whole *Body*, as to meet with generous and tender Usage at their *Hands*. Supported by which Expectation, I go on boldly to pursue those Adventures already so happily begun.

SECT. IV.

A TALE of a TUB.

I HAVE now with much Pains and Study, conducted the Reader to a Period, where he must expect to hear of great Revolutions. For no sooner had Our *Learned Brother*, so often mentioned, got a warm House of his own over his Head, than he began to look big, and to take mightily upon him; insomuch, that unless the Gentle Reader out of his great Candour, will please a little to exalt his Idea, I am afraid he will henceforth hardly know the *Hero* of the Play, when he happens to meet Him; his part, his Dress, and his Mien being so much altered.

HE told his Brothers, he would have them to know, that he was their Elder, and consequently his Father's sole Heir; Nay, a while after, he would not allow them to call Him, Brother, but Mr. *PETER*; And then he must be styl'd, *Father PETER*; and sometimes, *My Lord PETER*. To support this Grandeur, which he soon began to consider, could not be maintained without a Better *Fonde* than what he was born to; After much Thought, he cast about at last, to turn *Projector* and *Virtuoso*, wherein he so well succeeded, that many famous Discoveries, Projects and Machines, which bear great Vogue and Practice at present in the World, are owing entirely to *Lord Peter*'s Invention. I will deduce the best Account I have been able to collect of the Chief amongst them, without considering much the Order they came out in; because, I think, Authors are not well agreed as to that Point.

I hope, when this Treatise of mine shall be translated into Foreign Languages, (as I may without Vanity affirm, That the Labour of collecting, the Faithfulness in recounting, and the great Usefulness of the Matter to the Publick, will amply deserve that Justice) that the worthy Members of the several *Academies* abroad, especially those of *France* and *Italy*, will favourably accept these humble Offers, for the Advancement of Universal Knowledge. I do also advertise the most Reverend Fathers the *Eastern* Missionaries, that I have purely for their Sakes, made use of such Words and Phrases, as will best admit an easie Turn into any of the *Oriental* Languages, especially the *Chinese*. And so I proceed with great Content of Mind, upon reflecting, how much Emolument this whole Globe of Earth is like to reap by my Labours.

THE first Undertaking of Lord *Peter*, was to purchase a* Large Continent, lately said to have been discovered in *Terra Australis incognita*. This Tract of Land he bought at a very great Pennyworth from the Discoverers themselves, (tho' some pretended to doubt whether they had ever been there) and then retailed it into several Cantons to certain Dealers, who carried over Colonies, but were all Shipwreckt in the Voyage. Upon which, *Lord Peter* sold the said Continent to other Customers *again*, and *again*, and *again*, and *again*, with the same Success.

THE second Project I shall mention, was his † Sovereign Remedy for the *Worms*, especially those in the *Spleen*. || The Patient was to eat nothing after Supper for three Nights: as soon as he went to Bed, he was carefully to lye on one Side, and when he grew weary, to turn upon the other: He must also duly confine his two Eyes to the same Object; and by no means break Wind at both Ends together, without manifest Occasion. These Prescriptions diligently observed, the *Worms* would void insensibly by Perspiration, ascending thro' the *Brain*.

A third Invention, was the Erecting of a * *Whispering-Office*, for the Publick Good and Ease of all such as are Hypochondriacal, or troubled with the Cholick; as likewise of all Eves-droppers, Physicians, Midwives, small Politicians, Friends fallen out, Repeating Poets, Lovers Happy or in Despair, Bawds, Privy-

* *That is Purgatory.*

† Penance *and* Absolution *are plaid upon under the Notion of a* Sovereign Remedy for the Worms, *especially in the Spleen, which by observing* Peters *Prescription would void sensibly by Perspiration ascending thro' the Brain,* &c. W. Wotton.

|| *Here the Author ridicules the Penances of the Church of* Rome, *which may be made as easy to the Sinner as he pleases, provided he will pay for them accordingly.*

* *By his* Whispering-Office, *for the Relief of Eves-droppers, Physitians, Bawds, and Privy-counsellours, he ridicules Auricular Confession, and the Priest who takes it, is described by the Asses Head.* W. Wotton.

Counsellours, Pages, Parasites and Buffoons; In short, of all such as are in Danger of bursting with too much *Wind*. An *Asse*'s Head was placed so conveniently, that the Party affected might easily with his Mouth accost either of the Animal's Ears; which he was to apply close for a certain Space, and by a fugitive Faculty, peculiar to the Ears of that Animal, receive immediate Benefit, either by Eructation, or Expiration, or Evomition.

ANOTHER very beneficial Project of *Lord Peter*'s was an * *Office of Ensurance*, for Tobacco-Pipes, Martyrs of the Modern Zeal; Volumes of Poetry, Shadows, ———————— and Rivers: That these, nor any of these shall receive Damage by *Fire*. From whence our *Friendly Societies* may plainly find themselves, to be only Transcribers from this Original; tho' the one and the other have been of *great* Benefit to the Undertakers, as well as of *equal* to the Publick.

LORD Peter was also held the Original Author of † *Puppets* and *Raree-Shows*; the great Usefulness whereof being so generally known, I shall not enlarge farther upon this Particular.

BUT, another Discovery for which he was much renowned, was his famous Universal || *Pickle*. For having remark'd how your * Common *Pickle* in use among Huswives, was of no farther Benefit than to preserve dead Flesh, and certain kinds of Vegetables; *Peter*, with great Cost as well as Art, had contrived a *Pickle* proper for Houses, Gardens, Towns, Men, Women, Children, and Cattle; wherein he could preserve them as Sound as Insects in Amber. Now, this *Pickle* to the Taste, the Smell, and the Sight, appeared exactly the same, with what is in common Service for Beef, and Butter, and Herrings, (and has been often that way applied with great Success) but for its many Sove-

* *This I take to be the Office of* Indulgences, *the gross Abuses whereof first gave Occasion for the Reformation.*

† *I believe are the Monkeries and ridiculous Processions*, &c. *among the Papists.*

|| *Holy Water, he calls an* Universal Pickle *to preserve Houses, Gardens, Towns, Men, Women, Children and Cattle, wherein he could preserve them as sound as Insects in Amber.* W. Wotton.

* *This is easily understood to be Holy Water, composed of the same Ingredients with many other Pickles.*

reign Virtues was a quite different Thing. For *Peter* would put in a certain Quantity of his * *Powder Pimperlim pimp*, after which it never failed of Success. The Operation was performed by *Spargefaction* in a proper Time of the Moon. The Patient who was to be *pickled*, if it were a House, would infallibly be preserved from all Spiders, Rats and Weazels; If the Party affected were a Dog, he should be exempt from Mange, and Madness, and Hunger. It also infallibly took away all Scabs and Lice, and scall'd Heads from Children, never hindring the Patient from any Duty, either at Bed or Board.

BUT of all *Peter*'s Rarieties, he most valued a certain Set of † *Bulls*, whose Race was by great Fortune preserved in a lineal Descent from those that guarded the *Golden Fleece*. Tho' some who pretended to observe them curiously, doubted the Breed had not been kept entirely chast; because they had degenerated from their Ancestors in some Qualities and had acquired others very extraordinary, but a Forein Mixture. The *Bulls* of *Colchos* are recorded to have *brazen Feet*; But whether it happen'd by ill Pasture and Running, by an Allay from intervention of other Parents, from stolen Intrigues; Whether a Weakness in their Progenitors had impaired the seminal Virtue; Or by a Decline necessary thro' a long Course of Time, the Originals of Nature being depraved in these latter sinful Ages of the World; Whatever was the Cause, 'tis certain that *Lord Peter*'s *Bulls* were extreamely vitiated by the Rust of Time in the Mettal of their Feet, which was now sunk into common *Lead*. However the terrible *roaring* peculiar to their Lineage, was preserved; as likewise that Faculty of breathing out *Fire* from their Nostrils; which not-

* *And because Holy Water differs only in Consecration from common Water, therefore he tells us that his Pickle by the Powder of* Pimperlim-pimp *receives new Virtues though it differs not in Sight nor Smell from the common Pickle, which preserves Beef, and Butter, and Herrings.* W. Wotton.

† *The Papal* Bulls *are ridicul'd by Name, So that here we are at no loss for the Authors Meaning.* W. Wotton.

Ibid. *Here the Author has kept the Name, and means the* Popes Bulls, *or rather his Fulminations and Excommunications, of Heretical Princes, all sign'd with Lead and the Seal of the Fisherman.*

withstanding, many of their Detractors took to be a Feat of Art, and to be nothing so terrible as it appeared; proceeding only from their usual Course of Dyet, which was of * *Squibs* and *Crackers*. However, they had two peculiar Marks which extreamly distinguished them from the *Bulls of Jason*, and which I have not met together in the Description of any other Monster, beside that in *Horace*;

Varias inducere plumas,
and
Atrum desinit in piscem.

For, these had *Fishes Tails*, yet upon Occasion, could *out-fly* any Bird in the Air. *Peter* put these *Bulls* upon several Employs. Sometimes he would set them a *roaring* to fright † *Naughty Boys*, and make them quiet. Sometimes he would send them out upon Errands of great Importance; where it is wonderful to recount, and perhaps the cautious Reader may think much to believe it; An *Appetitus sensibilis*, deriving itself thro' the whole Family, from their Noble Ancestors, Guardians of the *Golden-Fleece*; they continued so extremely fond of *Gold*, that if *Peter* sent them abroad, though it were only upon a Compliment; they would *Roar*, and *Spit*, and *Belch*, and *Piss*, and *Fart*, and *Snivel* out *Fire*, and keep a perpetual Coyl, till you flung them a Bit of *Gold*; but then, *Pulveris exigui jactu*, they would grow calm and quiet as Lambs. In short, whether by secret Connivance, or Encouragement from their Master, or out of their own Liquorish Affection to Gold, or both; it is certain they were no better than a sort of sturdy, swaggering Beggars; and where they could not prevail to get an Alms, would make Women miscarry, and Children fall into Fits; who, to this very Day, usually call Sprites and Hobgoblins by the Name of *Bull-Beggars*. They grew at last so very troublesome to the Neighbourhood, that some Gentlemen of the *North-West*, got a Parcel of right *English Bull-Dogs*, and baited them so terribly, that they felt it ever after.

I must needs mention one more of *Lord Peter*'s Projects, which

* *These are the Fulminations of the Pope threatning Hell and Damnation to those Princes who offend him.*

† *That is Kings who incurr his Displeasure.*

was very extraordinary, and discovered him to be Master of a high Reach, and profound Invention. Whenever it happened that any Rogue of *Newgate* was condemned to be hang'd, *Peter* would offer him a Pardon for a certain Sum of Money, which when the poor Caitiff had made all Shifts to scrape up and send; *His Lordship* would return a * Piece of Paper in this Form.

TO all Mayors, Sheriffs, Jaylors, Constables, Bayliffs, Hangmen, &c. *Whereas we are informed that* A. B. *remains in the Hands of you, or any of you, under the Sentence of Death. We will and command you upon Sight hereof, to let the said Prisoner depart to his own Habitation, whether he stands condemned for Murder, Sodomy, Rape, Sacrilege, Incest, Treason, Blasphemy,* &c. *for which this shall be your sufficient Warrant: And if you fail hereof, G----- d----mn You and Yours to all Eternity. And so we bid you heartily Farewel.*

Your most Humble
Man's Man,
EMPEROR PETER.

THE Wretches trusting to this, lost their Lives and Money too.

I desire of those whom the *Learned* among Posterity will appoint for Commentators upon this elaborate Treatise; that they will proceed with great Caution upon certain dark points, wherein all who are not *Verè adepti*, may be in Danger to form rash and hasty Conclusions, especially in some mysterious Paragraphs, where certain *Arcana* are joyned for brevity sake, which in the Operation must be divided. And, I am certain, that future Sons of Art, will return large Thanks to my Memory, for so grateful, so useful an *Innuendo*.

IT will be no difficult Part to persuade the Reader, that so many worthy Discoveries met with great Success in the World; tho' I may justly assure him that I have related much the smallest Number; My Design having been only to single out such, as will be of most Benefit for Publick Imitation, or which best served to

* *This is a Copy of a General Pardon sign'd* Servus Servorum.

Ibid. *Absolution in* Articulo Mortis, *and the Tax* Cameræ Apostolicæ *are jested upon in Emperor* Peter'*s Letter*. W. Wotton.

give some Idea of the Reach and Wit of the Inventor. And therefore it need not be wondred, if by this Time, *Lord Peter* was become exceeding Rich. But alas, he had kept his Brain so long, and so violently upon the Rack, that at last it *shook* it self, and began to *turn round* for a little Ease. In short, what with Pride, Projects, and Knavery, poor *Peter* was grown distracted, and conceived the strangest Imaginations in the World. In the Height of his Fits (as it is usual with those who run mad out of Pride) He would call Himself * *God Almighty*, and sometimes *Monarch of the Universe*. I have seen him, (says my Author) take three old † *high-crown'd Hats*, and clap them all on his Head, three Story high, with a huge Bunch of || *Keys* at his Girdle, and an *Angling Rod* in his Hand. In which Guise, whoever went to take him by the Hand in the way of Salutation, *Peter* with much Grace, like a well educated Spaniel, would present them with his * *Foot*, and if they refused his Civility, then he would raise it as high as their Chops, and give them a damn'd Kick on the Mouth, which hath ever since been call'd a *Salute*. Whoever walkt by, without paying him their Compliments, having a wonderful strong Breath, he would blow their Hats off into the Dirt. Mean time, his Affairs at home went upside down; and his two Brothers had a wretched Time; Where his first † *Boutade* was, to kick both their || *Wives* one Morning out of Doors, and his own too, and in their stead, gave Orders to pick up the first three Strolers could be met with in the Streets. A while after, he nail'd up the

---

* *The Pope is not only allow'd to be the Vicar of* Christ, *but by several Divines is call'd* God upon Earth, *and other blasphemous Titles.*

† *The Triple Crown.*

|| *The Keys of the Church.*

Ibid. *The Pope's Universal Monarchy, and his Triple Crown, and Keys, and Fisher's Ring.* W. Wotton.

* *Neither does his arrogant way of requiring men to kiss his Slipper, escape Reflexion.* Wotton.

† *This Word properly signifies a sudden Jerk, or Lash of an Horse, when you do not expect it.*

|| *The* Celibacy of the *Romish* Clergy *is struck at in* Peter's *beating his own and Brothers Wives out of Doors.* W. Wotton.

Cellar-Door: and would not allow his Brothers a || Drop of *Drink* to their Victuals. Dining one Day at an Alderman's in the City, *Peter* observed him expatiating after the Manner of his Brethren, in the Praises of his Surloyn of Beef. *Beef*, said the Sage Magistrate, *is the King of Meat; Beef comprehends in it the Quintessence of Partridge, and Quail, and Venison, and Pheasant, and Plum-pudding and Custard.* When *Peter* came home, he would needs take the Fancy of cooking up this Doctrine into Use, and apply the Precept in default of a Surloyn, to his brown Loaf: *Bread*, says he, *Dear Brothers, is the Staff of Life; in which Bread is contained*, inclusivè, *the Quintessence of Beef, Mutton, Veal, Venison, Partridge, Plum-pudding, and Custard: And to render all compleat, there is intermingled a due Quantity of Water, whose Crudities are also corrected by Yeast or Barm, thro' which means it becomes a wholesome fermented Liquor, diffused thro' the* Mass *of the Bread.* Upon the Strength of these Conclusions, next Day at Dinner was the brown Loaf served up in all the Formality of a City Feast. *Come Brothers*, said *Peter*, *fall to, and spare not; here is excellent good* * *Mutton; or hold, now my Hand is in, I'll help you.* At which word, in much Ceremony, with Fork and Knife, he carves out two good Slices of the Loaf, and presents each on a Plate to his Brothers. The Elder of the two not suddenly entring into *Lord Peter*'s Conceit, began with very civil Language to examine the Mystery. *My Lord*, said he, *I doubt, with great Submission, there may be some Mistake. What*, says *Peter*, *you are pleasant; Come then, let us hear this Jest, your Head is so big with. None in the World, my Lord; but unless I am very much deceived, your Lordship was pleased a while ago, to let fall a Word about Mutton, and I would be glad to see it with all my Heart. How*, said *Peter*, appearing in great Surprise, *I do not comprehend this at all*— Upon which, the younger interposing,

|| *The Pope's refusing the Cup to the Laity, persuading them that the Blood is contain'd in the Bread, and that the Bread is the real and entire Body of* Christ.

* Transubstantiation. Peter *turns his Bread into Mutton, and according to the Popish Doctrine of Concomitants, his Wine too, which in his way he calls*, Pauming his damn'd Crusts upon the Brothers for Mutton. *W. Wotton.*

to set the Business right; *My Lord*, said he, *My Brother, I suppose is hungry, and longs for the Mutton, your Lordship hath promised us to Dinner. Pray*, said Peter, *take me along with you, either you are both mad, or disposed to be merrier than I approve of; If* You *there, do not like your Piece, I will carve you another, tho' I should take that to be the choice Bit of the whole Shoulder. What then, my Lord*, replied the first, *it seems this is a shoulder of Mutton all this while. Pray Sir*, says *Peter, eat your Vittles and leave off your Impertinence, if you please, for I am not disposed to relish it at present*: But the other could not forbear, being over-provoked at the affected Seriousness of *Peter*'s Countenance. *By G—, My Lord*, said he, *I can only say, that to my Eyes, and Fingers, and Teeth, and Nose, it seems to be nothing but a Crust of Bread*. Upon which, the second put in his Word: *I never saw a Piëce of Mutton in my Life, so nearly resembling a Slice from a Twelve-peny Loaf. Look ye, Gentlemen*, cries *Peter* in a Rage, *to convince you, what a couple of blind, positive, ignorant, wilful Puppies you are, I will use but this plain Argument; By G—, it is true, good, natural Mutton as any in* Leaden-Hall *Market; and G—, confound you both eternally, if you offer to believe otherwise.* Such a thundring Proof as this, left no farther Room for Objection: The two Unbelievers began to gather and pocket up their Mistake as hastily as they could. *Why, truly*, said the first, *upon more mature Consideration—Ay*, says the other, interrupting him, *now I have thought better on the Thing, your Lordship seems to have a great deal of Reason. Very well*, said *Peter. Here Boy, fill me a Beer-Glass of Claret. Here's to you both with all my Heart.* The two Brethren much delighted to see him so readily appeas'd returned their most humble Thanks, and said, they would be glad to pledge His Lordship. *That you shall*, said Peter, *I am not a Person to refuse you any Thing that is reasonable; Wine moderately taken, is a Cordial; Here is a Glass apiece for you; 'Tis true natural Juice from the Grape; none of your damn'd* Vintners *Brewings*. Having spoke thus, he presented to each of them another large dry Crust, bidding them drink it off, and not be bashful, for it would do them no Hurt. The two Brothers, after having performed the usual Office in such delicate Conjunctures, of staring a sufficient Period at *Lord Peter*, and each other; and finding how Matters were like to go, resolved not to enter on a new Dispute, but let him carry the

Point as he pleased; for he was now got into one of his mad Fits, and to Argue or Expostulate further, would only serve to render him a hundred times more untractable.

I have chosen to relate this worthy Matter in all its Circumstances, because it gave a principal Occasion to that great and famous * *Rupture*, which happened about the same time among these Brethren, and was never afterwards made up. But, of That, I shall treat at large in another Section.

HOWEVER, it is certain, that *Lord Peter*, even in his lucid Intervals, was very lewdly given in his common Conversation, extream wilful and positive, and would at any time rather argue to the Death, than allow himself to be once in an Error. Besides, he had an abominable Faculty of telling huge palpable *Lies* upon all Occasions; and swearing, not only to the Truth, but cursing the whole Company to Hell, if they pretended to make the least Scruple of believing Him. One time, he swore, he had a † *Cow* at home, which gave as much Milk at a Meal, as would fill three thousand Churches; and what was yet more extraordinary, would never turn Sower. Another time, he was telling of an old *Sign-Post* that belonged to his *Father*, with Nails and Timber enough on it, to build sixteen large Men of War. Talking one Day of *Chinese* Waggons, which were made so light as to sail over Mountains: Z----*nds*, said *Peter*, *where's the Wonder of that? By G-----, I saw a* * *Large House of Lime and Stone travel over Sea and Land* (*granting that it stopt sometimes to bait*) *above two thousand*

* *By this* Rupture *is meant the* Reformation.

† *The ridiculous Multiplying of the Virgin* Mary's Milk *among the Papists, under the Allegory of a* Cow, *which gave ás much Milk at a Meal, as would fill three thousand Churches.* W. Wotton.

|| *By this* Sign-Post *is meant the* Cross *of our Blessed Saviour.*

* *The Chappel of* Loretto. *He falls here only upon the ridiculous Inventions of Popery: The Church of* Rome *intended by these Things, to gull silly, superstitious People, and rook them of their Money; that the World had been too long in Slavery, our Ancestors gloriously redeem'd us from that Yoke. The Church of* Rome *therefore ought to be expos'd, and he deserves well of Mankind that does expose it.* W. Wotton.

Ibid. *The Chappel of* Loretto, *which travell'd from the* Holy Land *to* Italy.

German *Leagues*. And that which was the good of it, he would swear desperately all the while, that he never told a Lye in his Life; And at every Word; *By G---, Gentlemen, I tell you nothing but the Truth; And the D------l broil them eternally that will not believe me.*

In short, *Peter* grew so scandalous, that all the Neighbourhood began in plain Words to say, he was no better than a Knave. And his two Brothers long weary of his ill Usage, resolved at last to leave him; but first, they humbly desired a Copy of their Father's *Will*, which had now lain by neglected, time out of Mind. Instead of granting this Request, he called them *damn'd Sons of Whores, Rogues, Traytors*, and the rest of the vile Names he could muster up. However, while he was abroad one Day upon his Projects, the two Youngsters watcht their Opportunity, made a shift to come at the *Will*, * and took a *Copia vera*, by which they presently saw how grosly they had been abused; Their Father having left them equal Heirs, and strictly commanded, that whatever they got, should lye in common among them all. Pursuant to which, their next Enterprise was to break open the Cellar-Door, and get a little good † *Drink* to spirit and comfort their Hearts. In copying the *Will*, they had met another Precept against Whoring, Divorce, and separate Maintenance; Upon which, their next || Work was to discard their Concubines, and send for their Wives. Whilst all this was in agitation, there enters a Sollicitor from *Newgate*, desiring *Lord Peter* would please to procure a *Pardon* for a *Thief* that was to be *hanged* to morrow. But the two Brothers told him, he was a Coxcomb to seek Pardons from a Fellow, who deserv'd to be hang'd much better than his Client; and discovered all the Method of that Imposture, in the same Form I delivered it a while ago, advising the Sollicitor to put his Friend upon obtaining * *a Pardon from the King*. In the midst of all this Clutter and Revolution, in comes

---

* *Translated the Scriptures into the vulgar Tongues.*

† *Administred the Cup to the Laity at the Communion.*

|| *Allowed the Marriages of Priests.*

* *Directed Penitents not to trust to Pardons and Absolutions procur'd for Money, but sent them to implore the Mercy of God, from whence alone Remission is to be obtain'd.*

Peter with a File of * Dragoons at his Heels, and gathering from all Hands what was in the Wind, He and his Gang, after several Millions of Scurrilities and Curses, not very important here to repeat, by main Force, very fairly † kicks them both out of Doors, and would never let them come under his Roof from that Day to this.

* *By* Peter's *Dragoons, is meant the Civil Power which those Princes, who were bigotted to the Romish Superstition, employ'd against the Reformers.*

† *The Pope shuts all who dissent from him out of the Church.*

SECT. V.

A Digression in the Modern Kind.

WE whom the World is pleased to honor with the Title of *Modern Authors*, should never have been able to compass our great Design of an everlasting Remembrance, and never-dying Fame, if our Endeavours had not been so highly serviceable to the general Good of Mankind. This, *O Universe*, is the Adventurous Attempt of me thy Secretary;

> ———*Quemvis perferre laborem*
> *Suadet, & inducit noctes vigilare serenas.*

To this End, I have some Time since, with a World of Pains and Art, dissected the Carcass of *Humane Nature*, and read many useful Lectures upon the several Parts, both *Containing* and *Contained*; till at last it *smelt* so strong, I could preserve it no longer. Upon which, I have been at a great Expence to fit up all the Bones with exact Contexture, and in due Symmetry; so that I am ready to shew a very compleat Anatomy thereof to all curious *Gentlemen and others*. But not to Digress farther in the midst of a Digression, as I have known some Authors inclose Digressions in one another, like a Nest of Boxes; I do affirm, that having carefully cut up *Humane Nature*, I have found a very strange, new, and important Discovery; That the Publick Good of Mankind is performed by two Ways, *Instruction*, and *Diversion*. And I have farther proved in my said several Readings, (which, perhaps, the World may one day see, if I can prevail on any Friend to steal a Copy, or on certain Gentlemen of my Admirers, to be very Importunate) that, as Mankind is now disposed, he receives much greater Advantage by being *Diverted* than *Instructed*; His Epidemical Diseases being *Fastidiosity*, *Amorphy*, and *Oscitation*; whereas in the present universal Empire of Wit and Learning, there seems but little Matter left for *Instruction*. However, in Compliance with a Lesson of Great Age and Authority, I have attempted carrying the Point in all its Heights; and accordingly throughout this Divine Treatise, have skilfully kneaded up both together with a *Layer* of *Utile* and a *Layer* of *Dulce*.

WHEN I consider how exceedingly our Illustrious *Moderns* have eclipsed the weak glimmering Lights of the *Antients*, and turned them out of the Road of all fashionable Commerce, to a degree, that our choice * Town-Wits of most refined Accomplishments, are in grave Dispute, whether there have been ever any *Antients* or no: In which Point we are like to receive wonderful Satisfaction from the most useful Labours and Lucubrations of that Worthy *Modern*, Dr. *Bently*: I say, when I consider all this, I cannot but bewail, that no famous *Modern* hath ever yet attempted an universal System in a small portable Volume, of all Things that are to be Known, or Believed, or Imagined, or Practised in Life. I am, however, forced to acknowledge, that such an enterprise was thought on some Time ago by a great Philosopher of † *O. Brazile*. The Method he proposed, was by a certain curious *Receipt*, a *Nostrum*, which after his untimely Death, I found among his Papers; and do here out of my great Affection to the *Modern Learned*, present them with it, not doubting, it may one Day encourage some worthy Undertaker.

YOU take fair correct Copies, well bound in Calfs Skin, and Lettered at the Back, of all Modern Bodies of Arts and Sciences whatsoever, and in what Language you please. These you distil in balneo Mariæ, *infusing* Quintessence of Poppy Q. S. *together with three Pints of* Lethe, *to be had from the Apothecaries. You cleanse away carefully the* Sordes *and* Caput mortuum, *letting all that is volatile evaporate. You preserve only the first Running, which is again to be distilled seventeen times, till what remains will amount to about two Drams. This you keep in a Glass Viol* Hermetically *sealed, for one and twenty Days. Then you begin your Catholick Treatise, taking every Morning fasting, (first shaking the Viol) three Drops of this* Elixir, *snuffing it strongly up your Nose. It will dilate it self about the Brain (where there is any) in fourteen Minutes, and you immediately perceive in your Head an in-*

* *The Learned Person here meant by our Author, hath been endeavouring to annihilate so many Antient Writers, that until he is pleas'd to stop his hand it will be dangerous to affirm, whether there have been ever any Antients in the World.*

† *This is an imaginary Island, of Kin to that which is call'd the* Painters Wives Island, *placed in some unknown part of the Ocean, meerly at the Fancy of the Map-maker.*

finite Number of Abstracts, Summaries, Compendiums, Extracts, Collections, Medulla's, Excerpta quædam's, Florilegia's *and the like, all disposed into great Order, and reducible upon Paper.*

I must needs own, it was by the Assistance of this *Arcanum*, that I, tho' otherwise *impar*, have adventured upon so daring an Attempt; never atchieved or undertaken before, but by a certain Author called *Homer*, in whom, tho' otherwise a Person not without some Abilities, and *for an Ancient*, of a tolerable Genius; I have discovered many gross Errors, which are not to be forgiven his very Ashes, if by chance any of them are left. For whereas, we are assured, he design'd his Work for a * compleat Body of all Knowledge Human, Divine, Political, and Mechanick; it is manifest, he hath wholly neglected some, and been very imperfect in the rest. For, first of all, as eminent a *Cabbalist* as his Disciples would represent Him, his Account of the *Opus magnum* is extreamly poor and deficient; he seems to have read but very superficially, either *Sendivogius*, *Behmen*, or † *Anthroposophia Theomagica*. He is also quite mistaken about the *Sphæra Pyroplastica*, a neglect not to be attoned for; and (if the Reader will admit so severe a Censure) *Vix crederem Autorem hunc, unquam audivisse ignis vocem.* His Failings are not less prominent in several Parts of the *Mechanicks*. For, having read his Writings with the utmost Application usual among *Modern Wits*, I could never yet discover the least Direction about the Structure of that useful Instrument a *Save-all*. For want of which, if the *Moderns* had not lent their Assistance, we might yet have wandred *in the Dark*. But I have still behind, a Fault far more notorious to tax this Author with; I mean, || his gross Ignorance in the *Common Laws of this Realm*, and in the Doctrine as well as Discipline of the

* *Homerus omnes res humanas Poematis complexus est.* Xenoph. in conviv.

† *A Treatise written about fifty Years ago, by a* Welsh *Gentleman of* Cambridge, *his Name, as I remember, was* Vaughan, *as appears by the Answer to it, writ by the Learned Dr.* Henry Moor, *it is a Piece of the most unintelligible Fustian, that, perhaps, was ever publish'd in any Language.*

|| *Mr.* Wotton (*to whom our Author never gives any Quarter*) *in his Comparison of Antient and Modern Learning, Numbers Divinity, Law,* &c. *among those Parts of Knowledge wherein we excel the Antients.*

Church of *England*. A Defect indeed, for which both he and all the Ancients stand most justly censured by my worthy and ingenious Friend Mr. *Wotton*, Batchelor of Divinity, in his incomparable Treatise of *Ancient and Modern Learning*; A Book never to be sufficiently valued, whether we consider the happy Turns and Flowings of the Author's Wit, the great Usefulness of his sublime Discoveries upon the Subject of *Flies* and *Spittle*, or the laborious Eloquence of his Stile. And I cannot forbear doing that Author the Justice of my publick Acknowledgments, for the great *Helps* and *Liftings* I had out of his incomparable Piece, while I was penning this Treatise.

But, besides these Omissions in *Homer* already mentioned, the curious Reader will also observe several Defects in that Author's Writings, for which he is not altogether so accountable. For whereas every Branch of Knowledge has received such wonderful Acquirements since his Age, especially within these last three Years, or thereabouts; it is almost impossible, he could be so very perfect in Modern Discoveries, as his Advocates pretend. We freely acknowledge Him to be the Inventor of the *Compass*, of *Gun-Powder*, and the *Circulation of the Blood*: But, I challenge any of his Admirers to shew me in all his Writings, a compleat Account of the *Spleen*; Does he not also leave us wholly to seek in the Art of *Political Wagering*? What can be more defective and unsatisfactory than his long Dissertation upon *Tea*? and as to his Method of *Salivation without Mercury*, so much celebrated of late, it is to my own Knowledge and Experience, a Thing very little to be relied on.

It was to supply such momentous Defects, that I have been prevailed on after long Sollicitation, to take Pen in Hand; and I dare venture to Promise, the Judicious Reader shall find nothing neglected here, that can be of Use upon any Emergency of Life. I am confident to have included and exhausted all that Human Imagination can *Rise* or *Fall* to. Particularly, I recommend to the Perusal of the Learned, certain Discoveries that are wholly untoucht by others; whereof I shall only mention among a great many more; *My New help of Smatterers*, or the *Art of being Deep-learned, and Shallow-read. A curious Invention about Mouse-Traps. An Universal Rule of Reason, or Every Man his own Carver*; Together with a most useful Engine for *catching of Owls*. All which the judicious Reader will find largely treated on, in the several Parts of this Discourse.

I hold my self obliged to give as much Light as is possible, into the Beauties and Excellencies of what I am writing, because it is become the Fashion and Humor most applauded among the first Authors of this Polite and Learned Age, when they would correct the ill Nature of Critical, or inform the Ignorance of Courteous Readers. Besides, there have been several famous Pieces lately published both in Verse and Prose; wherein, if the Writers had not been pleas'd, out of their great Humanity and Affection to the Publick, to give us a nice Detail of the *Sublime*, and the *Admirable* they contain; it is a thousand to one, whether we should ever have discovered one Grain of either. For my own particular, I cannot deny, that whatever I have said upon this Occasion, had been more proper in a Preface, and more agreeable to the Mode, which usually directs it there. But I here think fit to lay hold on that great and honourable Privilege of being the *Last Writer*; I claim an absolute Authority in Right, as the *freshest Modern*, which gives me a Despotick Power over all Authors before me. In the Strength of which Title, I do utterly disapprove and declare against that pernicious Custom, of making the Preface a Bill of Fare to the Book. For I have always lookt upon it as a high Point of Indiscretion in *Monster-mongers* and other *Retailers of strange Sights*; to hang out a fair large Picture over the Door, drawn after the Life, with a most eloquent Description underneath: This hath saved me many a Threepence, for my Curiosity was fully satisfied, and I never offered to go in, tho' often invited by the urging and attending Orator, with his last *moving* and *standing* Piece of Rhetorick; *Sir, Upon my Word, we are just going to begin*. Such is exactly the Fate, at this Time, of *Prefaces*, *Epistles*, *Advertisements*, *Introductions*, *Prolegomena's*, *Apparatus*'s, *To-the-Reader*'s. This Expedient was admirable at first; Our Great *Dryden* has long carried it as far as it would go, and with incredible Success. He has often said to me in Confidence, that the World would have never suspected him to be so great a Poet, if he had not assured them so frequently in his Prefaces, that it was impossible they could either doubt or forget it. Perhaps it may be so; However, I much fear, his Instructions have edify'd out of their Place, and taught Men to grow Wiser in certain Points, where he never intended they should; For it is lamentable to behold, with what a lazy Scorn, many of the yawning Readers in our Age, do now a-days twirl over forty or fifty Pages of *Preface* and *Dedication*, (which is the usual *Modern* Stint) as if it were so much *Latin*. Tho' it must be also allowed on the other Hand that a very considerable Number is known to proceed *Criticks* and *Wits*, by reading nothing else. Into which two Factions, I think, all present Readers may justly be divided. Now, for my self, I profess to be of the former Sort; and therefore having the *Modern* Inclination to expatiate upon the Beauty of my own Productions, and display the bright Parts of my Discourse; I thought best to do it in the Body of the Work, where, as it now lies, it makes a very considerable Addition to the Bulk of the Volume, *a Circumstance by no means to be neglected by a skilful Writer*.

HAVING thus paid my due Deference and Acknowledgment to an establish'd Custom of our newest Authors, by *a long Digression unsought for*, and *an universal Censure unprovoked*; By forcing into the Light, with much Pains and Dexterity, my own Excellencies and other Mens Defaults, with great Justice to my self and Candor to them; I now happily resume my Subject, to the Infinite Satisfaction both of the Reader and the Author.

SECT. VI.

A TALE of a TUB.

WE left *Lord Peter* in open Rupture with his two Brethren; both for ever discarded from his House, and resigned to the wide World, with little or nothing to trust to. Which are Circumstances that render them proper Subjects for the Charity of a Writer's Pen to work on; Scenes of Misery, ever affording the fairest Harvest for great Adventures. And in this, the World may perceive the Difference between the Integrity of a generous Author, and that of a common Friend. The latter is observed to adhere close in Prosperity, but on the Decline of Fortune, to drop suddenly off. Whereas, the generous Author, just on the contrary, finds his Hero on the Dunghil, from thence by gradual Steps, raises Him to a Throne, and then immediately withdraws, expecting not so much as Thanks for his Pains: In imitation of which Example, I have placed *Lord Peter* in a Noble House, given Him a Title to wear, and Money to spend. There I shall leave Him for some Time; returning where common Charity directs me, to the Assistance of his two Brothers, at their lowest Ebb. However, I shall by no means forget my Character of an Historian, to follow the Truth, step by step, whatever happens, or where-ever it may lead me.

THE two Exiles so nearly united in Fortune and Interest, took a Lodging together; Where, at their first Leisure, they began to reflect on the numberless Misfortunes and Vexations of their Life past, and could not tell, on the sudden, to what Failure in their Conduct they ought to impute them; When, after some Recollection, they called to Mind the Copy of their Father's *Will*, which they had so happily recovered. This was immediately produced, and a firm Resolution taken between them, to alter whatever was already amiss, and reduce all their future Measures to the strictest Obedience prescribed therein. The main Body of the *Will* (as the Reader cannot easily have forgot) consisted in certain admirable Rules about the wearing of their Coats; in the Perusal whereof, the two Brothers at every Period duly comparing the Doctrine with the Practice, there was never seen a wider Difference between two Things; horrible downright Transgressions of every Point. Upon which, they both resolved without further Delay, to fall immediately upon reducing the Whole, exactly after their Father's Model.

BUT, here it is good to stop the hasty Reader, ever impatient to see the End of an Adventure, before We Writers can duly prepare him for it. I am to record, that these two Brothers began to be distinguished at this Time, by certain Names. One of them desired to be called * *MARTIN*, and the other took the Appellation of † *JACK*. These two had lived in much Friendship and Agreement under the Tyranny of their Brother *Peter*, as it is the Talent of Fellow-Sufferers to do; Men in Misfortune, being like Men in the Dark, to whom all Colours are the same: But when they came forward into the World, and began to display themselves to each other, and to the Light, their Complexions appear'd extreamly different; which the present Posture of their Affairs gave them sudden Opportunity to discover.

BUT, here the severe Reader may justly tax me as a Writer of short Memory, a Deficiency to which a true *Modern* cannot but of Necessity be a little subject. Because, *Memory* being an Employment of the Mind upon things past, is a Faculty, for which the Learned, in our Illustrious Age, have no manner of Occasion, who deal entirely with *Invention*, and strike all Things out of themselves, or at least, by Collision, from each other: Upon which Account we think it highly Reasonable to produce our great Forgetfulness, as an Argument unanswerable for our great Wit. I ought in Method, to have informed the Reader about fifty Pages ago, of a Fancy *Lord Peter* took, and infused into his Brothers, to wear on their Coats what ever Trimmings came up in Fashion; never pulling off any, as they went out of the Mode, but keeping on all together; which amounted in time to a Medley, the most Antick you can possibly conceive; and this to a Degree, that upon the Time of their falling out there was hardly a Thread of the Original Coat to be seen, but an infinite Quantity of *Lace*, and *Ribbands*, and *Fringe*, and *Embroidery*, and *Points*; (I

* *Martin Luther.*

† *John Calvin.*

mean, only those * *tagg'd with Silver*, for the rest fell off.) Now, this material Circumstance, having been forgot in due Place; as good Fortune hath ordered, comes in very properly here, when the two Brothers are just going to reform their Vestures into the Primitive State, prescribed by their Father's *Will*.

THEY both unanimously entred upon this great Work, looking sometimes on their Coats, and sometimes on the *Will*. *Martin* laid the first Hand; at one twitch brought off a large Handful of *Points*, and with a second pull, stript away ten dozen Yards of *Fringe*. But when He had gone thus far, he demurred a while: He knew very well, there yet remained a great deal more to be done; however, the first Heat being over, his Violence began to cool, and he resolved to proceed more moderately in the rest of the Work; having already very narrowly scap'd a swinging Rent in pulling off the *Points*, which being *tagged with Silver* (as we have observed before) the judicious Workman had with much Sagacity, double sown, to preserve them from *falling*. Resolving therefore to rid his Coat of a huge Quantity of *Gold Lace*; he pickt up the Stitches with much Caution, and diligently gleaned out all the loose Threads as he went, which proved to be a Work of Time. Then he fell about the embroidered *Indian* Figures of Men, Women and Children; against which, as you have heard in its due Place, their Father's Testament was extreamly exact and severe: These, with much Dexterity and Application, were after a while, quite eradicated, or utterly defaced. For the rest, where he observed the Embroidery to be workt so close, as not to be got away without damaging the Cloth, or where it served to hide or strengthen any Flaw in the Body of the Coat, contracted by the perpetual tampering of Workmen upon it; he concluded the wisest Course was to let it remain, resolving in no Case whatsoever, that the Substance of the Stuff should suffer Injury; which he thought the best Method for serving the true Intent and Meaning of his Father's *Will*. And this is the nearest Account I have been able to collect, of *Martin*'s Proceedings upon this great Revolution.

* *Points tagg'd with Silver, are those Doctrines that promote the Greatness and Wealth of the Church, which have been therefore woven deepest in the Body of Popery.*

But his Brother *Jack*, whose Adventures will be so extraordinary, as to furnish a great Part in the Remainder of this Discourse; entred upon the Matter with other Thoughts, and a quite different Spirit. For, the Memory of *Lord Peter*'s Injuries, produced a Degree of Hatred and Spight, which had a much greater Share of inciting Him, than any Regards after his Father's Commands, since these appeared at best, only Secondary and Subservient to the other. However, for this Meddly of Humor, he made a Shift to find a very plausible Name, honoring it with the Title of *Zeal*; which is, perhaps, the most significant Word that hath been ever yet produced in any Language; As, I think, I have fully proved in my excellent *Analytical* Discourse upon that Subject; wherein I have deduced a *Histori-theo-physi-logical* Account of *Zeal*, shewing how it first proceeded from a *Notion* into a *Word*, and from thence in a hot Summer, ripned into a *tangible Substance*. This Work containing three large Volumes in Folio, I design very shortly to publish by the *Modern* way of *Subscription*, not doubting but the Nobility and Gentry of the Land will give me all possible Encouragement, having already had such a Taste of what I am able to perform.

I record therefore, that Brother *Jack*, brimful of this miraculous Compound, reflecting with Indignation upon *PETER*'s Tyranny, and farther provoked by the Despondency of *Martin*; prefaced his Resolutions to this purpose. *What?* said he; *A Rogue that lock'd up his Drink, turned away our Wives, cheated us of our Fortunes; paumed his damned Crusts upon us for Mutton; and at last kickt us out of Doors; must we be in His Fashions with a Pox? a Rascal, besides, that all the Street cries out against*. Having thus kindled and enflamed himself as high as possible, and by Consequence, in a delicate Temper for beginning a Reformation, he set about the Work immediately, and in three Minutes, made more Dispatch than *Martin* had done in as many Hours. For, (Courteous Reader) you are given to understand, that *Zeal* is never so highly obliged, as when you set it a *Tearing*: and *Jack*, who doated on that Quality in himself, allowed it at this Time its full Swinge. Thus it happened, that stripping down a Parcel of *Gold Lace*, a little too hastily, he rent the *main Body* of his *Coat* from Top to Bottom; and whereas his Talent was not of the happiest in *taking up a Stitch*, he knew no better way, than to dern it again with *Packthred* and a *Scewer*. But the Matter was yet infinitely worse (I record it with Tears) when he proceeded to the *Embroidery*: For, being Clumsy by Nature, and of Temper, Impatient; withal, beholding Millions of Stitches, that required the nicest Hand, and sedatest Constitution, to extricate; in a great Rage, he tore off the whole Piece, Cloth and all, and flung it into the Kennel, and furiously thus continuing his Career; *Ah, Good Brother* Martin, said he, *do as I do, for the Love of God; Strip, Tear, Pull, Rent, Flay off all, that we may appear as unlike the Rogue* Peter, *as it is possible: I would not for a hundred Pounds carry the least Mark about me, that might give Occasion to the Neighbours, of suspecting I was related to such a Rascal*. But *Martin*, who at this Time happened to be extremely flegmatick and sedate, *begged his Brother of all Love, not to damage his Coat by any Means; for he never would get such another*: Desired him *to consider, that it was not their Business to form their Actions by any Reflection upon* Peter's, *but by observing the Rules prescribed in their Father's* Will. That *he should remember,* Peter *was still their Brother, whatever Faults or Injuries he had committed; and therefore they should by all means avoid such a Thought, as that of taking Measures for Good and Evil, from no other Rule, than of Opposition to him*. That *it was true, the Testament of their good Father was very exact in what related to the wearing of their* Coats; *yet was it no less penal and strict in prescribing Agreement, and Friendship, and Affection between them. And therefore, if straining a Point were at all dispensable, it would certainly be so, rather to the Advance of Unity, than Increase of Contradiction.*

MARTIN had still proceeded as gravely as he began; and doubtless, would have delivered an admirable Lecture of Morality, which might have exceedingly contributed to my Reader's *Repose, both of Body and Mind*: (the true ultimate End of *Ethicks*;) But *Jack* was already gone a Flight-shot beyond his Patience. And as in Scholastick Disputes, nothing serves to rouze the Spleen of him that *Opposes*, so much as a kind of Pedantick affected Calmness in the *Respondent*; Disputants being for the most part like unequal Scales, where the *Gravity* of one Side advances the *Lightness* of the Other, and causes it to fly up and kick the Beam; So it happened here, that the *Weight* of *Martin*'s

Arguments exalted *Jack*'s *Levity*, and made him fly out and spurn against his Brother's Moderation. In short, *Martin*'s *Patience* put *Jack* in a *Rage*; but that which most afflicted him was, to observe his Brother's Coat so well reduced into the State of Innocence; while his own was either wholly rent to his Shirt; or those Places which had scaped his cruel Clutches, were still in *Peter*'s Livery. So that he looked like a drunken *Beau*, half rifled by *Bullies*; Or like a fresh Tenant of *Newgate*, when he has refused the Payment of *Garnish*; Or like a discovered *Shoplifter*, left to the Mercy of *Exchange-Women*; Or like a *Bawd* in her old Velvet-Petticoat, resign'd into the secular Hands of the *Mobile*. Like any, or like all of these, a Meddley of *Rags*, and *Lace*, and *Rents*, and *Fringes*, unfortunate *Jack* did now appear: He would have been extremely glad to see his Coat in the Condition of *Martin*'s, but infinitely gladder to find that of *Martin*'s in the same Predicament with his. However, since neither of these was likely to come to pass, he thought fit to lend the whole Business another Turn, and to dress up Necessity into a Virtue. Therefore, after as many of the *Fox*'s Arguments, as he could muster up, for bringing *Martin* to *Reason*, as he called it; or, as he meant it, into his own ragged, bobtail'd Condition; and observing he said all to little purpose; what, alas, was left for the forlorn *Jack* to do, but after a Million of Scurrilities against his Brother, to run mad with Spleen, and Spight, and Contradiction. To be short, here began a mortal Breach between these two. *Jack* went immediately to *New Lodgings*, and in a few Days it was for certain reported, that he had run out of his Wits. In a short time after, he appeared abroad, and confirmed the Report, by falling into the oddest Whimsies that ever a sick Brain conceived.

AND now the little Boys in the Streets began to salute him with several Names. Sometimes they would call Him, * *Jack the Bald*; sometimes, † *Jack with a Lanthorn*; sometimes, || *Dutch Jack*; sometimes, * *French Hugh*; sometimes, † *Tom the Beggar*;

* *That is* Calvin, *from* Calvus, *Bald.*
† *All those who pretend to Inward Light.*
|| Jack *of* Leyden, *who gave Rise to the* Anabaptists.
* *The* Hugonots.
† *The* Gueuses, *by which Name some Protestants in* Flanders *were call'd.*

and sometimes, || *Knocking Jack of the North*. And it was under one, or some, or all of these Appellations (which I leave the Learned Reader to determine) that he hath given Rise to the most Illustrious and Epidemick Sect of *Æolists*, who with honourable Commemoration, do still acknowledge the Renowned *JACK* for their Author and Founder. Of whose Original, as well as Principles, I am now advancing to gratify the World with a very particular Account.

——*Mellæo contingens cuncta Lepore*.

|| John Knox, *the Reformer of* Scotland.

SECT. VII.

A Digression in Praise of Digressions.

I HAVE sometimes *heard* of an *Iliad* in a *Nut-shell*; but it hath been my Fortune to have much oftner *seen* a *Nut-shell* in an *Iliad*. There is no doubt, that Human Life has received most wonderful Advantages from both; but to which of the two the World is chiefly indebted, I shall leave among the Curious, as a Problem worthy of their utmost Enquiry. For the Invention of the latter, I think the Commonwealth of Learning is chiefly obliged to the great *Modern* Improvement of *Digressions*: The late Refinements in Knowledge, running parallel to those of Dyet in our Nation, which among Men of a judicious Taste, are drest up in various Compounds, consisting in *Soups* and *Ollio's*, *Fricassées* and *Ragousts*.

'Tis true, there is a sort of morose, detracting, ill-bred People, who pretend utterly to disrelish these polite Innovations: And as to the Similitude from Dyet, they allow the Parallel, but are so bold to pronounce the Example it self, a Corruption and Degeneracy of Taste. They tell us, that the Fashion of jumbling fifty Things together in a Dish, was at first introduced in Compliance to a depraved and *debauched Appetite*, as well as to a *crazy Constitution*; And to see a Man hunting thro' an *Ollio*, after the *Head* and *Brains* of a *Goose*, a *Wigeon*, or a *Woodcock*, is a Sign, he wants a Stomach and Digestion for more substantial Victuals. Farther, they affirm, that *Digressions* in a Book, are like *Forein Troops* in a *State*, which argue the Nation to want a *Heart* and *Hands* of its own, and often, either *subdue* the *Natives*, or drive them into the most *unfruitful Corners*.

But, after all that can be objected by these supercilious Censors; 'tis manifest, the Society of Writers would quickly be reduced to a very inconsiderable Number, if Men were put upon making Books, with the fatal Confinement of delivering nothing beyond what is to the Purpose. 'Tis acknowledged, that were the Case the same among Us, as with the *Greeks* and *Romans*, when Learning was in its *Cradle*, to be reared and fed, and cloathed by *Invention*; it would be an easy Task to fill up Volumes upon particular Occasions, without farther exspatiating from the Subject, than by moderate Excursions, helping to advance or clear the main Design. But with *Knowledge*, it has fared as with a numerous Army, encamped in a fruitful Country; which for a few Days maintains it self by the Product of the Soyl it is on; Till Provisions being spent, they send to forrage many a Mile, among Friends or Enemies it matters not. Mean while, the neighbouring Fields trampled and beaten down, become barren and dry, affording no Sustenance but Clouds of Dust.

THE whole Course of Things, being thus entirely changed between *Us* and the *Antients*; and the *Moderns* wisely sensible of it, we of this Age have discovered a shorter, and more prudent Method, to become *Scholars* and *Wits*, without the Fatigue of *Reading* or of *Thinking*. The most accomplisht Way of using Books at present, is twofold: Either first, to serve them as some Men do *Lords*, learn their *Titles* exactly, and then brag of their Acquaintance. Or Secondly, which is indeed the choicer, the profounder, and politer Method, to get a thorough Insight into the *Index*, by which the whole Book is governed and turned, like *Fishes* by the *Tail*. For, to enter the Palace of Learning at the *great Gate*, requires an Expence of Time and Forms; therefore Men of much Haste and little Ceremony, are content to get in by the *Back-Door*. For, the Arts are all in a *flying* March, and therefore more easily subdued by attacking them in the *Rear*. Thus Physicians discover the State of the whole Body, by consulting only what comes from *Behind*. Thus Men catch Knowledge by throwing their *Wit* on the *Posteriors* of a Book, as Boys do Sparrows with flinging *Salt* upon their *Tails*. Thus Human Life is best understood by the wise man's Rule of *Regarding the End*. Thus are the Sciences found like *Hercules*'s Oxen, by *tracing them Backwards*. Thus are *old Sciences* unravelled like *old Stockings*, by beginning at the *Foot*.

BESIDES all this, the Army of the Sciences hath been of late with a world of Martial Discipline, drawn into its *close Order*, so that a View, or a Muster may be taken of it with abundance of Expedition. For this great Blessing we are wholly indebted to

Systems and *Abstracts*, in which the *Modern* Fathers of Learning, like prudent Usurers, spent their Sweat for the Ease of Us their Children. For *Labor* is the Seed of *Idleness*, and it is the peculiar Happiness of our Noble Age to gather the *Fruit*.

Now the Method of growing Wise, Learned, and *Sublime*, having become so regular an Affair, and so established in all its Forms; the Number of Writers must needs have encreased accordingly, and to a Pitch that has made it of absolute Necessity for them to interfere continually with each other. Besides, it is reckoned, that there is not at this present, a sufficient Quantity of new Matter left in Nature, to furnish and adorn any one particular Subject to the Extent of a Volume. This I am told by a very skillful *Computer*, who hath given a full Demonstration of it from Rules of *Arithmetick*.

THIS, perhaps, may be objected against, by those, who maintain the Infinity of Matter, and therefore, will not allow that any *Species* of it can be exhausted. For Answer to which, let us examine the noblest Branch of *Modern* Wit or Invention, planted and cultivated by the present Age, and, which of all others, hath born the most, and the fairest Fruit. For tho' some Remains of it were left us by the *Antients*, yet have not any of those, as I remember, been translated or compiled into Systems for *Modern* Use. Therefore We may affirm, to our own Honor, that it has in some sort, been both invented, and brought to a Perfection by the same Hands. What I mean, is that highly celebrated Talent among the *Modern* Wits, of deducing Similitudes, Allusions, and Applications, very Surprizing, Agreeable, and Apposite, from the *Pudenda* of either Sex, together with *their proper Uses*. And truly, having observed how little Invention bears any Vogue, besides what is derived into these *Channels*, I have sometimes had a Thought, That the happy Genius of our Age and Country, was prophetically held forth by that antient * typical Description of the *Indian* Pygmies; *whose Stature did not exceed above two Foot; Sed quorum pudenda crassa, & ad talos usque pertingentia*. Now, I have been very curious to inspect the late Productions, wherein the Beauties of this kind have most prominently appeared. And altho' this *Vein* hath bled so freely, and all Endeavours have been used in the Power of Human

* *Ctesiæ fragm. apud Photium.*

Breath, to dilate, extend, and keep it open: Like the Scythians, * *who had a Custom, and an Instrument, to blow up the Privities of their Mares, that they might yield the more Milk*; Yet I am under an Apprehension, it is near growing dry, and past all Recovery; And that either some new *Fonde* of Wit should, if possible, be provided, or else that we must e'en be content with Repetition here, as well as upon all other Occasions.

* *Herodot*. L. 4.

THIS will stand as an uncontestable Argument, that our *Modern* Wits are not to reckon upon the Infinity of Matter, for a constant Supply. What remains therefore, but that our last Recourse must be had to large *Indexes*, and little *Compendiums*; *Quotations* must be plentifully gathered, and bookt in Alphabet; To this End, tho' Authors need be little consulted, yet *Criticks*, and *Commentators*, and *Lexicons* carefully must. But above all, those judicious Collectors of *bright Parts*, and *Flowers*, and *Observanda's*, are to be nicely dwelt on; by some called the *Sieves* and *Boulters* of Learning; tho' it is left undetermined, whether they dealt in *Pearls* or *Meal*; and consequently, whether we are more to value that which *passed thro'*, or what *staid behind*.

BY these Methods, in a few Weeks, there starts up many a Writer, capable of managing the profoundest, and most universal Subjects. For, what tho' his *Head* be empty, provided his *Common-place-Book* be full; And if you will bate him but the Circumstances of *Method*, and *Style*, and *Grammar*, and *Invention*; allow him but the common Priviledges of transcribing from others, and digressing from himself, as often as he shall see Occasion; He will desire no more Ingredients towards fitting up a Treatise, that shall make a very comely Figure on a Bookseller's Shelf, there to be preserved neat and clean, for a long Eternity, adorn'd with the Heraldry of its Title, fairly inscribed on a Label; never to be thumb'd or greas'd by Students, nor bound to everlasting Chains of Darkness in a Library: But when the Fulness of time is come, shall haply undergo the Tryal of Purgatory, in order *to ascend the Sky*.

WITHOUT these Allowances, how is it possible, we *Modern* Wits should ever have an Opportunity to introduce our Collections listed under so many thousand Heads of a different Nature? for want of which, the Learned World would be deprived of infinite Delight, as well as Instruction, and we our selves buried beyond Redress in an inglorious and undistinguisht Oblivion.

From such Elements as these, I am alive to behold the Day, wherein the Corporation of Authors can out-vie all its Brethren in the *Guild*. A Happiness derived to us with a great many others, from our *Scythian* Ancestors; among whom, the Number of *Pens* was so infinite, that the * *Grecian* Eloquence had no other way of expressing it, than by saying, *That in the Regions, far to the* North, *it was hardly possible for a Man to travel, the very Air was so replete with* Feathers.

* *Herodot.* L. 4.

The Necessity of this Digression, will easily excuse the Length; and I have chosen for it as proper a Place as I could readily find. If the judicious Reader can assign a fitter, I do here empower him to remove it into any other Corner he please. And so I return with great Alacrity to pursue a more important Concern.

SECT. VIII.

A TALE of a TUB.

THE Learned * *Æolists*, maintain the Original Cause of all Things to be *Wind*, from which Principle this whole Universe was at first produced, and into which it must at last be resolved; that the same Breath which had kindled, and blew *up* the Flame of Nature, should one Day blow it *out*.

Quod procul à nobis flectat Fortuna gubernans.

THIS is what the *Adepti* understand by their *Anima Mundi*; that is to say, the *Spirit*, or *Breath*, or *Wind* of the World: Or Examine the whole System by the Particulars of Nature, and you will find it not to be disputed. For, whether you please to call the *Forma informans* of Man, by the Name of *Spiritus*, *Animus*, *Afflatus*, or *Anima*; What are all these but several Appellations for *Wind*? which is the ruling *Element* in every Compound, and into which they all resolve upon their Corruption. Farther, what is Life itself, but as it is commonly call'd, the *Breath* of our Nostrils? Whence it is very justly observed by Naturalists, that *Wind* still continues of great Emolument in *certain Mysteries* not to be named, giving Occasion for those happy Epithets of *Turgidus*, and *Inflatus*, apply'd either to the *Emittent*, or *Recipient* Organs.

BY what I have gathered out of antient Records, I find the *Compass* of their Doctrine took in two and thirty Points, wherein it would be tedious to be very particular. However, a few of their most important Precepts, deducible from it, are by no means to be omitted; among which the following Maxim was of much Weight; That since *Wind* had the Master-Share, as well as Operation in every Compound, by Consequence, those Beings must be of chief Excellence, wherein that *Primordium* appears most prominently to abound; and therefore, *Man* is in highest Perfection of all created Things, as having by the great Bounty of Philosophers, been endued with three distinct *Anima's* or

* *All Pretenders to Inspiration whatsoever.*

Winds, to which the Sage *Æolists*, with much Liberality, have added a fourth of equal Necessity, as well as Ornament with the other three; by this *quartum Principium*, taking in the four Corners of the World; which gave Occasion to that Renowned *Cabbalist*, * *Bumbastus*, of placing the Body of Man, in due position to the four *Cardinal* Points.

In Consequence of this, their next Principle was, that *Man* brings with him into the World a peculiar Portion or Grain of *Wind*, which may be called a *Quinta essentia*, extracted from the other four. This *Quintessence* is of Catholick Use upon all Emergencies of Life, is improvable into all Arts and Sciences, and may be wonderfully refined, as well as enlarged by certain Methods in Education. This, when *blown* up to its Perfection, ought not to be covetously hoarded up, stifled, or hid under a Bushel, but freely communicated to Mankind. Upon these Reasons, and others of equal Weight, the Wise *Æolists*, affirm the Gift of BELCHING, to be the noblest Act of a Rational Creature. To cultivate which Art, and render it more serviceable to Mankind, they made Use of several Methods. At certain Seasons of the Year, you might behold the Priests amongst them in vast Numbers, with their † *Mouths gaping wide against a Storm.* At other times were to be seen several Hundreds link'd together in a circular Chain, with every Man a Pair of Bellows applied to his Neighbour's Breech, by which they blew up each other to the Shape and Size of a *Tun*; and for that Reason, with great Propriety of Speech, did usually call their Bodies, their *Vessels*. When, by these and the like Performances, they were grown sufficiently replete, they would immediately depart, and disembogue for the Publick Good, a plentiful Share of their Acquirements into their Disciples Chaps. For we must here observe, that all Learning was esteemed among them to be compounded from the same Principle. Because, First, it is generally affirmed, or confess'd that Learning *puffeth Men up*: And Secondly, they

* *This is one of the Names of* Paracelsus; *He was call'd* Christophorus, Theophrastus, Paracelsus, Bumbastus.

† *This is meant of those Seditious Preachers, who blow up the Seeds of Rebellion*, &c.

proved it by the following Syllogism; *Words are but Wind; and Learning is nothing but Words*; Ergo, *Learning is nothing but Wind.* For this Reason, the Philosophers among them, did in their Schools, deliver to their Pupils, all their Doctrines and Opinions by *Eructation*, wherein they had acquired a wonderful Eloquence, and of incredible Variety. But the great Characteristick, by which their chief Sages were best distinguished, was a certain Position of Countenance, which gave undoubted Intelligence to what Degree or Proportion, the Spirit agitated the inward Mass. For, after certain Gripings, the *Wind* and Vapours issuing forth; having first by their Turbulence and Convulsions within, caused an Earthquake in Man's little World; distorted the Mouth, bloated the Cheeks, and gave the Eyes a terrible kind of *Relievo.* At which Junctures, all their *Belches* were received for Sacred, the Sourer the better, and swallowed with infinite Consolation by their meager Devotes. And to render these yet more compleat, because the Breath of Man's Life is in his Nostrils, therefore, the choicest, most edifying, and most enlivening *Belches*, were very wisely conveyed thro' that Vehicle, to give them a Tincture as they passed.

THEIR Gods were the four *Winds*, whom they worshipped, as the Spirits that pervade and enliven the Universe, and as those from whom alone all *Inspiration* can properly be said to proceed. However, the Chief of these, to whom they performed the Adoration of *Latria*, was the *Almighty-North*. An antient Deity, whom the Inhabitants of *Megalopolis* in Greece, had likewise in highest Reverence. * *Omnium Deorum Boream maxime celebrant*. This God, tho' endued with Ubiquity, was yet supposed by the profounder *Æolists*, to possess one peculiar Habitation, or (to speak in Form) a *Cœlum Empyræum*, wherein he was more intimately present. This was situated in a certain Region, well known to the Antient *Greeks*, by them called, Σκοτία, or the *Land of Darkness*. And altho' many Controversies have arisen upon that Matter; yet so much is undisputed, that from a Region of the *like Denomination*, the most refined *Æolists* have borrowed their Original, from whence, in every Age, the zealous among their Priesthood, have brought over their choicest *Inspiration*, fetching it with their own Hands,

* *Pausan*. L.8.

from the Fountain Head, in certain *Bladders*, and disploding it among the Sectaries in all Nations, who did, and do, and ever will, daily Gasp and Pant after it.

Now, their Mysteries and Rites were performed in this Manner. 'Tis well known among the Learned, that the Virtuoso's of former Ages, had a Contrivance for carrying and preserving *Winds* in Casks or Barrels, which was of great Assistance upon long Sea Voyages; and the Loss of so useful an Art at present, is very much to be lamented, tho' I know not how, with great Negligence omitted by * *Pancirollus*. It was an Invention ascribed to *Æolus* himself, from whom this Sect is denominated, and who in Honour of their Founder's Memory, have to this Day preserved great Numbers of those *Barrels*, whereof they fix one in each of their Temples, first beating out the Top. Into this *Barrel*, upon Solemn Days, the Priest enters; where, having before duly prepared himself by the methods already described, a secret Funnel is also convey'd from his Posteriors, to the Bottom of the Barrel, which admits new Supplies of Inspiration from a *Northern* Chink or Crany. Whereupon, you behold him swell immediately to the Shape and Size of his *Vessel*. In this Posture he disembogues whole Tempests upon his Auditory, as the Spirit from beneath gives him Utterance; which issuing *ex adytis*, and *penetralibus*, is not performed without much Pain and Gripings. And the *Wind* in breaking forth, † deals with his Face, as it does with that of the Sea; first *blackning*, then *wrinkling*, and at last, *bursting it into a Foam*. It is in this Guise, the Sacred *Æolist* delivers his oracular *Belches* to his panting Disciples; Of whom, some are greedily gaping after the sanctified Breath; others are all the while hymning out the Praises of the *Winds*; and gently wafted to and fro by their own Humming, do thus represent the soft Breezes of their Deities appeased.

It is from this Custom of the Priests, that some Authors maintain these *Æolists*, to have been very antient in the World.

* *An Author who writ* De Artibus Perditis, &c. *of Arts lost, and of Arts invented.*

† *This is an exact Description of the Changes made in the Face by Enthusiastick Preachers.*

Because, the Delivery of their Mysteries, which I have just now mention'd, appears exactly the same with that of other antient Oracles, whose Inspirations were owing to certain subterraneous *Effluviums* of *Wind*, delivered with the *same* Pain to the Priest, and much about the *same* Influence on the People. It is true indeed, that these were frequently managed and directed by *Female* Officers, whose Organs were understood to be better disposed for the Admission of those Oracular *Gusts*, as entring and passing up thro' a Receptacle of greater Capacity, and causing also a Pruriency by the Way, such as with due Management, hath been refined from a Carnal, into a Spiritual Extasie. And to strengthen this profound Conjecture, it is farther insisted, that this Custom of * *Female* Priests is kept up still in certain refined Colleges of our *Modern Æolists*, who are agreed to receive their Inspiration, derived thro' the Receptacle aforesaid, like their Ancestors, the *Sibyls*.

And, whereas the mind of Man, when he gives the Spur and Bridle to his Thoughts, doth never stop, but naturally sallies out into both extreams of High and Low, of Good and Evil; His first Flight of Fancy, commonly transports Him to Idea's of what is most Perfect, finished, and exalted; till having soared out of his own Reach and Sight, not well perceiving how near the Frontiers of Height and Depth, border upon each other; With the same Course and Wing, he falls down plum into the lowest Bottom of Things; like one who travels the *East* into the *West*; or like a strait Line drawn by its own Length into a Circle. Whether a Tincture of Malice in our Natures, makes us fond of furnishing every bright Idea with its Reverse; Or, whether Reason reflecting upon the Sum of Things, can, like the Sun, serve only to enlighten one half of the Globe, leaving the other half, by Necessity, under Shade and Darkness: Or, whether Fancy, flying up to the imagination of what is Highest and Best, becomes over-shot, and spent, and weary, and suddenly falls like a dead Bird of Paradise, to the Ground. Or, whether after all these *Metaphysical* Conjectures, I have not entirely missed the true Reason; The Proposition, however, which hath stood me

* *Quakers who suffer their Women to preach and pray.*

in so much Circumstance, is altogether true; That, as the most unciviliz'd Parts of Mankind, have some way or other, climbed up into the Conception of a *God*, or Supream Power, so they have seldom forgot to provide their Fears with certain ghastly Notions, which instead of better, have served them pretty tolerably for a *Devil*. And this Proceeding seems to be natural enough; For it is with Men, whose Imaginations are lifted up very high, after the same Rate, as with those, whose Bodies are so; that, as they are delighted with the Advantage of a nearer Contemplation upwards, so they are equally terrified with the dismal Prospect of the Precipice below. Thus, in the Choice of a *Devil*, it hath been the usual Method of Mankind, to single out some Being, either in Act, or in Vision, which was in most Antipathy to the God they had framed. Thus also the Sect of *Æolists*, possessed themselves with a Dread, and Horror, and Hatred of two Malignant Natures, betwixt whom, and the Deities they adored, perpetual Enmity was established. The first of these, was the * *Camelion* sworn Foe to *Inspiration*, who in Scorn, devoured large Influences of their God; without refunding the smallest Blast by *Eructation*. The other was a huge terrible Monster, called *Moulinavent*, who with four strong Arms, waged eternal Battel with all their Divinities, dextrously turning to avoid their Blows, and repay them with Interest.

THUS furnisht, and set out with *Gods*, as well as *Devils*, was the renowned Sect of *Æolists*; which makes at this Day so illustrious a Figure in the World, and whereof, that Polite Nation of *Laplanders*, are beyond all Doubt, a most Authentick Branch; Of whom, I therefore cannot, without Injustice, here omit to make honourable Mention; since they appear to be so closely allied in Point of Interest, as well as Inclinations, with their Brother *Æolists* among Us, as not only to buy their *Winds* by wholesale from the *same* Merchants, but also to retail them after the *same* Rate and Method, and to Customers much alike.

NOW, whether the System here delivered, was wholly com-

* *I do not well understand what the Author aims at here, any more than by the terrible Monster, mention'd in the following Lines, called* Moulinavent, *which is the* French *Word for a Windmill.*

piled by *Jack*, or, as some Writers believe, rather copied from the Original at *Delphos*, with certain Additions and Emendations suited to Times and Circumstances, I shall not absolutely determine. This I may affirm, that *Jack* gave it at least a new Turn, and formed it into the same Dress and Model, as it lies deduced by me.

I have long sought after this Opportunity, of doing Justice to a Society of Men, for whom I have a peculiar Honour, and whose Opinions, as well as Practices, have been extreamly misrepresented, and traduced by the Malice or Ignorance of their Adversaries. For, I think it one of the greatest, and best of human Actions, to remove Prejudices, and place Things in their truest and fairest Light; which I therefore boldly undertake without any Regards of my own, beside the Conscience, the Honour, and the Thanks.

SECT. IX.

A Digression concerning the Original, the Use and Improvement of Madness *in a Commonwealth.*

NOR shall it any ways detract from the just Reputation of this famous Sect, that its Rise and Institution are owing to such an Author as I have described *Jack* to be; A Person whose Intellectuals were overturned, and his Brain shaken out of its Natural Position; which we commonly suppose to be a Distemper, and call by the Name of *Madness* or *Phrenzy*. For, if we take a Survey of the greatest Actions that have been performed in the World, under the Influence of Single Men; which are, *The Establishment of New Empires by Conquest: The Advance and Progress of New Schemes in Philosophy; and the contriving, as well as the propagating of New Religions*: We shall find the Authors of them all, to have been Persons, whose natural Reason hath admitted great Revolutions from their Dyet, their Education, the Prevalency of some certain Temper, together with the particular Influence of Air and Climate. Besides, there is something Individual in human Minds, that easily kindles at the accidental Approach and Collision of certain Circumstances, which tho' of paltry and mean Appearance, do often flame out into the greatest Emergencies of Life. For great Turns are not always given by strong Hands, but by lucky Adaption, and at proper Seasons; and it is of no import, where the Fire was kindled, if the Vapor has once got up into the Brain. For the *upper Region* of Man, is furnished like the *middle Region* of the Air; The Materials are formed from Causes of the widest Difference, yet produce at last the same Substance and Effect. Mists arise from the Earth, Steams from Dunghils, Exhalations from the Sea, and Smoak from Fire; yet all Clouds are the same in Composition, as well as Consequences: and the Fumes issuing from a Jakes, will furnish as comely and useful a Vapor, as Incense from an Altar. Thus far, I suppose, will easily be granted me; and then it will follow, that as the Face of Nature never produces Rain, but when it is overcast and disturbed, so Human Understanding, seated in the Brain, must be troubled and overspread by Vapours, ascending from the lower Faculties, to water the Invention, and render it fruitful. Now, altho' these Vapours (as it hath been already said) are of as various Original, as those of the Skies, yet the Crop they produce, differs both in Kind and Degree, meerly according to the Soil. I will produce two Instances to prove and Explain what I am now advancing.

* A certain Great Prince raised a mighty Army, filled his Coffers with infinite Treasures, provided an invincible Fleet, and all this, without giving the least Part of his Design to his greatest Ministers, or his nearest Favourites. Immediately the whole World was alarmed; the neighbouring Crowns, in trembling Expectation, towards what Point the Storm would burst; the small Politicians, every where forming profound Conjectures. Some believed he had laid a Scheme for Universal Monarchy: Others, after much Insight, determined the Matter to be a Project for pulling down the *Pope*, and setting up the *Reformed* Religion, which had once been his own. Some, again, of a deeper Sagacity, sent him into *Asia* to subdue the *Turk*, and recover *Palestine*. In the midst of all these Projects and Preparations; a certain † *State-Surgeon*, gathering the Nature of the Disease by these Symptoms, attempted the Cure, at one Blow performed the Operation, broke the Bag, and out flew the *Vapour*; nor did any thing want to render it a compleat Remedy, only, that the Prince unfortunately happened to Die in the Performance. Now, is the Reader exceeding curious to learn, from whence this *Vapour* took its Rise, which had so long set the Nations at a Gaze? What secret Wheel, what hidden Spring could put into Motion so wonderful an Engine? It was afterwards discovered, that the Movement of this whole Machine had been directed by an absent *Female*, whose Eyes had raised a Protuberancy, and before Emission, she was removed into an Enemy's Country. What should an unhappy Prince do in such ticklish Circumstances as these? He tried in vain the Poet's never-failing Receipt of *Corpora quæque*; For,

Idque petit corpus mens unde est saucia amore;
Unde feritur, eo tendit, gestitq; coire. Lucr.

---

* *This was* Harry *the Great of* France.

† Ravillac, *who stabb'd* Henry *the Great in his Coach.*

HAVING to no purpose used all peaceable Endeavours, the collected part of the *Semen*, raised and enflamed, became adust, converted to Choler, turned head upon the spinal Duct, and ascended to the Brain. The very same Principle that influences a *Bully* to break the Windows of a Whore, who has jilted him, naturally stirs up a Great Prince to raise mighty Armies, and dream of nothing but Sieges, Battles, and Victories.

———*Teterrima belli*
Causa————————

THE other * Instance is, what I have read somewhere, in a very antient Author, of a mighty King, who for the space of above thirty Years, amused himself to take and lose Towns; beat Armies, and be beaten; drive Princes out of their Dominions; fright Children from their Bread and Butter; burn, lay waste, plunder, dragoon, massacre Subject and Stranger, Friend and Foe, Male and Female. 'Tis recorded, that the Philosophers of each Country were in grave Dispute, upon Causes Natural, Moral, and Political, to find out where they should assign an original Solution of this *Phænomenon*. At last the *Vapour* or *Spirit*, which animated the Hero's Brain, being in perpetual Circulation, seized upon that Region of the Human Body, so renown'd for furnishing the † *Zibeta Occidentalis*, and gathering there into a Tumor, left the rest of the World for that Time in Peace. Of such mighty Consequence it is, where those Exhalations fix; and of so little, from whence they proceed. The same Spirits which in their superior Progress would conquer a Kingdom, descending upon the *Anus*, conclude in a *Fistula*.

LET us next examine the great Introducers of new Schemes in Philosophy, and search till we can find, from what Faculty of the Soul the Disposition arises in mortal Man, of taking it into his Head, to advance new Systems with such an eager Zeal, in

* *This is meant of the Present* French *King.*

† Paracelsus, *who was so famous for Chymistry, try'd an Experiment upon human Excrement, to make a Perfume of it, which when he had brought to Perfection, he called* Zibeta Occidentalis, *or* Western-Civet, *the back Parts of Man* (*according to his Division mention'd by the Author*, page [96].) *being the* West.

things agreed on all hands impossible to be known: from what Seeds this Disposition springs, and to what Quality of human Nature these Grand Innovators have been indebted for their Number of Disciples. Because, it is plain, that several of the chief among them, both *Antient* and *Modern*, were usually mistaken by their Adversaries, and indeed, by all, except their own Followers, to have been Persons Crazed, or out of their Wits, having generally proceeded in the common Course of their Words and Actions, by a Method very different from the vulgar Dictates of *unrefined* Reason: agreeing for the most Part in their several Models, with their present undoubted Successors in the *Academy* of *Modern Bedlam* (whose Merits and Principles I shall farther examine in due Place.) Of this Kind were *Epicurus*, *Diogenes*, *Apollonius*, *Lucretius*, *Paracelsus*, *Des Cartes*, and others; who, if they were now in the World, tied fast, and separate from their Followers, would in this our undistinguishing Age, incur manifest Danger of *Phlebotomy*, and *Whips*, and *Chains*, and *dark Chambers*, and *Straw*. For, what Man in the natural State, or Course of Thinking, did ever conceive it in his Power, to reduce the Notions of all Mankind, exactly to the same Length, and Breadth, and Heighth of his own? Yet this is the first humble and civil Design of all Innovators in the Empire of Reason. *Epicurus* modestly hoped, that one Time or other, a certain Fortuitous Concourse of all Mens Opinions, after perpetual Justlings, the Sharp with the Smooth, the Light and the Heavy, the Round and the Square, would by certain *Clinamina*, unite in the Notions of *Atoms* and *Void*, as these did in the Originals of all Things. *Cartesius* reckoned to see before he died, the Sentiments of all Philosophers, like so many lesser Stars in his *Romantick* System, rapt and drawn within his own *Vortex*. Now, I would gladly be informed, how it is possible to account for such Imaginations as these in particular Men, without Recourse to my *Phœnomenon* of *Vapours*, ascending from the lower Faculties to over-shadow the Brain, and thence distilling into Conceptions, for which the Narrowness of our Mother-Tongue has not yet assigned any other Name, besides that of *Madness* or *Phrenzy*. Let us therefore now conjecture how it comes to pass, that none of these great Prescribers, do ever fail providing themselves and their Notions, with a Number of implicite Disciples. And, I think, the Reason is easie to be assigned: For, there is a peculiar *String* in the Harmony of Human Understanding, which in several individuals is exactly of the same Tuning. This, if you can dexterously screw up to its right Key, and then strike gently upon it; Whenever you have the Good Fortune to light among those of the same Pitch, they will by a secret necessary Sympathy, strike exactly at the same time. And in this one Circumstance, lies all the Skill or Luck of the Matter; for if you chance to jar the String among those who are either above or below your own Height, instead of subscribing to your Doctrine, they will tie you fast, call you Mad, and feed you with Bread and Water. It is therefore a Point of the nicest Conduct to distinguish and adapt this noble Talent, with respect to the Differences of Persons and of Times. *Cicero* understood this very well, when writing to a Friend in *England*, with a Caution, among other Matters, to beware of being cheated by our *Hackney-Coachmen* (who, it seems, in those days, were as arrant Rascals as they are now) has these remarkable Words. * *Est quod gaudeas te in ista loca venisse, ubi aliquid sapere viderere.* For, to speak a bold Truth, it is a fatal Miscarriage, so ill to order Affairs, as to pass for a *Fool* in one Company, when in another you might be treated as a *Philosopher*. Which I desire *some certain Gentlemen of my Acquaintance*, to lay up in their Hearts, as a very seasonable *Innuendo*.

* *Epist. ad Fam. Trebatio.*

THIS, indeed, was the Fatal Mistake of that worthy Gentleman, my most ingenious Friend, Mr. *Wotton*: A Person, in appearance ordain'd for great Designs, as well as Performances; whether you will consider his *Notions* or his *Looks*. Surely, no Man ever advanced into the Publick, with fitter Qualifications of Body and Mind, for the Propagation of a new Religion. Oh, had those happy Talents misapplied to vain Philosophy, been turned into their proper Channels of *Dreams* and *Visions*, where *Distortion* of Mind and Countenance, are of such Sovereign Use; the base detracting World would not then have dared to report, that something is amiss, that his Brain hath undergone an unlucky Shake; which even his Brother *Modernists* themselves, like Ungrates, do whisper so loud, that it reaches up to the very *Garrat* I am writing in.

Lastly, Whosoever pleases to look into the Fountains of *Enthusiasm*, from whence, in all Ages, have eternally proceeded such fatning Streams, will find the Spring Head to have been as *troubled* and *muddy* as the Current; Of such great Emolument, is a Tincture of this *Vapour*, which the World calls *Madness*, that without its Help, the World would not only be deprived of those two great Blessings, *Conquests* and *Systems*, but even all Mankind would unhappily be reduced to the same Belief in Things Invisible. Now, the former *Postulatum* being held, that it is of no Import from what Originals this *Vapour* proceeds, but either in what *Angles* it strikes and spreads over the Understanding, or upon what *Species* of Brain it ascends; It will be a very delicate Point, to cut the Feather, and divide the several Reasons to a Nice and Curious Reader, how this numerical Difference in the Brain, can produce Effects of so vast a Difference from the same *Vapour*, as to be the sole Point of Individuation between *Alexander the Great*, *Jack of Leyden*, and Monsieur *Des Cartes*. The present Argument is the most abstracted that ever I engaged in, it strains my Faculties to their highest Stretch; and I desire the Reader to attend with utmost Perpensity; For, I now proceed to unravel this knotty Point.

†There is in Mankind a certain * * * * *
* * * * * * * * * *
* * * * * * * * * *
* * * * * * * * *Hic multa*
* * * * * * * * *desiderantur.*
* * * * * * * * * *
* * * And this I take to be a clear Solution of the Matter.

Having therefore so narrowly past thro' this intricate Difficulty, the Reader will, I am sure, agree with me in the Conclusion; that if the *Moderns* mean by *Madness*, only a Disturbance or Transposition of the Brain, by Force of certain *Vapours* issuing

†*Here is another Defect in the Manuscript, but I think the Author did wisely, and that the Matter which thus strained his Faculties, was not worth a Solution; and it were well if all Metaphysical Cobweb Problems were no otherwise answered.*

up from the lower Faculties; Then has this *Madness* been the Parent of all those mighty Revolutions, that have happened in *Empire*, in *Philosophy*, and in *Religion*. For, the Brain, in its natural Position and State of Serenity, disposeth its Owner to pass his Life in the common Forms, without any Thought of subduing Multitudes to his own *Power*, his *Reasons* or his *Visions*; and the more he shapes his Understanding by the Pattern of Human Learning, the less he is inclined to form Parties after his particular Notions; because that instructs him in his private Infirmities, as well as in the stubborn Ignorance of the People. But when a Man's Fancy gets *astride* on his Reason, when Imagination is at Cuffs with the Senses, and common Understanding, as well as common Sense, is Kickt out of Doors; the first Proselyte he makes, is Himself, and when that is once compass'd, the Difficulty is not so great in bringing over others; A strong Delusion always operating from *without*, as vigorously as from *within*. For, Cant and Vision are to the Ear and the Eye, the same that Tickling is to the Touch. Those Entertainments and Pleasures we most value in Life, are such as *Dupe* and play the Wag with the Senses. For, if we take an Examination of what is generally understood by *Happiness*, as it has Respect, either to the Understanding or the Senses, we shall find all its Properties and Adjuncts will herd under this short Definition: That, *it is a perpetual Possession of being well Deceived*. And first, with Relation to the Mind or Understanding; 'tis manifest, what mighty Advantages Fiction has over Truth; and the Reason is just at our Elbow; because Imagination can build nobler Scenes, and produce more wonderful Revolutions than Fortune or Nature will be at Expence to furnish. Nor is Mankind so much to blame in his Choice, thus determining him, if we consider that the Debate meerly lies between *Things past*, and *Things conceived*; and so the Question is only this; Whether Things that have Place in the *Imagination*, may not as properly be said to *Exist*, as those that are seated in the *Memory*; which may be justly held in the Affirmative, and very much to the Advantage of the former, since This is acknowledged to be the *Womb* of Things, and the other allowed to be no more than the *Grave*. Again, if we take this Definition of Happiness, and examine it with Reference to the

Senses, it will be acknowledged wonderfully adapt. How fade and insipid do all Objects accost us that are not convey'd in the Vehicle of *Delusion*? How shrunk is every Thing, as it appears in the Glass of Nature? So, that if it were not for the Assistance of Artificial *Mediums*, false Lights, refracted Angles, Varnish, and Tinsel; there would be a mighty Level in the Felicity and Enjoyments of Mortal Men. If this were seriously considered by the World, as I have a certain Reason to suspect it hardly will; Men would no longer reckon among their high Points of Wisdom, the Art of exposing weak Sides, and publishing Infirmities; an Employment in my Opinion, neither better nor worse than that of *Unmasking*, which I think, has never been allowed fair Usage, either in the *World* or the *Play-House*.

In the Proportion that Credulity is a more peaceful Possession of the Mind, than Curiosity, so far preferable is that Wisdom, which converses about the Surface, to that pretended Philosophy which enters into the Depth of Things, and then comes gravely back with Informations and Discoveries, that in the inside they are good for nothing. The two Senses, to which all Objects first address themselves, are the Sight and the Touch; These never examine farther than the Colour, the Shape, the Size, and whatever other Qualities dwell, or are drawn by Art upon the Outward of Bodies; and then comes Reason officiously, with Tools for cutting, and opening, and mangling, and piercing, offering to demonstrate, that they are not of the same consistence quite thro'. Now, I take all this to be the last Degree of perverting Nature; one of whose Eternal Laws it is, to put her best Furniture forward. And therefore, in order to save the Charges of all such expensive Anatomy for the Time to come; I do here think fit to inform the Reader, that in such Conclusions as these, Reason is certainly in the Right; and that in most Corporeal Beings, which have fallen under my Cognizance, the *Outside* hath been infinitely preferable to the *In*: Whereof I have been farther convinced from some late Experiments. Last Week I saw a Woman *flay'd*, and you will hardly believe, how much it altered her Person for the worse. Yesterday I ordered the Carcass of a *Beau* to be stript in my Presence; when we were all amazed to find so many unsuspected Faults under one Suit of Cloaths:

Then I laid open his *Brain*, his *Heart*, and his *Spleen*; But, I plainly perceived at every Operation, that the farther we proceeded, we found the Defects encrease upon us in Number and Bulk: from all which, I justly formed this Conclusion to my self; That whatever Philosopher or Projector can find out an Art to sodder and patch up the Flaws and Imperfections of Nature, will deserve much better of Mankind, and teach us a more useful Science, than that so much in present Esteem, of widening and exposing them (like him who held *Anatomy* to be the ultimate End of *Physick*.) And he, whose Fortunes and Dispositions have placed him in a convenient Station to enjoy the Fruits of this noble Art; He that can with *Epicurus* content his Ideas with the *Films* and *Images* that fly off upon his Senses from the *Superficies* of Things; Such a Man truly wise, creams off Nature, leaving the Sower and the Dregs, for Philosophy and Reason to lap up. This is the sublime and refined Point of Felicity, called, *the Possession of being well deceived*; The Serene Peaceful State of being a Fool among Knaves.

But to return to *Madness*. It is certain, that according to the System I have above deduced; every *Species* thereof proceeds from a Redundancy of *Vapour*; therefore, as some Kinds of *Phrenzy* give double Strength to the Sinews, so there are of other *Species*, which add Vigor, and Life, and Spirit to the Brain: Now, it usually happens, that these active Spirits, getting Possession of the Brain, resemble those that haunt other waste and empty Dwellings, which for want of Business, either vanish, and carry away a Piece of the House, or else stay at home and fling it all out of the Windows. By which are mystically display'd the two principal Branches of *Madness*, and which some Philosophers not considering so well as I, have mistook to be different in their Causes, over-hastily assigning the first to Deficiency, and the other to Redundance.

I think it therefore manifest, from what I have here advanced, that the main Point of Skill and Address, is to furnish Employment for this Redundancy of *Vapour*, and prudently to adjust the Seasons of it; by which means it may certainly become of Cardinal and Catholick Emolument in a Commonwealth. Thus one Man chusing a proper Juncture, leaps into a Gulph, from thence proceeds a Hero, and is called the Saver of his Country; Another atchieves the same Enterprise, but unluckily timing it, has left the Brand of *Madness*, fixt as a Reproach upon his Memory; Upon so nice a Distinction are we taught to repeat the Name of *Curtius* with Reverence and Love; that of *Empedocles*, with Hatred and Contempt. Thus, also it is usually conceived, that the Elder *Brutus* only personated the *Fool* and *Madman*, for the Good of the Publick: but this was nothing else, than a Redundancy of the same *Vapor*, long misapplied, called by the *Latins*, * *Ingenium par negotiis*: Or, (to translate it as nearly as I can) a sort of *Phrenzy*, never in its right Element, till you take it up in Business of the State.

* *Tacit.*

UPON all which, and many other Reasons of equal Weight, though not equally curious; I do here gladly embrace an Opportunity I have long sought for, of Recommending it as a very noble Undertaking, to Sir *Edward Seymour*, Sir *Christopher Musgrave*, Sir *John Bowls*, *John How*, Esq; and other Patriots concerned, that they would move for Leave to bring in a Bill, for appointing Commissioners to Inspect into *Bedlam*, and the Parts adjacent; who shall be empowered to *send for Persons, Papers, and Records*: to examine into the Merits and Qualifications of every Student and Professor; to observe with utmost Exactness their several Dispositions and Behaviour; by which means, duly distinguishing and adapting their Talents, they might produce admirable Instruments for the several Offices in a State, * * * * * * † *Civil* and *Military*; proceeding in such Methods as I shall here humbly propose. And, I hope the Gentle Reader will give some Allowance to my great Solicitudes in this important Affair, upon Account of that high Esteem I have ever born that honourable Society, whereof I had some Time the Happiness to be an unworthy Member.

Is any Student tearing his Straw in piece-meal, Swearing and Blaspheming, biting his Grate, foaming at the Mouth, and emptying his Pispot in the Spectator's Faces? Let the Right Worshipful, the *Commissioners of Inspection*, give him a Regiment of Dragoons, and send him into *Flanders* among the *Rest*. Is

† *Ecclesiastical.* H

another eternally talking, sputtering, gaping, bawling, in a Sound without Period or Article? What wonderful Talents are here mislaid! Let him be furnished immediately with a green Bag and Papers, and * *three Pence* in his Pocket, and away with Him to *Westminster-Hall.* You will find a Third, gravely taking the Dimensions of his Kennel; A Person of Foresight and Insight, tho' kept quite in the Dark; for why, like *Moses, Ecce* * *cornuta erat ejus facies.* He walks duly in one Pace, intreats your Penny with due Gravity and Ceremony; talks much of hard Times, and Taxes, and the *Whore of Babylon*; Bars up the woodden Window of his Cell constantly at eight a Clock: Dreams of *Fire*, and *Shop-lifters*, and *Court-Customers*, and *Priviledg'd Places.* Now, what a Figure would all these Acquirements amount to, if the Owner were sent into the *City* among his Brethren! Behold a Fourth, in much and deep Conversation with himself, biting his Thumbs at proper Junctures; His Countenance chequered with Business and Design; sometimes walking very fast, with his Eyes nailed to a Paper that he holds in his Hands: A great Saver of Time, somewhat thick of Hearing, very short of Sight, but more of Memory. A Man ever in Haste, a great Hatcher and Breeder of Business, and excellent at the Famous Art of *whispering Nothing.* A huge Idolater of Monosyllables and Procrastination; so ready to *Give* his Word to every Body, that he never *keeps* it. One that has forgot the common *Meaning* of Words, but an admirable Retainer of the *Sound.* Extreamly subject to the *Loosness*, for his *Occasions* are perpetually *calling him away.* If you approach his Grate in his familiar Intervals; *Sir*, says he, *Give me a Penny, and I'll sing you a Song: But give me the Penny first.* (Hence comes the common Saying, and commoner Practice of parting with Money for a *Song.*) What a compleat System of *Court-Skill* is here described in every Branch of it, and all utterly lost with wrong Application? Accost the Hole of another Kennel, first stopping your Nose, you will behold a surley, gloomy, nasty, slovenly Mortal, raking in his own Dung, and dabling in his Urine. The best Part of his Diet, is the

* *A Lawyer's Coach-hire.*

* Cornutus, *is either Horned or Shining, and by this Term,* Moses *is described in the vulgar* Latin *of the Bible.*

Reversion of his own Ordure, which exspiring into Steams, whirls perpetually about, and at last reinfunds. His Complexion is of a dirty Yellow, with a thin scattered Beard, exactly agreeable to that of his Dyet upon its first Declination; like other Insects, who having their Birth and Education in an Excrement, from thence borrow their Colour and their Smell. The Student of this Apartment is very sparing of his Words, but somewhat over-liberal of his Breath; He holds his Hand out ready to receive your Penny, and immediately upon Receipt, withdraws to his former Occupations. Now, is it not amazing to think, the Society of *Warwick-Lane*, should have no more Concern, for the Recovery of so useful a Member, who, if one may judge from these Appearances, would become the greatest Ornament to that Illustrious Body? Another Student struts up fiercely to your Teeth, puffing with his Lips, half squeezing out his Eyes, and very graciously holds you out his Hand to kiss. The *Keeper* desires you not to be afraid of this Professor, for he will do you no Hurt: To him alone is allowed the Liberty of the Anti-Chamber, and the *Orator* of the Place gives you to understand, that this solemn Person is a *Taylor* run mad with Pride. This considerable Student is adorned with many other Qualities, upon which, at present, I shall not farther enlarge. - - - - - - - * *Heark in your Ear* - - - - - - - - I am strangely mistaken, if all his Address, his Motions, and his Airs, would not then be very natural, and in their proper Element.

I shall not descend so minutely, as to insist upon the vast Number of *Beaux*, *Fidlers*, *Poets*, and *Politicians*, that the World might recover by such a Reformation; But what is more material, besides the clear Gain redounding to the Commonwealth, by so large an Acquisition of Persons to employ, whose Talents and Acquirements, if I may be so bold to affirm it, are now buried, or at least misapplied: It would be a mighty Advantage accruing to the Publick from this Enquiry, that all these would very much excel, and arrive at great Perfection in their several Kinds; which, I think, is manifest from what I have already

* *I cannot conjecture what the Author means here, or how this Chasm could be fill'd, tho' it is capable of more than one Interpretation.*

shewn; and shall inforce by this one plain Instance; That even, I my self, the Author of these momentous Truths, am a Person, whose Imaginations are hard-mouth'd, and exceedingly disposed to run away with his *Reason*, which I have observed from long Experience, to be a very light Rider, and easily shook off; upon which Account, my Friends will never trust me alone, without a solemn Promise, to vent my Speculations in this, or the like manner, for the universal Benefit of Human kind; which, perhaps, the gentle, courteous, and candid Reader, brimful of that *Modern* Charity and Tenderness, usually annexed to his *Office*, will be very hardly persuaded to believe.

SECT. X.

A TALE of a TUB.

IT is an unanswerable Argument of a very refined Age, the wonderful Civilities that have passed of late Years, between the Nation of *Authors*, and that of *Readers*. There can hardly pop out * a *Play*, a *Pamphlet*, or a *Poem*, without a Preface full of Acknowledgements to the World, for the general Reception and Applause they have given it, which the Lord knows where, or when, or how, or from whom it received. In due Deference to so laudable a Custom, I do here return my humble Thanks to *His Majesty*, and both Houses of *Parliament*; To the *Lords* of the King's most honourable Privy-Council, to the Reverend the *Judges*: To the *Clergy*, and *Gentry*, and *Yeomantry* of this Land: But in a more especial manner, to my worthy Brethren and Friends at *Will's Coffee-House*, and *Gresham-College*, and *Warwick-Lane*, and *Moor-Fields*, and *Scotland-Yard*, and *Westminster-Hall*, and *Guild-Hall*; In short, to all Inhabitants and Retainers whatsoever, either in Court, or Church, or Camp, or City, or Country; for their generous and universal Acceptance of this Divine Treatise. I accept their Approbation, and good Opinion with extream Gratitude, and to the utmost of my poor Capacity, shall take hold of all Opportunities to return the Obligation.

I am also happy, that Fate has flung me into so blessed an Age for the mutual Felicity of *Booksellers* and *Authors*, whom I may safely affirm to be at this Day the two only satisfied Parties in *England*. Ask an *Author* how his last Piece hath succeeded; *Why, truly he thanks his Stars, the World has been very favourable, and he has not the least* Reason *to complain: And yet, By G—, He writ it in a Week at Bits and Starts, when he could steal an Hour from his urgent Affairs*; as it is a hundred to one, you may see farther in the Preface, to which he refers you; and for the rest, to the Bookseller. There you go as a Customer, and make the same Question: *He blesses his God, the* Thing *takes wonderfully, he is just*

* *This is literally true, as we may observe in the Prefaces to most Plays, Poems,* &c.

Printing a Second Edition, and has but three left in his Shop. You beat down the Price: *Sir, we shall not differ*; and in hopes of your Custom another Time, lets you have it as reasonable as you please; *And, pray send as many of your Acquaintance as you will, I shall upon your Account furnish them all at the same Rate.*

Now, it is not well enough consider'd, to what Accidents and Occasions the World is indebted for the greatest Part of those noble Writings, which hourly start up to entertain it. If it were not for a *rainy Day, a drunken Vigil, a Fit of the Spleen, a Course of Physick, a sleepy Sunday, an ill Run at Dice, a long Taylor's Bill, a Beggar's Purse, a factious Head, a hot Sun, costive Dyet, Want of Books, and a just Contempt of Learning.* But for these Events, I say, and some Others too long to recite, (especially *a prudent Neglect of taking Brimstone inwardly,*) I doubt, the Number of *Authors*, and of *Writings* would dwindle away to a Degree most woful to behold. To confirm this Opinion, hear the Words of the famous *Troglodyte* Philosopher: *'Tis certain* (said he) *some Grains of Folly are of course annexed, as Part of the Composition of Human Nature, only the Choice is left us, whether we please to wear them* Inlaid *or* Embossed; *And we need not go very far to seek how that is usually determined, when we remember, it is with Human Faculties as with Liquors, the lightest will be ever at the Top.*

THERE is in this famous Island of *Britain* a certain paultry *Scribbler*, very voluminous, whose Character the Reader cannot wholly be a Stranger to. He deals in a pernicious Kind of Writings, called *Second Parts*, and usually passes under the Name of *The Author of the First*. I easily foresee, that as soon as I lay down my Pen, this nimble *Operator* will have stole it, and treat me as inhumanly as he hath already done Dr. *Blackmore*, *L'Estrange*, and many others who shall here be nameless, I therefore fly for Justice and Relief, into the Hands of that great *Rectifier of Saddles*, and *Lover of Mankind*, Dr. *Bently*, begging he will take this enormous Grievance into his most *Modern* Consideration: And if it should so happen, that the *Furniture of an Ass*, in the Shape of a *Second Part*, must for my Sins be clapt, by a Mistake upon my Back, that he will immediately please, in the Presence of the World, to lighten me of the Burthen, and take it home to *his own House*, till the *true Beast* thinks fit to call for it.

In the mean time I do here give this publick Notice, that my Resolutions are, to circumscribe within this Discourse the whole Stock of Matter I have been so many Years providing. Since my *Vein* is once opened, I am content to exhaust it all at a Running, for the peculiar Advantage of my dear Country, and for the universal Benefit of Mankind. Therefore hospitably considering the Number of my Guests, they shall have my whole Entertainment at a Meal; And I scorn to set up the *Leavings* in the Cupboard. What the *Guests* cannot eat may be given to the *Poor*, and the * *Dogs* under the Table may gnaw the *Bones*; This I understand for a more generous Proceeding, than to turn the Company's Stomachs, by inviting them again to morrow to a scurvy Meal of *Scraps*.

If the Reader fairly considers the Strength of what I have advanced in the foregoing Section, I am convinced it will produce a wonderful Revolution in his Notions and Opinions; And he will be abundantly better prepared to receive and to relish the concluding Part of this miraculous Treatise. Readers may be divided into three Classes, the *Superficial*, the *Ignorant*, and the *Learned*: And I have with much Felicity fitted my Pen to the Genius and Advantage of each. The *Superficial* Reader will be strangely provoked to *Laughter*; which clears the Breast and the Lungs, is Soverain against the *Spleen*, and the most innocent of all *Diureticks*. The *Ignorant* Reader (between whom and the former, the Distinction is extreamly nice) will find himself disposed to *Stare*; which is an admirable Remedy for ill Eyes, serves to raise and enliven the Spirits, and wonderfully helps *Perspiration*. But the Reader truly *Learned*, chiefly for whose Benefit I wake, when others sleep, and sleep when others wake, will here find sufficient Matter to employ his Speculations for the rest of his Life. It were much to be wisht, and I do here humbly propose for an Experiment, that every Prince in *Christendom* will take seven of the *deepest Scholars* in his Dominions, and shut them up close for *seven* Years, in *seven* Chambers, with a Command to write *seven* ample Commentaries on this comprehensive Discourse. I

* *By Dogs, the Author means common injudicious Criticks, as he explains it himself before in his* Digression upon Criticks, *Page* [64].

shall venture to affirm, that whatever Difference may be found in their several Conjectures, they will be all, without the least Distortion, manifestly deduceable from the Text. Mean time, it is my earnest Request, that so useful an Undertaking may be entered upon (if their Majesties please) with all convenient speed; because I have a strong Inclination, before I leave the World, to taste a Blessing, which we *mysterious* Writers can seldom reach, till we have got into our Graves. Whether it is, that *Fame* being a Fruit grafted on the Body, can hardly grow, and much less ripen, till the *Stock* is in the Earth: Or, whether she be a Bird of Prey, and is lured among the rest, to pursue after the Scent of a *Carcass*: Or, whether she conceives, her Trumpet sounds best and farthest, when she stands on a *Tomb*, by the Advantage of a rising Ground, and the Echo of a hollow Vault.

'Tis true, indeed, the Republick of *dark* Authors, after they once found out this excellent Expedient of *Dying*, have been peculiarly happy in the Variety, as well as Extent of their Reputation. For, *Night* being the universal Mother of Things, wise Philosophers hold all Writings to be *fruitful* in the Proportion they are *dark*; And therefore, the * *true illuminated* (that is to say, the *Darkest* of all) have met with such numberless Commentators, whose *Scholiastick* Midwifry hath deliver'd them of Meanings, that the Authors themselves, perhaps, never conceived, and yet may very justly be allowed the Lawful Parents of them: * The Words of such Writers being like Seed, which, however scattered at random, when they light upon a fruitful Ground, will multiply far beyond either the Hopes or Imagination of the Sower.

* *A Name of the* Rosycrucians.

And therefore in order to promote so useful a Work, I will here take Leave to glance a few *Innuendo*'s, that may be of great Assistance to those sublime Spirits, who shall be appointed to labor in a universal Comment upon this wonderful Discourse. And First, † I have couched a very profound Mystery in the

* *Nothing is more frequent than for Commentators to force Interpretation, which the Author never meant.*

† *This is what the* Cabbalists *among the* Jews *have done with the* Bible, *and pretend to find wonderful Mysteries by it.*

Number of O's multiply'd by *Seven*, and divided by *Nine*. Also, if a devout Brother of the *Rosy Cross* will pray fervently for sixty three Mornings, with a lively Faith, and then transpose certain Letters and Syllables according to Prescription, in the second and fifth Section; they will certainly reveal into a full Receit of the *Opus Magnum*. Lastly, Whoever will be at the Pains to calculate the whole Number of each Letter in this Treatise, and sum up the Difference exactly between the several Numbers, assigning the true natural Cause for every such Difference; the Discoveries in the Product, will plentifully reward his Labour. But then he must beware of † *Bythus* and *Sigè*, and be sure not to forget the Qualities of *Acamoth; A cujus lacrymis humecta prodit Substantia, à risu lucida, à tristitiâ solida, & à timore mobilis*, wherein * *Eugenius Philalethes* hath committed an unpardonable Mistake.

* *Vid. Anima magica abscondita*

† *I was told by an Eminent Divine, whom I consulted on this Point, that these two Barbarous Words, with that of* Acamoth *and its Qualities, as here set down, are quoted from* Irenæus. *This he discover'd by searching that Antient Writer for another Quotation of our Author, which he has placed in the Title Page, and refers to the Book and Chapter; the Curious were very Inquisitive, whether those Barbarous Words,* Basima Eacabasa, &c. *are really in* Irenæus, *and upon enquiry 'twas found they were a sort of Cant or Jargon of certain Hereticks, and therefore very properly prefix'd to such a Book as this of our Author.*

* *To the abovementioned Treatise, called* Anthroposophia Theomagica, *there is another annexed, called* Anima Magica Abscondita, *written by the same Author* Vaughan, *under the Name of* Eugenius Philalethes, *but in neither of those Treatises is there any mention of* Acamoth *or its Qualities, so that this is nothing but Amusement, and a Ridicule of dark, unintelligible Writers; only the Words,* A cujus lacrymis, &c. *are as we have said, transcribed from* Irenæus, *tho' I know not from what part. I believe one of the Authors Designs was to set curious Men a hunting thro' Indexes, and enquiring for Books out of the common Road.*

SECT. XI.

A TALE of a TUB.

AFTER so wide a Compass as I have wandred, I do now gladly overtake, and close in with my Subject, and shall henceforth hold on with it an even Pace to the End of my Journey, except some beautiful Prospect appears within sight of my Way; whereof, tho' at present I have neither Warning nor Expectation, yet upon such an Accident, come when it will, I shall beg my Readers Favour and Company, allowing me to conduct him thro' it along with my self. For in *Writing*, it is as in *Travelling*: If a Man is in haste to be at home, (which I acknowledge to be none of my Case, having never so little Business, as when I am there) if his *Horse* be tired with long Riding, and ill Ways, or be naturally a Jade, I advise him clearly to make the straitest and the commonest Road, be it ever so dirty; But, then surely, we must own such a man to be a scurvy Companion at best; He *spatters* himself and his Fellow-Travellers at every Step: All their Thoughts, and Wishes, and Conversation turn entirely upon the Subject of their Journey's End; and at every Splash, and Plunge, and Stumble, they heartily wish one another at the Devil.

ON the other side, when a Traveller and his *Horse* are in Heart and Plight, when his Purse is full, and the Day before him; he takes the Road only where it is clean or convenient; entertains his Company there as agreeably as he can; but upon the first Occasion, carries them along with him to every delightful Scene in View, whether of Art, of Nature, or of both; and if they chance to refuse out of Stupidity or Weariness; let them jog on by themselves, and be d—n'd; He'll overtake them at the next Town; at which arriving, he Rides furiously thro', the Men, Women, and Children run out to gaze, a hundred * *noisy Curs* run *barking* after him, of which, if he honors the boldest with a *Lash of his Whip*, it is rather out of Sport than Revenge: But should some *sourer*

* *By these are meant what the Author calls, The* True Criticks, *Page* [64].

Mungrel dare too near an Approach, he receives a *Salute* on the Chaps by an accidental Stroak from the Courser's Heels, (nor is any Ground lost by the Blow) which sends him yelping and limping home.

I now proceed to sum up the singular Adventures of my renowned *Jack*; the State of whose Dispositions and Fortunes, the careful Reader does, no doubt, most exactly remember, as I last parted with them in the Conclusion of a former Section. Therefore, his next Care must be from two of the foregoing, to extract a Scheme of Notions, that may best fit his Understanding for a true Relish of what is to ensue.

JACK had not only calculated the first Revolutions of his Brain so prudently, as to give Rise to that Epidemick Sect of *Æolists*, but succeeding also into a new and strange Variety of Conceptions, the Fruitfulness of his Imagination led him into certain Notions, which, altho' in Appearance very unaccountable, were not without their Mysteries and their Meanings, nor wanted Followers to countenance and improve them. I shall therefore be extreamly careful and exact in recounting such material Passages of this Nature, as I have been able to collect, either from undoubted Tradition, or indefatigable Reading; and shall describe them as graphically as it is possible, and as far as Notions of that Height and Latitude can be brought within the Compass of a Pen. Nor do I at all question, but they will furnish Plenty of noble Matter for such, whose converting Imaginations dispose them to reduce all Things into *Types*; who can make *Shadows*, no thanks to the Sun; and then mold them into Substances, no thanks to Philosophy; whose peculiar Talent lies in fixing Tropes and Allegories to the *Letter*, and refining what is Literal into Figure and Mystery.

JACK had provided a fair Copy of his Father's *Will*, engrossed in Form upon a large Skin of Parchment; and resolving to act the Part of a most dutiful Son, he became the fondest Creature of it imaginable. For, altho', as I have often told the Reader, it consisted wholly in certain plain, easy Directions about the management and wearing of their Coats, with Legacies and Penalties, in case of Obedience or Neglect; yet he began to entertain a Fancy, that the Matter was *deeper* and *darker*, and therefore must needs have a great deal more of Mystery at the Bottom. *Gentlemen*, said he, *I will prove this very Skin of Parchment to be Meat, Drink, and Cloth, to be the Philosopher's Stone, and the Universal Medicine.* * In consequence of which Raptures, he resolved to make use of it in the most necessary, as well as the most paltry Occasions of Life. He had a Way of working it into any Shape he pleased; so that it served him for a Night-cap when he went to Bed, and for an Umbrello in rainy Weather. He would lap a Piece of it about a sore Toe, or when he had Fits, burn two Inches under his Nose; or if any Thing lay heavy on his Stomach, scrape off, and swallow as much of the Powder as would lie on a silver Penny, they were all infallible Remedies. With Analogy to these Refinements, his common Talk and Conversation, † ran wholly in the Phrase of his Will, and he circumscribed the utmost of his Eloquence within that Compass, not daring to let slip a Syllable without Authority from thence. Once at a strange House, he was suddenly taken short, upon an urgent Juncture, whereon it may not be allowed too particularly to dilate; and being not able to call to mind, with that Suddenness, the Occasion required, an Authentick Phrase for demanding the Way to the Backside; he chose rather as the more prudent Course, to incur the Penalty in such Cases usually annexed. Neither was it possible for the united Rhetorick of Mankind to prevail with him to make himself clean again: Because having consulted the Will upon this Emergency, he met with a || Passage near the Bottom (whether foisted in by the Transcriber, is not known) which seemed to forbid it.

He made it a Part of his Religion, never to say * Grace to his

* *The Author here lashes those Pretenders to Purity, who place so much Merit in using Scripture Phrases on all Occasions.*

† *The* Protestant Dissenters *use* Scripture Phrases *in their serious Discourses, and Composures more than the* Church of England-Men, *accordingly* Jack *is introduced making his common Talk and Conversation to run wholly in the Phrase of his WILL.* W. Wotton.

|| *I cannot guess the Author's meaning here, which I would be very glad to know, because it seems to be of Importance.*

* *The slovenly way of Receiving the Sacrament among the Fanaticks.*

Meat, nor could all the World persuade him, as the common Phrase is, to * eat his Victuals *like a Christian.*

HE bore a strange kind of Appetite to † *Snap-Dragon*, and to the livid Snuffs of a burning Candle, which he would catch and swallow with an Agility, wonderful to conceive; and by this Procedure, maintained a perpetual Flame in his Belly, which issuing in a glowing Steam from both his Eyes, as well as his Nostrils, and his Mouth; made his Head appear in a dark Night, like the Scull of an Ass, wherein a roguish Boy hath conveyed a Farthing Candle, *to the Terror of His Majesty's Liege Subjects.* Therefore, he made use of no other Expedient to light himself home, but was wont to say, That *a Wise Man was his own Lanthorn.*

HE would shut his Eyes as he walked along the Streets, and if he happened to bounce his Head against a Post, or fall into the Kennel (as he seldom missed either to do one or both) he would tell the gibing Prentices, who looked on, that *he submitted with entire Resignation, as to a Trip, or a Blow of Fate, with whom he found, by long Experience, how vain it was either to wrestle or to cuff; and whoever durst undertake to do either, would be sure to come off with a swinging Fall, or a bloody Nose. It was ordained*, said he, *some few Days before the Creation, that my Nose and this very Post should have a Rencounter; and therefore, Nature thought fit to send us both into the World in the same Age, and to make us Country-men and Fellow-Citizens. Now, had my Eyes been open, it is very likely, the Business might have been a great deal worse; For, how many a confounded Slip is daily got by Man, with all his Foresight about him? Besides, the Eyes of the Understanding see best, when those of the Senses are out of the way; and therefore, blind Men are observed to tread their Steps with much more Caution, and Conduct, and Judgment, than those who rely with too much Confidence, upon the Virtue of the visual Nerve, which every little Accident shakes out of Order, and a Drop, or a Film, can*

* *This is a common Phrase to express Eating cleanlily, and is meant for an Invective against that undecent Manner among some People in Receiving the Sacrament, so in the Lines before, which is to be understood of the Dissenters refusing to kneel at the Sacrament.*

† *I cannot well find the Author's meaning here, unless it be the hot, untimely, blind Zeal of Enthusiasts.*

wholly disconcert; like a Lanthorn among a Pack of roaring Bullies, when they scower the Streets; exposing its Owner, and it self, to outward Kicks and Buffets, which both might have escaped, if the Vanity of Appearing would have suffered them to walk in the Dark. But, farther; if we examine the Conduct *of these boasted Lights, it will prove yet a great deal worse than their* Fortune: *'Tis true, I have broke my* Nose *against this Post, because Fortune either forgot, or did not think it convenient to twitch me by the Elbow, and give me notice to avoid it. But, let not this encourage either the present Age or Posterity, to trust their* Noses *into the keeping of their* Eyes, *which may prove the fairest Way of losing them for good and all. For, O ye Eyes, Ye blind Guides; miserable Guardians are Ye of our frail Noses; Ye, I say, who fasten upon the first Precipice in view, and then tow our wretched willing Bodies after You, to the very Brink of Destruction: But, alas, that Brink is rotten, our Feet slip, and we tumble down prone into a Gulph, without one hospitable Shrub in the Way to break the Fall; a Fall, to which not any Nose of mortal Make is equal, except that of the Giant* * Laurcalco, *who was Lord of the* Silver Bridge. *Most properly, therefore, O Eyes, and with great Justice, may You be compared to those foolish Lights, which conduct Men thro' Dirt and Darkness, till they fall into a deep Pit, or a noisom Bog.*

* *Vide* Don Quixot.

THIS I have produced, as a Scantling of *Jack*'s great Eloquence, and the Force of his Reasoning upon such abstruse Matters.

HE was besides, a Person of great Design and Improvement in Affairs of *Devotion*, having introduced a new Deity, who hath since met with a vast Number of Worshippers; by some called *Babel*, by others, *Chaos*; who had an antient Temple of *Gothick* Structure upon *Salisbury* Plain; famous for its Shrine, and Celebration by Pilgrims.

* WHEN he had some Roguish Trick to play, he would down with his Knees, up with his Eyes, and fall to Prayers, tho' in the midst of the Kennel. Then it was that those who understood his Pranks, would be sure to get far enough out of his Way; And

* *The Villanies and Cruelties committed by Enthusiasts and Phanaticks among us, were all performed under the Disguise of Religion and long Prayers.*

whenever Curiosity attracted Strangers to Laugh, or to Listen; he would of a sudden, with one Hand out with his *Gear*, and piss full in their Eyes, and with the other, all to-bespatter them with Mud.

* In Winter he went always loose and unbuttoned, and clad as thin as possible, to let *in* the ambient Heat; and in Summer, lapt himself close and thick to keep it *out*.

† In all Revolutions of Government, he would make his Court for the Office of *Hangman* General; and in the Exercise of that Dignity, wherein he was very dextrous, would make use of || no other *Vizard* than a long *Prayer*.

He had a Tongue so Musculous and Subtil, that he could twist it up into his Nose, and deliver a strange Kind of Speech from thence. He was also the first in these Kingdoms, who began to improve the *Spanish* Accomplishment of *Braying*; and having large Ears, perpetually exposed and arrect, he carried his Art to such a Perfection, that it was a Point of great Difficulty to distinguish either by the View or the Sound, between the *Original* and the *Copy*.

He was troubled with a Disease, reverse to that called the Stinging of the *Tarantula*; and would * run Dog-mad, at the Noise of *Musick*, especially a *Pair of Bag-Pipes*. But he would cure himself again, by taking two or three Turns in *Westminster-Hall*, or *Billingsgate*, or in a *Boarding-School*, or the *Royal-Exchange*, or a *State Coffee-House*.

He was a Person that † *feared* no *Colours*, but mortally *hated* all, and upon that Account, bore a cruel Aversion to *Painters*, insomuch, that in his Paroxysms, as he walked the Streets, he would have his Pockets loaden with Stones, to pelt at the *Signs*.

---

* *They affect Differences in Habit and Behaviour.*

† *They are severe Persecutors, and all in a Form of Cant and Devotion.*

|| Cromwell *and his Confederates went, as they called it*, to seek God, *when they resolved to murther the King.*

* *This is to expose our Dissenters Aversion to Instrumental Musick in Churches.* W. Wotton.

† *They quarrel at the most Innocent Decency and Ornament, and defaced the Statues and Paintings on all the Churches in* England.

HAVING from this manner of Living, frequent Occasion to *wash* himself, he would often leap over Head and Ears into the Water, tho' it were in the midst of the Winter, but was always observed to come out again much *dirtier*, if possible, than he went in.

HE was the first that ever found out the Secret of contriving a * *Soporiferous* Medicine to be convey'd in at the *Ears*; It was a Compound of *Sulphur* and *Balm of Gilead*, with a little *Pilgrim*'s *Salve*.

HE wore a large Plaister of artificial *Causticks* on his Stomach, with the Fervor of which, he could set himself a *groaning*, like the famous *Board* upon Application of a red-hot Iron.

† HE would stand in the Turning of a Street, and calling to those who passed by, would cry to One; *Worthy Sir, do me the Honour of a good Slap in the Chaps*: To another, *Honest Friend, pray favour me with a handsom Kick on the Arse: Madam, shall I entreat a small Box on the Ear, from your Ladyship's fair Hands? Noble Captain, Lend a reasonable Thwack, for the Love of God, with that Cane of yours, over these poor Shoulders*. And when he had by such earnest Sollicitations, made a shift to procure a Basting sufficient to swell up his Fancy and his Sides, He would return home extremely comforted, and full of terrible Accounts of what he had undergone for the *Publick Good. Observe this Stroak*, (said he, shewing his bare Shoulders) *a plaguy* Janisary *gave it me this very Morning at seven a Clock, as, with much ado, I was driving off the* Great Turk. *Neighbours mine, this broken Head deserves a Plaister; had poor* Jack *been tender of his Noddle, you would have seen the* Pope, *and the* French *King, long before this time of Day, among your Wives and your Ware-houses. Dear* Christians, *the* Great Mogul *was come as far as* White-Chappel, *and you may thank these poor Sides that he hath not (God bless us) already swallowed up Man, Woman, and Child.*

---

* *Fanatick Preaching, composed either of Hell and Damnation, or a fulsome Description of the Joys of Heaven, both in such a dirty, nauseous Style, as to be well resembled to Pilgrims Salve.*

† *The Fanaticks have always had a way of affecting to run into Persecution, and count vast Merit upon every little Hardship they suffer.*

* IT was highly worth observing, the singular Effects of that Aversion, or Antipathy, which *Jack* and his Brother *Peter* seemed, even to an Affectation, to bear toward each other. *Peter* had lately done *some Rogueries*, that forced him to abscond; and he seldom ventured to stir out before Night, for fear of Bayliffs. Their Lodgings were at the two most distant Parts of the Town from each other; and whenever their Occasions, or Humors called them abroad, they would make Choice of the oddest unlikely Times, and most uncouth Rounds they could invent; that they might be sure to avoid one another: Yet after all this, it was their perpetual Fortune to meet. The Reason of which, is easy enough to apprehend: For, the Phrenzy and the Spleen of both, having the same Foundation, we may look upon them as two Pair of Compasses, equally extended, and the fixed Foot of each, remaining in the same Center; which, tho' moving contrary Ways at first, will be sure to encounter somewhere or other in the Circumference. Besides, it was among the great Misfortunes of *Jack*, to bear a huge Personal Resemblance with his Brother *Peter*. Their Humours and Dispositions were not only the same, but there was a close Analogy in their Shape, their Size and their Mien. Insomuch, as nothing was more frequent than for a Bayliff to seize *Jack* by the Shoulders, and cry, *Mr.* Peter, *You are the King's Prisoner.* Or, at other Times, for one of *Peter*'s nearest Friends, to accost *Jack* with open Arms, *Dear* Peter, *I am glad to see thee, pray send me one of your best Medicines for the Worms.* This we may suppose, was a mortifying Return of those Pains and Proceedings, *Jack* had laboured in so long; And finding, how directly opposite all his Endeavours had answered to the sole End and Intention, which he had proposed to himself; How could it avoid having terrible Effects upon a Head and Heart so

* *The Papists and Fanaticks, tho' they appear the most Averse to each other, yet bear a near Resemblance in many things, as has been observed by Learned Men.*

Ibid. *The Agreement of our Dissenters and the Papists in that which Bishop* Stillingfleet *called,* The Fanaticism of the Church of Rome, *is ludicrously described for several Pages together by* Jack's *Likeness to* Peter, *and their being often mistaken for each other, and their frequent Meeting, when they least intended it.* W. Wotton.

furnished as his? However, the poor Remainders of his *Coat* bore all the Punishment; The orient Sun never entred upon his diurnal Progress, without missing a Piece of it. He hired a Taylor to stitch up the Collar so close, that it was ready to choak him, and squeezed out his Eyes at such a Rate, as one could see nothing but the White. What little was left of the main Substance of the Coat, he rubbed every day for two hours, against a rough-cast Wall, in order to grind away the Remnants of *Lace* and *Embroidery*; but at the same time went on with so much Violence, that he proceeded a *Heathen Philosopher*. Yet after all he could do of this kind, the Success continued still to disappoint his Expectation. For, as it is the Nature of Rags, to bear a kind of mock Resemblance to Finery; there being a sort of fluttering Appearance in both, which is not to be distinguished at a Distance, in the Dark, or by short-sighted Eyes: So, in those Junctures, it fared with *Jack* and his Tatters, that they offered to the first View a ridiculous Flanting, which assisting the Resemblance in Person and Air, thwarted all his Projects of Separation, and left so near a Similitude between them, as frequently deceived the very Disciples and Followers of both. * * * *

* * * * * * * * * *

* * * * * * * *

Desunt nonnulla. * * * * * * * *

* * * * * * * *

* * * * * * * * * *

THE old *Sclavonian* Proverb said well, That *it is with* Men, *as with* Asses; *whoever would keep them fast, may find a very good Hold at their Ears.* Yet, I think, we may affirm, and it hath been verified by repeated Experience, that,

Effugiet tamen hæc sceleratus vincula Proteus.

IT is good therefore, to read the Maxims of our Ancestors, with great Allowances to Times and Persons: For, if we look into Primitive Records, we shall find, that no Revolutions have been so great, or so frequent, as those of human *Ears*. In former Days, there was a curious Invention to catch and keep them; which, I think, we may justly reckon among the *Artes perditæ*: And how can it be otherwise, when in these latter Centuries, the very Species is not only diminished to a very lamentable Degree, but the poor Remainder is also degenerated so far, as to mock our skilfullest *Tenure*? For, if the only slitting of one *Ear* in a Stag, hath been found sufficient to propagate the Defect thro' a whole Forest; Why should we wonder at the greatest Consequences, from so many Loppings and Mutilations, to which the *Ears* of our Fathers and our own, have been of late so much exposed? 'Tis true, indeed, that while this *Island* of ours, was under the *Dominion of Grace*, many Endeavours were made to improve the Growth of *Ears* once more among us. The Proportion of Largeness, was not only lookt upon as an Ornament of the *Outward* Man, but as a Type of Grace in the *Inward*. Besides, it is held by Naturalists, that if there be a Protuberancy of Parts in the *Superiour* Region of the Body, as in the *Ears* and *Nose*, there must be a Parity also in the *Inferior*: And therefore in that truly pious Age, the *Males* in every Assembly, according as they were gifted, appeared very forward in exposing their *Ears* to view, and the Regions about them; because * *Hippocrates* tells us, that *when the Vein behind the Ear happens to be cut, a Man becomes a Eunuch*: And the *Females* were nothing backwarder in beholding and edifying by them: Whereof those who had already *used the Means*, lookt about them with great Concern, in hopes of conceiving a suitable Offspring by such a Prospect: Others, who stood Candidates for *Benevolence*, found there a plentiful Choice, and were sure to fix upon such as discovered the largest *Ears*, that the Breed might not dwindle between them. Lastly, the devouter Sisters, who lookt upon all extraordinary Dilatations of that Member, as Protrusions of Zeal, or spiritual Excrescencies, were sure to honor every Head they sat upon, as if they had been *Marks of Grace*; but, especially, that of the Preacher, whose *Ears* were usually of the prime Magnitude; which upon that Account, he was very frequent and exact in exposing with all Advantages to the People: in his Rhetorical *Paroxysms*, turning sometimes to *hold forth* the one, and sometimes to *hold forth* the other: From which Custom, the whole Operation of Preaching is to this very Day among their Professors, styled by the Phrase of *Holding forth*.

* *Lib. de aëre locis & aquis.*

SUCH was the Progress of the *Saints*, for advancing the Size of that Member; And it is thought, the Success would have been every way answerable, if in Process of time, a * cruel King had not arose, who raised a bloody Persecution against all *Ears*, above a certain Standard: Upon which, some were glad to hide their flourishing Sprouts in a black Border, others crept wholly under a Perewig: some were slit, others cropt, and a great Number sliced off to the Stumps. But of this, more hereafter, in my *general History of Ears*; which I design very speedily to bestow upon the Publick.

FROM this brief Survey of the falling State of *Ears*, in the last Age, and the small Care had to advance their antient Growth in the present, it is manifest, how little Reason we can have to rely upon a Hold so short, so weak, and so slippery; and that, whoever desires to catch Mankind fast, must have Recourse to some other Methods. Now, he that will examine Human Nature with Circumspection enough, may discover several *Handles*, whereof the † *Six* Senses afford one apiece, beside a great Number that are screw'd to the Passions, and some few riveted to the Intellect. Among these last, *Curiosity* is one, and of all others, affords the firmest Grasp: *Curiosity*, that Spur in the side, that Bridle in the Mouth, that Ring in the Nose, of a lazy, an impatient, and a grunting Reader. By this *Handle* it is, that an Author should seize upon his Readers; which as soon as he hath once compast, all Resistance and struggling are in vain; and they become his Prisoners as close as he pleases, till Weariness or Dullness force him to let go his Gripe.

† *Including* Scaliger's.

AND therefore, I the Author of this miraculous Treatise, having hitherto, beyond Expectation, maintained by the aforesaid *Handle*, a firm Hold upon my gentle Readers; It is with great Reluctance, that I am at length compelled to remit my Grasp; leaving them in the Perusal of what remains, to that natural *Oscitancy* inherent in the Tribe. I can only assure thee, Courteous Reader, for both our Comforts, that my Concern is altogether equal to thine, for my Unhappiness in losing, or mislaying

* *This was King* Charles *the Second, who at his Restauration, turned out all the Dissenting Teachers that would not conform.*

among my Papers the remaining Part of these Memoirs; which consisted of Accidents, Turns, and Adventures, both New, Agreeable, and Surprizing; and therefore, calculated in all due Points, to the delicate Taste of this our noble Age. But, alas, with my utmost Endeavours, I have been able only to retain a few of the Heads. Under which, there was a full Account, how *Peter* got a *Protection* out of the *King's-Bench*; And of a * Reconcilement between *Jack* and Him, upon a Design they had in a certain *rainy Night*, to trepan Brother *Martin* into a *Spunging-house*, and there strip him to the Skin. How *Martin*, with much ado, shew'd them both a fair pair of Heels. How a *new Warrant* came out against *Peter*: upon which, how *Jack* left him in the lurch, *stole his Protection, and made use of it himself*. How *Jack*'s Tatters came into Fashion in *Court* and *City*; How *he* † *got upon a great Horse, and eat* || *Custard*. But the Particulars of all these, with several others, which have now slid out of my Memory, are lost beyond all Hopes of Recovery. For which Misfortune, leaving my Readers to condole with each other, as far as they shall find it to agree with their several Constitutions; but conjuring them by all the Friendship that hath passed between Us, from the Title-Page to this, not to proceed so far as to injure their Healths, for an Accident past Remedy; I now go on to the Ceremonial Part of an accomplish'd Writer, and therefore, by a Courtly *Modern*, least of all others to be omitted.

* *In the Reign of King* James *the Second, the Presbyterians by the King's Invitation, joined with the Papists, against the Church of* England, *and Addrest him for Repeal of the Penal-Laws and Test. The King by his Dispensing Power, gave Liberty of Conscience, which both Papists and Presbyterians made use of, but upon the Revolution, the Papists being down of Course, the Presbyterians freely continued their Assemblies, by Virtue of King* James's *Indulgence, before they had a Toleration by Law; this I believe the Author means by* Jack's *stealing* Peter's *Protection, and making use of it himself.*

† *Sir* Humphry Edwyn, *a Presbyterian, was some Years ago Lord-Mayor of* London, *and had the Insolence to go in his Formalities to a Conventicle, with the Ensigns of his Office.*

|| *Custard is a famous Dish at a Lord-Mayors Feast.*

THE
CONCLUSION.

GOING *too long* is a Cause of Abortion as effectual, tho' not so frequent, as *Going too short*; and holds true especially in the *Labors* of the Brain. Well fare the Heart of that Noble * *Jesuit*, who first adventur'd to confess in Print, that Books must be suited to their several Seasons, like Dress, and Dyet, and Diversions: And better fare our noble Nation, for refining upon this, among other *French* Modes. I am living fast, to see the Time, when a *Book* that misses its Tide, shall be neglected, as the *Moon* by day, or like *Mackarel* a Week after the Season. No Man hath more nicely observed our Climate, than the Bookseller who bought the Copy of this Work; He knows to a Tittle what Subjects will best go off in a *dry Year*, and which it is proper to expose foremost, when the Weather-glass is fallen to *much Rain*. When he had seen this Treatise, and consulted his *Almanack* upon it; he gave me to understand, that he had maturely considered the two Principal Things, which were the *Bulk*, and the *Subject*; and found, it would never *take*, but after a long Vacation, and then only, in case it should happen to be a hard Year for Turnips. Upon which I desired to know, *considering my urgent Necessities*, what he thought might be acceptable this Month. He lookt *Westward*, and said, *I doubt we shall have a Fit of bad Weather; However, if you could prepare some pretty little* Banter (but not in Verse) *or a small Treatise upon the —— it would run like Wild-Fire. But*, if it hold up, *I have already hired an Author to write something against* Dr. Bentley, *which, I am sure, will turn to Account*.

* *Pere d' Orleans*.

AT length we agreed upon this Expedient; That when a Customer comes for one of these, and desires in Confidence to know the Author; he will tell him very privately, as a Friend, naming which ever of the Wits shall happen to be that Week in the Vogue; and if *Durfy*'s last Play should be in Course, I had as lieve he may be the Person as *Congreve*. This I mention, because I am wonderfully well acquainted with the present Relish of Courteous Readers; and have often observed, with singular Pleasure, that a *Fly* driven from a *Honey-pot*, will immediately, with very good Appetite alight, and finish his Meal on an *Excrement*.

I have one Word to say upon the Subject of *Profound Writers*, who are grown very numerous of late; And, I know very well, the judicious World is resolved to list me in that Number. I conceive therefore, as to the Business of being *Profound*, that it is with *Writers*, as with *Wells*; A Person with good Eyes may see to the Bottom of the deepest, provided any *Water* be there; and, that often, when there is nothing in the World at the Bottom, besides *Dryness* and *Dirt*, tho' it be but a Yard and half under Ground, it shall pass, however, for wondrous *Deep*, upon no wiser a Reason than because it is wondrous *Dark*.

I am now trying an Experiment very frequent among Modern Authors; which is, to *write upon Nothing*; When the Subject is utterly exhausted, to let the Pen still move on; by some called, the Ghost of Wit, delighting to walk after the Death of its Body. And to say the Truth, there seems to be no Part of Knowledge in fewer Hands, than That of Discerning *when to have Done*. By the Time that an Author has writ out a Book, he and his Readers are become old Acquaintance, and grow very loth to part: So that I have sometimes known it to be in Writing, as in Visiting, where the Ceremony of taking Leave, has employ'd more Time than the whole Conversation before. The Conclusion of a Treatise, resembles the Conclusion of Human Life, which hath sometimes been compared to the End of a Feast; where few are satisfied to depart, *ut plenus vitæ conviva*: For Men will sit down after the fullest Meal, tho' it be only to *doze*, or to *sleep* out the rest of the Day. But, in this latter, I differ extreamly from other Writers; and shall be too proud, if by all my Labors, I can have any ways contributed to the *Repose* of Mankind in * Times so turbulent

* *This was writ before the Peace of* Riswick.

and unquiet as these. Neither, do I think such an Employment so very alien from the Office of a *Wit*, as some would suppose. For among a very Polite Nation in **Greece*, there were the *same* Temples built and consecrated to *Sleep* and the *Muses*, between which two Deities, they believed the strictest Friendship was established.

* *Trezenii* *Pausan.* l. 2.

I have one concluding Favour, to request of my Reader; that he will not expect to be equally diverted and informed by every Line, or every Page of this Discourse; but give some Allowance to the Author's Spleen, and short Fits or Intervals of Dullness, as well as his own; And lay it seriously to his Conscience, whether, if he were walking the Streets, in dirty Weather, or a rainy Day; he would allow it fair Dealing in Folks at their Ease from a Window, to Critick his Gate, and ridicule his Dress at such a Juncture.

In my Disposure of Employments of the Brain, I have thought fit to make *Invention* the *Master*, and to give *Method* and *Reason*, the Office of its *Lacquays*. The Cause of this Distribution was, from observing it my peculiar Case, to be often under a Temptation of being *Witty*, upon Occasions, where I could be neither *Wise* nor *Sound*, nor any thing to the Matter in hand. And, I am too much a Servant of the *Modern* Way, to neglect any such Opportunities, whatever Pains or Improprieties I may be at, to introduce them. For, I have observed, that from a laborious Collection of Seven Hundred Thirty Eight *Flowers*, and *shining Hints* of the best *Modern* Authors, digested with great Reading, into my Book of *Common-places*; I have not been able after five Years to draw, hook, or force into common Conversation, any more than a Dozen. Of which Dozen, the one Moiety failed of Success, by being dropt among unsuitable Company; and the other cost me so many Strains, and Traps, and *Ambages* to introduce, that I at length resolved to give it over. Now, this Disappointment, (to discover a Secret) I must own, gave me the first Hint of setting up for an *Author*; and, I have since found among some particular Friends, that it is become a very general Complaint, and has produced the same Effects upon many others. For, I have remarked many a *towardly Word*, to be wholly neglected or despised in *Discourse*, which hath passed very smoothly, with some Consideration and Esteem, after its Preferment and Sanction in *Print*. But now, since by the Liberty and Encouragement of the Press, I am grown absolute Master of the Occasions and Opportunities, to expose the Talents I have acquired; I already discover, that the *Issues* of my *Observanda* begin to grow too large for the *Receipts*. Therefore, I shall here pause awhile, till I find, by feeling the World's Pulse, and my own, that it will be of absolute Necessity for us both, to resume my Pen.

FINIS.

A

Full and True Account

OF THE

BATTEL

Fought laſt *FRIDAY*,

Between the

Antient and the *Modern*

BOOKS

IN

St. *JAMES*'s

LIBRARY.

LONDON:

Printed in the Year, MDCCX.

THE

BOOKSELLER

TO THE

READER.

THE following Discourse, as it is unquestionably of the same Author, so it seems to have been written about the same time with the former, I mean, the Year 1697, when the famous Dispute was on Foot, about *Antient and Modern Learning*. The Controversy took its Rise from an Essay of Sir *William Temple*'s, upon that Subject; which was answer'd by *W. Wotton*, B.D. with an Appendix by Dr. *Bently*, endeavouring to destroy the Credit of *Æsop* and *Phalaris*, for Authors, whom Sir *William Temple* had in the Essay before-mentioned, highly commended. In that Appendix, the Doctor falls hard upon a new Edition of *Phalaris*, put out by the Honourable *Charles Boyle* (now *Earl* of *Orrery*) to which, Mr. *Boyle* replyed at large, with great Learning and Wit; and the Doctor, voluminously, rejoyned. In this Dispute, the Town highly resented to see a Person of Sir *William Temple*'s Character and Merits, roughly used by the two Reverend Gentlemen aforesaid, and without any manner of Provocation. At length, there appearing no End of the Quarrel, our Author tells us, that the BOOKS in St. *James*'s Library, looking upon themselves as Parties principally concerned, took up the Controversie, and came to a decisive Battel; But, the Manuscript, by the Injury of Fortune, or Weather, being in several Places imperfect, we cannot learn to which side the Victory fell.

I must warn the Reader, to beware of applying to Persons what is here meant, only of Books in the most literal Sense. So, when *Virgil* is mentioned, we are not to understand the Person of a famous Poet, call'd by that Name, but only certain Sheets of Paper, bound up in Leather, containing in Print, the Works of the said Poet, and so of the rest.

THE
PREFACE
OF THE
AUTHOR.

S*ATYR is a sort of* Glass, *wherein Beholders do generally discover every body's Face but their Own; which is the chief* Reason *for that kind of* Reception *it meets in the* W*orld, and that so very few are offended with it. But if it should happen otherwise, the Danger is not great; and, I have learned from long Experience, never to apprehend Mischief from those Understandings, I have been able to provoke;* For, *Anger and Fury, though they add Strength to the* Sinews *of the* Body, *yet are found to relax those of the* Mind, *and to render all its Efforts feeble and impotent.*

THERE *is a* Brain *that will endure but one* Scumming: *Let the Owner gather it with Discretion, and manage his little Stock with Husbandry; but of all things, let him beware of bringing it under the* Lash *of his* Betters; *because, That will make it all bubble up into Impertinence, and he will find no new Supply: Wit, without knowledge, being a Sort of* Cream, *which gathers in a Night to the Top, and by a skilful Hand, may be soon* whipt *into* Froth; *but once scumm'd away, what appears underneath will be fit for nothing, but to be thrown to the Hogs.*

A Full and True

ACCOUNT

OF THE

BATTEL

Fought last FRIDAY, &c.

WHOEVER examines with due Circumspection into the * *Annual Records* of *Time*, will find it remarked, that *War is the Child of Pride*, and *Pride the Daughter of Riches*; The former of which Assertions may be soon granted; but one cannot so easily subscribe to the latter: For *Pride* is nearly related to Beggary and *Want*, either by Father or Mother, and sometimes by both; And, to speak naturally, it very seldom happens among Men to fall out, when all have enough: Invasions usually travelling from *North* to *South*, that is to say, from Poverty upon Plenty. The most antient and natural Grounds of Quarrels, are *Lust* and *Avarice*; which, tho' we may allow to be Brethren or collateral Branches of *Pride*, are certainly the Issues of *Want*. For, to speak in the Phrase of Writers upon the Politicks, we may observe in the Republick of *Dogs*, (which in its Original seems to be an Institution of the *Many*) that the whole State is ever in the profoundest Peace, after a full Meal; and, that Civil Broils arise among them, when it happens For one great *Bone* to be seized on by some *leading Dog*, who either divides it among the *Few*, and then it falls to an *Oligarchy*, or keeps it to Himself, and then it runs up to a *Tyranny*. The same Reasoning also, holds Place among them, in those Dissensions we behold upon a Turgescency in any of their Females. For, the Right of Possession lying in common (it being impossible to establish a Property in so delicate a Case)

*Riches produceth Pride; Pride is War's Ground, &c. Vid. Ephem. de *Mary Clarke*; opt. Edit.

Jealousies and Suspicions do so abound, that the whole Commonwealth of that Street, is reduced to a manifest *State of War*, of every *Citizen* against every *Citizen*; till some One of more Courage, Conduct, or Fortune than the rest, seizes and enjoys the Prize; Upon which, naturally arises Plenty of Heart-burning, and Envy, and Snarling against the *Happy Dog*. Again, if we look upon any of these Republicks engaged in a Forein War, either of Invasion or Defence, we shall find, the same Reasoning will serve, as to the Grounds and Occasions of each; and, that *Poverty*, or *Want*, in some Degree or other, (whether Real, or in Opinion, which makes no Alteration in the Case) has a great Share, as well as *Pride*, on the Part of the Aggressor.

Now, whoever will please to take this Scheme, and either reduce or adapt it to an Intellectual State, or Commonwealth of Learning, will soon discover the first Ground of Disagreement between the two great Parties at this Time in Arms; and may form just Conclusions upon the Merits of either Cause. But the Issue or Events of this War are not so easie to conjecture at: For, the present Quarrel is so enflamed by the warm Heads of either Faction, and the Pretensions *somewhere or other* so exorbitant, as not to admit the least Overtures of Accommodation: This Quarrel first began (as I have heard it affirmed by an old Dweller in the Neighbourhood) about a small Spot of Ground, *lying* and *being* upon one of the two Tops of the Hill *Parnassus*; the highest and largest of which, had it seems, been time out of Mind, in quiet Possession of certain Tenants, call'd the *Antients*; And the other was held by the *Moderns*. But, these disliking their present Station, sent certain Ambassadors to the *Antients*, complaining of a great Nuisance, how the Height of that Part of *Parnassus*, quite spoiled the Prospect of theirs, especially towards the *East*; and therefore, to avoid a War, offered them the Choice of this Alternative; either that the *Antients* would please to remove themselves and their Effects down to the lower Summity, which the *Moderns* would graciously surrender to them, and advance in their Place; or else, that the said *Antients* will give leave to the *Moderns* to come with Shovels and Mattocks, and level the said Hill, as low as they shall think it convenient. To which, the *Antients* made Answer: How little they expected such a Message as this, from a Colony, whom they had admitted out of their own Free Grace, to so near a Neighbourhood. That, as to their own Seat, they were *Aborigines* of it, and therefore, to talk with them of a Removal or Surrender, was a Language they did not understand. That, if the Height of the Hill, on their side, shortned the Prospect of the *Moderns*, it was a Disadvantage they could not help, but desired them to consider, whether that Injury (if it be any) were not largely recompenced by the *Shade* and *Shelter* it afforded them. That, as to levelling or digging down, it was either Folly or Ignorance to propose it, if they did, or did not know, how that side of the Hill was an entire Rock, which would break their Tools and Hearts; without any Damage to itself. That they would therefore advise the *Moderns*, rather to raise their own side of the Hill, than dream of pulling down that of the *Antients*, to the former of which, they would not only give Licence, but also largely contribute. All this was rejected by the *Moderns*, with much Indignation, who still insisted upon one of the two Expedients; And so this Difference broke out into a long and obstinate War, maintain'd on the one Part, by Resolution, and by the Courage of certain Leaders and Allies; but, on the other, by the greatness of their Number, upon all Defeats, affording continual Recruits. In this Quarrel, whole Rivulets of *Ink* have been exhausted, and the Virulence of both Parties enormously augmented. Now, it must here be understood, that *Ink* is the great missive Weapon, in all Battels of the *Learned*, which, convey'd thro' a sort of Engine, call'd a *Quill*, infinite Numbers of these are darted at the Enemy, by the Valiant on each side, with equal Skill and Violence, as if it were an Engagement of *Porcupines*. This malignant Liquor was compounded by the Engineer, who invented it, of two Ingredients, which are *Gall* and *Copperas*, by its Bitterness and Venom, to *Suit* in some Degree, as well as to *Foment* the Genius of the Combatants. And as the *Grecians*, after an Engagement, when they could not *agree* about the Victory, were wont to set up Trophies on both sides, the beaten Party being content to be at the same Expence, to keep it self in Countenance (A laudable and antient Custom, happily reviv'd of late, in the Art of War) so the *Learned*, after a sharp and bloody Dispute, do on both sides hang out their Trophies too, which-ever comes by the worst. These Trophies have largely inscribed on them the Merits of the Cause; a full impartial Account of such a Battel, and how the Victory fell clearly to the Party that set them up. They are known to the World under several Names; As, *Disputes*, *Arguments*, *Rejoynders*, *Brief Considerations*, *Answers*, *Replies*, *Remarks*, *Reflexions*, *Objections*, *Confutations*. For a very few Days they are fixed up in all Publick Places, either by themselves or their * Representatives, for Passengers to gaze at: From whence the chiefest and largest are removed to certain Magazines, they call, *Libraries*, there to remain in a Quarter purposely assign'd them, and from thenceforth, begin to be called, *Books of Controversie*.

* *Their Title-Pages.*

In these Books, is wonderfully instilled and preserved, the Spirit of each Warrier, while he is alive; and after his Death, his Soul transmigrates there, to inform them. This, at least, is the more common Opinion; But, I believe, it is with Libraries, as with other Cœmeteries, where some Philosophers affirm, that a certain Spirit, which they call *Brutum hominis*, hovers over the Monument, till the Body is corrupted, and turns to *Dust*, or to *Worms*, but then vanishes or dissolves: So, we may say, a restless Spirit haunts over every B*ook*, till *Dust* or *Worms* have seized upon it; which to some, may happen in a few Days, but to others, later; And therefore, *Books* of Controversy, being of all others, haunted by the most disorderly Spirits, have always been confined in a separate Lodge from the rest; and for fear of mutual violence against each other, it was thought Prudent by our Ancestors, to bind them to the Peace with strong Iron Chains. Of which Invention, the original Occasion was this: When the Works of *Scotus* first came out, they were carried to a certain great Library, and had Lodgings appointed them; But this Author was no sooner settled, than he went to visit his Master *Aristotle*, and there both concerted together to seize *Plato* by main Force, and turn him out from his antient Station among the *Divines*, where he had peaceably dwelt near Eight Hundred Years. The Attempt succeeded, and the two Usurpers have reigned ever since in his stead: But to maintain Quiet for the future, it was decreed, that all *Polemicks* of the larger Size ,should be held fast with a Chain.

By this Expedient, the publick Peace of Libraries, might certainly have been preserved, if a new Species of controversial Books had not arose of late Years, instinct with a most malignant Spirit, from the War above-mentioned, between the *Learned*, about the higher Summity of *Parnassus*.

When these Books were first admitted into the Publick Libraries, I remember to have said upon Occasion, to several Persons concerned, how I was sure, they would create Broyls wherever they came, unless a World of Care were taken: And therefore, I advised, that the Champions of each side should be coupled together, or otherwise mixt, that like the blending of contrary Poysons, their Malignity might be employ'd among themselves. And it seems, I was neither an ill Prophet, nor an ill Counsellor; for it was nothing else but the Neglect of this Caution, which gave Occasion to the terrible Fight that happened on *Friday* last between the *Antient* and *Modern Books* in the *King*'s *Library*. Now, because the Talk of this Battel is so fresh in every body's Mouth, and the Expectation of the Town so great to be informed in the Particulars; I, being possessed of all Qualifications requisite in an *Historian*, and retained by neither Party; have resolved to comply with the urgent *Importunity of my Friends*, by writing down a full impartial Account thereof.

The *Guardian* of the *Regal Library*, a Person of great Valor, but chiefly renowned for his * *Humanity*, had been a fierce Champion for the *Moderns*, and in an Engagement upon *Parnassus*, had vowed, with his own Hands, to knock down two of the *Antient* Chiefs, who guarded a small Pass on the superior Rock; but endeavouring to climb up, was cruelly obstructed by his own unhappy Weight, and tendency towards his Center; a Quality, to which, those of the *Modern* Party, are extreme subject; For, being light-headed, they have in Speculation, a wonderful Agility, and conceive nothing too high for them to mount; but in reducing to Practice, discover a mighty Pressure about their Posteriors and their Heels. Having thus failed in his Design, the

* *The Honourable Mr*. Boyle, *in the Preface to his Edition of* Phalaris, *says, he was refus'd a Manuscript by the Library-Keeper*, pro solita Humanitate suâ.

disappointed Champion bore a cruel Rancour to the *Antients*, which he resolved to gratifie, by shewing all Marks of his Favour to the *Books* of their Adversaries, and lodging them in the fairest Apartments; when at the same time, whatever *Book* had the boldness to own it self for an Advocate of the *Antients*, was buried alive in some obscure Corner, and threatned upon the least Displeasure, to be turned out of Doors. Besides, it so happened, that about this time, there was a strange Confusion of Place among all the *Books* in the Library; for which several Reasons were assigned. Some imputed it to a great heap of *learned Dust*, which a perverse Wind blew off from a Shelf of *Moderns* into the *Keeper*'s Eyes. Others affirmed, He had a Humour to pick the *Worms* out of the *Schoolmen*, and swallow them fresh and fasting; whereof some fell upon his *Spleen*, and some climbed up into his Head, to the great Perturbation of both. And lastly, others maintained, that by walking much in the dark about the Library, he had quite lost the Situation of it out of his Head; And therefore, in replacing his *Books*, he was apt to mistake, and clap *Des-Cartes* next to *Aristotle*; Poor *Plato* had got between *Hobbes* and the *Seven Wise Masters*, and *Virgil* was hemm'd in with *Dryden* on one side, and *Withers* on the other.

MEAN while, those *Books* that were Advocates for the *Moderns*, chose out one from among them, to make a Progress thro' the whole Library, examine the Number and Strength of their Party, and concert their Affairs. This Messenger performed all things very industriously, and brought back with him a List of their Forces, in all Fifty Thousand, consisting chiefly of *light Horse*, *heavy-armed Foot*, and *Mercenaries*; Whereof the *Foot* were in general but sorrily armed, and worse clad; Their *Horses* large, but extremely out of Case and Heart; However, some few by trading among the *Antients*, had furnisht themselves tolerably enough.

WHILE Things were in this Ferment; *Discord* grew extremely high, hot Words passed on both sides, and ill blood was plentifully bred. Here a solitary *Antient*, squeezed up among a whole Shelf of *Moderns*, offered fairly to dispute the Case, and to prove by manifest Reasons, that the Priority was due to them, from long Possession, and in regard of their Prudence, Antiquity, and above all, their great Merits towards the *Moderns*. But these denied the Premises, and seemed very much to wonder, how the *Antients* could pretend to insist upon their Antiquity, when it was so plain (if they went to that) that the *Moderns* were much the more * *Antient* of the two. As for any Obligations they owed to the *Antients*, they renounced them all. *'Tis true*, said they, *we are informed, some few of our Party have been so mean to borrow their Subsistence from You; But the rest, infinitely the greater Number (and especially, we* French *and* English) *were so far from stooping to so base an Example, that there never passed, till this very hour, six Words between us. For, our* Horses *are of our own breeding, our* Arms *of our own forging, and our* Cloaths *of our own cutting out and sowing. Plato* was by chance upon the next Shelf, and observing those that spoke to be in the ragged Plight, mentioned a while ago; their *Jades* lean and foundred, their *Weapons* of rotten Wood, their *Armour* rusty, and nothing but Raggs underneath; he laugh'd loud, and in his pleasant way, swore, *By G——, he believ'd them.*

* *According to the Modern Paradox.*

Now, the *Moderns* had not proceeded in their late Negotiation, with Secrecy enough to escape the Notice of the Enemy. For, those Advocates, who had begun the Quarrel, by setting first on Foot the Dispute of Precedency, talkt so loud of coming to a Battel, that *Temple* happened to over-hear them, and gave immediate Intelligence to the *Antients*; who thereupon drew up their scattered Troops together, resolving to act upon the defensive; Upon which, several of the *Moderns* fled over to their Party, and among the rest, *Temple* himself. This *Temple* having been educated and long conversed among the *Antients*, was, of all the *Moderns*, their greatest Favorite, and became their greatest Champion.

THINGS were at this Crisis, when a material Accident fell out. For, upon the highest Corner of a large Window, there dwelt a certain *Spider*, swollen up to the first Magnitude, by the Destruction of infinite Numbers of *Flies*, whose Spoils lay scattered before the Gates of his Palace, like human Bones before the Cave of some Giant. The Avenues to his Castle were guarded with Turn-pikes, and Palissadoes, all after the *Modern* way of Fortification. After you had passed several Courts, you came to the Center, wherein you might behold the *Constable* himself in his own Lodgings, which had Windows fronting to each Avenue, and Ports to sally out upon all Occasions of Prey or Defence. In this Mansion he had for some Time dwelt in Peace and Plenty, without Danger to his *Person* by *Swallows* from above, or to his *Palace* by *Brooms* from below: When it was the Pleasure of Fortune to conduct thither a wandring *Bee*, to whose Curiosity a broken Pane in the Glass had discovered it self; and in he went, where expatiating a while, he at last happened to alight upon one of the outward Walls of the *Spider*'s Cittadel; which yielding to the unequal Weight, sunk down to the very Foundation. Thrice he endeavoured to force his Passage, and Thrice the Center shook. The *Spider* within, feeling the terrible Convulsion, supposed at first, that *Nature* was approaching to her final Dissolution; or else, that *Beelzebub* with all his Legions, was come to revenge the Death of many thousands of his Subjects, whom his Enemy had slain and devoured. However, he at length valiantly resolved to issue forth, and meet his Fate. Mean while, the *Bee* had acquitted himself of his Toils, and posted securely at some Distance, was employed in cleansing his Wings, and disengaging them from the ragged Remnants of the Cobweb. By this Time the *Spider* was adventured out, when beholding the Chasms, and Ruins, and Dilapidations of his Fortress, he was very near at his Wit's end, he stormed and swore like a Mad-man, and swelled till he was ready to burst. At length, casting his Eye upon the *Bee*, and wisely gathering Causes from Events, (for they knew each other by Sight) *A Plague split you*, said he, *for a giddy Son of a Whore; Is it you, with a Vengeance, that have made this Litter here? Could you not look before you, and be d——n'd? Do you think I have nothing else to do (in the Devil's Name) but to Mend and Repair after your Arse? Good Words, Friend*, said the *Bee*, (having now pruned himself, and being disposed to drole) *I'll give you my Hand and Word to come near your Kennel no more; I was never in such a confounded Pickle since I was born. Sirrah*, replied the *Spider*, *if it were not for breaking an old Custom in our Family, never to stir abroad against an Enemy, I should come and teach you better Manners. I pray, have Patience*, said the *Bee*, *or you will spend your Substance, and for ought I see, you may stand in need of it all*, *towards the Repair of your House.* Rogue, Rogue, replied the *Spider*, *yet, methinks, you should have more Respect to a Person, whom all the World allows to be so much your Betters. By my Troth*, said the *Bee*, *the Comparison will amount to a very good Jest, and you will do me a Favour, to let me know the Reasons, that all the World is pleased to use in so hopeful a Dispute.* At this, the *Spider* having swelled himself into the Size and Posture of a Disputant, began his Argument in the true Spirit of Controversy, with a Resolution to be heartily scurrilous and angry, to urge *on* his own Reasons, without the least Regard to the Answers or Objections of his Opposite; and fully predetermined in his Mind against all Conviction.

NOT *to disparage my self*, said he, *by the Comparison with such a Rascal; What art thou but a Vagabond without House or Home, without Stock or Inheritance? Born to no Possession of your own, but a Pair of Wings, and a Drone-Pipe. Your Livelihood is an universal Plunder upon Nature; a Freebooter over Fields and Gardens; and for the sake of Stealing, will rob a Nettle as readily as a Violet. Whereas I am a domestick Animal, furnisht with a Native Stock within my self. This large Castle (to shew my Improvements in the Mathematicks) is all built with my own Hands, and the Materials extracted altogether out of my own Person.*

I am glad, answered the *Bee*, *to hear you grant at least, that I am come honestly by my Wings and my Voice, for then, it seems, I am obliged to Heaven alone for my Flights and my Musick; and Providence would never have bestowed me two such Gifts, without designing them for the noblest Ends. I visit, indeed, all the Flowers and Blossoms of the Field and the Garden, but whatever I collect from thence, enriches my self, without the least Injury to their Beauty, their Smell, or their Taste. Now, for you and your Skill in Architecture, and other Mathematicks, I have little to say: In that Building of yours, there might, for ought I know, have been Labor and Method enough, but by woful Experience for us both, 'tis too plain, the Materials are nought, and I hope, you will henceforth take Warning, and consider Duration and matter, as well as method and Art. You, boast, indeed, of being obliged to no other Creature, but of drawing, and spinning out all from your self; That is to say, if we may judge of the Liquor in the Vessel by what issues out, You possess a good plentiful Store of Dirt and Poison in your Breast; And, tho' I would by no means, lessen or disparage your genuine Stock of either, yet, I doubt you are somewhat obliged for an Encrease of both, to a little foreign Assistance. Your inherent Portion of Dirt, does not fail of Acquisitions, by Sweepings exhaled from below: and one Insect furnishes you with a share of Poison to destroy another. So that in short, the Question comes all to this; Whether is the nobler Being of the two, That which by a lazy Contemplation of four Inches round; by an overweening Pride, which feeding and engendering on it self, turns all into Excrement and Venom; producing nothing at last, but Fly-bane and a Cobweb: Or That, which, by an universal Range, with long Search, much Study, true Judgment, and Distinction of Things, brings home Honey and Wax.*

THIS Dispute was managed with such Eagerness, Clamor, and Warmth, that the two Parties of *Books* in Arms below, stood Silent a while, waiting in Suspense what would be the Issue; which was not long undetermined: For the *Bee* grown impatient at so much loss of Time, fled strait away to a bed of Roses, without looking for a Reply; and left the *Spider* like an Orator, *collected* in himself, and just prepared to burst out.

IT happened upon this Emergency, that *Æsop* broke silence first. He had been of late most barbarously treated by a strange Effect of the *Regent*'s *Humanity*, who had tore off his Title-page, sorely defaced one half of his Leaves, and chained him fast among a Shelf of *Moderns*. Where soon discovering how high the Quarrel was like to proceed, He tried all his Arts, and turned himself to a thousand Forms: At length in the borrowed Shape of an *Ass*, the *Regent* mistook Him for a *Modern*; by which means, he had Time and Opportunity to escape to the *Antients*, just when the *Spider* and the *Bee* were entring into their Contest; to which He gave His Attention with a world of Pleasure; and when it was ended, swore in the loudest Key, that in all his Life, he had never known two Cases so parallel and adapt to each other, as That in the Window, and this upon the Shelves. The *Disputants*, said he, *have admirably managed the Dispute between them, have taken in the full Strength of all that is to be said on both sides, and exhausted the Substance of every Argument* pro *and* con. *It is but to adjust the Reasonings of both to the present Quarrel, then to compare and apply the Labors and Fruits of each, as the* Bee *has learnedly deduced them; and we shall find the Conclusions fall plain and close upon the* Moderns *and* Us. *For, pray Gentlemen, was ever any thing so* Modern *as the* Spider *in his Air, his Turns, and his Paradoxes? He argues in the Behalf of* You *his Brethren, and Himself, with many Boastings of his native Stock, and great Genius; that he Spins and Spits wholly from himself, and scorns to own any Obligation or Assistance from without. Then he displays to you his great Skill in Architecture, and Improvement in the Mathematicks. To all this, the* Bee, *as an Advocate, retained by us the* Antients, *thinks fit to Answer; That if one may judge of the great Genius or Inventions of the* Moderns, *by what they have produced, you will hardly have Countenance to bear you out in boasting of either. Erect your Schemes with as much Method and Skill as you please; yet, if the materials be nothing but Dirt, spun out of your own Entrails (the Guts of* Modern *Brains) the Edifice will conclude at last in a* Cobweb: *The Duration of which, like that of other* Spiders *Webs, may be imputed to their being forgotten, or neglected, or hid in a Corner. For any Thing else of Genuine, that the* Moderns *may pretend to, I cannot recollect; unless it be a large Vein of Wrangling and Satyr, much of a Nature and Substance with the* Spider*'s Poison; which, however they pretend to spit wholly out of themselves, is improved by the same Arts, by feeding upon the* Insects *and* Vermin *of the Age. As for* Us, *the* Antients, *We are content with the* Bee, *to pretend to Nothing of our own, beyond our* Wings *and our* Voice: *that is to say, our* Flights *and our* Language; *For the rest, whatever we have got, has been by infinite Labor, and search, and ranging thro' every Corner of Nature: The Difference is, that instead of* Dirt *and* Poison, *we have rather chose to fill our Hives with* Honey *and* Wax, *thus furnishing Mankind with the two Noblest of Things, which are* Sweetness *and* Light.

'Tis wonderful to conceive the Tumult arisen among the *Books*, upon the Close of this long Descant of *Æsop*; Both Parties took the Hint, and heightened their Animosities so on a sudden, that they resolved it should come to a Battel. Immediately, the two main Bodies withdrew under their several Ensigns, to the farther Parts of the Library, and there entred into Cabals, and Consults upon the present Emergency. The *Moderns* were in very warm Debates upon the Choice of their *Leaders*, and nothing less than the Fear impending from their Enemies, could have kept them from Mutinies upon this Occasion. The Difference was greatest among the *Horse*, where every private *Trooper* pretended to the chief Command, from *Tasso* and *Milton*, to *Dryden* and *Withers*. The *Light-Horse* were Commanded by *Cowly*, and *Despreaux*. There, came the *Bowmen* under their valiant Leaders, *Des-Cartes*, *Gassendi*, and *Hobbes*, whose Strength was such, that they could shoot their Arrows beyond the *Atmosphere*, never to fall down again, but turn like that of *Evander*, into *Meteors*, or like the *Canon-ball* into *Stars*. *Paracelsus* brought a *Squadron* of *Stink-Pot-Flingers* from the snowy Mountains of *Rhœtia*. There, came a vast Body of *Dragoons*, of different Nations, under the leading of *Harvey*, their great *Aga*: Part armed with *Scythes*, the Weapons of Death; Part with *Launces* and long *Knives*, all steept in *Poison*; Part shot *Bullets* of a most malignant Nature, and used *white Powder* which infallibly killed without *Report*. There, came several Bodies of *heavy-armed Foot*, all *Mercenaries*, under the Ensigns of *Guiccardine*, *Davila*, *Polydore Virgil*, *Buchanan*, *Mariana*, *Cambden*, and others. The *Engineers* were commanded by *Regiomontanus* and *Wilkins*. The rest were a confused Multitude, led by *Scotus*, *Aquinas*, and *Bellarmine*; of mighty Bulk and Stature, but without either Arms, Courage, or Discipline. In the last Place, came infinite Swarms of * *Calones*, a disorderly Rout led by *Lestrange*; Rogues and Raggamuffins, that follow the Camp for nothing but the Plunder; All without *Coats* to cover them.

THE Army of the *Antients* was much fewer in Number; *Homer* led the *Horse*, and *Pindar* the *Light-Horse; Euclid* was chief *Engineer: Plato* and *Aristotle* commanded the *Bowmen*, *Herodotus* and *Livy* the *Foot*, *Hippocrates* the *Dragoons*. The *Allies*, led by *Vossius* and *Temple*, brought up the Rear.

ALL things violently tending to a decisive Battel; *Fame*, who much frequented, and had a large Apartment formerly assigned her in the *Regal Library*, fled up strait to *Jupiter*, to whom she delivered a faithful account of all that passed between the two Parties below. (For, among the Gods, she always tells Truth.) *Jove* in great concern, convokes a Council in the *Milky-Way*. The Senate assembled, he declares the Occasion of convening

* *These are Pamphlets, which are not bound or cover'd.*

them; a bloody Battel just impendent between two mighty Armies of *Antient* and *Modern* Creatures, call'd *Books*, wherein the Celestial Interest was but too deeply concerned. *Momus*, the Patron of the *Moderns*, made an Excellent Speech in their Favor, which was answered by *Pallas* the Protectress of the *Antients*. The Assembly was divided in their affections; when *Jupiter* commanded the Book of Fate to be laid before Him. Immediately were brought by *Mercury*, three large Volumes in Folio, containing Memoirs of all Things past, present, and to come. The Clasps were of Silver, double Gilt; the Covers, of Celestial Turky-leather, and the Paper such as here on Earth might almost pass for Vellum. *Jupiter* having silently read the Decree, would communicate the Import to none, but presently shut up the Book.

WITHOUT the Doors of this Assembly, there attended a vast Number of light, nimble Gods, menial Servants to *Jupiter*: These are his ministring Instruments in all Affairs below. They travel in a Caravan, more or less together, and are fastened to each other like a Link of Gally-slaves, by a light Chain, which passes from them to *Jupiter*'s great Toe: And yet in receiving or delivering a Message, they may never approach above the lowest Step of his Throne, where he and they whisper to each other thro' a long hollow Trunk. These Deities are call'd by mortal Men, *Accidents*, or *Events*; but the Gods call them, *Second Causes*. *Jupiter* having delivered his Message to a certain Number of these Divinities, they flew immediately down to the Pinnacle of the Regal Library, and consulting a few Minutes, entered unseen, and disposed the Parties according to their Orders.

MEAN while, *Momus* fearing the worst, and calling to mind an antient Prophecy, which bore no very good Face to his Children the *Moderns*; bent his Flight to the Region of a malignant Deity, call'd *Criticism*. She dwelt on the Top of a snowy Mountain in *Nova Zembla*; there *Momus* found her extended in her Den, upon the Spoils of numberless Volumes half devoured. At her right Hand sat *Ignorance*, her Father and Husband, blind with Age; at her left, *Pride* her Mother, dressing her up in the Scraps of Paper herself had torn. There, was *Opinion* her Sister, light of Foot, hoodwinkt, and headstrong, yet giddy and perpetually turning. About her play'd her Children, *Noise* and *Impudence*, *Dullness* and *Vanity*, *Positiveness*, *Pedantry*, and *Ill-Manners*. The Goddess herself had Claws like a Cat: Her Head, and Ears, and Voice, resembled those of an *Ass*; Her Teeth fallen out before; Her Eyes turned inward, as if she lookt only upon herself: Her Diet was the overflowing of her own *Gall*: Her *Spleen* was so large, as to stand prominent like a Dug of the first Rate, nor wanted Excrescencies in form of Teats, at which a Crew of ugly Monsters were greedily sucking; and, what is wonderful to conceive, the bulk of Spleen encreased faster than the Sucking could diminish it. *Goddess*, said *Momus*, *can you sit idly here, while our devout Worshippers, the* Moderns, *are this Minute entring into a cruel Battel, and, perhaps, now lying under the Swords of their Enemies; Who then hereafter, will ever sacrifice, or build Altars to our Divinities? Haste therefore to the* British Isle, *and, if possible, prevent their Destruction, while I make Factions among the Gods, and gain them over to our Party.*

MOMUS having thus delivered himself, staid not for an answer, but left the Goddess to her own Resentment; Up she rose in a Rage, and as it is the Form upon such Occasions, began a Soliloquy. *'Tis I* (said she) *who give Wisdom to Infants and Idiots; By Me, Children grow wiser than their Parents. By Me,* Beaux *become Politicians; and* School-boys, *Judges of Philosophy. By Me, Sophisters debate, and conclude upon the Depths of Knowledge; and Coffee-house Wits instinct by Me, can correct an Author's Style, and display his minutest Errors, without understanding a Syllable of his Matter or his Language. By Me, Striplings spend their Judgment, as they do their Estate, before it comes into their Hands. 'Tis I, who have deposed Wit and Knowledge from their Empire over* Poetry, *and advanced my self in their stead. And shall a few* upstart Antients *dare to oppose me?—But, come, my aged Parents, and you, my Children dear, and thou my beauteous Sister; let us ascend my Chariot, and haste to assist our devout* Moderns, *who are now sacrificing to us a* Hecatomb, *as I perceive by that grateful Smell, which from thence reaches my Nostrils.*

The Goddess and her Train having mounted the Chariot, which was drawn by *tame Geese*, flew over infinite Regions, shedding her Influence in due Places, till at length, she arrived at her beloved Island of *Britain*; but in hovering over its *Metropolis*, what Blessings did she not let fall upon her Seminaries of

Gresham and *Covent-Garden*? And now she reach'd the fatal Plain of St. *James*'s Library, at what time the two Armies were upon the Point to engage; where entring with all her Caravan, unseen, and landing upon a Case of Shelves, now desart, but once inhabited by a Colony of *Virtuoso's*, she staid a while to observe the Posture of both Armies.

But here, the tender Cares of a Mother began to fill her Thoughts, and move in her Breast. For, at the Head of a Troop of *Modern Bow-men*, she cast her Eyes upon her Son *Wotton*; to whom the Fates had assigned a very short Thread. *Wotton*, a young Hero, whom an unknown Father of mortal Race, begot by stollen Embraces with this Goddess. He was the Darling of his Mother, above all her Children, and she resolved to go and comfort Him. But first, according to the good old Custom of Deities, she cast about to change her Shape; for fear the Divinity of her Countenance might dazzle his Mortal Sight, and overcharge the rest of his Senses. She therefore gathered up her Person into an *Octavo* Compass: Her Body grew white and arid, and split in pieces with Driness; the thick turned into Pastboard, and the thin into Paper, upon which, her Parents and Children, artfully strowed a Black Juice, or Decoction of Gall and Soot, in Form of Letters; her Head, and Voice, and Spleen, kept their primitive Form, and that which before, was a Cover of Skin, did still continue so. In which Guise, she march'd on towards the *Moderns*, undistinguishable in Shape and Dress from the *Divine Bentley*, *Wotton*'s dearest Friend. *Brave Wotton*, said the Goddess, *Why do our Troops stand idle here, to spend their present Vigour and Opportunity of the Day? Away, let us haste to the Generals, and advise to give the Onset immediately*. Having spoke thus, she took the ugliest of her Monsters, full glutted from her Spleen, and flung it invisibly into his Mouth; which flying strait up into his Head, squeez'd out his Eye-Balls, gave him a distorted Look, and half over-turned his Brain. Then she privately ordered two of her beloved Children, *Dulness* and *Ill-Manners*, closely to attend his Person in all Encounters. Having thus accoutred him, she vanished in a Mist, and the *Hero* perceived it was the Goddess, his Mother.

The destined Hour of Fate, being now arrived, the Fight

began; whereof, before I dare adventure to make a particular Description, I must, after the Example of other Authors, petition for a hundred Tongues, and Mouths, and Hands, and Pens; which would all be too little to perform so immense a Work. Say, Goddess, that presidest over History; who it was that first advanced in the Field of Battel. *Paracelsus*, at the Head of his *Dragoons*, observing *Galen* in the adverse Wing, darted his Javelin with a mighty Force, which the brave *Antient* received upon his Shield, the Point breaking in the second fold. * * *

Hic pauca desunt. * * * * * * * *
* * * * * * * *

They bore the wounded *Aga*, on their Shields to his Chariot *
* * * * * * * *

Desunt nonnulla. * * * * * * * *
* * * * * * * *
* * * * * * * * * *

THEN *Aristotle* observing *Bacon* advance with a furious Mien, drew his Bow to the Head, and let fly his Arrow, which mist the valiant *Modern*, and went hizzing over his Head; but *Des-Cartes* it hit; The Steel Point quickly found a *Defect* in his *Head-piece*; it pierced the Leather and the Past-board, and went in at his Right Eye. The Torture of the Pain, whirled the valiant *Bow-man* round, till Death, like a Star of superior Influence, drew him into his own *Vortex*. * * * * * *
* * * * * * * *

Ingens hiatus hic in MS. * * * * * * * *
* * * * * * * *

when *Homer* appeared at the Head of the Cavalry, mounted on a furious Horse, with Difficulty managed by the Rider himself, but which no other Mortal durst approach; He rode among the Enemies Ranks, and bore down all before him. Say, Goddess, whom he slew first, and whom he slew last. First, *Gondibert* advanced against Him, clad in heavy Armour, and mounted on a staid sober Gelding, not so famed for his Speed as his Docility in kneeling, whenever his Rider would mount or alight. He had made a Vow to *Pallas*, that he would never leave the Field, till he had spoiled * *Homer* of his Armour; Madman, who had never once *seen* the Wearer, nor under-

* *Vid. Homer.*

stood his Strength. Him *Homer* overthrew, Horse and Man to the Ground, there to be trampled and choak'd in the Dirt. Then, with a long Spear, he slew *Denham*, a stout *Modern*, who from his * Father's side, derived his Lineage from *Apollo*, but his Mother was of Mortal Race. He fell, and bit the Earth. The Celestial Part *Apollo* took, and made it a Star, but the Terrestrial lay wallowing upon the Ground. Then *Homer* slew *Wesley* with a kick of his Horse's heel; He took *Perrault* by mighty Force out of his Saddle, then hurl'd him at *Fontenelle*, with the same Blow dashing out both their Brains.

On the left Wing of the Horse, *Virgil* appeared in shining Armor, compleatly fitted to his Body; He was mounted on a dapple grey Steed, the slowness of whose Pace, was an Effect of the highest Mettle and Vigour. He cast his Eye on the adverse Wing, with a desire to find an Object worthy of his valour, when behold, upon a sorrel Gelding of a monstrous Size, appear'd a Foe, issuing from among the thickest of the Enemy's Squadrons; But his Speed was less than his Noise; for his Horse, old and lean, spent the Dregs of his Strength in a high Trot, which tho' it made slow advances, yet caused a loud Clashing of his Armor, terrible to hear. The two Cavaliers had now approached within the Throw of a Lance, when the Stranger desired a Parley, and lifting up the Vizard of his Helmet, a Face hardly appeared from within, which after a pause, was known for that of the renowned *Dryden*. The brave *Antient* suddenly started, as one possess'd with Surprize and Disappointment together: For, the Helmet was nine times too large for the Head, which appeared Situate far in the hinder Part, even like the Lady in a Lobster, or like a Mouse under a Canopy of State, or like a shrivled Beau from within the Pent-house of a modern Perewig: And the voice was suited to the Visage, sounding weak and remote. *Dryden* in a long Harangue soothed up the good *Antient*, called him *Father*, and by a large deduction of Genealogies, made it plainly appear, that they were nearly related. Then he humbly proposed an Ex-

* *Sir* John Denham's *Poems are very Unequal, extremely Good, and very Indifferent, so that his Detractors said, he was not the real Author of* Coopers-Hill.

change of Armor, as a lasting Mark of Hospitality between them. *Virgil* consented (for the Goddess *Diffidence* came unseen, and cast a Mist before his Eyes) tho' his was of Gold, and cost a hundred Beeves, the others but of rusty Iron. However, this glittering Armor became the *Modern* yet worse than his Own. Then, they agreed to exchange Horses; but when it came to the Trial, *Dryden* was afraid, and utterly unable to mount. * * * * * *

Vid. Homer.

Alter hiatus in MS. * * * * * * * *
* * * * * * * *

* * * * *Lucan* appeared upon a fiery Horse, of admirable Shape, but head-strong, bearing the Rider where he list, over the Field; he made a mighty Slaughter among the Enemy's Horse; which Destruction to stop, *Blackmore*, a famous *Modern* (but one of the *Mercenaries*) strenuously opposed himself; and darted a Javelin, with a strong Hand, which falling short of its Mark, struck deep in the Earth. Then *Lucan* threw a Lance; but *Æsculapius* came unseen, and turn'd off the Point. *Brave* Modern, *said* Lucan, *I perceive some God protects you, for never did my Arm so deceive me before; But, what Mortal can contend with a God? Therefore, let us Fight no longer, but present Gifts to each other.* *Lucan* then bestowed the *Modern a Pair of Spurs*, and *Blackmore* gave *Lucan* a *Bridle*.

* * * * * * * *
Pauca desunt. * * * * * * * *

Creech; But, the Goddess *Dulness* took a Cloud, formed into the Shape of *Horace*, armed and mounted, and placed it in a flying Posture before Him. Glad was the Cavalier, to begin a Combat with a flying Foe, and pursued the Image, threatning loud; till at last it led him to the peaceful Bower of his Father *Ogleby*, by whom he was disarmed, and assigned to his Repose.

THEN *Pindar* slew——, and ——, and *Oldham*, and —— and *Afra* the *Amazon* light of foot; Never advancing in a direct Line, but wheeling with incredible Agility and Force, he made a terrible Slaughter among the Enemies *Light-Horse*. Him, when *Cowley* observed, his generous Heart burnt within him, and he advanced against the fierce *Antient*, imitating his Address, and Pace, and Career, as well as the Vigour of his Horse, and his own

Skill would allow. When the two Cavaliers had approach'd within the Length of three Javelins; first *Cowley* threw a Lance, which miss'd *Pindar*, and passing into the Enemy's Ranks, fell ineffectual to the Ground. Then *Pindar* darted a Javelin, so large and weighty, that scarce a dozen *Cavaliers*, as *Cavaliers* are in our degenerate Days, could raise it from the Ground: yet he threw it with Ease, and it went by an unerring Hand, singing through the Air; Nor could the *Modern* have avoided present Death, if he had not luckily opposed the Shield that had been given Him by *Venus*. And now both Hero's drew their Swords, but the *Modern* was so aghast and disordered, that he knew not where he was; his Shield dropt from his Hands; thrice he fled, and thrice he could not escape; at last he turned, and lifting up his Hands, in the Posture of a Suppliant, *God-like* Pindar, said he, *spare my Life, and possess my Horse with these Arms; besides the Ransom which my Friends will give, when they hear I am alive, and your Prisoner. Dog*, said Pindar, *Let your Ransom stay with your Friends; But your Carcass shall be left for the* Fowls of the Air, *and the* Beasts of the Field. With that, he raised his Sword, and with a mighty Stroak, cleft the wretched *Modern* in twain, the Sword pursuing the Blow; and one half lay panting on the Ground, to be trod in pieces by the Horses Feet, the other half was born by the frighted Steed thro' the Field. This * *Venus* took, and wash'd it seven times in *Ambrosia*, then struck it thrice with a Sprig of *Amarant*; upon which, the Leather grew round and soft, the Leaves turned into Feathers, and being gilded before, continued gilded still; so it became a *Dove*, and She harness'd it to her Chariot.

* * * * * * * * * *
* * * * * * *
* * * * * * *
* * * * * * * * * *

Hiatus valdè deflendus in MS.

The Episode of Bentley *and* Wotton.

DAY being far spent, and the numerous Forces of the *Moderns* half inclining to a Retreat, there issued forth from a Squadron of their *heavy armed Foot*, a Captain, whose Name was *Bentley*; in Person, the

* *I do not approve the Author's Judgment in this, for I think* Cowley's *Pindaricks are much preferable to his* Mistress.

most deformed of all the *Moderns*; Tall, but without Shape or Comeliness; Large, but without Strength or Proportion. His Armour was patch'd up of a thousand incoherent Pieces; and the Sound of it, as he march'd, was loud and dry, like that made by the Fall of a Sheet of Lead, which an *Etesian* Wind blows suddenly down from the Roof of some Steeple. His Helmet was of old rusty Iron, but the Vizard was Brass, which tainted by his Breath, corrupted into Copperas, nor wanted Gall from the same Fountain; so, that whenever provoked by Anger or Labour, an atramentous Quality, of most malignant Nature, was seen to distil from his Lips. In his * right Hand he grasp'd a Flail, and (that he might never be unprovided of an *offensive* Weapon) a Vessel full of *Ordure* in his Left: Thus, compleatly arm'd, he advanc'd with a slow and heavy Pace, where the *Modern* Chiefs were holding a Consult upon the Sum of Things; who, as he came onwards, laugh'd to behold his crooked Leg, and hump Shoulder, which his Boot and Armour vainly endeavouring to hide were forced to comply with, and expose. The Generals made use of him for his Talent of Railing; which kept within Government, proved frequently of great Service to their Cause, but at other times did more Mischief than Good; For at the least Touch of Offence, and often without any at all, he would, like a wounded Elephant, convert it against his Leaders. Such, at this Juncture, was the Disposition of *Bentley*, grieved to see the Enemy prevail, and dissatisfied with every Body's Conduct but his own. He humbly gave the *Modern* Generals to understand, that he conceived, with great Submission, they were all a Pack of *Rogues*, and *Fools*, and *Sons of Whores*, and *d——mn'd Cowards*, and *confounded Loggerheads*, and *illiterate Whelps*, and *nonsensical Scoundrels*; That if Himself had been constituted General, those *presumptuous Dogs*, the *Antients*, would long before this, have been beaten out of the Field. *You*, said he, *sit here idle, but, when I, or any other valiant* Modern, *kill an Enemy, you are sure to seize the Spoil. But, I will not march one Foot against the Foe, till you all swear*

Vid. Homer. de Thersite.

The Person here spoken of, is famous for letting fly at every Body without Distinction, and using mean and foul Scurrilities.

to me, that, whomever I take or kill, his Arms I shall quietly possess. Bentley having spoke thus, *Scaliger* bestowing him a sower Look; *Miscreant* Prater, said he, *Eloquent only in thine own Eyes, Thou railest without Wit, or Truth, or Discretion. The Malignity of thy Temper perverteth Nature; Thy* Learning *makes thee more* Barbarous, *thy Study of* Humanity, *more* Inhuman; *Thy* Converse *amongst Poets more* groveling, miry, *and* dull. *All Arts of* civilizing *others, render thee* rude *and* untractable; Courts *have taught thee* ill Manners, *and* polite Conversation *has finish'd thee a* Pedant. *Besides, a greater Coward burtheneth not the Army. But never despond, I pass my Word, whatever Spoil thou takest, shall certainly be thy own; though, I hope, that vile Carcass will first become a prey to Kites and Worms.*

BENTLEY durst not reply; but half choaked with Spleen and Rage, withdrew, in full Resolution of performing some great Achievment. With him, for his Aid and Companion, he took his beloved *Wotton*; resolving by Policy or Surprize, to attempt some neglected Quarter of the *Antients* Army. They began their March over Carcasses of their slaughtered Friends; then to the Right of their own Forces: then wheeled Northward, till they came to *Aldrovandus*'s Tomb, which they pass'd on the side of the declining Sun. And now they arrived with Fear towards the Enemy's Out-guards; looking about, if haply, they might spy the Quarters of the Wounded, or some straggling Sleepers, unarm'd and remote from the rest. As when two *Mungrel-Curs*, whom *native Greediness*, and *domestick Want*, provoke, and join in Partnership, though fearful, nightly to invade the Folds of some rich Grazier; They, with Tails depress'd, and lolling Tongues, creep soft and slow; mean while, the conscious *Moon*, now in her *Zenith*, on their guilty Heads, darts perpendicular Rays; Nor dare they bark, though much provok'd at her refulgent Visage, whether seen in Puddle by Reflexion, or in Sphear direct; but one surveys the Region round, while t'other scouts the Plain, if haply, to discover at distance from the Flock, some *Carcass* half devoured, the Refuse of gorged Wolves, or ominous Ravens. So march'd this lovely, loving Pair of Friends, nor with less Fear and Circumspection; when, at distance, they might perceive two shining Suits of Armor, hanging upon an Oak, and the Owners not far off in a profound Sleep. The two

Friends drew Lots, and the pursuing of this Adventure, fell to *Bentley*; On he went, and in his Van *Confusion* and *Amaze*; while *Horror* and *Affright* brought up the Rear. As he came near; Behold two Hero's of the *Antients* Army, *Phalaris* and *Æsop*, lay fast asleep: *Bentley* would fain have dispatch'd them both, and stealing close, aimed his Flail at *Phalaris*'s Breast. But, then, the Goddess *Affright* interposing, caught the *Modern* in her icy Arms, and dragg'd him from the Danger she foresaw; For both the dormant Hero's happened to turn at the same Instant, tho' soundly Sleeping, and busy in a Dream. * For *Phalaris* was just that Minute dreaming, how a most vile *Poetaster* had lampoon'd him, and how he had got him roaring in his *Bull*. And *Æsop* dream'd, that as he and the *Antient Chiefs* were lying on the Ground, a *Wild Ass* broke loose, ran about trampling and kicking, and dunging in their Faces. *Bentley* leaving the two Hero's asleep, seized on both their Armors, and withdrew in quest of his Darling *Wotton*.

He, in the mean time, had wandred long in search of some Enterprize, till at length, he arrived at a small *Rivulet*, that issued from a Fountain hard by, call'd in the Language of mortal Men, *Helicon*. Here he stopt, and, parch'd with thirst, resolved to allay it in this limpid Stream. Thrice, with profane Hands, he essay'd to raise the Water to his Lips, and thrice it slipt all thro' his Fingers. Then he stoop'd prone on his Breast, but e'er his Mouth had kiss'd the liquid Crystal, *Apollo* came, and, in the Channel, held his *Shield* betwixt the *Modern* and the Fountain, so that he drew up nothing but *Mud*. For, altho' no Fountain on Earth can compare with the Clearness of *Helicon*, yet there lies at Bottom, a thick sediment of *Slime* and *Mud*; For, so *Apollo* begg'd of *Jupiter*, as a Punishment to those who durst attempt to taste it with unhallowed Lips, and for a Lesson to all, not to *draw too deep*, or *far from the Spring*.

At the Fountain Head, *Wotton* discerned two Hero's; The one he could not distinguish, but the other was soon known for *Temple*, General of the *Allies* to the *Antients*. His Back was

* *This is according to* Homer, *who tells the Dreams of those who were kill'd in their Sleep*.

turned, and he was employ'd in Drinking large Draughts in his Helmet, from the Fountain, where he had withdrawn himself to rest from the Toils of the War. *Wotton*, observing him, with quaking Knees, and trembling Hands, spoke thus to Himself: *Oh, that I could kill this Destroyer of our Army, what* Renown *should I purchase among the Chiefs! But to issue out against Him, Man for Man, Shield against Shield, and Launce against Launce; what* Modern *of us dare? For, he fights like a God, and* Pallas *or* Apollo *are ever at his Elbow. But, Oh,* Mother! *if what Fame reports, be true, that I am the Son of so great a Goddess, grant me to Hit* Temple *with this Launce, that the Stroak may send Him to Hell, and that I may return in Safety and Triumph, laden with his Spoils.* The first Part of his Prayer, the Gods granted, at the Intercession of His *Mother* and of *Momus*; but the rest, by a perverse Wind sent from *Fate*, was scattered in the Air. Then *Wotton* grasp'd his Launce, and brandishing it thrice over his head, darted it with all his Might, the *Goddess*, his *Mother*, at the same time, adding Strength to his Arm. Away the Launce went hizzing, and reach'd even to the Belt of the averted *Antient*, upon which, lightly grazing, it fell to the Ground. *Temple* neither felt the Weapon touch him, nor heard it fall; And *Wotton*, might have escaped to his Army, with the Honor of having remitted his Launce against so great a Leader, unrevenged; But, *Apollo* enraged, that a Javelin, flung by the Assistance of so foul a *Goddess*, should pollute his Fountain, put on the shape of——, and softly came to young *Boyle*, who then accompanied *Temple*: He pointed, first to the Launce, then to the distant *Modern* that flung it, and commanded the young Hero to take immediate Revenge. *Boyle*, clad in a suit of Armor which had been *given him by all the Gods*, immediately advanced against the trembling Foe, who now fled before him. As a young Lion, in the *Libyan Plains*, or *Araby Desart*, sent by his aged Sire to hunt for Prey, or Health, or Exercise; He scours along, wishing to meet some Tiger from the Mountains, or a furious Boar; If Chance, a *Wild Ass*, with Brayings importune, affronts his Ear, the generous Beast, though loathing to distain his Claws with Blood so vile, yet much provok'd at the offensive Noise; which *Echo*, foolish Nymph, like her *ill-judging Sex*, repeats much louder, and with

Vid. Homer.

more Delight than *Philomela's* Song: He vindicates the Honor of the Forest, and hunts the noisy, long-ear'd Animal. So *Wotton* fled, so *Boyle* pursued. But *Wotton* heavy-arm'd, and slow of foot, began to slack his Course; when his Lover *Bentley* appeared, returning laden with the Spoils of the two sleeping *Antients*. *Boyle* observed him well, and soon discovering the Helmet and Shield of *Phalaris*, his Friend, both which he had lately with his own Hands, new polish'd and gilded; Rage sparkled in His Eyes, and leaving his Pursuit after *Wotton*, he furiously rush'd on against this new Approacher. Fain would he be revenged on both; but both now fled different Ways: * And as a Woman in a little House, that gets a painful Livelihood by Spinning; if chance her *Geese* be scattered o'er the Common, she courses round the Plain from side to side, compelling here and there, the Straglers to the Flock; They cackle loud, and flutter o'er the Champain. So *Boyle* pursued, so fled this Pair of Friends: finding at length, their Flight was vain, they bravely joyn'd, and drew themselves in *Phalanx*. First, *Bentley* threw a Spear with all his Force, hoping to pierce the Enemy's Breast; But *Pallas* came unseen, and in the Air took off the Point, and clap'd on one of *Lead*, which after a dead Bang against the Enemy's Shield, fell blunted to the Ground. Then *Boyle* observing well his Time, took a Launce of wondrous Length and sharpness; and as this Pair of Friends compacted stood close Side to Side, he wheel'd him to the right, and with unusual Force, darted the Weapon. *Bentley* saw his Fate approach, and flanking down his Arms, close to his Ribs, hoping to save his Body; in went the Point, passing through Arm and Side, nor stopt, or spent its Force, till it had also pierc'd the valiant *Wotton*, who going to sustain his dying Friend, shared his Fate. As, when a skilful Cook has truss'd a Brace of *Woodcocks*, He, with Iron Skewer, pierces the tender Sides of both, their Legs and Wings close pinion'd to their Ribs; So was this pair of Friends transfix'd, till down they fell, joyn'd in their Lives, joyn'd in

Vid. Homer.

* *This is also, after the manner of* Homer; *the Woman's getting a painful Livelihood by Spinning, has nothing to do with the Similitude, nor would be excusable without such an Authority.*

their Deaths; so closely joyn'd, that *Charon* would mistake them both for one, and waft them over *Styx* for half his Fare. Farewel, beloved, loving Pair; Few Equals have you left behind: And happy and immortal shall you be, if all my Wit and Eloquence can make you.

AND, now * * * * * * *
* * * * * * * * * *
* * * * * *
* * * * *Desunt cætera.*

FINIS.

A DISCOURSE Concerning the Mechanical Operation OF THE SPIRIT IN A LETTER *To a FRIEND.* A FRAGMENT.

LONDON:
Printed in the Year, MDCCX.

THE

BOOKSELLER's
Advertisement.

THE *following Discourse came into my Hands perfect and entire. But there being several Things in it, which the present Age would not very well bear, I kept it by me some Years, resolving it should never see the Light. At length, by the Advice and Assistance of a judicious Friend, I retrench'd those Parts that might give most Offence, and have now ventured to publish the Remainder; Concerning the Author, I am wholly ignorant; neither can I conjecture, whether it be the same with That of the two foregoing Pieces, the Original having been sent me at a different Time, and in a different Hand. The Learned Reader will better determine; to whose Judgment I entirely submit it.*

A DISCOURSE Concerning the Mechanical Operation of the SPIRIT, &c.

For T.H. *Esquire, at his Chambers in the Academy of the* Beaux Esprits *in* New-Holland.

SIR,

IT is now a good while since I have had in my Head something, not only very material, but absolutely necessary to my Health, that the World should be informed in. For, to tell you a Secret, I am able to *contain* it no longer. However, I have been perplexed for some time, to resolve what would be the most proper Form to send it abroad in. To which End, I have three Days been coursing thro' *Westminster-Hall*, and St. *Paul*'s *Church-yard*, and *Fleet-street*, to peruse *Titles*; and, I do not find any which holds so general a Vogue, as that of *A Letter to a Friend*: Nothing is more common than to meet with long Epistles address'd to Persons and Places, where, at first thinking, one would be apt to imagine it not altogether so necessary or Convenient; Such as, *a Neighbour at next Door, a mortal Enemy, a perfect Stranger*, or *a*

This Discourse is not altogether equal to the two Former, the best Parts of it being omitted; whether the Bookseller's Account be true, that he durst not print the rest, I know not, nor indeed is it easie to determine whether he may be rely'd on, in any thing he says of this, or the former Treatises, only as to the Time they were writ in, which, however, appears more from the Discourses themselves than his Relation.

Person of Quality in the Clouds; and these upon Subjects, in appearance, the least proper for Conveyance by the Post; as, *long Schemes in Philosophy; dark and wonderful Mysteries of State; Laborious Dissertations in Criticism and Philosophy*, *Advice to Parliaments*, and the like.

Now, Sir, to proceed after the Method in present Wear. (For, let me say what I will to the contrary, I am afraid you will publish this *Letter*, as soon as ever it comes to your Hands;) I desire you will be my Witness to the World, how careless and sudden a Scribble it has been; That it was but Yesterday, when You and I began accidentally to fall into Discourse on this Matter: That I was not very well, when we parted; That the Post is in such haste, I have had no manner of Time to digest it into Order, or correct the Style; And if any other Modern Excuses, for Haste and Negligence, shall occur to you in Reading, I beg you to insert them, faithfully promising they shall be thankfully acknowledged.

PRAY, Sir, in your next Letter to the *Iroquois Virtuosi*, do me the Favour to present my humble Service to that illustrious Body, and assure them, I shall send an Account of those *Phænomena*, as soon as we can determine them at *Gresham*.

I have not had a Line from the *Literati* of *Tobinambou*, these three last Ordinaries.

AND now, Sir, having dispatch'd what I had to say of Forms, or of Business, let me intreat, you will suffer me to proceed upon my Subject; and to pardon me, if I make no farther Use of the Epistolary Stile, till I come to conclude.

SECTION I.

TIS recorded of *Mahomet*, that upon a Visit he was going to pay in *Paradise*, he had an Offer of several Vehicles to conduct him upwards; as fiery Chariots, wing'd Horses, and celestial Sedans; but he refused them all, and would be born to Heaven upon nothing but his *Ass*. Now, this Inclination of *Mahomet*, as singular as it seems, hath been since taken up by a great Number of devout *Christians*; and doubtless, with very good Reason. For, since That *Arabian* is known to have borrowed a Moiety of his Religious System from the *Christian* Faith; it is but just he should pay Reprisals to such as would Challenge them; wherein the good People of *England*, to do them all Right, have not been backward. For, tho' there is not any other Nation in the World, so plentifully provided with Carriages for that Journey, either as to Safety or Ease; yet there are abundance of us, who will not be satisfied with any other Machine, beside this of *Mahomet*.

For my own part, I must confess to bear a very singular Respect to this Animal, by whom I take human Nature to be most admirably held forth in all its Qualities as well as Operations: And therefore, whatever in my small Reading, occurs, concerning this our Fellow-Creature, I do never fail to set it down, by way of Common-place; and when I have occasion to write upon Human Reason, Politicks, Eloquence, or Knowledge; I lay my *Memorandums* before me, and insert them with a wonderful Facility of Application. However, among all the Qualifications, ascribed to this distinguish'd Brute, by Antient or Modern Authors; I cannot remember this Talent, of bearing his Rider to Heaven, has been recorded for a Part of his Character, except in the two Examples mentioned already; Therefore, I conceive the Methods of this Art, to be a Point of useful Knowledge in very few Hands, and which the Learned World would gladly be better informed in. This is what I have undertaken to perform in the following Discourse. For, towards the Operation already mentioned, many peculiar Properties are required, both in the *Rider* and the *Ass*; which I shall endeavour to set in as clear a Light as I can.

But, because I am resolved, by all means, to avoid giving Offence to any Party whatever; I will leave off discoursing so closely to the *Letter* as I have hitherto done, and go on for the future by way of Allegory, tho' in such a manner, that the judicious Reader, may without much straining, make his Applications as often as he shall think fit. Therefore, if you please from hence forward, instead of the Term, *Ass*, we shall make use of *Gifted*, or *enlightned Teacher*; And the Word *Rider*, we will exchange for that of *Fanatick Auditory*, or any other Denomination of the like Import. Having settled this weighty Point; the great Subject of Enquiry before us, is to examine, by what Methods this *Teacher* arrives at his *Gifts* or *Spirit*, or *Light*; and by what Intercourse between him and his Assembly, it is cultivated and supported.

In all my Writings, I have had constant Regard to this great End, not to suit and apply them to particular Occasions and Circumstances of Time, of Place, or of Person; but to calculate them for universal Nature, and Mankind in general. And of such Catholick use, I esteem this present Disquisition: For I do not remember any other Temper of Body, or Quality of Mind, wherein all Nations and Ages of the World have so unanimously agreed, as That of a *Fanatick* Strain, or Tincture of *Enthusiasm*; which improved by certain Persons or Societies of Men, and by them practised upon the rest, has been able to produce Revolutions of the greatest Figure in History; as will soon appear to those who know any thing of *Arabia*, *Persia*, *India*, or *China*, of *Morocco* and *Peru*: Farther, it has possessed as great a Power in the Kingdom of Knowledge, where it is hard to assign one Art or Science, which has not annexed to it some *Fanatick* Branch: Such are the *Philosopher's Stone; * The Grand Elixir; The Planetary Worlds; The Squaring of the Circle; The Summum bonum*; Utopian *Commonwealths*; with some others of less or subordinate Note; which all serve for nothing else, but to employ or amuse this Grain of *Enthusiasm*, dealt into every Composition.

* Some Writers hold them for the same, others not.

But, if this Plant has found a Root in the Fields of *Empire*, and of *Knowledge*, it has fixt deeper, and spread yet farther upon *Holy Ground*. Wherein, though it hath pass'd under the general Name of *Enthusiasm*, and perhaps arisen from the same Original, yet hath it produced certain Branches of a very different Nature, however often mistaken for each other. The Word in its universal Acceptation, may be defined, *A lifting up of the Soul or its Faculties above Matter*. This Description will hold good in general; but I am only to understand it, as applied to *Religion*; wherein there are three general Ways of ejaculating the Soul, or transporting it beyond the Sphere of Matter. The first, is the immediate Act of God, and is called, *Prophecy* or *Inspiration*. The second, is the immediate Act of the Devil, and is termed *Possession*. The third, is the Product of natural Causes, the effect of strong Imagination, Spleen, violent Anger, Fear, Grief, Pain, and the like. These three have been abundantly treated on by Authors, and therefore shall not employ my Enquiry. But, the fourth Method of *Religious Enthusiasm*, or launching out the Soul, as it is purely an Effect of Artifice and *Mechanick Operation*, has been sparingly handled, or not at all, by any Writer; because tho' it is an Art of great Antiquity, yet having been confined to few Persons, it long wanted those Advancements and Refinements, which it afterwards met with, since it has grown so Epidemick, and fallen into so many cultivating Hands.

It is therefore upon this *Mechanical Operation of the Spirit*, that I mean to treat, as it is at present performed by our *British Workmen*. I shall deliver to the Reader the Result of many judicious Observations upon the Matter; tracing, as near as I can, the whole Course and Method of this *Trade*, producing parallel Instances, and relating certain Discoveries that have luckily fallen in my way.

I have said, that there is one Branch of *Religious Enthusiasm*, which is purely an Effect of Nature; whereas, the Part I mean to handle, is wholly an Effect of Art, which, however, is inclined to work upon certain Natures and Constitutions, more than others. Besides, there is many an Operation, which in its Original, was purely an Artifice, but through a long Succession of Ages, hath grown to be natural. *Hippocrates*, tells us, that among our Ancestors, the *Scythians*, there was a Nation call'd, * *Longheads*, which at first began by a Custom among Midwives and Nurses, of molding, and squeezing, and bracing up the Heads of Infants; by which means, Nature shut out at one Passage, was forc'd to seek another, and finding room above, shot upwards, in the Form of a Sugar-Loaf; and being diverted that way, for some Generations, at last found it out of her self, needing no Assistance from the Nurse's Hand. This was the Original of the *Scythian Long-heads*, and thus did Custom, from being a second Nature proceed to be a first. To all which, there is something very analogous among Us of this Nation, who are the undoubted Posterity of that refined People. For, in

* *Macrocephali.*

the Age of our Fathers, there arose a Generation of Men in this Island, call'd *Round-heads*, whose Race is now spread over three Kingdoms, yet in its Beginning, was meerly an Operation of Art, produced by a pair of Cizars, a Squeeze of the Face, and a black Cap. These Heads, thus formed into a perfect Sphere in all Assemblies, were most exposed to the view of the Female Sort, which did influence their Conceptions so effectually, that Nature, at last, took the Hint, and did it of her self; so that a *Round-head* has been ever since as familiar a Sight among Us, as a *Long-head* among the *Scythians*.

UPON these Examples, and others easy to produce, I desire the curious Reader to distinguish, First between an Effect grown from *Art* into *Nature*, and one that is natural from its Beginning; Secondly, between an Effect wholly natural, and one which has only a natural Foundation, but where the Superstructure is entirely Artificial. For, the first and the last of these, I understand to come within the Districts of my Subject. And having obtained these allowances, they will serve to remove any objections that may be raised hereafter against what I shall advance.

THE Practitioners of this famous Art, proceed in general upon the following Fundamental; That, *the Corruption of the Senses is the Generation of the Spirit*: Because the *Senses* in Men are so many Avenues to the Fort of *Reason*, which in this Operation is wholly block'd up. All Endeavours must be therefore used, either to divert, bind up, stupify, fluster, and amuse the *Senses*, or else to justle them out of their Stations; and while they are either absent, or otherwise employ'd or engaged in a Civil War against each other, the *Spirit* enters and performs its Part.

Now, the usual Methods of managing the Senses upon such Conjunctures, are what I shall be very particular in delivering, as far as it is lawful for me to do; but having had the Honour to be Initiated into the Mysteries of every Society, I desire to be excused from divulging any Rites, wherein the *Profane* must have no Part.

BUT here, before I can proceed farther, a very dangerous Objection must, if possible, be removed: For, it is positively denied by certain Criticks, that the *Spirit* can by any means be introduced into an Assembly of Modern Saints, the Disparity being so great in many material Circumstances, between the Primitive Way of Inspiration, and that which is practised in the present Age. This they pretend to prove from the second Chapter of the *Acts*, where comparing both, it appears; First, that *the Apostles were gathered together with one accord in one place*; by which is meant, an universal Agreement in Opinion, and Form of Worship; a Harmony (say they) so far from being found between any two Conventicles among Us, that it is in vain to expect it between any two Heads in the same. Secondly, the *Spirit* instructed the Apostles in the Gift of speaking several Languages; a Knowledge so remote from our Dealers in this Art, that they neither understand Propriety of Words, or Phrases in their own. Lastly, (say these Objectors) The Modern Artists do utterly exclude all Approaches of the *Spirit*, and bar up its antient Way of entring, by covering themselves so close, and so industriously a top. For, they will needs have it as a Point clearly gained, that the *Cloven Tongues* never sat upon the Apostles Heads, while their Hats were on.

Now, the Force of these Objections, seems to consist in the different Acceptation of the Word, *Spirit*: which if it be understood for a supernatural Assistance, approaching from without, the Objectors have Reason, and their Assertions may be allowed; But the *Spirit* we treat of here, proceeding entirely from within, the Argument of these Adversaries is wholly eluded. And upon the same Account, our Modern Artificers, find it an Expedient of absolute Necessity, to cover their Heads as close as they can, in order to prevent Perspiration, than which nothing is observed to be a greater Spender of Mechanick Light, as we may, perhaps, farther shew in convenient Place.

To proceed therefore upon the *Phænomenon* of *Spiritual Mechanism*, It is here to be noted, that in forming and working up the *Spirit*, the Assembly has a considerable Share, as well as the Preacher; The Method of this *Arcanum*, is as follows. They violently strain their Eye balls inward, half closing the Lids; Then, as they sit, they are in a perpetual Motion of *See-saw*, making long Hums at proper Periods, and continuing the Sound at equal Height, chusing their Time in those Intermissions, while the Preacher is at Ebb. Neither is this Practice, in any part of it, so singular or improbable, as not to be traced in distant Regions, from Reading and Observation. For, first, the * *Jauguis*, or enlightened Saints of *India*, see all their Visions, by help of an acquired straining and pressure of the Eyes. Secondly, the Art of *See-saw* on a Beam, and swinging by Session upon a Cord, in order to raise artificial Extasies, hath been derived to Us, from our † *Scythian* Ancestors, where it is practised at this Day, among the Women. Lastly, the whole Proceeding, as I have here related it, is performed by the Natives of *Ireland*, with a considerable Improvement; And it is granted, that this noble Nation, hath of all others, admitted fewer Corruptions, and degenerated least from the Purity of the Old *Tartars*. Now it is usual for a Knot of *Irish*, Men and Women, to abstract themselves from Matter, bind up all their Senses, grow visionary and spiritual, by Influence of a short Pipe of Tobacco, handed round the Company; each preserving the Smoak in his Mouth, till it comes again to his Turn to take in fresh: At the same Time, there is a Consort of a continued gentle Hum, repeated and renewed by Instinct, as Occasion requires, and they move their Bodies up and down, to a Degree, that sometimes their Heads and Points lie parallel to the Horizon. Mean while, you may observe their Eyes turn'd up in the Posture of one, who endeavours to keep himself awake; by which, and many other Symptoms among them, it manifestly appears, that the Reasoning Faculties are all suspended and superseded, that Imagination hath usurped the Seat, scattering a thousand Deliriums over the Brain. Returning from this Digression, I shall describe the Methods, by which the *Spirit* approaches. The Eyes being disposed according to Art, at first, you can see nothing, but after a short pause, a small glimmering Light begins to appear, and dance before you. Then, by frequently moving your Body up and down, you perceive the Vapors to ascend very fast, till you are perfectly dosed and flustred like one who drinks too much in a Morning. Mean while, the Preacher is also at work; He begins a loud Hum, which pierces you quite thro'; This is immediately returned by the Audience, and you find your self prompted to imitate them, by a meer spontaneous Impulse, without knowing what you do.

* *Bernier, Mem. de Mogol.*

† *Guagnini Hist. Sarmat.*

The *Interstitia* are duly filled up by the Preacher, to prevent too long a Pause, under which the *Spirit* would soon faint and grow languid.

This is all I am allowed to discover about the Progress of the *Spirit*, with relation to that part, which is born by the *Assembly*; But in the Methods of the Preacher, to which I now proceed, I shall be more large and particular.

SECTION II.

YOU will read it very gravely remarked in the Books of those illustrious and right eloquent Pen-men, the Modern Travellers; that the fundamental Difference in Point of Religion, between the wild *Indians* and Us, lies in this; that We worship *God*, and they worship the *Devil*. But, there are certain Criticks, who will by no means admit of this Distinction; rather believing, that all Nations whatsoever, adore the *true God*, because, they seem to intend their Devotions to some invisible Power, of greatest *Goodness* and *Ability* to help them, which perhaps will take in the brightest Attributes ascribed to the Divinity. Others, again, inform us, that those Idolaters adore two *Principles*; the *Principle* of *Good*, and That of *Evil*: Which indeed, I am apt to look upon as the most Universal Notion, that Mankind, by the meer Light of Nature, ever entertained of Things Invisible. How this Idea hath been managed by the *Indians* and Us, and with what Advantage to the Understandings of either, may well deserve to be examined. To me, the difference appears little more than this, That They are put oftener upon their Knees by their *Fears*, and We by our *Desires*; That the former set them a *Praying*, and Us a *Cursing*. What I applaud them for, is their Discretion, in limiting their Devotions and their Deities to their several Districts, nor ever suffering the Liturgy of the *white* God, to cross or interfere with that of the *Black*. Not so with Us, who pretending by the Lines and Measures of our Reason, to extend the Dominion of one invisible Power, and contract that of the other, have discovered a gross Ignorance in the Natures of Good and Evil, and most horribly confounded the Frontiers of both.

After Men have lifted up the Throne of their Divinity to the *Cœlum Empyræum*, adorned him with all such Qualities and Accomplishments, as themselves seem most to value and possess: After they have sunk their *Principle* of *Evil* to the lowest Center, bound him with Chains, loaded him with Curses, furnish'd him with viler Dispositions than any *Rake-hell* of the Town, accoutred him with Tail, and Horns, and huge Claws, and Sawcer Eyes; I laugh aloud, to see these Reasoners, at the same time, engaged in wise Dispute, about certain Walks and Purlieus, whether they are in the Verge of God or the Devil, seriously debating, whether such and such Influences come into Mens Minds, from above or below, or whether certain Passions and Affections are guided by the Evil Spirit or the Good.

> *Dum fas atque nefas exiguo fine libidinum*
> *Discernunt avidi*——

Thus do Men establish a Fellowship of *Christ* with *Belial*, and such is the Analogy they make between *cloven Tongues*, and *cloven Feet*. Of the like Nature is the Disquisition before us: It hath continued these hundred Years an even Debate, whether the Deportment and the Cant of our *English* Enthusiastick Preachers, were *Possession*, or *Inspiration*, and a World of Argument has been drained on either side, perhaps, to little Purpose. For, I think, it is in *Life* as in *Tragedy*, where, it is held, a Conviction of great Defect, both in Order and Invention, to interpose the Assistance of preternatural Power, without an absolute and last Necessity. However, it is a Sketch of Human Vanity, for every Individual, to imagine the whole Universe is interess'd in his meanest Concern. If he hath got cleanly over a Kennel, some Angel, unseen, descended on purpose to help him by the Hand; if he hath knockt his Head against a Post, it was the Devil, for his Sins, let loose from Hell, on purpose to buffet him. Who, that sees a little paultry Mortal, droning, and dreaming, and drivelling to a Multitude, can think it agreeable to common good Sense, that either Heaven or Hell should be put to the Trouble of Influence or Inspection upon what he is about? Therefore, I am resolved immediately, to weed this Error out of Mankind, by making it clear, that this Mystery, of venting spiritual Gifts is nothing but a *Trade*, acquired by as much Instruction, and mastered by equal Practice and Application as others are. This will best appear, by describing and deducing the whole Process of the Operation, as variously as it hath fallen under my Knowledge or Experience.

* * * * * * * * * *
* * * * * * * * * *
* * * * * * * * * *

Here the whole Scheme of spiritual Mechanism was deduced and explained, with an Appearance of great reading and observation; but it was thought neither safe nor Convenient to Print it.

* * * * * * * * * *

HERE it may not be amiss, to add a few Words upon the laudable Practice of wearing *quilted Caps*; which is not a Matter of meer Custom, Humor, or Fashion, as some would pretend, but an Institution of great Sagacity and Use; these, when moistned with Sweat, stop all Perspiration, and by reverberating the Heat, prevent the Spirit from evaporating any way, but at the Mouth; even as a skilful Housewife, that covers her Still with a wet Clout, for the same Reason, and finds the same Effect. For, it is the Opinion of Choice *Virtuosi*, that the Brain is only a Crowd of little Animals, but with Teeth and Claws extremely sharp, and therefore, cling together in the Contexture we behold, like the Picture of *Hobbes*'s *Leviathan*, or like Bees in perpendicular swarm upon a Tree, or like a Carrion corrupted into Vermin, still preserving the Shape and Figure of the Mother Animal. That all Invention is formed by the Morsure of two or more of these Animals, upon certain capillary Nerves, which proceed from thence, whereof three Branches spread into the Tongue, and two into the right Hand. They hold also, that these Animals are of a Constitution extremely cold; that their Food is the Air we attract, their Excrement Phlegm; and that what we vulgarly call Rheums, and Colds, and Distillations, is nothing else but an Epidemical Looseness, to which that little Commonwealth is very subject, from the Climate it lyes under. Farther, that nothing less than a violent Heat, can disentangle these Creatures from their hamated Station of Life, or give them Vigor and Humor, to imprint the Marks of their little Teeth. That if the Morsure be Hexagonal, it produces Poetry; the Circular gives Eloquence; If the Bite hath been Conical, the Person, whose Nerve is so affected, shall be disposed to write upon the Politicks; and so of the rest.

I shall now Discourse briefly, by what kind of Practices the Voice is best governed, towards the Composition and Improvement of the *Spirit*; for, without a competent Skill in tuning and toning each Word, and Syllable, and Letter, to their due Cadence, the whole Operation is incompleat, misses entirely of its effect on the Hearers, and puts the Workman himself to continual Pains for new Supplies, without Success. For, it is to be understood, that in the Language of the Spirit, *Cant* and *Droning* supply the Place of *Sense* and *Reason*, in the Language of Men: Because, in Spiritual Harangues, the Disposition of the Words according to the Art of Grammar, hath not the least Use, but the Skill and Influence wholly lye in the Choice and Cadence of the Syllables; Even as a discreet *Composer*, who in setting a Song, changes the Words and Order so often, that he is forced to make it *Nonsense*, before he can make it *Musick*. For this Reason, it hath been held by some, that the Art of Canting is ever in greatest Perfection, when managed by *Ignorance*: Which is thought to be enigmatically meant by *Plutarch*, when he tells us, that the best Musical Instruments were made from the Bones of an *Ass*. And the profounder Criticks upon that Passage, are of Opinion, the Word in its genuine Signification, means no other than a *Jaw-bone*: tho' some rather think it to have been the *Os sacrum*; but in so nice a Case, I shall not take upon me to decide: The Curious are at Liberty, to *pick* from it whatever they please.

THE first Ingredient, towards the Art of Canting, is a competent Share of *Inward Light*: that is to say, a large Memory, plentifully fraught with Theological Polysyllables, and mysterious Texts from holy Writ, applied and digested by those Methods, and Mechanical Operations already related: The Bearers of this *Light*, resembling *Lanthorns*, compact of Leaves from old *Geneva* Bibles; Which Invention, Sir *Humphry Edwyn*, during his Mayoralty, of happy Memory, highly approved and advanced; affirming, the Scripture to be now fulfilled, where it says, *Thy Word is a Lanthorn to my Feet, and a Light to my Paths.*

Now, the Art of *Canting* consists in skilfully adapting the Voice, to whatever Words the Spirit delivers, that each may strike the Ears of the Audience, with its most significant Cadence. The Force, or Energy of this Eloquence, is not to be found, as among antient Orators, in the Disposition of Words to a Sentence, or the turning of long Periods; but agreeable to the Modern Refinements in Musick, is taken up wholly in dwelling, and dilating upon Syllables and Letters. Thus it is frequent for a single *Vowel* to draw Sighs from a Multitude; and for a whole Assembly of Saints to sob to the Musick of one solitary *Liquid.* But these are Trifles; when even Sounds inarticulate are observed to produce as forcible Effects. A Master Work-man shall *blow his Nose so powerfully*, as to pierce the Hearts of his People, who are disposed to receive the *Excrements* of his Brain with the same Reverence, as the *Issue* of it. Hawking, Spitting, and Belching, the Defects of other Mens Rhetorick, are the Flowers, and Figures, and Ornaments of his. For, the *Spirit* being the same in all, it is of no Import through what Vehicle it is convey'd.

It is a Point of too much Difficulty, to draw the Principles of this famous Art within the Compass of certain adequate Rules. However, perhaps, I may one day, oblige the World with my Critical Essay upon the Art of *Canting, Philosophically, Physically, and Musically considered.*

But, among all Improvements of the *Spirit*, wherein the Voice hath born a Part, there is none to be compared with That of *conveying the Sound thro' the Nose*, which under the Denomination of **Snuffling*, hath passed with so great Applause in the World. The Originals of this Institution are very dark; but having been initiated into the Mystery of it, and Leave being given me to publish it to the World, I shall deliver as direct a Relation as I can.

This Art, like many other famous Inventions, owed its Birth, or at least, Improvement and Perfection, to an Effect of Chance,

* *The* Snuffling *of Men, who have lost their Noses by lewd Courses, is said to have given Rise to that Tone, which our Dissenters did too much Affect.* W. Wotton.

but was established upon solid Reasons, and hath flourished in this Island ever since, with great Lustre. All agree, that it first appeared upon the Decay and Discouragement of *Bag-pipes*, which having long suffered under the Mortal Hatred of the *Brethren*, tottered for a Time, and at last fell with *Monarchy*. The Story is thus related.

As yet, *Snuffling* was not; when the following Adventure happened to a *Banbury Saint*. Upon a certain Day, while he was far engaged among the Tabernacles of the *Wicked*, he felt the Outward Man put into odd Commotions, and strangely prick'd forward by the Inward: An Effect very usual among the Modern Inspired. For, some think, that the *Spirit* is apt to feed on the *Flesh*, like hungry Wines upon raw Beef. Others rather believe, there is a perpetual Game at *Leap-Frog* between both; and, sometimes, the *Flesh* is uppermost, and sometimes the *Spirit*; adding, that the former, while it is in the State of a *Rider*, wears huge *Rippon* Spurs, and when it comes to the Turn of being *Bearer*, is wonderfully headstrong, and hard-mouth'd. However it came about, the *Saint* felt his *Vessel* full *extended* in every Part (a very natural Effect of strong *Inspiration*;) and the Place and Time falling out so unluckily, that he could not have the Convenience of Evacuating upwards, by Repetition, Prayer, or Lecture; he was forced to open an inferior Vent. In short, he wrestled with the Flesh so long, that he at length subdued it, coming off with honourable Wounds, all *before*. The Surgeon had now cured the Parts, primarily affected; but the Disease driven from its Post, flew up into his Head; And, as a skilful General, valiantly attack'd in his Trenches, and beaten from the Field, by flying Marches withdraws to the Capital City, breaking down the Bridges to prevent Pursuit; So the Disease repell'd from its first Station, fled before the *Rod* of *Hermes*, to the upper Region, there fortifying it self; but, finding the Foe making Attacks at the *Nose*, broke down the *Bridge*, and retir'd to the *Head*-Quarters. Now, the Naturalists observe, that there is in human Noses, an *Idiosyncrasy*, by Virtue of which, the more the Passage is obstructed, the more our Speech delights to go through, as the Musick of a Flagelate is made by the *Stops*. By this Method, the Twang of the Nose, becomes perfectly to resemble the *Snuffle* of a Bag-pipe, and is found to be equally attractive of *British* Ears; whereof the Saint had sudden Experience, by practising his new Faculty with wonderful Success in the Operation of the *Spirit*: For, in a short Time, no Doctrine pass'd for Sound and Orthodox, unless it were delivered thro' the Nose. Strait, every Pastor copy'd after this Original; and those, who could not otherwise arrive to a Perfection, spirited by a noble Zeal, made use of the same Experiment to acquire it. So that, I think, it may be truly affirmed, the *Saints* owe their Empire to the *Snuffling* of one *Animal*, as *Darius* did his, to the *Neighing* of another; and both Stratagems were performed by the same Art; for we read, how the * *Persian Beast* acquired his Faculty, by *covering a Mare* the Day Before.

* *Herodot.*

I should now have done, if I were not convinced, that whatever I have yet advanced upon this Subject, is liable to great Exception. For, allowing all I have said to be true, it may still be justly objected, that there is in the Commonwealth of *artificial Enthusiasm*, some real Foundation for Art to work upon in the Temper and Complexion of Individuals, which other Mortals seem to want. Observe, but the Gesture, the Motion, and the Countenance, of some choice Professors, tho' in their most familiar Actions, you will find them of a different Race from the rest of human Creatures. Remark your commonest Pretender to a Light *within*, how dark, and dirty, and gloomy he is *without*; As Lanthorns, which the more Light they bear in their Bodies, cast out so much the more Soot, and Smoak, and fuliginous Matter to adhere to the Sides. Listen, but to their ordinary Talk, and look on the Mouth that delivers it; you will imagine you are hearing some antient Oracle, and your Understanding will be *equally* informed. Upon these, and the like Reasons, certain Objectors pretend to put it beyond all Doubt, that there must be a sort of preternatural *Spirit*, possessing the Heads of the Modern Saints; And some will have it to be the *Heat* of Zeal, working upon the *Dregs* of Ignorance, as other *Spirits* are produced from *Lees*, by the Force of Fire. Some again think, that when our earthly Tabernacles are disordered and desolate, shaken and out of Repair; the *Spirit* delights to dwell within them, as Houses are said to be haunted, when they are forsaken and gone to Decay.

To set this Matter in as fair a Light as possible; I shall here, very briefly, deduce the History of *Fanaticism*, from the most early Ages to the present. And if we are able to fix upon any one material or fundamental Point, wherein the chief Professors have universally agreed, I think we may reasonably lay hold on That, and assign it for the great Seed or Principle of the *Spirit*.

THE most early Traces we meet with, of *Fanaticks*, in antient Story, are among the *Ægyptians*, who instituted those Rites, known in *Greece* by the Names of *Orgya*, *Panegyres*, and *Dionysia*, whether introduced there by *Orpheus* or *Melampus*, we shall not dispute at present, nor in all likelihood, at any time for the future. These Feasts were celebrated to the Honor of *Osyris*, whom the *Grecians* called *Dionysius*, and is the same with *Bacchus*: Which has betray'd some superficial Readers to imagine, that the whole Business was nothing more than a Set of roaring, scouring Companions, overcharg'd with Wine; but this is a scandalous Mistake foisted on the World, by a sort of Modern Authors, who have too *literal* an Understanding; and, because Antiquity is to be traced *backwards*, do therefore, like *Jews*, begin their Books at the wrong End, as if Learning were a sort of *Conjuring*. These are the Men, who pretend to understand a Book, by scouting thro' the *Index*, as if a Traveller should go about to describe a *Palace*, when he had seen nothing but the *Privy*; or like certain Fortune-tellers in *Northern America*, who have a Way of reading a Man's Destiny, by peeping in his *Breech*. For, at the Time of instituting these Mysteries, * there was not one Vine in all *Egypt*, the Natives drinking nothing but *Ale*; which Liquor seems to have been far more antient than Wine, and has the Honor of owing its Invention and Progress, not only to the † *Egyptian Osyris*, but to the *Grecian Bacchus*, who in their famous Expedition, carried the Receipt of it along with them, and gave it to the Nations they visited or subdued. Besides, *Bacchus* himself, was very seldom, or never Drunk: For, it is recorded of him, that he was the first * Inventor of the *Mitre*, which he wore con-

Diod. Sic. L. I. *Plut. de Iside & Osyride.*

* *Herod.* L.2.

† *Diod. Sic.* L. I. & 3.

* *Id.* L. 4.

tinually on his Head (as the whole Company of *Bacchanals* did) to prevent Vapors and the Head-ach, after hard Drinking. And for this Reason (say some) the *Scarlet Whore*, when she makes the Kings of the Earth drunk with her Cup of Abomination, is always sober her self, tho' she never balks the Glass in her Turn, being, it seems, kept upon her Legs by the Virtue of her *Triple Mitre*. Now, these Feasts were instituted in imitation of the famous Expedition *Osyris* made thro' the World, and of the Company that attended him, whereof the *Bacchanalian* Ceremonies were so many Types and Symbols. From which Account, it is manifest, that the Fanatick Rites of these *Bacchanals*, cannot be imputed to Intoxications by Wine, but must needs have had a deeper Foundation. What this was, we may gather large Hints from certain Circumstances in the Course of their Mysteries. For, in the first Place, there was in their Processions, an entire *Mixture and Confusion of Sexes*; they affected to ramble about Hills and Desarts: Their Garlands were of *Ivy* and *Vine*, Emblems of Cleaving and Clinging; or of *Fir*, the Parent of *Turpentine*. It is added, that they imitated *Satyrs*, were attended by *Goats*, and rode upon *Asses*, all Companions of great Skill and Practice in Affairs of Gallantry. They bore for their Ensigns, certain curious Figures, perch'd upon long Poles, made into the Shape and Size of the *Virga genitalis*, with its *Appurtenances*, which were so many Shadows and Emblems of the whole Mystery, as well as Trophies set up by the Female Conquerors. Lastly, in a certain Town of *Attica*, the whole Solemnity * stript of all its Types, was performed in *puris naturalibus*, the Votaries, not flying in Coveys, but sorted into Couples. The same may be farther conjectured from the Death of *Orpheus*, one of the Institutors of these Mysteries, who was torn in Pieces by Women, because he refused to † *communicate his Orgyes* to them; which others explained, by telling us, he had *castrated* himself upon Grief, for the Loss of his Wife.

See the Particulars in Diod. Sic. L. 1. & 3.

* *Dionysia Brauronia.*

† *Vid. Photium in excerptis è Conone.*

Omitting many others of less Note, the next *Fanaticks* we meet with, of any Eminence, were the numerous Sects of *Hereticks* appearing in the five first Centuries of the *Christian Æra*, from *Simon Magus* and his Followers, to those of *Eutyches*. I have collected their Systems from infinite Reading, and comparing them with those of their Successors in the several Ages since, I find there are certain Bounds set even to the Irregularities of Human Thought, and those a great deal narrower than is commonly apprehended. For, as they all frequently interfere, even in their wildest Ravings; So there is one fundamental Point, wherein they are sure to meet, as Lines in a Center, and that is the *Community of Women*: Great were their Sollicitudes in this Matter, and they never fail'd of certain Articles in their Schemes of Worship, on purpose to establish it.

THE last *Fanaticks* of Note, were those which started up in *Germany*, a little after the *Reformation* of *Luther*; Springing, as *Mushrooms* do at the *End of a Harvest*; Such were *John* of *Leyden*, *David George*, *Adam Neuster*, and many others; whose Visions and Revelations, always terminated in *leading about half a dozen Sisters, apiece*, and making That Practice a fundamental Part of their System. For, Human Life is a continual Navigation, and, if we expect our *Vessels* to pass with Safety, thro' the Waves and Tempests of this fluctuating World, it is necessary to make a good Provision of the *Flesh*, as Sea-men lay in store of *Beef* for a long Voyage.

Now from this brief Survey of some Principal Sects, among the *Fanaticks*, in all Ages (having omitted the *Mahometans* and others, who might also help to confirm the Argument I am about) to which I might add several among our selves, such as the *Family of Love*, *Sweet Singers of Israel*, and the like: And from reflecting upon that fundamental Point in their Doctrines, about *Women*, wherein they have so unanimously agreed; I am apt to imagine, that the Seed or Principle, which has ever put Men upon *Visions* in Things *Invisible*, is of a Corporeal Nature: For the profounder Chymists inform us, that the Strongest *Spirits* may be extracted from *Human Flesh*. Besides, the Spinal Marrow, being nothing else but a Continuation of the Brain, must needs create a very free Communication between the Superior Faculties and those below: And thus the *Thorn in the Flesh* serves for a *Spur* to the *Spirit*. I think, it is agreed among Physicians, that nothing affects the Head so much, as a tentiginous Humor, repelled and elated to the upper Region, found by daily practice, to run frequently up into Madness. A very eminent Member of the Faculty, assured me, that when the *Quakers* first appeared, he seldom was without some Female Patients among them, for the *furor*——. Persons of a visionary Devotion, either Men or Women, are in their Complexion, of all others, the most amorous: For, *Zeal* is frequently kindled from the same Spark with other Fires, and from inflaming Brotherly Love, will proceed to raise That of a Gallant. If we inspect into the usual Process of modern Courtship, we shall find it to consist in a devout Turn of the Eyes, called *Ogling*; an artificial Form of Canting and Whining by rote, every Interval, for want of other Matter, made up with a Shrug, or a Hum, a Sigh or a Groan; The Style compact of insignificant Words, Incoherences and Repetition. These, I take, to be the most accomplish'd Rules of Address to a Mistress; and where are these performed with more Dexterity, than by the *Saints*? Nay, to bring this Argument yet closer, I have been informed by certain Sanguine Brethren of the first Class, that in the Height and *Orgasmus* of their Spiritual exercise it has been frequent with them * * * * *; immediately after which, they found the *Spirit* to relax and flag of a sudden with the Nerves, and they were forced to hasten to a Conclusion. This may be farther Strengthened, by observing, with Wonder, how unaccountably all Females are attracted by Visionary or Enthusiastick Preachers, tho' never so contemptible in their *outward Men*; which is usually supposed to be done upon Considerations, purely Spiritual, without any carnal Regards at all. But I have Reason to think, the *Sex* hath certain Characteristicks, by which they form a truer Judgment of Human Abilities and Performings, than we our selves can possibly do of each other. Let That be as it will, thus much is certain, that however Spiritual Intrigues begin, they generally conclude like all others; they may branch upwards toward Heaven, but the Root is in the Earth. Too intense a Contemplation is not the Business of Flesh and Blood; it must by the necessary Course of Things, in a little Time, let go its Hold, and fall into *Matter*. Lovers, for the sake of Celestial Converse, are but another sort of *Platonicks*, who pretend to see Stars and Heaven in Ladies Eyes, and to look or think no lower; but the same *Pit* is provided for both; and they seem a perfect Moral to the Story of that Philosopher, who, while his Thoughts and Eyes were fixed upon the *Constellations*, found himself seduced by his *lower Parts* into a *Ditch*.

I had somewhat more to say upon this Part of the Subject; but the Post is just going, which forces me in great Haste to conclude,

SIR,

Yours, &c.

Pray, burn this Letter as soon as it comes to your Hands.

FINIS.

A

MEDITATION

UPON A

Broom-Stick,

AND

Somewhat Beside;

OF

The Same AUTHOR's.

——*Utile dulci.*

LONDON:

Printed for E. *Curll*, at the *Dial* and *Bible* against St. *Dunstan's* Church in *Fleetstreet*; and sold by *J. Harding*, at the *Post-Office* in St. *Martins-Lane*. 1710.

(Price 6 *d.*)

Given me by John Cliffe Esq, who had them of the Bp of Killala in Ireland, whose Daughter he married & was my Lodger — E. Curll.

A

MEDITATION

UPON A

BROOM-STICK:

ACCORDING TO

The Style and Manner of the Honourable Robert Boyle's *Meditations*.

Written in the YEAR 1703.

THIS single Stick, which you now behold ingloriously lying in that neglected Corner, I once knew in a flourishing State in a Forest: It was full of Sap, full of Leaves, and full of Boughs: But now, in vain does the busy Art of Man pretend to vye with Nature, by tying that withered Bundle of Twigs to its sapless Trunk: It is now at best but the Reverse of what it was; a Tree turned upside down, the Branches on the Earth, and the Root in the Air: It is now handled by every dirty Wench, condemned to do her Drugery; and by a capricious Kind of Fate, destined to make other Things clean, and be nasty it self. At length, worn to the Stumps in the Service of the Maids, it is either thrown out of Doors, or condemned to its last Use of kindling a Fire. When I beheld this, I sighed, and said within my self SURELY MORTAL MAN IS A BROOMSTICK; Nature sent him into the World strong and lusty, in a thriving Condition, wearing his own Hair on his Head, the proper Branches of this reasoning Vegetable; till the Axe of Intemperance has lopped off his Green Boughs, and left him a withered Trunk: He then flies to Art, and puts on a *Perriwig*; valuing himself upon an unnatural Bundle of Hairs, all covered with Powder, that never grew on his Head: But now, should this our *Broom-stick* pretend to enter the Scene, proud of those *Birchen* Spoils it never bore, and all covered with Dust, though the Sweepings of the finest Lady's Chamber; we should be apt to ridicule and despise its Vanity. Partial Judges that we are of our own Excellencies, and other Mens Defaults!

But a *Broom-stick*, perhaps you will say, is an Emblem of a Tree standing on its Head; and pray what is Man but a topsy-turvy Creature? His Animal Faculties perpetually mounted on his Rational; his Head where his Heels should be, groveling on the Earth. And yet, with all his Faults, he sets up to be a universal Reformer and Correcter of Abuses; a Remover of Grievances; rakes into every Slut's Corner of Nature, bringing hidden Corruptions to the Light, and raiseth a mighty Dust where there was none before; sharing deeply all the while in the very same Pollutions he pretends to sweep away. His last Days are spent in Slavery to Women, and generally the least deserving; till worn to the Stumps, like his Brother *Bezom*, he is either kicked out of Doors, or made use of to kindle Flames for others to warm themselves by.

A

Tritical Essay upon the Faculties of the Mind

To - - - - - - - -

Sir,

BEING so great a Lover of Antiquities, it was reasonable to suppose you would be very much obliged with any Thing that was new. I have been of late offended with many Writers of Essays and moral Discourses, for running into stale Topicks and thread-bare Quotations, and not handling their Subject fully and closely: All which Errors I have carefully avoided in the following Essay, which I have proposed as a Pattern for young Writers to imitate. The Thoughts and Observations being entirely new, the Quotations untouched by others, the Subject of mighty Importance, and treated with much Order and Perspicuity: It hath cost me a great deal of Time; and I desire you will accept and consider it as the utmost Effort of my Genius.

A

Tritical ESSAY, &c.

PHILOSOPHERS say, that Man is a Microcosm or little World, resembling in Miniature every Part of the great: And, in my Opinion, the Body Natural may be compared to the Body Politick: And if this be so, how can the *Epicureans* Opinion be true, that the Universe was formed by a fortuitous

Concourse of Atoms; which I will no more believe, than that the accidental Jumbling of the Letters in the Alphabet, could fall by Chance into a most ingenious and learned Treatise of Philosophy, *Risum teneatis Amici*, HOR. This false Opinion must needs create many more; it is like an Error in the first Concoction, which cannot be corrected in the second; the Foundation is weak, and whatever Superstructure you raise upon it, must of Necessity fall to the Ground. Thus Men are led from one Error to another, till with *Ixion* they embrace a Cloud instead of *Juno*; or, like the Dog in the Fable, lose the Substance in gaping at the Shadow. For such Opinions cannot cohere; but like the Iron and Clay in the Toes of *Nebuchadnezzar*'s Image, must separate and break in Pieces. I have read in a certain Author, that *Alexander* wept because he had no more Worlds to conquer; which he need not have done, if the fortuitous Concourse of Atoms could create one: But this is an Opinion fitter for that many-headed Beast, the Vulgar, to entertain, than for so wise a Man as *Epicurus*; the corrupt Part of his Sect only borrowed his Name, as the Monkey did the Cat's Claw, to draw the Chesnut out of the Fire.

HOWEVER, the first Step to the Cure is to know the Disease; and although Truth may be difficult to find, because, as the Philosopher observes, she lives in the Bottom of a Well; yet we need not, like blind Men, grope in open Day-light. I hope, I may be allowed, among so many far more learned Men, to offer my Mite, since a Stander-by may sometimes, perhaps, see more of the Game than he that plays it. But I do not think a Philosopher obliged to account for every Phænomenon in Nature; or drown himself with *Aristotle*, for not being able to solve the Ebbing and Flowing of the Tide, in that fatal Sentence he passed upon himself, *Quia te non capio, tu capies me*.

WHEREIN he was at once the Judge and the Criminal, the Accuser and Executioner. *Socrates*, on the other Hand, who said he knew nothing, was pronounced by the Oracle to be the wisest Man in the World.

BUT to return from this Digression; I think it as clear as any Demonstration in *Euclid*, that Nature does nothing in vain; if we were able to dive into her secret Recesses, we should find that the smallest Blade of Grass, or most contemptible Weed, has its particular Use; but she is chiefly admirable in her minutest Compositions, the least and most contemptible Insect most discovers the Art of Nature, if I may so call it; although Nature, which delights in Variety, will always triumph over Art: And as the Poet observes,

Naturam expellas furcâ licet, usque recurret. Hor.

BUT the various Opinions of Philosophers, have scattered through the World as many Plagues of the Mind, as *Pandora*'s Box did those of the Body; only with this Difference, that they have not left Hope at the Bottom. And if Truth be not fled with *Astræa*, she is certainly as hidden as the Source of *Nile*, and can be found only in *Utopia*. Not that I would reflect on those wise Sages, which would be a Sort of Ingratitude; and he that calls a Man ungrateful, sums up all the Evil that a Man can be guilty of.

Ingratum si dixeris, omnia dicis.

BUT what I blame the Philosophers for, (although some may think it a Paradox) is chiefly their Pride; nothing less than an *ipse dixit*, and you must pin your Faith on their Sleeve. And, although *Diogenes* lived in a Tub, there might be, for ought I know, as much Pride under his Rags, as in the fine spun Garment of the Divine *Plato*. It is reported of this *Diogenes*, that when *Alexander* came to see him, and promised to give him whatever he would ask; the *Cynick* only answered, *Take not from me, what thou canst not give me*; *but stand from between me and the Light*; which was almost as extravagant as the Philosopher that flung his Money into the Sea, with this remarkable Saying, ———

HOW different was this Man from the Usurer, who being told his Son would spend all he had got, replied, *He cannot take more Pleasure in spending, than I did in getting it*. These Men could see the Faults of each other, but not their own; those they flung into the Bag behind; *Non videmus id manticæ quod in tergo est*. I may, perhaps, be censured for my free Opinions, by those carping *Momus*'s, whom Authors worship as the *Indians* do the Devil, for fear. They will endeavour to give my Reputation as many

Wounds as the Man in the Almanack; but I value it not; and perhaps, like Flies, they may buz so often about the Candle, till they burn their Wings. They must pardon me, if I venture to give them this Advice, not to rail at what they cannot understand; it does but discover that self-tormenting Passion of Envy; than which, the greatest Tyrant never invented a more cruel Torment.

Invidia Siculi non invenere Tyranni
Tormentum majus.——— Juven.

I MUST be so bold, to tell my Criticks and Witlings, that they are no more Judges of this, than a Man that is born blind can have any true Idea of Colours. I have always observed, that your empty Vessels sound loudest: I value their Lashes as little, as the Sea did when *Xerxes* whipped it. The utmost Favour a Man can expect from them, is that which *Polyphemus* promised *Ulysses*, that he would devour him the last: They think to subdue a Writer, as *Cæsar* did his Enemy, with a *Veni, vidi, vici*. I confess, I value the Opinion of the judicious Few, a *Rymer*, a *Dennis*, or a *Walsh*; but for the rest, to give my Judgment at once; I think the long Dispute among the Philosophers about a *Vacuum*, may be determined in the Affirmative, that it is to be found in a Critick's Head. They are, at best, but the Drones of the learned World, who devour the Honey, and will not work themselves; and a Writer need no more regard them, than the Moon does the Barking of a little sensless Cur. For, in spight of their terrible Roaring, you may with half an Eye discover the *Ass* under the *Lyon*'s Skin.

BUT to return to our Discourse: *Demosthenes* being asked, what was the first Part of an Orator, replied, *Action*: What was the Second, *Action*: What was the Third, *Action*: And so on *ad infinitum*. This may be true in Oratory; but Contemplation, in other Things, exceeds Action. And, therefore, a wise Man is never less alone, than when he is alone:

Nunquam minus solus, quàm cum solus.

AND *Archimedes*, the famous Mathematician, was so intent upon his Problems, that he never minded the Soldier who came to kill him. Therefore, not to detract from the just Praise which belongs to Orators; they ought to consider that Nature, which gave us two Eyes to see, and two Ears to hear, hath given us but one Tongue to speak; wherein, however, some do so abound; that the *Virtuosi*, who have been so long in Search for the perpetual Motion, may infallibly find it there.

SOME Men admire Republicks; because, Orators flourish there most, and are the great Enemies of Tyranny: But my Opinion is, that one Tyrant is better than an Hundred. Besides, these Orators inflame the People, whose Anger is really but a short Fit of Madness.

Ira furor brevis est.——— Horat.

AFTER which, Laws are like Cobwebs, which may catch small Flies, but let Wasps and Hornets break through. But in Oratory, the greatest Art is to hide Art.

Artis est celare Artem.

BUT this must be the Work of Time; we must lay hold on all Opportunities, and let slip no Occasion, else we shall be forced to weave *Penelope*'s Web; unravel in the Night what we spun in the Day. And, therefore, I have observed that Time is painted with a Lock before, and bald behind; signifying thereby, that we must take Time (as we say) by the Forelock; for when it is once past, there is no recalling it.

THE Mind of Man is, at first, (if you will pardon the Expression) like a *Tabula rasa*; or like Wax, which while it is soft, is capable of any Impression, until Time hath hardened it. And at length Death, that grim Tyrant, stops us in the Midst of our Career. The greatest Conquerors have at last been conquered by Death, which spares none from the Sceptre to the Spade.

Mors omnibus communis.

ALL Rivers go to the Sea, but none return from it. *Xerxes* wept when he beheld his Army; to consider that in less than an Hundred Years they would all be dead. *Anacreon* was choqued with a Grape-stone; and violent Joy kills as well as violent Grief.

There is nothing in this World constant, but Inconstancy; yet *Plato* thought, that if Virtue would appear to the World in her own native Dress, all Men would be enamoured with her. But now, since Interest governs the World, and Men neglect the Golden Mean, *Jupiter* himself, if he came on the Earth, would be despised, unless it were as he did to *Danaæ*, in a golden Shower. For Men, now-a-days, worship the rising Sun, and not the setting.

Donec eris fœlix, multos numerabis amicos.

THUS have I, in Obedience to your Commands, ventured to expose my self to Censure in this Critical Age. Whether I have done Right to my Subject, must be left to the Judgment of the learned Reader: However, I cannot but hope, that my attempting of it may be an Encouragement for some able Pen to perform it with more Success.

Mr. C——ns's DISCOURSE OF Free-Thinking,

Put into plain *English*, by way of

ABSTRACT,

FOR THE

Use of the Poor.

By a Friend of the AUTHOR.

LONDON

Printed for *John Morphew*, near *Stationers-Hall* 1713. Price 4 *d.*

OUR *Party having failed, by all their Political Arguments, to re-establish their Power; the wise Leaders have determined, that the last and principal* Remedy *should be made use of, for opening the Eyes of this blinded Nation; and that a short, but perfect, System of their* Divinity, *should be publish'd, to which we are all of us ready to subscribe, and which we lay down as a Model, bearing a close Analogy to our Schemes in* Religion. *Crafty designing Men, that they might keep the World in Awe, have, in their several Forms of Government, placed a* Supream Power *on* Earth, *to keep human Kind in fear of being* Hanged; *and a* Supream Power *in* Heaven, *for fear of being* Damned. *In order to cure Mens Apprehensions of the former, several of our learned Members have writ many profound Treatises in* Anarchy; *but a brief compleat Body of* Atheology *seemed yet wanting, till this irrefragable Discourse appeared. However it so happens, that our ablest Brethren, in their elaborate Disquisitions upon this Subject, have written with so much Caution, that ignorant* Unbelievers *have edified very little by them. I grant that those daring Spirits, who first adventured to write against the direct* Rules *of the Gospel, the Current of Antiquity, the* Religion *of the Magistrate, and the* Laws *of the* Land, *had some Measures to keep; and particularly when they railed at* Religion, *were in the right to use little artful Disguises, by which a Jury could only find them guilty of abusing Heathenism or Popery. But the* Mystery *is now* revealed, *that there is no such Thing as* Mystery *or* Revelation; *and though our Friends are out of Place and Power, yet we may have so much Confidence in the present Ministry to be secure, that those who suffer so many* Free Speeches *against their Sovereign and themselves to pass unpunished, will never resent our expressing the* freest Thoughts *against their Religion; but think with* Tiberius, *That if there be a God, he is able enough to revenge any Injuries done to himself, without expecting the* Civil Power *to interpose.*

By these Reflections I was brought to think, that the most ingenious Author of the Discourse upon Free Thinking, *in a Letter to* Somebody, Esq; *although he hath used less reserve than any of his Predecessors, might yet have been more free and open. I considered, that several* Well-willers *to* Infidelity *might be discouraged by a shew of Logick, and multiplicity of Quotations, scattered through his*

Book, which to Understandings of that Size might carry an appearance of something like Book-learning, *and consequently fright them from reading for their Improvement: I could see no* Reason *why these great Discoveries should be hid from our Youth of Quality, who frequent* White*'s and* Tom*'s; why they should not be adapted to the Capacities of the* Kit-Cat *and* Hannover *Clubs, who might* then *be able to read Lectures on them to their several* Toasts: *And it will be allowed on all Hands, that nothing can sooner help to restore our abdicated Cause, than a firm universal Belief of the Principles laid down by this sublime Author.*

For I am sensible that nothing would more contribute to the continuance of the War, *and the Restoration of the late Ministry, than to have the Doctrines delivered in this Treatise well infused into the People. I have therefore compiled them into the following Abstract, wherein I have adhered to the very Words of our Author, only adding some few Explanations of my own, where the Terms happen to be too learned, and consequently a little beyond the Comprehension of those for whom the Work was principally intended, I mean the Nobility and Gentry of our Party. After which I hope it will be impossible for the Malice of a* Jacobite, High-flying, Priest-ridden Faction, *to misrepresent us. The few Additions I have made, are for no other use than to help the Transition, which could not otherwise be kept in an Abstract; but I have not presumed to advance any thing of my own; which besides would be needless to an Author, who hath so fully handled and demonstrated every Particular. I shall only add, that though this Writer, when he speaks of* Priests, *desires chiefly to be understood to mean the* English *Clergy, yet he includes all* Priests *whatsoever, except the antient and modern* Heathens, *the* Turks, Quakers, *and* Socinians.

The LETTER.

SIR,

I Send you this Apology for *Free Thinking*, without the least hopes of doing good, but purely to comply with your Request; for those Truths which no Body can deny, will do no good to those who deny them. The Clergy, who are so impudent to teach the People the Doctrines of Faith, are all either cunning Knaves or mad Fools; for none but artificial designing Men, and crackt-brained Enthusiasts, presume to be Guides to others in matters of Speculation, which all the Doctrines of Christianity are; and whoever has a mind to learn the Christian Religion, naturally chuses such Knaves and Fools to teach them. Now the *Bible*, which contains the Precepts of the Priests Religion, is the most difficult Book in the World to be understood; It requires a thorow Knowledge in Natural, Civil, Ecclesiastical History, Law, Husbandry, Sailing, Physick, Pharmacy, Mathematicks, Metaphysicks, Ethicks, and every thing else that can be named: And every Body who believes it, ought to understand it, and must do so by force of his own *Free Thinking*, without any Guide or Instructor.

How can a Man *think* at all, if he does not think freely? A Man who does not eat and drink freely, does not eat and drink at all. Why may not I be deny'd the liberty of *Free-seeing*, as well as *Free-thinking?* Yet no body pretends that the first is unlawful, for a Cat may look on a King; though you be near-sighted, or have weak or soar Eyes, or are blind, you may be a *Free-seer*; you ought to see for your self, and not trust to a Guide to chuse the Colour of your Stockings, or save you from falling into a Ditch.

In like manner there ought to be no restraint at all on *thinking freely* upon any Proposition, however impious or absurd. There is not the least hurt in the wickedest Thoughts, provided they be free; nor in telling those Thoughts to every Body, and endeavouring to convince the World of them; for all this is included in the Doctrine of *Free-thinking*, as I shall plainly shew you in what follows; and therefore you are all along to understand the Word *Free-thinking* in this Sense.

If you are apt to be afraid of the Devil, *think freely* of him, and you destroy him and his Kingdom. *Free-thinking* has done him more Mischief than all the Clergy in the World ever could do; they *believe in the Devil*, they have an *Interest* in him, and therefore are the great Supports of his Kingdom. The Devil was in the *States General* before they began to be *Free-thinkers*. For *England* and *Holland* were formerly the *Christian* Territories of the Devil; I told you how he left *Holland*; and *Free-thinking* and the *Revolution* banish'd him from *England*; I defy all the Clergy to shew me when they ever had such Success against him. My Meaning is, that to think freely of the Devil, is to think there is no Devil at all; and he that thinks so, the Devil's in him if he be afraid of the Devil.

But within these two or three Years the Devil has come into *England* again, and Dr. *Sacheverell* has given him Commission to appear in the shape of a *Cat*, and carry old Women about upon Broomsticks: And the Devil has now so many *Ministers ordained to his Service*, that they have rendred *Free-thinking* odious, and nothing but the Second Coming of *Christ* can restore it.

The Priests tell me I am to believe the *Bible*, but *Free-thinking* tells me otherwise in many Particulars: The *Bible* says, the *Jews* were a Nation favoured by God; but I who am a *Free-thinker* say, that cannot be, because the *Jews* lived in a *Corner* of the Earth, and *Free-thinking* makes it clear, that those who live in *Corners* cannot be Favourites of God. The *New Testament* all along asserts the Truth of Christianity, but *Free-thinking* denies it; because Christianity was communicated but to a few; and whatever is communicated but to a few, cannot be true; for that is like *Whispering*, and the Proverb says, that there is no Whispering without Lying.

Here is a Society in *London* for propagating *Free-thinking* throughout the World, encouraged and supported by the Queen and many others. You say perhaps, it is for propagating the Gospel. Do you think the Missionaries we send, will tell the Heathens that they must not *think freely?* No surely; why then, 'tis manifest those Missionaries must be *Free-thinkers*, and make the Heathens so too. But why should not the King of *Siam*, whose Religion is Heathenism and Idolatry, send over a parcel of his Priests to convert us to *his Church*, as well as we send Missionaries there? Both Projects are exactly of a Piece, and equally reasonable; and if those Heathen Priests were here, it would be our Duty to hearken to them, and *think freely* whether *they* may not be in the right rather than we. I heartily wish a Detachment of such Divines as Dr. *Atterbury*, Dr. *Smalridge*, Dr. *Swift*, Dr. *Sacheverell*, and some others, were sent every Year to the furthest part of the Heathen World, and that we had a Cargo of their Priests in return, who would spread *Free-thinking* among us; then the War would go on, the late Ministry be restored, and Faction cease, which our Priests inflame by haranguing upon Texts, and falsly call that preaching the Gospel.

I have another Project in my Head which ought to be put in execution, in order to make us *Free-thinkers:* It is a great Hardship and Injustice, that our Priests must not be disturbed while they are prating in their Pulpit. For Example: Why should not *William Penn* the Quaker, or any *Anabaptist*, *Papist*, *Muggletonian*, *Jew* or *Sweet Singer*, have liberty to come into St. *Paul*'s Church, in the midst of Divine Service, and endeavour to convert first the Aldermen, then the Preacher, and Singing-Men? Or pray, why might not poor Mr. *Whiston*, who denies the Divinity of Christ, be allow'd to come into the Lower House of Convocation, and convert the Clergy? But alas we are over-run with such false Notions, that if *Penn* or *Whiston* should do their Duty, they would be reckoned Fanaticks, and Disturbers of the Holy Synod, although they have as good a Title to it, as St. *Paul* had to go into the Synagogues of the *Jews*; and their Authority is full as Divine as his.

Christ himself commands us to be *Free-thinkers*, for he bids us search the Scriptures, and take heed what and whom we hear; by which he plainly warns us, not to believe our Bishops and Clergy; for *Jesus Christ*, when he consider'd that all the *Jewish* and *Heathen* Priests, whose Religion he came to abolish, were his Enemies, rightly concluded that those appointed by him to preach his own Gospel, would probably be so too; and could not be secure, that any Sett of Priests, of the Faith he deliver'd, would ever be otherwise; therefore it is fully demonstrated that the Clergy of the Church of *England* are mortal Enemies to Christ, and ought not to be believ'd.

But without the Priviledge of *Free-thinking*, how is it possible to know which is the right *Scripture?* Here are perhaps twenty Sorts of *Scriptures* in the several Parts of the World, and every Sett of Priests contends that their *Scripture* is the true One. The *Indian Bramines* have a Book of Scripture call'd the *Shaster*; the *Persees* their *Zundivastaw*; the *Bonzes* in *China* have theirs, written by the Disciples of *Fo-he*, whom they call *God and Saviour of the World, who was born to teach the way of Salvation, and to give satisfaction for all Men's Sins*. Which you see is directly the same with what our *Priests* pretend of *Christ*; And must we not *think freely* to find out which are in the right, whether the *Bishops* or the *Bonzes?* But the *Talapoins* or *Heathen* Clergy of *Siam* approach yet nearer to the System of our Priests; they have a Book of *Scripture* written by *Sommonocodum*, who, the *Siamese* say, was *born of a Virgin*, and was *the God expected by the Universe*; just as our *Priests* tell us, that *Jesus Christ* was born of the *Virgin Mary*, and was the *Messiah* so long expected. The *Turkish* Priests or *Dervises* have their Scripture, which they call the *Alcoran*. The *Jews* have the *Old Testament* for their Scripture, and the *Christians* have both the Old and the New. Now among all these Scriptures there cannot above one be right; and how is it possible to know which is that, without reading them all, and then *thinking freely*, every one of us for our selves, without following the Advice or Instruction of any Guide, before we venture to chuse? The Parliament ought to be at the Charge of finding a sufficient number of these *Scriptures* for every one of Her Majesty's Subjects, for there are Twenty to One against us, that we may be in the wrong: But a great deal of *Free-thinking* will at last set us all right, and every one will adhere to the *Scripture* he likes best; by which means Religion, Peace, and Wealth, will be for ever secured in Her Majesty's Realms.

And it is the more necessary that the good People of *England* should have liberty to chuse some other *Scripture*, because all *Christian* Priests differ so much about the Copies of theirs, and about the various Readings of the several Manuscripts, which quite destroys the Authority of the Bible: For what Authority can a Book pretend to, where there are various Readings? And for this reason, it is manifest that no Man can know the Opinions of *Aristotle* or *Plato*, or believe the Facts related by *Thucidydes* or *Livy*, or be pleased with the Poetry of *Homer* and *Virgil*, all which Books are utterly useless, upon account of their various Readings. Some Books of *Scripture* are said to be lost, and this utterly destroys the Credit of those that are left: Some we reject, which the *Africans* and *Copticks* receive; and why may we not *think freely*, and reject the rest? Some think the Scriptures wholly inspired, some partly; and some not at all. Now this is just the very Case of the *Bramines*, *Persees*, *Bonzes*, *Talapoins*, *Dervizes*, *Rabbi*'s, and all *other Priests* who build their Religion upon Books, as our Priests do upon their Bibles; they all equally differ about the Copies, various Readings and Inspirations, of their several Scriptures, and God knows which are in the right; *Free-thinking* alone can determine it.

It would be endless to shew in how many Particulars the Priests of the *Heathen* and *Christian Churches* differ about the Meaning even of those Scriptures which they universally receive as Sacred. But to avoid Prolixity, I shall confine my self to the different Opinions among the Priests of the Church of *England*, and here only give you a Specimen, because even these are too many to be enumerated.

I have found out a Bishop (though indeed his Opinions are condemn'd by all his Brethren) who allows the Scriptures to be so difficult, that God has left them rather as a Trial of our Industry than a Repository of our Faith, and Furniture of *Creeds* and Articles of *Belief*; with several other admirable

Schemes of *Free-thinking*, which you may consult at your leisure.

The Doctrine of the *Trinity* is the most fundamental Point of the whole *Christian* Religion. Nothing is more easie to a *Free-thinker*, yet what different Notions of it do the *English* Priests pretend to deduce from Scripture, explaining it by *specifick Unities*, *eternal Modes of Subsistance*, and the like unintelligible Jargon? Nay, 'tis a Question whether this Doctrine be Fundamental or no; for though Dr. *South* and Bishop *Bull* affirm it, yet Bishop *Taylor* and Dr. *Wallis* deny it. And that excellent *Free-thinking* Prelate, Bishop *Taylor*, observes, that *Athanasius*'s Example was followed with too much greediness; by which means it has happened, that the greater number of our Priests are in that Sentiment, and think it necessary to believe the *Trinity*, and Incarnation of *Christ*.

Our Priests likewise dispute several Circumstances about the Resurrection of the Dead, the Nature of our Bodies after the Resurrection, and in what manner they shall be united to our Souls. They also attack one another *very weakly with great Vigour*, about Predestination. And it is certainly true, (for Bishop *Taylor* and Mr. *Whiston* the Socinian say so) that all Churches in Prosperity alter their Doctrines every Age, and are neither satisfy'd with themselves, nor their own Confessions; neither does any Clergymen of Sense believe the Thirty nine Articles.

Our Priests differ about the Eternity of Hell-Torments. The famous Dr. *Henry Moor*, and the most pious and rational of all Priests Doctor *Tillotson*, (both *Free-thinkers*) believe them to be not Eternal. They differ about keeping the Sabbath, the Divine Right of Episcopacy, and the Doctrine of Original Sin; which is the Foundation of the whole Christian Religion; for if Men are not liable to be damned for *Adam*'s Sin, the Christian Religion is an Imposture: Yet this is now disputed among them; so is Lay-Baptism; so was formerly the lawfulness of Usury, but now the Priests are common Stock-jobbers, Attorneys and Scriveners. In short there is no end of disputing among Priests, and therefore I conclude, that there ought to be no such Thing in the World as Priests, Teachers, or Guides, for instructing ignorant People in Religion; but that every Man ought to *think freely* for himself.

I will tell you my meaning in all this; the Priests dispute every Point in the Christian Religion, as well as almost every Text in the Bible; and the force of my Argument lies here, that whatever Point is disputed by one or two Divines, however condemned by the Church, not only that particular Point, but the whole Article to which it relates, may lawfully be received or rejected by any *Free Thinker*. For Instance, suppose *Moor* and *Tillotson* deny the Eternity of Hell Torments, a *Free Thinker* may deny all future Punishments whatsoever. The Priests dispute about explaining the *Trinity*; therefore a *Free Thinker* may reject one or two, or the whole three *Persons*; at least he may reject Christianity, because the *Trinity* is the most fundamental Doctrine of that Religion. So I affirm Original Sin, and that Men are now liable to be damned for *Adam*'s Sin, to be the Foundation of the whole Christian Religion; but this Point was formerly, and is now disputed, therefore a *Free Thinker* may deny the whole. And I cannot help giving you one further Direction, how I insinuate all along, that the wisest *Free Thinking* Priests, whom you may distinguish by the Epithets I bestow them, were those who differed most from the generality of their Brethren.

But besides, the Conduct of our Priests, in many other Points, makes *Free Thinking* unavoidable; for some of them own, that the Doctrines of the Church are contradictory to one another, as well as to Reason: Which I thus prove; Dr. *Sacheverell* says in his Speech at his Tryal, that by abandoning Passive Obedience we must render our selves the most inconsistent Church in the World: Now 'tis plain, that one Inconsistency could not make the most inconsistent Church in the World; *ergo*, there must have been a great many Inconsistencies and contradictory Doctrines in the Church before. Dr. *South* describes the Incarnation of Christ, as an astonishing Mystery, impossible to be conceived by Mans Reason; *ergo*, it is contradictory to it self, and to Reason, and ought to be exploded by all *Free Thinkers*.

Another Instance of the Priests Conduct, which multiplies

Free Thinkers, is their acknowledgments of Abuses, Defects, and false Doctrines in the Church; particularly that of eating *Black Pudding*, which is so plainly forbid in the *Old* and *New Testament*, that I wonder those who pretend to believe a Syllable in either, will presume to taste it. Why should I mention the want of Discipline, and of a Side-board at the Altar, with Complaints of other great Abuses and Defects made by some of the Priests, which no Man can *think* on without *Free Thinking*, and consequently rejecting Christianity?

When I see an honest Free Thinking Bishop endeavour to destroy the Power and Privileges of the Church, and Dr. *Atterbury* angry with him for it, and calling it *dirty Work*, what can I conclude, by vertue of being a *Free Thinker*, but that Christianity is all a Cheat?

Mr. *Whiston* has publish'd several Tracts, wherein he absolutely denies the Divinity of *Christ:* A Bishop tells him, *Sir, in any Matter where you have the Church's Judgment against you, you should be careful not to break the Peace of the Church, by Writing against it, though you are sure you are in the right.* Now my Opinion is directly contrary; and I affirm, that if Ten thousand Free Thinkers thought differently from the received Doctrine, and from each other, they would be all in Duty bound to publish their Thoughts (provided they were all sure of being in the right) though it broke the Peace of the Church and State, Ten thousand times.

And here I must take leave to tell you, although you cannot but have perceived it from what I have already said, and shall be still more amply convinced by what is to follow; That *Free Thinking* signifies nothing, without *Free Speaking* and *Free Writing.* It is the indispensable Duty of a *Free Thinker*, to endeavour *forcing* all the World to think as he does, and by that means make them *Free Thinkers* too. You are also to understand, that I allow no Man to be a *Free Thinker*, any further than as he differs from the received Doctrines of Religion. Where a Man falls in, though by perfect Chance, with what is generally believed, he is in that Point a confined and limited Thinker; and you shall see by and by, that I celebrate those for the noblest *Free Thinkers* in every Age, who differed from the

Religion of their Countries in the most fundamental Points, and especially in those which bear any Analogy to the chief Fundamentals of Religion among us.

Another Trick of the Priests, is to charge all Men with Atheism, who have more Wit than themselves; which therefore I expect will be my Case for Writing this Discourse: This is what makes them so implacable against Mr. *Gildon*, Dr. *Tindal*, Mr. *Toland*, and my self, and when they call us *Wits* Atheists, it provokes us to be *Free Thinkers*.

Again; The Priests cannot agree when their Scripture was wrote. They differ about the number of Canonical Books, and the various Readings. Now those few among us who understand Latin, are careful to tell this to our Disciples, who presently fall a *Free Thinking*, that the Bible is a Book not to be depended upon in any thing at all.

There is another Thing that mightily spreads *Free Thinking*, which I believe you would hardly guess: The Priests have got a way of late of Writing Books against *Free Thinking*; I mean Treatises in Dialogue, where they introduce *Atheists*, *Deists*, *Scepticks* and *Socinians* offering their several Arguments. Now these *Free Thinkers* are too hard for the Priests themselves in their own Books; and how can it be otherwise? For if the Arguments usually offered by *Atheists*, are fairly represented in these Books, they must needs convert every Body that reads them; because *Atheists*, *Deists*, *Scepticks* and *Socinians*, have certainly better Arguments to maintain their Opinions, than any the Priests can produce to maintain the contrary.

Mr. *Creech*, a Priest, translated *Lucretius* into *English*, which is a compleat System of Atheism; and several Young Students, who were afterwards Priests, writ Verses in Praise of this Translation. The Arguments against Providence in that Book are so strong, that they have added mightily to the Number of *Free Thinkers*.

What should I mention the pious Cheats of the Priests, who in the *New Testament* translate the Word *Ecclesia* sometimes the *Church*, and sometimes the *Congregation*; and *Episcopus*, sometimes a *Bishop*, and sometimes an *Overseer*? A Priest translating a Book, left out a whole Passage that reflected on the *King*, by which he was an Enemy to *Political Free Thinking*, a most considerable Branch of our System. Another Priest translating a Book of Travels, left out a lying Miracle, out of meer Malice to conceal an Argument for *Free Thinking*. In short, these Frauds are very common in all Books which are published by *Priests:* But however, I love to excuse them whenever I can: And as to this Accusation, they may plead the Authority of the Ancient Fathers of the Church for Forgery, Corruption, and mangling of Authors, with more Reason than for any of their Articles of Faith. St. *Jerom*, St. *Hilary*, *Eusebius Vercellensis*, *Victorinus*, and several others, were all guilty of arrant Forgery and Corruption: For when they translated the Works of several *Free-thinkers*, whom they called *Hereticks*, they omitted all their Heresies or *Free-thinkings*, and had the Impudence to own it to the World.

From these many notorious Instances of the Priests' Conduct, I conclude they are not to be relied on in any one thing relating to Religion, but that every Man must think freely for himself.

But to this it may be objected, that the Bulk of Mankind is as well qualified for *flying* as *thinking*, and if every Man thought it his Duty to *think freely*, and trouble his Neighbour with his Thoughts (which is an essential Part of *Free-thinking*,) it would make wild work in the World. I answer; whoever cannot *think freely*, may let it alone if he pleases, by virtue of his Right to *think freely*; that is to say, if such a Man *freely thinks* that he cannot *think freely*, of which every Man is a sufficient Judge, why then he need not *think freely*, unless he *thinks* fit.

Besides, if the Bulk of Mankind cannot *think freely* in Matters of Speculation, as the Being of a God, the Immortality of the Soul, *&c.* why then, *Free-thinking* is indeed no Duty: But then the *Priests* must allow, that Men are not concerned to believe whether there is a God or no. But still those who are disposed to *think freely*, may *think freely* if they please.

It is again objected, that *Free-thinking* will produce endless Divisions in Opinion, and by consequence disorder Society. To which I answer,

When every single Man comes to have a different Opinion

every Day from the whole World, and from himself, by Virtue of *Free-thinking*, and thinks it his Duty to convert every Man to his own *Free-thinking* (as all we *Free-thinkers* do) how can that possibly create so great a Diversity of Opinions, as to have a Sett of Priests agree among themselves to teach the same Opinions in their several Parishes to all who will come to hear them? Besides, if all People were of the same Opinion, the Remedy would be worse than the Disease; I will tell you the Reason some other time.

Besides, difference in Opinion, especially in Matters of great Moment, breeds no Confusion at all. Witness *Papist* and *Protestant*, *Roundhead* and *Cavalier*, and *Whig* and *Tory* now among us. I observe, the *Turkish* Empire is more at Peace *within it self* than *Christian* Princes are *with one another*. Those noble *Turkish* Virtues of Charity and Toleration, are what contribute chiefly to the flourishing State of that happy Monarchy. There *Christians* and *Jews* are tolerated, and live at ease, if they can hold their Tongues and *think freely*, provided they never set foot within the *Moschs*, nor write against *Mahomet:* A few Plunderings now and then by their *Janisaries* are all they have to fear.

It is objected, that by *Free-thinking*, Men will *think* themselves into *Atheism*; and indeed I have allowed all along, that Atheistical Books convert Men to *Free-thinking*. But suppose that be true; I can bring you two Divines who affirm Superstition and Enthusiasm to be worse than Atheism, and more mischievous to Society, and in short it is necessary that the Bulk of the People should be Atheists or Superstitious.

It is objected, that Priests ought to be relied on by the People, as Lawyers and Physicians, because it is their Faculty.

I answer, 'Tis true, a Man who is no Lawyer is not suffered to plead for himself; But every Man may be his own Quack if he pleases, and he only ventures his Life; but in the other Case the Priest tells him he must be damned; therefore do not trust the Priest, but *think freely* for your self, and if you happen to think there is no Hell, there certainly is none, and consequently you cannot be damned; I answer further, that wherever there is no *Lawyer*, *Physician*, or *Priest*, that Country is *Paradise*.

Besides, all Priests (except the Orthodox, and those are not ours, nor any that I know) are hired by the Publick to lead Men into Mischief; but *Lawyers* and *Physicians* are not, you hire them your self.

It is objected (by Priests no doubt, but I have forgot their Names) that false Speculations are necessary to be imposed upon Men, in order to assist the Magistrate in keeping the Peace, and that Men ought therefore to be deceived like Children, for their own Good. I answer, that Zeal for imposing Speculations, whether true or false (under which Name of Speculations I include all Opinions of Religion, as the Belief of a God, Providence, Immortality of the Soul, future Rewards and Punishments, *&c.*) has done more hurt than it is possible for Religion to do good. It puts us to the Charge of maintaining Ten thousand Priests in *England*, which is a Burthen upon Society never felt on any other occasion; and a greater Evil to the Publick than if these Ecclesiasticks were only employed in the most innocent Offices of Life, which I take to be *Eating* and *Drinking*. Now if you offer to impose any thing on Mankind besides what relates to moral Duties, as to pay your Debts, not pick Pockets, nor commit Murder, and the like; that is to say, if besides this, you oblige them to believe in God and Jesus Christ, what you add to their Faith will take just so much off from their Morality. By this Argument it is manifest that a perfect moral Man must be a perfect Atheist, every Inch of Religion he gets, loses him an Inch of Morality: For there is a certain *Quantum* belongs to every Man, of which there is nothing to spare. This is clear from the common Practice of all our Priests, they never once Preach to you to love your Neighbour, to be just in your Dealings, or to be Sober and Temperate: The Streets of *London* are full of Common Whores, publickly tolerated in their Wickedness; yet the Priests make no Complaints against this Enormity, either from the Pulpit or the Press: I can affirm, that neither you nor I Sir, have ever heard one Sermon against Whoring since we were Boys. No, the Priests allow all these Vices, and love us the better for them, provided we will promise not to *harangue upon a Text*, nor to sprinkle a little Water in a Child's Face, which they call Baptizing, and would engross it all to themselves.

Besides, the *Priests* engage all the Rogues, Villains and Fools in their Party, in order to make it as large as they can: By this means they seduced *Constantine the Great* over to their Religion, who was the first Christian Emperor, and so horrible a Villain, that the *Heathen* Priests told him they could not expiate his Crimes in their Church; so he was at a loss to know what to do, till an *Ægyptian* Bishop assured him that there was no Villainy so great, but was to be expiated by the Sacraments of the Christian Religion; upon which he became a Christian, and to him that Religion owes its first Settlement.

It is objected, that *Free-thinkers* themselves are the most infamous, wicked and senseless of all Mankind.

I answer, First, We say the same of *Priests* and other Believers. But the Truth is, Men of all Sects are equally good and bad; for no Religion whatsoever contributes in the least to mend Mens Lives.

I answer, Secondly, That *Free-thinkers* use their Understanding, but those who have Religion, do not, therefore the first have more Understanding than the others; Witness *Toland*, *Tindal*, *Gildon*, *Clendon*, *Coward*, and my self. For, use Legs and have Legs.

I answer, Thirdly, That *Free-thinkers* are the most virtuous Persons in the World; for every *Free-thinker* must certainly differ from the *Priests*, and from Nine hundred ninety nine of a Thousand of those among whom they live; and are therefore Virtuous of course, because every Body hates them.

I answer, Fourthly, That the most virtuous People in all Ages have been *Free-thinkers*; of which I shall produce several Instances.

Socrates was a *Free-thinker*; for he disbelieved the Gods of his Country, and the common *Creeds* about them, and declared his Dislike when he heard Men attribute *Repentance*, *Anger*, *and other Passions to the Gods*, *and talk of Wars and Battles in Heaven*, *and of the Gods getting Women with Child*, and such like fabulous and blasphemous Stories. I pick out these Particulars, because they are the very same with what the Priests have in their

Bibles, where *Repentance* and *Anger* are attributed to God, where it is said, there was *War in Heaven*; and that the *Virgin* Mary *was with Child by the Holy Ghost*, whom the Priests call God; all fabulous and blasphemous Stories. Now, I affirm *Socrates* to have been a true *Christian*. You will ask perhaps how that can be, since he lived Three or four hundred Years before Christ? I answer with *Justin Martyr*, that *Christ* is nothing else but *Reason*, and I hope you do not think *Socrates* lived before *Reason*. Now, this true Christian *Socrates* never made Notions, Speculations, or Mysteries any Part of his Religion, but demonstrated all Men to be Fools who troubled themselves with Enquiries into heavenly Things. Lastly, 'tis plain that *Socrates* was a *Free-thinker*, because he was calumniated for an *Atheist*, as *Free-thinkers* generally are, only because he was an Enemy to all Speculations and Enquiries into heavenly Things. For I argue thus, that if I never trouble my self to think whether there be a God or no, and forbid others to do it, I am a *Free-thinker*, but not an *Atheist*.

Plato was a *Free-thinker*, and his Notions are so like some in the Gospel, that a Heathen charged Christ with borrowing his Doctrine from *Plato*. But *Origen* defends Christ very well against this Charge, by saying he did not understand *Greek*, and therefore could not borrow his Doctrines from *Plato*. However their two Religions agreed so well, that it was common for Christians to turn *Platonists*, and *Platonists* Christians. When the Christians found out this, one of their zealous Priests (worse than any Atheist) forged several Things under *Plato*'s Name, but conformable to Christianity, by which the Heathens were fraudulently converted.

Epicurus was the greatest of all *Free-thinkers*, and consequently the most virtuous Man in the World. His Opinions in Religion were the most compleat System of Atheism that ever appeared. Christians ought to have the greatest Veneration for him, because he taught a higher Point of Virtue than Christ; I mean the Virtue of *Friendship*, which in the Sense we usually understand it, is not so much as named in the New Testament.

Plutarch was a *Free-thinker*, notwithstanding his being a

Priest; but indeed he was a *Heathen Priest.* His *Free-thinking* appears by shewing the Innocence of Atheism (which at worst is only false Reasoning) and the Mischiefs of Superstition; and explains what Superstition is, by calling it a Conceit of immortal Ills after Death, the Opinion of Hell Torments, dreadful Aspects, doleful Groans, and the like. He is likewise very Satyrical upon the publick Forms of Devotion in his own Country (a *Qualification* absolutely necessary to a *Free-thinker*) yet those Forms which he ridicules, are the very same that now pass for *true Worship* in almost all Countries: I am sure some of them do so in ours; such as abject Looks, Distortions, wry Faces, beggarly Tones, Humiliation, and Contrition.

Varro the most Learned among the *Romans* was a *Free-thinker*; for he said, the Heathen Divinity contained many Fables below the Dignity of Immortal Beings; such for Instance as Gods BEGOTTEN and PROCEEDING from other Gods. These two Words I desire you will particularly remark, because they are the very Terms made use of by our Priests in their Doctrine of the *Trinity:* He says likewise, that there are many Things false in Religion, and so say all *Free-thinkers*; but then he adds; *Which the Vulgar ought not to know, but it is Expedient they should believe.* In this last he indeed discovers the whole Secret of a Statesman and Politician, by denying the Vulgar the Priviledge of *Free-thinking*, and here I differ from him. However it is manifest from hence, that the *Trinity* was an Invention of Statesmen and Politicians.

The Grave and Wise *Cato* the Censor will for ever live in that noble *Free-thinking* Saying; I wonder, said he, how one of your Priests can forbear laughing when he sees another. (For Contempt of Priests is another grand Characteristick of a Free-thinker). This shews that *Cato* understood the whole Mystery of the *Roman* Religion, *as by Law Established.* I beg you Sir, not to overlook these last Words, *Religion as by Law Established.* I translate *Haruspex* into the general Word, *Priest:* Thus I apply the Sentence to our *Priests* in *England*, and when Dr. *Smalridge* sees Dr. *Atterbury*, I wonder how either of them can forbear laughing at the Cheat they put upon the People, by making them believe their *Religion as by Law Established.*

Cicero, that consummate Philosopher, and noble Patriot, though he were a *Priest*, and consequently more likely to be a *Knave*; gave the greatest Proofs of his *Free-thinking.* First, He professed the *Sceptick* Philosophy, which doubts of every thing. Then, he wrote two Treatises; in the first, he shews the Weakness of the *Stoicks* Arguments for the Being of the Gods: In the latter, he has destroyed the whole *reveal'd* Religion of the *Greeks* and *Romans* (for why should not theirs be a *reveal'd* Religion as well as that of Christ?) *Cicero* likewise tells us, as his own Opinion, that they who study Philosophy, do not believe there are any Gods: He denies the Immortality of the Soul, and says, there can be nothing after Death.

And because the Priests have the Impudence to quote *Cicero* in their Pulpits and Pamphlets, against *Free-thinking*; I am resolved to disarm them of his Authority. You must know, his Philosophical Works are generally in Dialogues, where People are brought in disputing against one another: Now the Priests when they see an Argument to prove a God, offered perhaps by a *Stoick*, are such Knaves or Blockheads, to quote it as if it were *Cicero*'s own; whereas *Cicero* was so noble a *Free-thinker*, that he believed nothing at all of the Matter, nor ever shews the least Inclination to favour Superstition, or the Belief of God, and the Immortality of the Soul; unless what he throws out sometimes to save himself from Danger, in his Speeches to the *Roman* Mob; whose Religion was, however, much more Innocent and less Absurd, than that of *Popery* at least: And I could say more,—but you understand me.

Seneca was a great *Free-thinker*, and had a noble Notion of the Worship of the Gods, for which our Priests would call any Man an Atheist: He laughs at Morning-Devotions, or Worshipping upon Sabbath-Days; he says God has no need of *Ministers* and *Servants*, because he himself *serves* Mankind. This religious Man, like his religious Brethren the *Stoicks*, denies the Immortality of the Soul, and says, all that is feign'd to be so terrible in Hell, is but a Fable: Death puts an end to all our Misery, *&c.* Yet the Priests were anciently so fond of

Seneca, that they forged a Correspondence of Letters between him and St. *Paul*.

Solomon himself, whose Writings are called the Word of God, was such a *Free Thinker*, that if he were now alive, nothing but his Building of Churches could have kept our Priests from calling him an Atheist. He affirms the Eternity of the World almost in the same manner with *Manilius* the *Heathen* Philosophical Poet (which Opinion entirely overthrows the History of the Creation by *Moses*, and all the *New Testament*): He denies the Immortality of the Soul, assures us that Men die like Beasts, and that both go to one Place.

The Prophets of the *Old Testament* were generally *Free Thinkers:* You must understand, that their way of learning to Prophesie was by *Musick* and *Drinking*. These Prophets writ against the *Established Religion* of the *Jews*, (which those People looked upon as the Institution of God himself) as if they believed it was all a Cheat: That is to say, with as great liberty against the Priests and Prophets of *Israel*, as Dr. *Tindall* did lately against the Priests and Prophets of our *Israel*, who has clearly shewn them and their Religion to be Cheats. To prove this, you may read several Passages in *Isaiah*, *Ezekiel*, *Amos*, *Jeremiah*, *&c.* wherein you will find such Instances of *Free Thinking*, that if any *Englishman* had talked so in our Days, their Opinions would have been Registred in Dr. *Sacheverell*'s Tryal, and in the Representation of the Lower House of Convocation, and produced as so many Proofs of the Prophaneness, Blasphemy, and Atheism of the Nation; there being nothing more Prophane, Blasphemous, or Atheistical in those Representations, than what these Prophets have spoke, whose Writings are yet called by our Priests the *Word of God*. And therefore these Prophets are as much *Atheists* as my self, or as any of my Free-thinking Brethren, whom I lately named to you.

Josephus was a great *Free-thinker:* I wish he had chosen a better Subject to write on, than those ignorant, barbarous, ridiculous Scoundrels the *Jews*, whom God (if we may believe the Priests) thought fit to chuse for his own People. I will give you some Instances of his *Free-thinking*. He says, *Cain* travelled through several Countries, and kept Company with Rakes and profligate Fellows, he corrupted the Simplicities of former Times, *&c.* which plainly supposes Men before *Adam*, and consequently that the Priests' History of the Creation by *Moses*, is an Imposture. He says, the *Israelites* passing through the Red Sea, was no more than *Alexander*'s passing at the *Pamphilion* Sea; that as for the appearance of God at Mount *Sinai*, the Reader may believe it as he pleases; that *Moses* persuaded the *Jews*, he had God for his Guide, just as the *Greeks* pretended they had their Laws from *Apollo*. These are noble Strains of *Free Thinking*, which the Priests know not how to solve, but by *thinking* as *freely*; for one of them says, that *Josephus* writ this to make his Work acceptable to the *Heathen*, by striking out every thing that was incredible.

Origen, who was the first Christian that had any Learning, has left a noble Testimony of his *Free Thinking*; for a general Council has determined him to be damn'd; which plainly shews he was a *Free Thinker:* And was no *Saint*; for People were only Sainted because of their want of Learning and excess of Zeal; so that all the Fathers, who are called *Saints* by the Priests, were worse than Atheists.

Minutius Fœlix seems to be a true, Modern, Latitudinarian, *Free Thinking* Christian, for he is against Altars, Churches, publick Preaching, and publick Assemblies; and likewise against Priests; for he says, there were several great flourishing Empires before there were any Orders of Priests in the World.

Synesius, who had too much Learning and too little Zeal for a *Saint*, was for some time a great *Free Thinker*; he could not believe the Resurrection till he was made a Bishop, and then pretended to be convinced by a Lying Miracle.

To come to our own Country: My Lord *Bacon* was a great *Free Thinker*, when he tells us, that whatever has the least Relation to Religion, is particularly liable to Suspicion, by which he seems to suspect all the Facts whereon most of the Superstitions (that is to say, what the Priests call the Religions) of the World are grounded. He also prefers Atheism before Superstition.

Mr. *Hobbs* was a Person of great Learning, Virtue and *Free Thinking*, except in his *High-Church* Politicks.

But *Arch Bishop Tillotson* is the Person whom all *English Free Thinkers* own as their Head; and his Virtue is indisputable for this manifest Reason, that Dr. *Hicks*, a Priest, calls him an Atheist; says, he caused several to turn Atheists, and to ridicule the Priesthood and Religion. These must be allowed to be noble effects of *Free Thinking*. This great Prelate assures us, that all the Duties of the Christian Religion, with respect to God, are no other but what natural Light prompts Men to, except the two Sacraments, and praying to God in the Name and Mediation of Christ: As a Priest and Prelate he was obliged to say something of Christianity; but pray observe, Sir, how he brings himself off. He justly affirms that even these things are of less Moment than natural Duties; and because Mothers nursing their Children is a natural Duty, it is of more Moment than the two Sacraments, or than praying to God in the Name and by the Mediation of Christ. This *Free Thinking* Archbishop could not allow a Miracle sufficient to give Credit to a Prophet who taught any thing contrary to our natural Notions: By which it is plain, he rejected at once all the Mysteries of Christianity.

I could name one and twenty more great Men, who were all *Free Thinkers*; but that I fear to be tedious. For, 'tis certain that all Men of Sense depart from the Opinions commonly received; and are consequently more or less Men of Sense, according as they depart more or less from the Opinions commonly received; neither can you name an Enemy to *Free Thinking*, however he be dignify'd or distinguish'd, whether *Archbishop*, *Bishop*, *Priest* or *Deacon*, who has not been either a *crack-brain'd Enthusiast*, a *diabolical Villain*, or a most *profound ignorant Brute*.

Thus, Sir, I have endeavour'd to execute your Commands, and you may print this Letter if you please; but I would have you conceal your Name, For my Opinion of Virtue is, that we ought not to venture doing our selves harm, by endeavouring to do good. I am

Yours, *&c.*

I have here given the Publick a brief, but faithful Abstract, of this most excellent Essay; wherein I have all along religiously adhered to our Author's Notions, and generally to his Words, without any other Addition than that of explaining a few necessary Consequences, foı the sake of ignorant Readers; For, to those who have the least degree of Learning, I own they will be wholly useless. I hope I have not, in any single Instance, misrepresented the Thoughts of this admirable Writer. If I have happened to mistake through Inadvertency, I entreat he will condescend to inform me, and point out the Place, upon which I will immediately beg Pardon both of him and the World. The Design of his Piece is to recommend Free-thinking, *and one chief Motive is the Example of many Excellent Men who were of that Sect. He produces as the principal Points of their* Free-thinking; *That they denied the Being of a God, the Torments of Hell, the Immortality of the Soul, the Trinity, Incarnation, the History of the Creation by* Moses, *with many other such* fabulous and blasphemous Stories, *as he judiciously calls them: And he asserts, that whoever denies the most of these, is the compleatest* Free-thinker, *and consequently the wisest and most virtuous Man. The Author, sensible of the Prejudices of the Age, does not directly affirm himself an Atheist; he goes no further than to pronounce that Atheism is the most perfect degree of* Free-thinking; *and leaves the Reader to form the Conclusion. However, he seems to allow, that a Man may be a tolerable* Free-thinker, *tho' he does believe a God; provided he utterly rejects* Providence, Revelation, the Old and New Testament, Future Rewards *and* Punishments, *the* Immortality of the Soul, *and other the like impossible Absurdities. Which Mark of superabundant Caution, sacrificing* Truth *to the* Superstition *of Priests, may perhaps be* forgiven, *but ought not to be* imitated *by any who would arrive (even in this Author's Judgment) at the true Perfection of* Free-thinking.

FINIS.

AN

ARGUMENT

To prove, That the

Abolishing of CHRISTIANITY

IN

ENGLAND,

May, as Things now Stand, be attended with some Inconveniencies, and perhaps, not produce those many good Effects proposed thereby.

Written in the YEAR 1708.

I AM very sensible what a Weakness and Presumption it is, to reason against the general Humour and Disposition of the World. I remember it was with great Justice, and a due Regard to the Freedom both of the Publick and the Press, forbidden upon severe Penalties to write or discourse, or lay Wagers against the *Union*, even before it was confirmed by Parliament: Because that was looked upon as a Design to oppose the Current of the People; which besides the Folly of it, is a manifest Breach of the Fundamental Law, that makes this Majority of Opinion the Voice of God. In like Manner, and for the very same Reasons, it may perhaps be neither safe nor prudent to argue against the Abolishing of Christianity, at a Juncture when all Parties appear so unanimously determined upon the Point; as we cannot but allow from their Actions, their Discourses, and their Writings. However, I know not how, whether from the Affectation of Singularity, or the Perverseness of human Nature; but so it unhappily falls out, that I cannot be entirely of this Opinion.

Nay, although I were sure an Order were issued out for my immediate Prosecution by the Attorney-General; I should still confess, that in the present Posture of our Affairs at home or abroad, I do not yet see the absolute Necessity of extirpating the Christian Religion from among us.

THIS perhaps may appear too great a Paradox, even for our wise and paradoxical Age to endure: Therefore I shall handle it with all Tenderness, and with the utmost Deference to that great and profound Majority, which is of another Sentiment.

AND yet the Curious may please to observe, how much the Genius of a Nation is liable to alter in half an Age: I have heard it affirmed for certain by some very old People, that the contrary Opinion was even in their Memories as much in Vogue as the other is now; and, that a Project for the Abolishing of Christianity would then have appeared as singular, and been thought as absurd, as it would be at this Time to write or discourse in its Defence.

THEREFORE I freely own, that all Appearances are against me. The System of the Gospel, after the Fate of other Systems is generally antiquated and exploded; and the Mass or Body of the common People, among whom it seems to have had its latest Credit, are now grown as much ashamed of it as their Betters: Opinions, like Fashions always descending from those of Quality to the middle Sort, and thence to the Vulgar, where at length they are dropt and vanish.

BUT here I would not be mistaken; and must therefore be so bold as to borrow a Distinction from the Writers on the other Side, when they make a Difference between nominal and real *Trinitarians*. I hope, no Reader imagines me so weak to stand up in the Defence of *real* Christianity; such as used in primitive Times (if we may believe the Authors of those Ages) to have an Influence upon Mens Belief and Actions: To offer at the Restoring of that, would indeed be a wild Project; it would be to dig up Foundations; to destroy at one Blow *all* the Wit, and *half* the Learning of the Kingdom; to break the entire Frame and Constitution of Things; to ruin Trade, extinguish Arts and Sciences with the Professors of them; in short, to turn our Courts, Exchanges and Shops into Desarts: And would be full as absurd as the Proposal of *Horace*, where he advises the *Romans*, all in a Body, to leave their City, and seek a new Seat in some remote Part of the World, by Way of Cure for the Corruption of their Manners.

THEREFORE, I think this Caution was in it self altogether unnecessary, (which I have inserted only to prevent all Possibility of cavilling) since every candid Reader will easily understand my Discourse to be intended only in Defence of *nominal* Christianity; the other having been for some Time wholly laid aside by general Consent, as utterly inconsistent with our present Schemes of Wealth and Power.

BUT why we should therefore cast off the Name and Title of Christians, although the general Opinion and Resolution be so violent for it; I confess I cannot (with Submission) apprehend the Consequence necessary. However, since the Undertakers propose such wonderful Advantages to the Nation by this Project; and advance many plausible Objections against the System of Christianity; I shall briefly consider the Strength of both; fairly allow them their greatest Weight, and offer such Answers as I think most reasonable. After which I will beg leave to shew what Inconveniencies may possibly happen by such an Innovation, in the present Posture of our Affairs.

First, ONE great Advantage proposed by the Abolishing of Christianity is, That it would very much enlarge and establish Liberty of Conscience, that great Bulwark of our Nation, and of the *Protestant* Religion, which is still too much limited by *Priest-Craft*, notwithstanding all the good Intentions of the Legislature; as we have lately found by a severe Instance. For it is confidently reported, that two young Gentlemen of great Hopes, bright Wit, and profound Judgment, who upon a thorough Examination of Causes and Effects, and by the meer Force of natural Abilities, without the least Tincture of Learning; having made a Discovery, that there was no God, and generously communicating their Thoughts for the Good of the Publick; were some Time ago, by an unparalleled Severity, and upon I know not what *obsolete* Law, broke *only* for *Blasphemy*. And as it hath been wisely observed; if Persecution once begins, no Man alive knows how far it may reach, or where it will end.

In Answer to all which, with Deference to wiser Judgments; I think this rather shews the Necessity of a *nominal* Religion among us. Great Wits love to be free with the highest Objects; and if they cannot be allowed a *God* to revile or renounce; they will *speak Evil of Dignities*, abuse the Government, and reflect upon the Ministry; which I am sure, few will deny to be of much more pernicious Consequence; according to the Saying of *Tiberius*; *Deorum offensa Diis curæ*. As to the particular Fact related, I think it is not fair to argue from one Instance; perhaps another cannot be produced; yet (to the Comfort of all those, who may be apprehensive of Persecution) Blasphemy we know is freely spoke a Million of Times in every Coffee-House and Tavern, or where-ever else *good Company* meet. It must be allowed indeed, that to break an *English Free-born* Officer only for Blasphemy, was, to speak the gentlest of such an Action, a very high Strain of absolute Power. Little can be said in Excuse for the General; perhaps he was afraid it might give Offence to the Allies, among whom, for ought I know, it may be the Custom of the Country to believe a God. But if he argued, as some have done, upon a mistaken Principle, that an Officer who is guilty of speaking Blasphemy, may, some Time or other, proceed so far as to raise a Mutiny; the Consequence is, by no Means, to be admitted: For, surely the Commander of an *English* Army is like to be but ill obeyed, whose Soldiers fear and reverence him as little as they do a Deity.

It is further objected against the Gospel System, that it obliges Men to the Belief of Things too difficult for Free-Thinkers, and such who have shaken off the Prejudices that usually cling to a confined Education. To which I answer, that Men should be cautious how they raise Objections, which reflect upon the Wisdom of the Nation. Is not every Body freely allowed to believe whatever he pleaseth; and to publish his Belief to the World whenever he thinks fit; especially if it serve to strengthen the Party which is in the Right? Would any indifferent Foreigner, who should read the Trumpery lately written by *Asgill*, *Tindall*, *Toland*, *Coward*, and Forty more, imagine the Gospel to be our Rule of Faith, and confirmed by Parliaments? Does any Man either believe, or say he believes, or desire to have it thought that he says he believes one Syllable of the Matter? And is any Man worse received upon that Score; or does he find his Want of *Nominal* Faith a Disadvantage to him, in the Pursuit of any Civil, or Military Employment? What if there be an old dormant Statute or two against him? Are they not now obsolete, to a Degree, that *Empson* and *Dudley* themselves, if they were now alive, would find it impossible to put them in Execution?

IT is likewise urged, that there are, by Computation, in this Kingdom, above ten Thousand Parsons; whose Revenues added to those of my Lords the Bishops, would suffice to maintain, at least, two Hundred young Gentlemen of Wit and Pleasure, and Free-thinking; Enemies to Priest-craft, narrow Principles, Pedantry, and Prejudices; who might be an Ornament to the Court and Town: And then again, so great a Number of able (bodied) Divines might be a Recruit to our Fleet and Armies. This, indeed, appears to be a Consideration of some Weight: But then, on the other Side, several Things deserve to be considered likewise: As, First, Whether it may not be thought necessary, that in certain Tracts of Country, like what we call Parishes, there should be *one* Man at least, of Abilities to read and write. Then, it seems a wrong Computation, that the Revenues of the Church throughout this Island, would be large enough to maintain two Hundred young Gentlemen, or even Half that Number, after the present refined Way of Living; that is, to allow each of them such a Rent, as, in the modern Form of Speech, would make them *easy*. But still, there is in this Project a greater Mischief behind; and we ought to beware of the Woman's Folly, who killed the Hen, that every Morning laid her a Golden Egg. For, pray, what would become of the Race of Men in the next Age, if we had nothing to trust to, besides the scrophulous consumptive Productions furnished by our Men of Wit and Pleasure; when having squandered away their Vigour, Health, and Estates; they are forced, by some disagreeable Marriage, to piece up their broken Fortunes, and entail Rottenness and Politeness on their Posterity? Now, here are ten Thousand Persons reduced by the wise Regulations of *Henry* the Eighth, to the Necessity of a low Diet, and moderate Exercise, who are the only great Restorers of our Breed; without which, the Nation would, in an Age or two, become but one great Hospital.

ANOTHER Advantage proposed by the abolishing of Christianity, is, the clear Gain of one Day in Seven, which is now entirely lost, and consequently the Kingdom one Seventh less considerable in Trade, Business, and Pleasure; beside the Loss to the Publick of so many stately Structures now in the Hands of the Clergy; which might be converted into Theatres, Exchanges, Market-houses, common Dormitories, and other publick Edifices.

I HOPE I shall be forgiven a hard Word, if I call this a perfect Cavil. I readily own there hath been an old Custom, Time out of Mind, for People to assemble in the Churches every *Sunday*, and that Shops are still frequently shut; in order, as it is conceived, to preserve the Memory of that antient Practice; but how this can prove a Hindrance to Business, or Pleasure, is hard to imagine. What if the Men of Pleasure are forced, one Day in the Week, to game at home, instead of the *Chocolate-House*? Are not the *Taverns* and *Coffee-Houses* open? Can there be a more convenient Season for taking a Dose of Physick? Are fewer Claps got upon *Sundays* than other Days? Is not that the chief Day for Traders to sum up the Accounts of the Week; and for Lawyers to prepare their Briefs? But I would fain know how it can be pretended, that the Churches are misapplied. Where are more Appointments and Rendezvouzes of Gallantry? Where more Care to appear in the foremost Box with greater Advantage of Dress? Where more Meetings for Business? Where more Bargains driven of all Sorts? And where so many Conveniences, or Incitements to sleep?

THERE is one Advantage, greater than any of the foregoing, proposed by the abolishing of Christianity; that it will utterly extinguish Parties among us, by removing those factious Distinctions of High and Low Church, of *Whig* and *Tory*, *Presbyterian* and *Church-of-England*; which are now so many grievous Clogs upon publick Proceedings, and dispose Men to prefer the gratifying themselves, or depressing their Adversaries, before the most important Interest of the State.

I CONFESS, if it were certain that so great an Advantage

would redound to the Nation by this Expedient, I would submit and be silent: But, will any Man say, that if the Words *Whoring*, *Drinking*, *Cheating*, *Lying*, *Stealing*, were, by Act of Parliament, ejected out of the *English* Tongue and Dictionaries; we should all awake next Morning chaste and temperate, honest and just, and Lovers of Truth. Is this a fair Consequence? Or if the Physicians would forbid us to pronounce the Words *Pox*, *Gout*, *Rheumatism*, and *Stone*; would that Expedient serve like so many *Talismans* to destroy the Diseases themselves? Are Party and Faction rooted in Mens Hearts no deeper than Phrases borrowed from Religion; or founded upon no firmer Principles? And is our Language so poor, that we cannot find other Terms to express them? Are Envy, Pride, Avarice and Ambition, such ill Nomenclators, that they cannot furnish Appellations for their Owners? Will not *Heydukes* and *Mamalukes*, *Mandarins*, and *Potshaws*, or any other Words formed at Pleasure, serve to distinguish those who are in the *Ministry* from others, who *would be in* it *if they could*? What, for Instance, is easier than to vary the Form of Speech; and instead of the Word *Church*, make it a Question in Politicks, Whether the *Monument* be in Danger? Because Religion was nearest at Hand to furnish a few convenient Phrases; is our Invention so barren, we can find no others? Suppose, for Argument Sake, that the *Tories* favoured * *Margarita*, the *Whigs* Mrs. *Tofts*, and the *Trimmers Valentini*; would not *Margaritians*, *Toftians*, and *Valentinians*, be very tolerable Marks of Distinction? The *Prasini* and *Veneti*, two most virulent Factions in *Italy*, began (if I remember right) by a Distinction of Colours in Ribbonds; which we might do, with as good a Grace, about the Dignity of the *Blue* and the *Green*; and would serve as properly to divide the Court, the Parliament, and the Kingdom between them, as any Terms of Art whatsoever, borrowed from Religion. Therefore, I think there is little Force in this Objection against *Christianity*; or Prospect of so great an Advantage as is proposed in the Abolishing of it.

It is again objected, as a very absurd, ridiculous Custom, that a Set of Men should be suffered, much less employed, and hired

* Italian *Singers then in Vogue.*

to bawl one Day in Seven, against the Lawfulness of those Methods most in Use towards the Pursuit of Greatness, Riches, and Pleasure; which are the constant Practice of all Men alive on the other Six. But this Objection is, I think, a little unworthy so refined an Age as ours. Let us argue this Matter calmly. I appeal to the Breast of any polite Free-Thinker, whether in the Pursuit of gratifying a predominant Passion, he hath not always felt a wonderful Incitement, by reflecting it was a Thing forbidden: And therefore we see, in order to cultivate this Taste, the Wisdom of the Nation hath taken special Care, that the Ladies should be furnished with prohibited Silks, and the Men with prohibited Wine: And, indeed, it were to be wished, that some other Prohibitions were promoted, in order to improve the Pleasures of the Town; which, for want of such Expedients, begin already, as I am told, to flag and grow languid; giving way daily to cruel Inroads from the Spleen.

IT is likewise proposed, as a great Advantage to the Publick, that if we once discard the System of the Gospel, all Religion will, of Course, be banished for ever; and consequently along with it, those grievous Prejudices of Education; which, under the Names of Virtue, Conscience, Honour, Justice, and the like, are so apt to disturb the Peace of human Minds; and the Notions whereof are so hard to be eradicated by right Reason, or Free-thinking, sometimes during the whole Course of our Lives.

HERE, first, I observe how difficult it is to get rid of a Phrase, which the World is once grown fond of, although the Occasion that first produced it, be entirely taken away. For several Years past, if a Man had but an ill-favoured Nose, the Deep-Thinkers of the Age would, some way or other, contrive to impute the Cause to the Prejudice of his Education. From this Fountain are said to be derived all our foolish Notions of Justice, Piety, Love of our Country; all our Opinions of God, or a future State, Heaven, Hell, and the like: And there might formerly, perhaps, have been some Pretence for this Charge. But so effectual Care hath been since taken, to remove those Prejudices by an entire Change in the Methods of Education; that (with Honour I mention it to our polite Innovators) the young Gentlemen, who are now on the Scene, seem to have not the least Tincture left of those Infusions, or String of those Weeds; and, by Consequence, the Reason for abolishing *Nominal* Christianity upon that Pretext, is wholly ceased.

FOR the rest, it may perhaps admit a Controversy, whether the Banishing all Notions of Religion whatsoever, would be convenient for the Vulgar. Not that I am in the least of Opinion with those, who hold Religion to have been the Invention of Politicians, to keep the lower Part of the World in Awe, by the Fear of invisible Powers; unless Mankind were then very different from what it is now: For I look upon the Mass, or Body of our People here in *England*, to be as Free-Thinkers, that is to say, as stanch Unbelievers, as any of the highest Rank. But I conceive some scattered Notions about a superior Power to be of singular Use for the common People, as furnishing excellent Materials to keep Children quiet, when they grow peevish; and providing Topicks of Amusement in a tedious Winter Night.

LASTLY, It is proposed as a singular Advantage, that the Abolishing of Christianity, will very much contribute to the uniting of *Protestants*, by enlarging the Terms of Communion, so as to take in all Sorts of *Dissenters*; who are now shut out of the Pale upon Account of a few Ceremonies, which all Sides confess to be Things indifferent: That this alone will effectually answer the great Ends of a Scheme for Comprehension, by opening a large noble Gate, at which all Bodies may enter; whereas the chaffering with *Dissenters*, and dodging about this or the other Ceremony, is but like opening a few Wickets, and leaving them at jar, by which no more than one can get in at a Time, and that not without stooping and sideling, and squeezing his Body.

To all this I answer, That there is one darling Inclination of Mankind, which usually affects to be a Retainer to Religion, although she be neither its Parent, its Godmother, or its Friend; I mean the Spirit of Opposition, that lived long before Christianity, and can easily subsist without it. Let us, for Instance, examine wherein the Opposition of Sectaries among us consists; we shall find Christianity to have no Share in it at all. Does the

Gospel any where prescribe a starched squeezed Countenance, a stiff formal Gait, a Singularity of Manners and Habit, or any affected Modes of Speech, different from the reasonable Part of Mankind? Yet, if Christianity did not lend its Name, to stand in the Gap, and to employ or divert these Humours, they must of Necessity be spent in Contraventions to the Laws of the Land, and Disturbance of the publick Peace. There is a Portion of Enthusiasm assigned to every Nation, which if it hath not proper Objects to work on, will burst out, and set all in a Flame. If the Quiet of a State can be bought by only flinging Men a few Ceremonies to devour, it is a Purchase no wise Man would refuse. Let the Mastiffs amuse themselves about a Sheep-skin stuffed with Hay, provided it will keep them from worrying the Flock. The Institution of Convents abroad, seems in one Point a Strain of great Wisdom; there being few Irregularities in human Passions, that may not have recourse to vent themselves in some of those Orders; which are so many Retreats for the Speculative, the Melancholy, the Proud, the Silent, the Politick and the Morose, to spend themselves, and evaporate the noxious Particles; for each of whom, we in this Island are forced to provide a several Sect of Religion, to keep them quiet. And whenever Christianity shall be abolished, the Legislature must find some other Expedient to employ and entertain them. For what imports it, how large a Gate you open, if there will be always left a Number, who place a Pride and a Merit in refusing to enter?

HAVING thus considered the most important Objections against Christianity, and the chief Advantages proposed by the Abolishing thereof; I shall now with equal Deference and Submission to wiser Judgments as before, proceed to mention a few Inconveniences that may happen, if the Gospel should be repealed; which perhaps the Projectors may not have sufficiently considered.

AND first, I am very sensible how much the Gentlemen of Wit and Pleasure are apt to murmur, and be choqued at the sight of so many daggled-tail Parsons, who happen to fall in their Way, and offend their Eyes: But at the same Time these wise Reformers do not consider what an Advantage and Felicity it is, for great Wits to be always provided with Objects of Scorn and Contempt, in order to exercise and improve their Talents, and divert their Spleen from falling on each other, or on themselves; especially when all this may be done without the least imaginable *Danger to their Persons*.

AND to urge another Argument of a parallel Nature: If Christianity were once abolished, how would the Free-Thinkers, the strong Reasoners, and the Men of profound Learning be able to find another Subject so calculated in all Points whereon to display their Abilities. What wonderful Productions of Wit should we be deprived of, from those whose Genius, by continual Practice hath been wholly turned upon Raillery and Invectives against Religion; and would therefore never be able to shine or distinguish themselves upon any other Subject. We are daily complaining of the great Decline of Wit among us; and would we take away the greatest, perhaps the only Topick we have left? Who would ever have suspected *Asgill* for a Wit, or *Toland* for a Philosopher, if the inexhaustible Stock of Christianity had not been at hand to provide them with Materials? What other Subject through all Art or Nature could have produced *Tindal* for a profound Author, or furnished him with Readers? It is the wise Choice of the Subject that alone adorns and distinguishes the Writer. For had an hundred such Pens as these been employed on the Side of Religion, they would have immediately sunk into Silence and Oblivion.

NOR do I think it wholly groundless, or my Fears altogether imaginary; that the Abolishing of Christianity may perhaps bring the Church in Danger; or at least put the Senate to the Trouble of another Securing Vote. I desire, I may not be mistaken; I am far from presuming to affirm or think, that the Church is in Danger at present, or as Things now stand; but we know not how soon it may be so, when the Christian Religion is repealed. As plausible as this Project seems, there may a dangerous Design lurk under it. Nothing can be more notorious, than that the *Atheists*, *Deists*, *Socinians*, *Anti-Trinitarians*, and other Subdivisions of Free-Thinkers, are Persons of little Zeal for the present Ecclesiastical Establishment: Their declared Opinion is for repealing the Sacramental Test; they are very indifferent with regard to Ceremonies; nor do they hold the *Jus Divinum* of Episcopacy. Therefore this may be intended as one politick Step towards altering the Constitution of the Church Established, and setting up *Presbytery* in the stead; which I leave to be further considered by those at the Helm.

IN the last Place, I think nothing can be more plain, than that by this Expedient, we shall run into the Evil we chiefly pretend to avoid; and that the Abolishment of the Christian Religion, will be the readiest Course we can take to introduce Popery. And I am the more inclined to this Opinion, because we know it hath been the constant Practice of the *Jesuits* to send over Emissaries, with Instructions to personate themselves Members of the several prevailing Sects amongst us. So it is recorded, that they have at sundry Times appeared in the Guise of *Presbyterians*, *Anabaptists*, *Independents*, and *Quakers*, according as any of these were most in Credit: So, since the Fashion hath been taken up of exploding Religion, the *Popish* Missionaries have not been wanting to mix with the Free-Thinkers; among whom, *Toland*, the great Oracle of the *Anti-Christians*, is an *Irish* Priest, the Son of an *Irish* Priest; and the most learned and ingenious Author of a Book, called the *Rights of the Christian Church*, was, in a proper Juncture, reconciled to the *Romish* Faith; whose true Son, as appears by an Hundred Passages in his Treatise, he still continues. Perhaps I could add some others to the Number; but the Fact is beyond Dispute; and the Reasoning they proceed by, is right: For, supposing Christianity to be extinguished, the People will never be at Ease, till they find out some other Method of Worship; which will as infallibly produce Superstition, as this will end in *Popery*.

AND therefore, if, notwithstanding all I have said, it shall still be thought necessary to have a Bill brought in for repealing Christianity; I would humbly offer an Amendment, that instead of the Word *Christianity*, may be put *Religion* in general; which I conceive, will much better answer all the good Ends proposed by the Projectors of it. For, as long as we leave in Being a God, and his Providence, with all the necessary Consequences, which curious and inquisitive Men will be apt to draw from such Premises; we do not strike at the Root of the Evil, although we should ever so effectually annihilate the present Scheme of the Gospel. For, of what Use is Freedom of Thought, if it will not produce Freedom of Action; which is the sole End, how remote soever, in Appearance, of all Objections against Christianity? And therefore, the Free-Thinkers consider it as a Sort of Edifice, wherein all the Parts have such a mutual Dependance on each other, that if you happen to pull out one single Nail, the whole Fabrick must fall to the Ground. This was happily expressed by him, who had heard of a Text brought for Proof of the Trinity, which in an antient Manuscript was differently read; he thereupon immediately took the Hint, and by a sudden Deduction of a long *Sorites*, most logically concluded; Why, if it be as you say, I may safely whore and drink on, and defy the Parson. From which, and many the like Instances easy to be produced, I think nothing can be more manifest, than that the Quarrel is not against any particular Points of hard Digestion in the Christian System; but against Religion in general; which, by laying Restraints on human Nature, is supposed the great Enemy to the Freedom of Thought and Action.

UPON the whole; if it shall still be thought for the Benefit of Church and State, that Christianity be abolished; I conceive, however, it may be more convenient to defer the Execution to a Time of Peace; and not venture in this Conjuncture to disoblige our Allies; who, as it falls out, are all Christians; and many of them, by the Prejudices of their Education, so bigotted, as to place a Sort of Pride in the Appellation. If, upon being rejected by them, we are to trust to an Alliance with the *Turk*, we shall find our selves much deceived: For, as he is too remote, and generally engaged in War with the *Persian* Emperor; so his People would be more scandalized at our Infidelity, than our Christian Neighbours. Because, the *Turks* are not only strict Observers of religious Worship; but, what is worse, believe a God; which is more than is required of us, even while we preserve the Name of Christians.

To conclude: Whatever some may think of the great Advantages to Trade, by this favourite Scheme; I do very much apprehend, that in six Months Time, after the Act is past for the Extirpation of the Gospel, the Bank and *East-India* Stock may fall, at least, One *per Cent*. And, since that is Fifty Times more than ever the Wisdom of our Age thought fit to venture for the *Preservation* of Christianity, there is no Reason we should be at so great a Loss, meerly for the Sake of *destroying* it.

THE
INTELLIGENCER

NUMBER III

——— *Ipse per omnes*
Ibit personas, & turbam reddet in unam.

Written in *Ireland* in the Year 1728

THE *Players* having now almost done with the Comedy called the *Beggar's Opera*, for the Season; it may be no unpleasant Speculation, to reflect a little upon this *Dramatick Piece*, so singular in the Subject and Manner, so much an Original, and which hath frequently given so very agreeable an Entertainment.

ALTHOUGH an evil *Taste* be very apt to prevail, both here and in *London*; yet there is a Point which whoever can rightly touch, will never fail of pleasing a very great Majority; so great, that the Dislikers, out of Dulness or Affectation, will be silent, and forced to fall in with the Herd: The Point I mean, is what we call *Humour*; which, in its Perfection, is allowed to be much preferable to *Wit*; if it be not rather the most useful, and agreeable Species of it.

I AGREE with Sir *William Temple*, that the Word is peculiar to our *English Tongue*; but I differ from him in the Opinion, that the Thing it self is peculiar to the *English Nation*, because the contrary may be found in many *Spanish*, *Italian*, and *French* Productions: And particularly, whoever hath a *Taste* for *true Humour*, will find an Hundred Instances of it, in those Volumes printed in *France*, under the name of *Le Theatre Italien:* To say nothing of *Rabelais*, *Cervantes*, and many others.

NOW I take the *Comedy*, or *Farce*, (or whatever Name the *Criticks* will allow it) called the *Beggar's Opera*, to excel in this

Article of *Humour*; and upon that Merit to have met with such prodigious Success, both here and in *England*.

As to *Poetry*, *Eloquence*, and *Musick*, which are said to have most Power over the Minds of Men; it is certain, that very few have a *Taste* or *Judgment* of the Excellencies of the two former; and if a Man succeed in either, it is upon the Authority of those *few Judges*, that lend their *Taste* to the Bulk of Readers, who have none of their own. I am told, there are as few good Judges in *Musick*; and that among those who crowd the *Opera's*, Nine in Ten go thither merely out of *Curiosity*, *Fashion*, or *Affectation*.

But a *Taste* for *Humour*, is in some Manner fixed to the very Nature of Man, and generally obvious to the Vulgar, except upon Subjects too refined, and superior to their Understanding.

And, as this *Taste* of *Humour* is purely natural, so is *Humour* it self; neither is it a *Talent* confined to Men of *Wit*, or *Learning*; for we observe it sometimes among common Servants, and the meanest of the People, while the very Owners are often ignorant of the Gift they possess.

I know very well, that this happy *Talent* is contemptibly treated by *Criticks*, under the Name of *low Humour*, or *low Comedy*; but I know likewise, that the *Spaniards* and *Italians*, who are allowed to have the most Wit of any *Nation* in *Europe*, do most excel in it, and do most esteem it.

By what Disposition of the Mind, what Influence of the Stars, or what Situation of the *Climate*, this Endowment is bestowed upon Mankind, may be a Question fit for *Philosophers* to discuss. It is certainly the best Ingredient towards that Kind of Satyr, which is most useful, and gives the least Offence; which, instead of lashing, laughs Men out of their Follies, and Vices; and is the Character that gives *Horace* the Preference to *Juvenal*.

And, although some Things are too serious, solemn, or sacred to be turned into Ridicule, yet the Abuses of them are certainly not; since it is allowed, that Corruptions in *Religion*, *Politicks*, and *Law*, may be proper *Topicks* for this Kind of *Satyr*.

There are two Ends that Men propose in writing Satyr; one of them less noble than the other, as regarding nothing further than the private Satisfaction, and Pleasure of the Writer; but without any View towards *personal Malice:* The other is a *publick Spirit*, prompting Men of *Genius* and Virtue, to mend the World as far as they are able. And as both these Ends are innocent, so the latter is highly commendable. With regard to the former, I demand, whether I have not as good a Title to laugh, as Men have to be ridiculous; and to expose Vice, as another hath to be vicious. If I ridicule the Follies and Corruptions of a *Court*, a *Ministry*, or a *Senate*, are they not amply paid by *Pensions*, *Titles*, and *Power*; while I expect, and desire no other Reward, than that of laughing with a few Friends in a Corner? Yet, if those who take Offence, think me in the Wrong, I am ready to change the Scene with them, whenever they please.

But, if my Design be to make Mankind better; then I think it is my Duty; at least, I am sure it is the Interest of those very *Courts* and *Ministers*, whose Follies or Vices I ridicule, to reward me for my good Intentions: For if it be reckoned a high Point of Wisdom to get the Laughers on our Side; it is much more easy, as well as wise, to get those on our Side, who can make Millions laugh when they please.

My Reason for mentioning *Courts*, and *Ministers*, (*whom I never think on, but with the most profound Veneration*) is, because an Opinion obtains, that in the *Beggar's Opera*, there appears to be some Reflection upon *Courtiers* and *Statesmen*, whereof I am by no Means a Judge.

It is true, indeed, that Mr. Gay, the Author of this Piece, hath been somewhat singular in the Course of his Fortunes; for it hath happened, that after Fourteen Years attending the *Court*, with a large Stock of real Merit, a modest and agreeable Conversation, a *Hundred Promises*, and *five Hundred Friends*, he hath failed of Preferment; and upon a very weighty Reason. He lay under the Suspicion of having written a Libel, or Lampoon against a great * Minister. It is true, that great Minister was demonstratively convinced, and publickly owned

* Sir Robert Walpole.

his Conviction, that Mr. GAY was not the Author; but having lain under the Suspicion, it seemed very just, that he should suffer the punishment; because in this most reformed Age, the Virtues of a Prime Minister are no more to be suspected, than the Chastity of *Cæsar*'s Wife.

IT must be allowed, That the *Beggar's Opera* is not the first of Mr. GAY's Works, wherein he hath been faulty, with Regard to *Courtiers* and *Statesmen*. For to omit his other Pieces; even in his Fables, published within two Years past, and dedicated to the Duke of CUMBERLAND, for which he was *promised* a Reward, he hath been thought somewhat too bold upon the *Courtiers*. And although it be highly probable, he meant only the *Courtiers* of former Times, yet he acted unwarily, by not considering that the Malignity of some People might misinterpret what he said, to the Disadvantage of present *Persons* and Affairs.

BUT I have now done with Mr. GAY as a Politician; and shall consider him henceforward only as Author of the *Beggar's Opera*, wherein he hath by a Turn of *Humour*, entirely new, placed Vices of all Kinds in the strongest and most odious Light; and thereby, done eminent Service, both to *Religion* and *Morality*. This appears from the unparallelled Success he hath met with. All *Ranks*, *Parties*, and *Denominations* of Men, either crowding to see his *Opera*, or reading it with Delight in their Closets; even *Ministers* of State, whom he is thought to have most offended (next to those whom the Actors represent) appearing frequently at the *Theatre*, from a Consciousness of their own Innocence, and to convince the World how unjust a Parallel, *Malice*, *Envy*, and *Disaffection to the Government have made*.

I AM assured that several worthy *Clergy-Men* in this *City*, went privately to see the *Beggar's Opera* represented; and that the *fleering Coxcombs* in the *Pit*, amused themselves with making Discoveries, and spreading the Names of those Gentlemen round the Audience.

I SHALL not pretend to vindicate a *Clergy-Man*, who would appear openly in his Habit at a *Theatre*, with such a vicious Crew, as might probably stand round him, at such *Comedies*, and profane *Tragedies* as are often represented. Besides, I know very well, that Persons of their Function are bound to avoid the Appearance of Evil, or of giving Cause of Offence. But when the *Lords Chancellors*, who are Keepers of the King's Conscience; when the *Judges* of the Land, whose Title is *Reverend*; when *Ladies*, who are bound by the Rules of their Sex to the strictest Decency, appear in the *Theatre* without Censure; I cannot understand, why a young *Clergy-Man*, who comes concealed, out of Curiosity to see an innocent and moral Play, should be so highly condemned: Nor do I much approve the Rigour of a great Prelate, who said, *he hoped none of his Clergy were there*. I am glad to hear there are no weightier Objections against that Reverend Body planted in this City, and I wish there never may. But I should be very sorry, that any of them should be so weak, as to imitate a **Court-Chaplain* in ENGLAND, who preached against the *Beggar's Opera*; which will probably do more Good, than a thousand Sermons of so stupid, so injudicious, and so prostitute a Divine.

IN this happy Performance of Mr. GAY's, all the Characters are just, and none of them carried beyond Nature, or hardly beyond Practice. It discovers the whole System of that Common-Wealth, or that *Imperium in Imperio* of Iniquity, established among us, by which neither our Lives nor our Properties are secure, either in the High-ways, or in publick Assemblies, or even in our own Houses. It shews the miserable Lives and the constant Fate of those abandoned Wretches: For how little they sell their Lives and Souls; betrayed by their *Whores*, their *Comrades*, and the *Receivers* and *Purchasers* of those Thefts and Robberies. This *Comedy* contains likewise a *Satyr*, which, without enquiring whether it affects the present Age, may possibly be useful in Times to come. I mean, where the Author takes the Occasion of comparing those *common Robbers of the Publick*, and their several Stratagems of betraying, undermining and hanging each other, to the several Arts of *Politicians* in Times of Corruption.

THIS *Comedy* likewise exposeth with great Justice, that unnatural Taste for *Italian* Musick among us, which is wholly

* Dr. Herring, *Chaplain to the Society at Lincoln's Inn.*

unsuitable to our Northern *Climate*, and the *Genius* of the *People*, whereby we are over-run with *Italian Effeminacy*, and *Italian* Nonsense. An old Gentleman said to me, that many Years ago, when the Practice of an unnatural Vice grew frequent in *London*, and many were prosecuted for it, he was sure it would be a Fore-runner of *Italian* Opera's and Singers; and then we should want nothing but Stabbing or Poisoning, to make us perfect *Italians*.

UPON the whole, I deliver my Judgment, That nothing but servile Attachment to a Party, Affectation of Singularity, lamentable Dullness, mistaken Zeal, or studied Hypocrisy, can have the least reasonable Objection against this excellent moral Performance of the *Celebrated Mr.* GAY.

HINTS

TOWARDS

AN ESSAY

ON

CONVERSATION.

I HAVE observed few obvious Subjects to have been so seldom, or, at least, so slightly handled as this; and, indeed, I know few so difficult, to be treated as it ought, nor yet upon which there seemeth to be so much to be said.

MOST Things, pursued by Men for the Happiness of publick or private Life, our Wit or Folly have so refined, that they seldom subsist but in Idea; a true Friend, a good Marriage, a perfect Form of Government, with some others, require so many Ingredients, so good in their several Kinds, and so much Niceness in mixing them, that for some thousands of Years Men have despaired of reducing their Schemes to Perfection: But in Conversation, it is, or might be otherwise; for here we are only to avoid a Multitude of Errors, which, although a Matter of some Difficulty, may be in every Man's Power, for Want of which it remaineth as meer an Idea as the other. Therefore it seemeth to me, that the truest Way to understand Conversation, is to know the Faults and Errors to which it is subject, and from thence, every Man to form Maxims to himself whereby it may be regulated; because it requireth few Talents to which most Men are not born, or at least may not acquire without any great Genius or Study. For Nature hath left every Man a Capacity of being agreeable, though not of shining in Company, and there are an hundred Men sufficiently qualified for both, who by a very few Faults, that they might correct in half an Hour, are not so much as tolerable.

I WAS prompted to write my Thoughts upon this Subject by mere Indignation, to reflect that so useful and innocent a Pleasure, so fitted for every Period and Condition of Life, and so much in all Men's Power, should be so much neglected and abused.

AND in this Discourse it will be necessary to note those Errors that are obvious, as well as others which are seldomer observed, since there are few so obvious or acknowledged, into which most Men, some Time or other, are not apt to run.

FOR Instance: Nothing is more generally exploded than the Folly of Talking too much, yet I rarely remember to have seen five People together, where some one among them hath not been predominant in that Kind, to the great Constraint and Disgust of all the rest. But among such as deal in Multitudes of Words, none are comparable to the sober deliberate Talker, who proceedeth with much Thought and Caution, maketh his Preface, brancheth out into several Digressions, findeth a Hint that putteth him in Mind of another Story, which he promiseth to tell you when this is done; cometh back regularly to his Subject, cannot readily call to Mind some Person's Name, holdeth his Head, complaineth of his Memory; the whole Company all this while in Suspence; at length says, it is no Matter, and so goes on. And, to crown the Business, it perhaps proveth at last a Story the Company hath heard fifty Times before; or, at best, some insipid Adventure of the Relater.

ANOTHER general Fault in Conversation is, That of those who affect to talk of themselves: Some, without any Ceremony, will run over the History of their Lives; will relate the Annals of their Diseases, with the several Symptoms and Circumstances of them; will enumerate the Hardships and Injustice they have suffered in Court, in Parliament, in Love, or in Law. Others are more dexterous, and with great Art will lie on the Watch to hook in their own Praise: They will call a Witness to remember, they always foretold what would happen in such a

Case, but none would believe them; they advised such a Man from the Beginning, and told him the Consequences just as they happened; but he would have his own Way. Others make a Vanity of telling their Faults; they are the strangest Men in the World; they cannot dissemble, they own it is a Folly; they have lost Abundance of Advantages by it; but, if you would give them the World they cannot help it; there is something in their Nature that abhors Insincerity and Constraint; with many other unsufferable Topicks of the same Altitude.

OF such mighty Importance every Man is to himself, and ready to think he is so to others; without once making this easy and obvious Reflection, that his Affairs can have no more Weight with other Men, than theirs have with him; and how little that is, he is sensible enough.

WHERE Company hath met, I often have observed two Persons discover, by some Accident, that they were bred together at the same School or University; after which the rest are condemned to Silence, and to listen while these two are refreshing each other's Memory with the arch Tricks and Passages of themselves and their Comrades.

I KNOW a Great Officer of the Army, who will sit for some time with a supercilious and impatient Silence, full of Anger and Contempt for those who are talking; at length of a sudden demand Audience, decide the Matter in a short dogmatical Way; then withdraw within himself again, and vouchsafe to talk no more, until his Spirits circulate again to the same Point.

THERE are some Faults in Conversation, which none are so subject to as the Men of Wit, nor ever so much as when they are with each other. If they have opened their Mouths, without endeavouring to say a witty Thing, they think it is so many Words lost; it is a Torment to the Hearers, as much as to themselves, to see them upon the Rack for Invention, and in perpetual Constraint, with so little Success. They must do something extraordinary, in order to acquit themselves, and answer their Character; else the Standers-by may be disappointed, and be apt to think them only like the rest of Mortals. I have known two Men of Wit industriously brought together, in order to entertain the Company, where they have made a very ridiculous Figure, and provided all the Mirth at their own Expence.

I KNOW a Man of Wit, who is never easy but where he can be allowed to dictate and preside; he neither expecteth to be informed or entertained, but to display his own Talents. His Business is to be good Company, and not good Conversation; and, therefore, he chuseth to frequent those who are content to listen, and profess themselves his Admirers. And, indeed, the worst Conversation I ever remember to have heard in my Life, was that at *Will*'s Coffee-house, where the Wits (as they were called) used formerly to assemble; that is to say, five or six Men, who had writ Plays, or at least Prologues, or had Share in a Miscellany, came thither, and entertained one another with their trifling Composures, in so important an Air, as if they had been the noblest Efforts of human Nature, or that the Fate of Kingdoms depended on them; and they were usually attended with an humble Audience of young Students from the Inns of Courts, or the Universities, who, at due Distance, listened to these Oracles, and returned Home with great Contempt for their Law and Philosophy, their Heads filled with Trash, under the Name of Politeness, Criticism and Belles Lettres.

BY these Means the Poets, for many Years past, were all over-run with Pedantry. For, as I take it, the Word is not properly used; because Pedantry is the too frequent or unseasonable obtruding our own Knowledge in common Discourse, and placing too great a Value upon it; by which Definition Men of the Court or the Army may be as guilty of Pedantry as a Philosopher, or a Divine; and, it is the same Vice in Women, when they are over-copious upon the Subject of their Petticoats, or their Fans, or their China: For which Reason, although it be a Piece of Prudence, as well as good Manners, to put Men upon talking on Subjects they are best versed in, yet that is a Liberty a wise Man could hardly take; because, beside the Imputation of Pedantry, it is what he would never improve by.

THIS great Town is usually provided with some Player,

Mimick, or Buffoon, who hath a general Reception at the good Tables; familiar and domestick with Persons of the first Quality, and usually sent for at every Meeting to divert the Company; against which I have no Objection. You go there as to a Farce, or a Puppet-Show; your Business is only to laugh in Season, either out of Inclination or Civility, while this merry Companion is acting his Part. It is a Business he hath undertaken, and we are to suppose he is paid for his Day's Work. I only quarrel, when in select and private Meetings, where Men of Wit and Learning are invited to pass an Evening, this Jester should be admitted to run over his Circle of Tricks, and make the whole Company unfit for any other Conversation, besides the Indignity of confounding Men's Talents at so shameful a Rate.

RAILLERY is the finest Part of Conversation; but, as it is our usual Custom to counterfeit and adulterate whatever is dear to us, so we have done with this, and turned it all into what is generally called Repartee, or being smart; just as when an expensive Fashion cometh up, those who are not able to reach it, content themselves with some paltry Imitation. It now passeth for Raillery to run a Man down in Discourse, to put him out of Countenance, and make him ridiculous, sometimes to expose the Defects of his Person, or Understanding; on all which Occasions he is obliged not to be angry, to avoid the Imputation of not being able to take a Jest. It is admirable to observe one who is dexterous at this Art, singling out a weak Adversary, getting the Laugh on his Side, and then carrying all before him. The *French*, from whom we borrow the Word, have a quite different Idea of the Thing, and so had we in the politer Age of our Fathers. Raillery was to say something that at first appeared a Reproach, or Reflection; but, by some Turn of Wit unexpected and surprising, ended always in a Compliment, and to the Advantage of the Person it was addressed to. And, surely, one of the best Rules in Conversation is, never to say a Thing which any of the Company can reasonably wish we had rather left unsaid; nor can there any Thing be well more contrary to the Ends for which

People meet together, than to part unsatisfied with each other, or themselves.

THERE are two Faults in Conversation, which appear very different, yet arise from the same Root, and are equally blameable; I mean, an Impatience to interrupt others, and the Uneasiness at being interrupted ourselves. The two chief Ends of Conversation are to entertain and improve those we are among, or to receive those Benefits ourselves; which whoever will consider, cannot easily run into either of those two Errors; because when any Man speaketh in Company, it is to be supposed he doth it for his Hearer's Sake, and not his own; so that common Discretion will teach us not to force their Attention, if they are not willing to lend it; nor on the other Side, to interrupt him who is in Possession, because that is in the grossest Manner to give the Preference to our own good Sense.

THERE are some People, whose good Manners will not suffer them to interrupt you; but what is almost as bad, will discover Abundance of Impatience, and lye upon the Watch until you have done, because they have started something in their own Thoughts which they long to be delivered of. Mean Time, they are so far from regarding what passes, that their Imaginations are wholely turned upon what they have in Reserve, for fear it should slip out of their Memory; and thus they confine their Invention, which might otherwise range over a hundred Things full as good, and that might be much more naturally introduced.

THERE is a Sort of rude Familiarity, which some People, by practising among their Intimates, have introduced into their general Conversation, and would have it pass for innocent Freedom, or Humour, which is a dangerous Experiment in our Northern Climate, where all the little Decorum and Politeness we have are purely forced by Art, and are so ready to lapse into Barbarity. This among the *Romans*, was the Raillery of Slaves, of which we have many Instances in *Plautus*. It seemeth to have been introduced among us by *Cromwell*, who, by preferring the Scum of the People, made it a Court Entertainment, of which I have heard many Particulars; and, considering all

Things were turned upside down, it was reasonable and judicious; although it was a Piece of Policy found out to ridicule a Point of Honour in the other Extream, when the smallest Word misplaced among Gentlemen ended in a Duel.

THERE are some Men excellent at telling a Story, and provided with a plentiful Stock of them, which they can draw out upon Occasion in all Companies; and, considering how low Conversation runs now among us, it is not altogether a contemptible Talent; however, it is subject to two unavoidable Defects; frequent Repetition, and being soon exhausted; so that whoever valueth this Gift in himself, hath need of a good Memory, and ought frequently to shift his Company, that he may not discover the Weakness of his Fund; for those who are thus endowed, have seldom any other Revenue, but live upon the main Stock.

GREAT Speakers in Publick, are seldom agreeable in private Conversation, whether their Faculty be natural, or acquired by Practice and often venturing. Natural Elocution, although it may seem a Paradox, usually springeth from a Barrenness of Invention and of Words, by which Men who have only one Stock of Notions upon every Subject, and one Set of Phrases to express them in, they swim upon the Superficies, and offer themselves on every Occasion; therefore, Men of much Learning, and who know the Compass of a Language, are generally the worst Talkers on a sudden, until much Practice hath inured and emboldened them, because they are confounded with Plenty of Matter, Variety of Notions, and of Words, which they cannot readily chuse, but are perplexed and entangled by too great a Choice; which is no Disadvantage in private Conversation; where, on the other Side, the Talent of Haranguing is, of all others, most insupportable.

NOTHING hath spoiled Men more for Conversation, than the Character of being Wits, to support which, they never fail of encouraging a Number of Followers and Admirers, who list themselves in their Service, wherein they find their Accounts on both Sides, by pleasing their mutual Vanity. This hath given the former such an Air of Superiority, and made the latter so pragmatical, that neither of them are well to be endured. I say nothing here of the Itch of Dispute and Contradiction, telling of Lies, or of those who are troubled with the Disease called the Wandering of the Thoughts, that they are never present in Mind at what passeth in Discourse; for whoever labours under any of these Possessions, is as unfit for Conversation as a Mad-man in Bedlam.

I THINK I have gone over most of the Errors in Conversation, that have fallen under my Notice or Memory, except some that are merely personal, and others too gross to need exploding; such as lewd or prophane Talk; but I pretend only to treat the Errors of Conversation in general, and not the several Subjects of Discourse, which would be infinite. Thus we see how human Nature is most debased, by the Abuse of that Faculty which is held the great Distinction between Men and Brutes; and how little Advantage we make of that which might be the greatest, the most lasting, and the most innocent, as well as useful Pleasure of Life: In Default of which, we are forced to take up with those poor Amusements of Dress and Visiting, or the more pernicious ones of Play, Drink and Vicious Amours, whereby the Nobility and Gentry of both Sexes are entirely corrupted both in Body and Mind, and have lost all Notions of Love, Honour, Friendship, Generosity; which, under the Name of Fopperies, have been for some Time laughed out of Doors.

THIS Degeneracy of Conversation, with the pernicious Consequences thereof upon our Humours and Dispositions, hath been owing, among other Causes, to the Custom arisen, for some Years past, of excluding Women from any Share in our Society, further than in Parties at Play, or Dancing, or in the Pursuit of an Amour. I take the highest Period of Politeness in *England* (and it is of the same Date in *France*) to have been the peaceable Part of King *Charles* the First's Reign; and from what we read of those Times, as well as from the Accounts I have formerly met with from some who lived in that Court, the Methods then used for raising and cultivating Conversation, were altogether different from ours: Several Ladies, whom we find celebrated by the Poets of that Age, had Assemblies at their Houses, where Persons of the best Understanding, and of both Sexes, met to pass the Evenings in discoursing upon whatever agreeable Subjects were occasionally started; and, although we are apt to ridicule the sublime Platonic Notions they had, or personated, in Love and Friendship, I conceive their Refinements were grounded upon Reason, and that a little Grain of the Romance is no ill Ingredient to preserve and exalt the Dignity of human Nature, without which it is apt to degenerate into every Thing that is sordid, vicious and low. If there were no other Use in the Conversation of Ladies, it is sufficient that it would lay a Restraint upon those odious Topicks of Immodesty and Indecencies, into which the Rudeness of our Northern Genius is so apt to fall. And, therefore, it is observable in those sprightly Gentlemen about the Town, who are so very dexterous at entertaining a Vizard Mask in the Park or the Playhouse, that, in the Company of Ladies of Virtue and Honour, they are silent and disconcerted, and out of their Element.

THERE are some People who think they sufficiently acquit themselves, and entertain their Company with relating of Facts of no Consequence, nor at all out of the Road of such common Incidents as happen every Day; and this I have observed more frequently among the *Scots* than any other Nation, who are very careful not to omit the minutest Circumstances of Time or Place; which Kind of Discourse, if it were not a little relieved by the uncouth Terms and Phrases, as well as Accent and Gesture peculiar to that Country, would be hardly tolerable. It is not a Fault in Company to talk much; but to continue it long, is certainly one; for, if the Majority of those who are got together be naturally silent or cautious, the Conversation will flag, unless it be often renewed by one among them, who can start new Subjects, provided he doth not dwell upon them, but leaveth Room for Answers and Replies.

A MODEST
PROPOSAL
FOR

Preventing the Children of poor People in Ireland, *from being a Burden to their Parents or Country; and for making them beneficial to the Publick.*

Written in the Year 1729

IT is a melancholly Object to those, who walk through this great Town, or travel in the Country; when they see the *Streets*, the *Roads*, and *Cabbin-doors* crowded with *Beggars* of the Female Sex, followed by three, four, or six Children, *all in Rags*, and importuning every Passenger for an Alms. These *Mothers*, instead of being able to work for their honest Livelyhood, are forced to employ all their Time in stroling to beg Sustenance for their *helpless Infants*; who, as they grow up, either turn *Thieves* for want of Work; or leave their *dear Native Country*, *to fight for the Pretender in* Spain, or sell themselves to the *Barbadoes*.

I THINK it is agreed by all Parties, that this prodigious Number of Children in the Arms, or on the Backs, or at the *Heels* of their *Mothers*, and frequently of their *Fathers*, is *in the present deplorable State of the Kingdom*, a very great additional Grievance; and therefore, whoever could find out a fair, cheap, and easy Method of making these Children sound and useful Members of the Commonwealth, would deserve so well of the Publick, as to have his Statue set up for a Preserver of the Nation.

BUT my Intention is very far from being confined to provide only for the Children of *professed Beggars*: It is of a much greater

Extent, and shall take in the whole Number of Infants at a certain Age, who are born of Parents, in effect as little able to support them, as those who demand our Charity in the Streets.

As to my own Part, having turned my Thoughts for many Years, upon this important Subject, and maturely weighed the several *Schemes of other Projectors*, I have always found them grosly mistaken in their Computation. It is true a Child, *just dropt from its Dam*, may be supported by her Milk, for a Solar Year with little other Nourishment; at most not above the Value of two Shillings; which the Mother may certainly get, or the Value in *Scraps*, by her lawful Occupation of *Begging*: And, it is exactly at one Year old, that I propose to provide for them in such a Manner, as, instead of being a Charge upon their *Parents*, or the *Parish*, or *wanting Food and Raiment* for the rest of their Lives; they shall, on the contrary, contribute to the Feeding, and partly to the Cloathing, of many Thousands.

THERE is likewise another great Advantage in my *Scheme*, that it will prevent those *voluntary Abortions*, and that horrid Practice of *Women murdering their Bastard Children*; alas! too frequent among us; sacrificing the *poor innocent Babes*, I doubt, more to avoid the Expence than the Shame; which would move Tears and Pity in the most Savage and inhuman Breast.

THE Number of Souls in *Ireland* being usually reckoned one Million and a half; of these I calculate there may be about Two hundred Thousand Couple whose Wives are Breeders; from which Number I subtract thirty thousand Couples, who are able to maintain their own Children; although I apprehend there cannot be so many, under *the present Distresses of the Kingdom*; but this being granted, there will remain an Hundred and Seventy Thousand Breeders. I again subtract Fifty Thousand, for those Women who miscarry, or whose Children die by Accident, or Disease, within the Year. There only remain an Hundred and Twenty Thousand Children of poor Parents, annually born: The Question therefore is, How this Number shall be reared, and provided for? Which, as I have already said, under the present Situation of Affairs, is utterly impossible, by all the Methods hitherto proposed: For we can *neither employ them in Handicraft* or *Agriculture*; we neither build Houses, (I mean in the Country) nor cultivate Land: They can very seldom pick up a Livelyhood *by Stealing* until they arrive at six Years old; except where they are of towardly Parts; although, I confess, they learn the Rudiments much earlier; during which Time, they can, however, be properly looked upon only as *Probationers*; as I have been informed by a principal Gentleman in the County of *Cavan*, who protested to me, that he never knew above one or two Instances under the Age of six, even in a Part of the Kingdom *so renowned for the quickest Proficiency in that Art*.

I AM assured by our Merchants, that a Boy or a Girl before twelve Years old, is no saleable Commodity; and even when they come to this Age, they will not yield above Three Pounds, or Three Pounds and half a Crown at most, on the Exchange; which cannot turn to Account either to the Parents or the Kingdom; the Charge of Nutriment and Rags, having been at least four Times that Value.

I SHALL now therefore humbly propose my own Thoughts; which I hope will not be liable to the least Objection.

I HAVE been assured by a very knowing *American* of my Acquaintance in *London*; that a young healthy Child, well nursed, is, at a Year old, a most delicious, nourishing, and wholesome Food; whether *Stewed*, *Roasted*, *Baked*, or *Boiled*; and, I make no doubt, that it will equally serve in a *Fricasie*, or *Ragoust*.

I DO therefore humbly offer it to *publick Consideration*, that of the Hundred and Twenty Thousand Children, already computed, Twenty thousand may be reserved for Breed; whereof only one Fourth Part to be Males; which is more than we allow to *Sheep*, *black Cattle*, or *Swine*; and my Reason is, that these Children are seldom the Fruits of Marriage, *a Circumstance not much regarded by our Savages*; therefore, *one Male* will be sufficient to serve *four Females*. That the remaining Hundred thousand, may, at a Year old, be offered in Sale to the *Persons of Quality* and *Fortune*, through the Kingdom; always advising the Mother to let them suck plentifully in the last Month, so as to render them plump, and fat for a good

Table. A Child will make two Dishes at an Entertainment for Friends; and when the Family dines alone, the fore or hind Quarter will make a reasonable Dish; and seasoned with a little Pepper or Salt, will be very good Boiled on the fourth Day, especially in *Winter*.

I HAVE reckoned upon a Medium, that a Child just born will weigh Twelve Pounds; and in a solar Year, if tolerably nursed, encreaseth to twenty eight Pounds.

I GRANT this Food will be somewhat dear, and therefore very *proper for Landlords*; who, as they have already devoured most of the Parents, seem to have the best Title to the Children.

INFANTS Flesh will be in Season throughout the Year; but more plentiful in *March*, and a little before and after: For we are told by a grave * Author, an eminent *French* Physician, that *Fish being a prolifick Dyet*, there are more Children born in *Roman Catholick Countries* about Nine Months after *Lent*, than at any other Season: Therefore reckoning a Year after *Lent*, the Markets will be more glutted than usual; because the Number of *Popish Infants*, is, at least, three to one in this Kingdom; and therefore it will have one other Collateral Advantage, by lessening the Number of *Papists* among us.

I HAVE already computed the Charge of nursing a Beggar's Child (in which List I reckon all *Cottagers*, *Labourers*, and Four fifths of the *Farmers*) to be about two Shillings *per Annum*, Rags included; and I believe, no Gentleman would repine to give Ten Shillings for the *Carcase of a good fat Child*; which, as I have said, will make four Dishes of excellent nutritive Meat, when he hath only some particular Friend, or his own Family, to dine with him. Thus the Squire will learn to be a good Landlord, and grow popular among his Tenants; the Mother will have Eight Shillings net Profit, and be fit for Work until she produceth another Child.

THOSE who are more thrifty (*as I must confess the Times require*) may flay the Carcase; the Skin of which, artificially dressed, will make admirable *Gloves for Ladies*, and *Summer Boots for fine Gentlemen*.

As to our City of *Dublin*; Shambles may be appointed for

* Rabelais.

this Purpose, in the most convenient Parts of it; and Butchers we may be assured will not be wanting; although I rather recommend buying the Children alive, and dressing them hot from the Knife, as we do *roasting Pigs*.

A VERY worthy Person, *a true Lover of his Country*, and whose Virtues I highly esteem, was lately pleased, in discoursing on this Matter, to offer a Refinement upon my Scheme. He said, that many Gentlemen of this Kingdom, having of late destroyed their Deer; he conceived, that the Want of Venison might be well supplied by the Bodies of young Lads and Maidens, not exceeding fourteen Years of Age, nor under twelve; so great a Number of both Sexes in every County being now ready to starve, for Want of Work and Service: And these to be disposed of by their Parents, if alive, or otherwise by their nearest Relations. But with due Deference to so excellent a Friend, and so deserving a Patriot, I cannot be altogether in his Sentiments. For as to the Males, my *American* Acquaintance assured me from frequent Experience, that their Flesh was generally tough and lean, like that of our School-boys, by continual Exercise, and their Taste disagreeable; and to fatten them would not answer the Charge. Then, as to the Females, it would, I think, with humble Submission, *be a Loss to the Publick*, because they soon would become Breeders themselves: And besides it is not improbable, that some scrupulous People might be apt to censure such a Practice (although indeed very unjustly) as a little bordering upon Cruelty; which, I confess, hath always been with me the strongest Objection against any Project, how well soever intended.

BUT in order to justify my Friend; he confessed, that this Expedient was put into his Head by the famous *Salmanaazor*, a Native of the Island *Formosa*, who came from thence to *London*, above twenty Years ago, and in Conversation told my Friend, that in his Country, when any young Person happened to be put to Death, the Executioner sold the Carcase to *Persons of Quality*, as a prime Dainty; and that, in his Time, the Body of a plump Girl of fifteen, who was crucified for an Attempt to poison the Emperor, was sold to his Imperial

Majesty's prime Minister of State, and other great *Mandarins* of the Court, *in Joints from the Gibbet*, at Four hundred Crowns. Neither indeed can I deny, that if the same Use were made of several plump young girls in this Town, who, without one single Groat to their Fortunes, cannot stir Abroad without a Chair, and appear at the *Play-house*, and *Assemblies* in foreign Fineries, which they never will pay for; the Kingdom would not be the worse.

SOME Persons of a desponding Spirit are in great Concern about that vast Number of poor People, who are Aged, Diseased, or Maimed; and I have been desired to employ my Thoughts what Course may be taken, to ease the Nation of so grievous an Incumbrance. But I am not in the least Pain upon that Matter; because it is very well known, that they are every Day *dying*, and *rotting*, by *Cold* and *Famine*, and *Filth*, and *Vermin*, as fast as can be reasonably expected. And as to the younger Labourers, they are now in almost as hopeful a Condition: They cannot get Work, and consequently pine away for Want of Nourishment, to a Degree, that if at any Time they are accidentally hired to common Labour, they have not Strength to perform it; and thus the Country, and themselves, are in a fair Way of being soon delivered from the Evils to come.

I HAVE too long digressed; and therefore shall return to my Subject. I think the Advantages by the Proposal which I have made, are obvious, and many, as well as of the highest Importance.

FOR, *First*, as I have already observed, it would greatly lessen the *Number of Papists*, with whom we are yearly over-run; being the principal Breeders of the Nation, as well as our most dangerous Enemies; and who stay at home on Purpose, with a Design to *deliver the Kingdom to the Pretender*; hoping to take their Advantage by the Absence *of so many good Protestants*, who have chosen rather to leave their Country, than stay at home, and pay Tithes against their Conscience, to an idolatrous *Episcopal Curate*.

SECONDLY, The poorer Tenants will have something valuable of their own, which, by Law, may be made liable to

Distress, and help to pay their Landlord's Rent; their Corn and Cattle being already seized, and *Money a Thing unknown.*

THIRDLY, Whereas the Maintenance of an Hundred Thousand Children, from two Years old, and upwards, cannot be computed at less than ten Shillings a Piece *per Annum*, the Nation's Stock will be thereby encreased Fifty Thousand Pounds *per Annum*; besides the Profit of a new Dish, introduced to the Tables of all *Gentlemen of Fortune* in the Kingdom, who have any Refinement in Taste; and the Money will circulate among ourselves, the Goods being entirely of our own Growth and Manufacture.

FOURTHLY, The constant Breeders, besides the Gain of Eight Shillings *Sterling per Annum*, by the Sale of their Children, will be rid of the Charge of maintaining them after the first Year.

FIFTHLY, This Food would likewise bring great *Custom to Taverns*, where the Vintners will certainly be so prudent, as to procure the best Receipts for dressing it to Perfection; and consequently, have their Houses frequented by all the *fine Gentlemen*, who justly value themselves upon their Knowledge in good Eating; and a skilful Cook, who understands how to oblige his Guests, will contrive to make it as expensive as they please.

SIXTHLY, This would be a great Inducement to Marriage, which all wise Nations have either encouraged by Rewards, or enforced by Laws and Penalties. It would encrease the Care and Tenderness of Mothers towards their Children, when they were sure of a Settlement for Life, to the poor Babes, provided in some Sort by the Publick, to their annual Profit instead of Expence. We should soon see an honest Emulation among the married Women, *which of them could bring the fattest Child to the Market.* Men would become as *fond* of their Wives, during the Time of their Pregnancy, as they are now of their *Mares* in Foal, their *Cows* in Calf, or *Sows* when they are ready to farrow; nor offer to beat or kick them, (as it is too *frequent* a Practice) for fear of a Miscarriage.

MANY other Advantages might be enumerated. For instance, the Addition of some Thousand Carcasses in our

Exportation of barrelled Beef: The Propagation of *Swines Flesh*, and Improvement in the Art of making good *Bacon*; so much wanted among us by the great Destruction of *Pigs*, too frequent at our Tables, and are no way comparable in Taste, or Magnificence, to a well-grown fat yearling Child; which, roasted whole, will make a considerable Figure at a *Lord Mayor's Feast*, or any other publick Entertainment. But this, and many others, I omit; being studious of Brevity.

SUPPOSING that one Thousand Families in this City, would be constant Customers for Infants Flesh; besides others who might have it at *merry Meetings*, particularly *Weddings* and *Christenings*; I compute that *Dublin* would take off, annually, about Twenty Thousand Carcasses; and the rest of the Kingdom (where probably they will be sold somewhat cheaper) the remaining Eighty Thousand.

I CAN think of no one Objection, that will possibly be raised against this Proposal; unless it should be urged, that the Number of People will be thereby much lessened in the Kingdom. This I freely own; and it was indeed one principal Design in offering it to the World. I desire the Reader will observe, that I calculate my Remedy *for this one individual Kingdom of* IRELAND, *and for no other that ever was, is, or I think ever can be upon Earth.* Therefore, let no man talk to me of other Expedients: *Of taxing our Absentees at five Shillings a Pound: Of using neither Cloaths, nor Houshold Furniture except what is of our own Growth and Manufacture: Of utterly rejecting the Materials and Instruments that promote foreign Luxury: Of curing the Expensiveness of Pride, Vanity, Idleness, and Gaming in our Women: Of introducing a Vein of Parsimony, Prudence and Temperance: Of learning to love our Country, wherein we differ even from* LAPLANDERS, *and the Inhabitants of* TOPINAMBOO: *Of quitting our Animosities, and Factions; nor act any longer like the* Jews, *who were murdering one another at the very Moment their City was taken: Of being a little cautious not to sell our Country and Consciences for nothing: Of teaching Landlords to have, at least, one Degree of Mercy towards their Tenants.* Lastly, *Of putting a Spirit of Honesty, Industry, and Skill into our Shop-keepers; who, if a Resolution could now be taken to buy only our native Goods, would immediately unite to cheat and exact upon us in the Price, the Measure, and the Goodness; nor could ever yet be brought to make one fair Proposal of just Dealing, though often and earnestly invited to it.*

THEREFORE I repeat, let no Man talk to me of these and the like Expedients; till he hath, at least, a Glimpse of Hope, that there will ever be some hearty and sincere Attempt to put *them in Practice.*

BUT, as to my self; having been wearied out for many Years with offering vain, idle, visionary Thoughts; and at length utterly despairing of Success, I fortunately fell upon this Proposal; which, as it is wholly new, so it hath something *solid* and *real*, of no Expence, and little Trouble, full in our own Power; and whereby we can incur no Danger in *disobliging* ENGLAND: For, this Kind of Commodity will not bear Exportation; the Flesh being of too tender a Consistence, to admit a long Continuance in Salt; *although, perhaps, I could name a Country, which would be glad to eat up our whole Nation without it.*

AFTER all, I am not so violently bent upon my own Opinion, as to reject any Offer proposed by wise Men, which shall be found equally innocent, cheap, easy, and effectual. But before something of that Kind shall be advanced, in Contradiction to my Scheme, and offering a better; I desire the Author, or Authors, will be pleased maturely to consider two Points. *First*, As Things now stand, how they will be able to find Food and Raiment, for a Hundred Thousand useless Mouths and Backs? And *secondly*, There being a round Million of Creatures in human Figure, throughout this Kingdom; whose whole Subsistence, put into a common Stock, would leave them in Debt two Millions of Pounds *Sterling*; adding those, who are Beggars by Profession, to the Bulk of Farmers, Cottagers, and Labourers, with their Wives and Children, who are Beggars in Effect; I desire those Politicians, who dislike my Overture, and may perhaps be so bold to attempt an Answer, that they will first ask the Parents of these Mortals, Whether they would not, at this Day, think it a great Happiness to have been sold for Food at a Year old, in the Manner I prescribe; and thereby have avoided such a perpetual Scene of Misfortunes, as they have since gone through; by the *Oppres-*

sion of Landlords; the Impossibility of paying Rent, without Money or Trade; the Want of common Sustenance, with neither House nor Cloaths, to cover them from the Inclemencies of Weather; and the most inevitable Prospect of intailing the like, or greater Miseries upon their Breed for ever.

I PROFESS, in the Sincerity of my Heart, that I have not the least personal Interest, in endeavouring to promote this necessary Work; having no other Motive than the *publick Good of my Country*, *by advancing our Trade*, *providing for Infants*, *relieving the Poor*, *and giving some Pleasure to the Rich*. I have no Children, by which I can propose to get a single Penny; the youngest being nine Years old, and my Wife past Child-bearing.

The NOTES.

A Tale of a Tub

1.5. *two or three Treatises:* William King's *Remarks on the Tale of a Tub* (1704) and William Wotton's *Observations upon the Tale of a Tub* (1705). Swift's *Apology* was first printed in the 1710 edition of the *Tale*, and in this edition he also includes some of Wotton's remarks in the form of footnotes.

2.24. *Nondum . . . Hostis:* Lucan, *De bello civili*, i. 23: 'You have never yet been lacking for an enemy.'

3.13. *another Book: A Letter concerning Enthusiasm to My Lord* *** [Somers], by the Third Earl of Shaftesbury. Published 1708.

3.25. *the tritest Maxim: Corruptio optimi pessima* (The best, corrupted, becomes the worst), a very ancient saying.

3.32. *L'Estrange:* Sir Roger L'Estrange (1616–1704), journalist.

3.35. *one of his Prefaces: Discourse Concerning Satire* (prefixed to his translation of Juvenal).

4.35. *his Book about the Contempt of the Clergy:* John Eachard's *The Grounds & Occasions of the Contempt of the Clergy and Religion Enquired into* (1670). The book gave rise to many attacks, to which Eachard replied in a further publication.

5.2. *Marvel's Answer to Parker:* Samuel Parker (later Bishop of Oxford) published in 1670 *A Discourse of Ecclesiastical Politie*; Andrew Marvell's answer was *The Rehearsal Transpos'd* (1672–1673).

5.3. *The Earl of Orrery's Remarks: Dr. Bentley's Dissertations on the Epistles of Phalaris, and the Fables of Aesop, examin'd by the Honourable Charles Boyle, Esq.* (1698). Boyle became Fourth Earl of Orrery in 1703.

5.17. *One . . . from an unknown hand:* King's *Remarks*.

5.29. *The other . . . of a graver Character:* William Wotton, who was in holy orders.

6.1. *had . . . drawn his Pen against a certain Great Man:* Wotton in *Reflections upon Ancient and Modern Learning* (1694) attacked Sir William Temple, who had supported the Ancients in his *Essay upon Ancient and Modern Learning* (1692).

6.9 *Idem trecenti juravimus:* Florus, *Epitoma*, i. 10. 6: 'We three hundred have made the same vow.'

6.12. *another Antagonist:* Richard Bentley.

7.4. *a Letter of . . . Buckingham:* Buckingham's letter 'To Mr. Clifford, on his Humane Reason'.

7.13. *Alsatia:* Part of Whitefriars. Swift attributes to this district the origin of slang terms such as 'banter'.

8.5. *the Answerer and his Friend:* Wotton and Bentley.

8.28. *Min-ellius . . . Farnaby:* Jean Minell (1625–83), a Dutch classical scholar; Thomas Farnaby (1575?–1647), classical scholar and grammarian.

8.30. *Optat . . . piger:* Horace, *Ep.* I. xiv. 43: 'The slow ox wishes for the trappings of the horse.'

9.15. *the Bookseller's Preface:* See *The Bookseller to the Reader*, p. 17.

9.31. *A Fragment: A Discourse Concerning the Mechanical Operation of the Spirit. A Fragment.*

10.28. *White-Fryars:* See note 7.13, above.

12.1. *a Prostitute Bookseller . . . a foolish paper:* Edmund Curll's *Complete Key* to the *Tale* (1710). Curll was a publisher of pirated editions.

13. LORD SOMMERS: Lord Somers was Chancellor of England in 1697, and a great patron of learning.

14.2. *Detur dignissimo:* 'Let it be given to the worthiest.' An adaptation of a common Latin phrase.

14.21. *prodigious Number of . . . Stairs:* It was usual to speak of unsuccessful writers as forced by poverty to live in garret rooms.

15.18ff. *an old Beaten Story . . . :* Somers was noted for his calm good humour.

15.28. *your Enemies . . . :* Somers was impeached, but acquitted, in 1701.

15.33. *a late Reign:* William III's.

17.5. *the second* [*Treatise*]: *The Battle of the Books.*

17.24. *Don Quixot . . . and other Authors:* Several translations of such works claimed to adapt them to contemporary taste.

19.5. *the Person* (*it seems*) *to whose care . . . :* Time.

19.34. *the Center:* the centre of the earth: a usual meaning at that time.

20.20. *Great Numbers . . . to Moloch:* Children were burned alive as sacrifices to Moloch.

20.28. *the Laurel:* poetic fame, or perhaps more precisely the Poet Laureateship.

21.6. *uncontroulable:* irrefutable. Compare the title of Swift's *Maxims Controlled in Ireland.*

21.12. *The Originals were posted . . . :* The title pages of new books were pasted up by way of advertisement.

22.14. *Nahum Tate:* appointed Poet Laureate in 1692.

22.19. *Tom Durfey:* popular dramatist and song writer (1653–1723).

22.21. Rymer and Dennis were well-known literary critics.

22.23. *a full and true Account:* Bentley's preface to the 1699 edition of his *Dissertation on the Epistles of Phalaris.*

22.29. *a good sizeable Volume against . . . : Reflections upon Ancient and Modern Learning* (1697) against Temple, who as supporter of the Ancients is also the friend of Time.

23.1. *A Character of the present Set of Wits . . . :* See the first of the 'Treatises wrote by the same Author'.

24.22ff. Among the many Modern errors laughed at in the *Tale* is the theory that the universe, including man, is nothing but matter in motion, and that man is motivated wholly by self-love. The influential Thomas Hobbes formulated this theory in *Leviathan* (1651), and built upon it an argument for political absolutism. Hobbes's attitudes are parodied in Chapter II, the Clothes philosophy.

25.3. *a Tale of a Tub:* The phrase meant a nonsensical story.

25.23. *the School of Salivation:* a reference to the prevalence of venereal disease, treated by inducing salivation by means of mercury.

26.6. *Insigne . . . ore alio:* Horace, *Odes* III. xxv. 7–8.

26.19. *Mercury:* used here as (a) a common metaphor for wit, (b) the metal. To 'fix' is to convert it to a solid. The term is taken from alchemy, to which Modern wit is thus compared.

26.30. *Refiners:* another alchemical term.

28.12 *Leicester-Fields:* now Leicester Square.

29.26. *first Monarch of this Island:* James I, first monarch of the whole island (Scotland as well as England).

30.33. *all Pork, with a little variety of Sawce:* the same common material, however disguised. The story exists in many forms and had become proverbial.

31.19f. '*That all are gone astray . . .*': Psalm xiv. 3.

31.24. *Splendida bilis:* Horace, *Sat.* II. iii. 141.

31.28. *Covent-Garden:* A place notorious for assignations.

31.29. *White Hall:* then a royal palace, and a centre of government accordingly.

31.30. *Inns of Court:* Law centre.

31.31. *City:* the commercial section of London.

32.15. *A Panegyrick upon the World:* See the fifth of the 'Treatises wrote by the same Author'.

33.9–10. Virgil, *Aeneid* VI. 128–9. The translation is Dryden's.

33.12. *Edifices in the Air:* philosophic systems.

33.15. *suspended in a Basket . . . :* Aristophanes, *The Clouds*.

34.26. *Senes . . . recedant:* Horace, *Sat.* I. i. 31: 'So that old men may sink into a secure repose'.

34.36. *some proper mystical Number:* Mystical or hermetical writers often regarded a particular number or numbers as the key to the universe. Three, seven, and nine were especially favoured.

35.7. *a Panegyrical Essay . . . :* See the fourth of the 'Treatises wrote by the same Author'.

35.13. *That made of Timber from the Sylva Caledonia:* The allusion is to the Scottish Church, much favoured by the Dissenters.

35.23. *Ladders:* those to the gallows. Condemned men often made lengthy farewell speeches.

35.30. Dunton (1659–1733) was editor of the *Athenian Mercury*.

36.20–21. Lucretius, *De Rerum Natura*, iv. 526–7. The translation is by Creech.

37.14ff. *Now this Physico-logical Scheme . . . :* a mockery of those writers of the seventeenth century and earlier to whom everything was a type or symbol.

38.1ff. *Of Poetry, because . . . :* A psalm was sung at executions.

38.11. *Grub-Street:* a real street near Moorfields, but used metaphorically to apply to the hack writers who lived poorly in such streets.

38.26. *Gresham:* The Royal Society met in Gresham College until 1710.

39.23. *Briguing:* intriguing (from French *briguer*).

40.25. *Pythagoras . . . Socrates:* all said to have been ugly men.

40.35. *Exantlation: exantlare*, to draw out, as water from a well.

40.38. *the History of Reynard the Fox:* an old series of beast stories, often used for political satire.

41.12. *of Tom Thumb:* another old popular story.

41.16. *Artephius:* a skilled alchemist ('Adeptus'). The terms that follow are alchemical: Reincrudation = reduction; *via humida* = the humid way; Dragons = sulphur and mercury.

41.26ff. *The Hind and the Panther:* Dryden's Catholic apologia. Tommy Potts is a character in a popular ballad.

42.16. *Meal-Tubs:* the Meal-tub Plot of 1679; one of the apparently invented plots of the time.

43.24. *a Multiplicity of God-fathers:* Dryden's translation of Virgil was dedicated to three patrons.

44. Note †. *Lambin:* a learned French writer of commentaries on classical authors, who lived from 1516 to 1572. The note of course is Swift's.

45.14. *Bulks:* a bulk is a stall outside a shop.

45.17. *Locket's:* a fashionable eating-house at Charing Cross.

46.12. *a Goose for his Ensign:* the tailor's iron, whose handle was shaped like a goose's neck.

46.14. *Jupiter Capitolinus:* The sacred geese at Jupiter's temple on the Capitoline Hill saved Rome from attack by giving the alarm.

46.15. *Hell:* a term used for the place where the tailor throws scraps of cloth.

46.21. *that Creature . . . humane Gore:* the louse, alluding to the proverbial phrase 'to prick a louse' = to be a tailor.

47.5. *Water-Tabby:* watered silk.

48.6. *ex traduce:* the theological doctrine of traduction, according to which the soul is transmitted from the parents, as is the body. The opponents of the doctrine held that the soul is newly created at birth.

48.7ff. *proved by Scripture:* Acts 17: 28; 1 Cor. 15: 28.

48.24. *Race:* characteristic flavour (strictly, applied to wines; and here, like 'vein', metaphorical).

49.13. *Ruelles:* properly, the passage between bed and wall. In France, where it was fashionable for ladies to receive in their bedrooms, it came to mean such a bedroom or boudoir.

49.19. *Sculler:* Scullers or sculls were slower boats, with consequently cheaper fare.

50.3. *Temper:* middle course.

51.25. *Nuncupatory:* by word of mouth; referring here to Church tradition as opposed to the written word for Scripture.

55.1. *Points:* laces used for fastening.

57.14. *Zoilus . . . Tigellius:* Zoilus was a critic of Homer, Tigellius of Horace. Both were regarded as carping and fault-finding.

58.1ff. The references in this paragraph are to various labours of Hercules.

61.2. *our Scythian Ancestors:* The Scots were thought to have been probably descended from the Scythians.

61.13–14. Lucretius, vi. 786–7. The translation is Creech's.

62.31. *the Composition of a Man:* alluding to the proverbial 'Nine tailors make a man'.

65.16. *Fonde:* foundation.

65.17. *Projector:* a particularly pejorative word in Swift. In the usage of the time it includes makers of mechanical, scientific, and financial 'projects'.

66.7. *at a very great Penny-worth:* very cheaply.

66.27. *Repeating Poets:* poets who love to recite their own verses.

67.8ff. *an Office of Ensurance:* Indulgences are here seen as insurance against hell-fire, and so parallel to the fire insurance companies, of which the Friendly Society was one.

68.2. *Pimperlin pimp:* a corruption of a French term for an imaginary powder of magical power.

68.4. *Spargefaction:* sprinkling.

68.25. *the Mettall of their Feet:* their leaden seals (*bullae*).

69.8–10. Horace, *Ars Poetica* 2–4. He gives as an example of muddled creation a hypothetical painting in which varied feathers are added to other creatures and a woman is given a fish's tail.

68.11. *Fishes Tails:* The allusion is properly to Papal Briefs (less formal than Bulls) which were sealed not with the leaden *bulla* but with the Pope's private seal of St Peter the Fisherman and the words *sub annulo piscatoris*.

70.16. *Man's Man: servus servorum Dei*, servant of the servants of God; a title used by the Pope.

71.22. *Boutade:* a sudden movement, as a sudden jerk by a horse.

77.7–8. Lucretius, i. 141–2: 'It persuades one to undertake any labour and to stay awake through the peaceful nights.'

77.19ff. *a very strange, new and important Discovery:* not, of course, new at all, but a version of the Horatian commonplace that literature should both instruct and please.

78.5f. *in grave Dispute . . . :* The supporters of Modern achievement sometimes claimed that the Moderns were the true Ancients, since the modern world is some centuries older than the ancient world. The reference is also to Bentley's refutation of the genuineness of texts attributed to the Ancients Aesop and Phalaris.

78.21f. *balneo Mariae: bain-marie,* double saucepan. *Q.S.: quantum sufficit.*

78.28. *Catholick:* universally applicable.

79.16. *Opus magnum:* the alchemical 'Great Work', the transmutation of metals.

79.21f. *Vix crederem . . . vocem:* 'I would scarcely have believed that this author even heard the sound that fire makes.' The *Sphaera Pyroplastica* is the sphere of fire.

79.26. *a Save-all:* a candle-holder which enabled candle stubs to be burned to the end.

80.20. *the Compass . . . :* All these are modern inventions, on which the Moderns based many of their claims to equality with the Ancients.

84.15. *Complexions:* characters, temperaments.

86.25. *that lock'd up his Drink:* presumably the denial of the cup, in the Communion service, to the laity.

87.8. *Kennel:* gutter.

87.26. *dispensable:* permissible.

88.9. *Garnish:* money extorted from new prisoners, to provide drinks for the rest or as a jailer's fee.

88.11. *Mobile: mobile vulgus,* or mob. Swift detested the shortening of the term.

89.9. A near-quotation from Lucretius, i. 934, which reads 'Musaeo' for 'Mellaeo': 'Touching all things with the charm of the Muse.'

90.1. *an Iliad in a Nut-shell:* There is a story in Pliny about a minutely written *Iliad.*

91.31. *like Hercules's Oxen:* Cacus stole cattle from Hercules and drove them backwards to confuse the search.

92.34f. *Sed quorum pudenda . . . pertingentia:* 'but whose genitals were thick, and reached to their heels'.

93.32. *everlasting Chains of Darkness:* books in libraries were still often chained in place. In the Bodleian they began to be unchained in the mid-eighteenth century.

95.6. Lucretius, v. 107: 'May governing Fortune turn this far from us' ('Heaven forbid').

95.7. *Anima Mundi:* The hermeticist Thomas Vaughan, especially ridiculed by Swift, refers to the '*Anima Mundi*, or the universall *spirit* of Nature'.

95.31. *three distinct Anima's:* Compare the traditional vegetative, sensitive, and rational souls.

96.26. *Vessels:* a usual term, of Biblical origin, among the Dissenters.

97.25. *the Adoration of Latria:* worship of a supreme God. In view of the imagery which is developed in this chapter, it is likely that a reference to *latrina* is also present. The *Almighty-North* is the wind from Scotland.

97.27f. *Omnium . . . celebrant:* 'Of all the Gods they chiefly worship Boreas' (the North Wind).

97.33. *Σκοτία:* Scotland.

98.13. *Barrels:* The Dissenters' pulpits were often called tubs on account of their shape. The title of the *Tale* alludes to them.

98.22f. *ex adytis, and penetralibus:* 'from the holy of holies'.

99.34. *like a dead Bird of Paradise:* It was anciently believed that the Bird of Paradise had no feet and so continued on the wing till death.

100.18. *the Camelion sworn Foe to Inspiration:* popularly supposed to live on air, and hence (like the windmill) the enemy of the Aeolist deity. The chameleon has been interpreted by some as the Church of England, and the windmill as the monarchy.

100.27. *Laplanders:* The Lapland witches captured and sold winds.

101.2. *Delphos:* a form of Delphi, where the oracular priestess breathed vapours from the earth.

103.6. *A certain Great Prince:* Henry IV of France.

103.29. *an absent Female:* The reference is presumably to Henriette, Princesse de Condé.

103.34–35. Lucretius, iv. 1058 and 1055: 'He seeks that body by which his mind is wounded with love. He seeks that which wounded him, and desires to unite with it.'

104. 8–9. 'The most hateful cause of the war' (a woman). Horace, *Sat.* I. iii. 107.

104.11. *a mighty King:* Louis XIV.

105.26. *Clinamena: Clinamen* is Lucretius' word for the bias, or deviation from a straight course, to which Epicurus attributed the concourse of atoms.

106.19f. *Est quod gaudeas . . . viderere:* 'There is reason for you to be glad that you came to the place where your knowledge was recognized.'

107.13. *to cut the Feather:* to make nice distinctions.

107.17. *Jack of Leyden:* Johann Bockholdt, known as John or Jack of Leyden, leader of the

Anabaptist sect in the sixteenth century.

111.10. *Ingenium par negotiis:* a good head for business.

111.19. *Bedlam:* the insane asylum, originally Bethlehem Hospital.

111.25. The omission of the word 'Ecclesiastical' here was suggested in the eighteenth century.

113.11. *Warwick-Lane:* the Royal College of Physicians was in Warwick Lane from 1674 to 1825.

115.13f. *Will's Coffee-House . . . Moor-Fields:* Will's was the resort of the wits, Gresham College the home of the Royal Society. Bedlam was situated in Moorfields.

116.31. *Rectifier of Saddles:* The allusion is to the proverbial phrase about putting the saddle on the right horse.

122.25ff. *a Passage . . . which seemed to forbid it:* Guthkelch and Smith suggest Rev. 22: 11.

124.28ff. *an antient Temple:* Stonehenge. *Gothick:* barbarous.

125.15. *the Spanish Accomplishment:* Spanish because of the aldermen who bray in *Don Quixote*.

126.2. *would often leap . . . into the Water:* baptismal immersion.

128.25. Horace, *Sat.* II. iii. 71: 'Yet the wicked Proteus will escape all these bonds.'

129.10. *improve the Growth of Ears:* The reference is to the Puritans who cut their hair very close (hence called Roundheads) and so made their ears seem unduly large.

130.9. *general History of Ears:* See the seventh of the 'Treatises wrote by the same Author'.

131.9. *a Spunging-house:* for the confinement of debtors.

131.14f. *How he got upon a great Horse:* The Dissenter Edwin, Lord Mayor in 1697, would have ridden in the procession the city horse, as the state coach was not yet in use.

132.3ff. *that Noble Jesuit . . . :* The reference is to the *Avertissement* to the *Histoire de M. Constance . . . Par le Père d'Orléans, de la Compagnie de Jésus* (1690).

133.32 *ut plenus vitae conviva:* Lucretius, iii. 938: 'A contented guest after the meal of life.'

THE BATTLE OF THE BOOKS

139.5ff. *an Essay of Sir William Temple's: Essay upon the Ancient and Modern Learning* (1690). *answer'd by . . . with an Appendix by . . . :* the second edition of Wotton's *Reflections upon Ancient and Modern Learning* (1697). The appendix is *Dissertations upon the Epistles of Phalaris* in which the *Epistles* are shown to be spurious.

139.12. *to which, Mr. Boyle replyed at large: Dr. Bentley's Dissertations*

. . . *Examin'd by the Honourable Charles Boyle, Esq.* (1698).

139.18. *the Books in St. James's Library:* Bentley was librarian at the Royal Library in St James's Palace.

141.1ff. The marginal reference is to Vincent Wing's almanac, printed by Mary Clark. *Ephem.* = *ephemeris. opt. Edit.* = *optima Editio* (a phrase more proper to a learned work).

142.30. . . . *especially towards the East:* The reference is to Temple's argument that the learning of the ancient East reached the Moderns through the medium of Greek and Latin authors.

144.15. *Soul transmigrates . . . to inform them:* inform with spirit, animate.

144.38. *held fast with a Chain:* large and important volumes in libraries were chained until the eighteenth century.

145.24. *chiefly renowned for his Humanity:* Bentley was in fact famous equally for his learning and for his roughness and lack of courtesy or 'humanity'.

145.26f. *two of the Antient Chiefs:* Phalaris and Aesop, whose attributed works Bentley showed to be spurious.

146.21. *Withers:* George Wither (1588–1667), a minor poet whose later work was bad enough to arouse derision in Swift's time.

146.27f. *light Horse:* poets. *heavy-armed Foot:* historians.

147.2ff. See above, *A Tale of a Tub*, n. 78.5f.

147.36ff. . . . *after the Modern way of Fortification:* The supporters of the Moderns used this art as an example of their superiority to the Ancients in mathematical skills. The *Spider* later refers to this.

150.4ff. *So that in short . . . :* The *Bee* gives, in its own terms, a version of the classical aesthetic.

150.26 *mistook Him for a Modern:* The reference is to Bentley's view that the *Fables* are late and spurious work.

152.4. *Despreaux:* Nicolas Boileau Despreaux, poet and critic (1636–1711). *Bowmen:* Philosophers.

152.8. *Paracelsus:* natural philosopher and alchemist (c. 1490–1541)

152.11. *Harvey:* William Harvey (1578–1657), discoverer of the circulation of the blood, leads the Dragoons (medical writers).

152.16f. *Giuccardine . . . Cambden:* all historians of the fifteenth and sixteenth centuries.

152.18. *Regiomontanus:* Johann Muller of Königsberg (1436–1476), astronomer. *John Wilkins:* author of *The Discovery of a World in the Moone* (1614–1704).

152.22. *Lestrange:* See above, *A Tale of a Tub*, n. 3.32.

152.29. *Vossius:* Isaak Vossius (1618–89) and his father Gerhard were both fine scholars.

155.1. *Gresham and Covent-Garden:*

The Royal Society met at Gresham College. Will's, the coffee-house where the wits met, was in Covent Garden.

156.13ff. *Des-Cartes . . . into his own Vortex:* Descartes at death is drawn into his own hypothesis of vortices.

156.23. *Gondibert:* Sir William Davenant's epic poem (1650), of which its author had a high opinion.

157.7ff. *Wesley:* Samuel Wesley (1662–1735), versifier and father of John and Charles. His most ambitious poem was an epic on the life of Christ. *Perrault . . . Fontenelle:* Charles Perrault (1628–1703) and Bernard de Fontenelle (1657–1757), leading French supporters of the Moderns.

157.28. *the Lady in a Lobster:* part of the stomach of a lobster.

158.9ff. Sir Richard Blackmore (c. 1650–1729) was a writer of very long and dull epics. Aesculapius saves him because of his skill as a physician.

158.22. *Creech:* Thomas Creech (1659–1700) translated Horace and Lucretius.

158.26. *Ogleby:* John Ogleby (1600–1676), whose translations of Homer and Virgil were much ridiculed.

158.28. *Oldham:* John Oldham (1653–83), satirist and writer of Pindaric odes.

158.29. *Afra the Amazon:* Aphra Behn (1640–89), novelist, dramatist, writer of Pindarics.

159.9ff. The shield of Venus is *The Mistress*, the collected love poems of Abraham Cowley (1618–67) who also wrote Pindaric odes.

160.3. *a thousand incoherent Pieces:* because Bentley's work contained numerous quotations, and because he studied the fragmentary remains of Greek poets.

160.5. *an Etesian Wind:* a north-west wind which blows in summer in the Mediterranean.

160.10. *atramentous:* inky, dark.

161.2. *Scaliger:* Joseph Justus Scaliger (1540–1609), a great scholar and literary critic, son of J. C. Scaliger.

161.20. *Aldrovandus:* Ulisse Aldrovandi (1522–1605), writer of a number of folio volumes on natural history.

162.10ff. Phalaris (c. 570 B.C.), tyrant of Sicily, was reputed to have roasted victims in a brazen bull. He was the supposed author of the *Epistles* shown by Bentley to be spurious. Aesop's beast fables were also exposed by Bentley as later work.

162.33f. *The one he could not distinguish:* Charles Boyle.

163.23ff. *Apollo enraged . . . put on the shape of —:* Guthkelch and Smith suggest that the reference is to Atterbury, who helped Boyle with the *Examination*.

164.6ff. Boyle's edition of the *Epistles* of Phalaris (1693).

164.18f. *first Bentley threw a Spear:* Bentley's first *Dissertation* (1697), a very learned work which in fact was not, of course, refuted by Boyle's reply.

A DISCOURSE CONCERNING THE MECHANICAL OPERATION OF THE SPIRIT

171. NEW-HOLLAND: the name given at this time to Australia, the western shore of which had been navigated by the Dutch by 1665. The joke is carried on below in the references to *Iroquois Virtuosi* and the *Literati* of *Tobinambou* (the latter are a Brazilian tribe).

173.22. *the two Examples mentioned already:* As well as that of Mahomet, perhaps Balaam's ass (Num. xxii: 21) is hinted at here.

174.21. *The Planetary Worlds:* included in this list of hopeless and unrealistic endeavours because of the idea that the planets might be inhabited. See in particular *The Discovery of a World in the Moone* (1638) by John Wilkins, one of the founders of the Royal Society and later Bishop of Chester.

174.27. *upon Holy Ground:* Guthkelch and Smith suggest a reference to Exod. iii: 5.

175.27. *the Scythians:* Thought by some historians to be the ancestors of the Scots, whom Swift thinks of as especially proficient in the Mechnical Operation.

176.2ff. *Round-heads . . . pair of Cizars:* The short-cropped hair of the seventeenth-century Puritans earned them their name.

176.21ff. *the following Fundamental . . . :* Compare Sir Thomas Browne, *Vulgar Errors*, III. ix: 'that axiom in Philosophy that the generation of one thing, is the corruption of another'. The idea derives from Aristotle.

176.38. *Assembly of Modern Saints:* The Dissenters often called themselves the saints.

178.3. *Jauguis:* The footnote reference is to *Suite des Memoires du St Bernier, sur l'Empire du grand Mogol* (Paris, 1671), pp. 57, 60–1.

180.14–15. Horace, *Odes*, I. xviii. 10–11: 'When in their desire they distinguish right and wrong only by the narrow line of their passions'.

181.17. *the Picture of Hobbes's Leviathan:* See the engraved title-page of *Leviathan* (1651).

182.1. *hamated:* furnished with hooks.

183.2. *Thy Word is a Lanthorn . . . :* Psalm cxix, v. 105. Edwin was a Presbyterian.

184.8. *a Banbury Saint:* Banbury was a famous centre of Puritanism.

184.17. *Rippon Spurs:* Ripon was famous for its manufacture of spurs.

185.12ff. *for we read, how the Persian Beast . . . :* Herodotus, iii. 85–6.

186.14ff. *These Feasts were celebrated . . . :* Diodorus Siculus, i. 97. 286.

186.29. *there was not one Vine in all Egypt:* Herodotus, ii. 77.

186.33. *the Egyptian Osyris:* Diodorus Siculus, i. 15; iii. 62.

186.38. *first inventor of the Mitre:* Ibid., iv. 4.

187.26ff. *in a certain Town of Attica . . . :* the festival in honour of Dionysus at Brauron.

188.14f. *John of Leyden:* Johann Bockholdt, Anabaptist leader. *David George:* or Joris (1501–1556), Anabaptist and founder of the Family of Love. *Adam Neuster:* German theologian, coverted to Mohammedanism (d. 1576).

188.27. *Family of Love, Sweet Singers of Israel:* These two sects won over some converts from among the Puritans in sixteenth- and seventeenth-century England.

190.2ff. *the Story of that Philosopher:* This philosopher is an ancient example. The story was sometimes attached to Thales. See Diogenes Laertius, I. i. 8. 34; Plato, *Theatetus.*

A Meditation upon a Broom-Stick

193. BOYLE: A son of the first Earl of Cork, he was a founding member of the Royal Society, a brilliant physicist and an actively pious moralist (1627–1691).

193.14. *Surely Mortal Man is a Broomstick:* The comparison of man to an inverted tree was a Platonic commonplace.

A Tritical Essay upon the Faculties of the Mind

195. TRITICAL: because it is a tissue of 'stale Topicks and thread-bare Quotations'.

196.4. Horace, *De Arte Poetica,* 5. *Spectatum admissi risum teneatis amici?:* 'Once you saw this, my friends, could you keep from laughing?'

197.7. 'You may drive Nature out with a pitch-fork, but she will soon return.' Horace, *Epistles* I. x. 24.

200.9. 'As long as you are fortunate, you will be well provided with friends.' Ovid, *Tristia,* I. 9.5.

MR COLLINS'S DISCOURSE OF FREE-THINKING

204.6. *the Kit-Cat and Hannover Clubs:* These were places of Whig resort.

206.21. *Dr. Sacheverell:* Henry Sacheverell (1674–1724), a High Church Anglican clergyman, delivered two strongly Tory sermons in 1709; he was impeached by the Whig government and became a Tory hero.

207.13f. *such Divines as . . . :* all High Church Tory divines.

207.25f. *William Penn . . . Muggletonian:* The former (1644–1718) was an advocate of toleration and founder of Pennsylvania: his book, *The New Witnesses proved old Hereticks* (1672), was provoked by Lodowick Muggleton (1609–1698), an obscure sectarian leader, who attacked the Quakers.

207.29. *Mr. Whiston:* William Whiston (1667–1752), a distinguished mathematician who held a chair at Cambridge. In 1710 he was expelled from the University for Arianism.

210. 27f. *Dr. Henry Moor . . . Doctor Tillotson:* Henry More (1614–1687), one of the Cambridge Platonists, and John Tillotson (1630–94), Archbishop of Canterbury from 1691. Neither, of course, was a 'free-thinker' in the meaning implied here.

211.29. *Passive Obedience:* to the reigning monarch.

213.7f. *Mr. Gildon . . . Mr. Toland:* all prominent Deists, of whom John Toland (1670–1722), was perhaps the most able. His *Christianity not Mysterious* (1696) created a great sensation and was burned by the public hangman in Ireland.

213.28. *Mr. Creech:* Thomas Creech (1650–1700), headmaster at Sherborne and rector of Welwyn.

AN ARGUMENT AGAINST ABOLISHING CHRISTIANITY

225.5f. *lay wagers against the Union:* the Act of Union between England and Scotland, 1707. In 1708 an Act of Parliament was introduced to prevent laying wagers 'of great sums of money, upon several contingencies relating to the present war, and other matters relating to government'.

226.28f. *nominal and real Trinitarians:* Swift discusses such distinctions in his sermon *On the Trinity*.

227.1. *the Proposal of Horace:* Horace's *Epode* XVI; in *Odes*, II, xvi, Horace points out that changing the sky over one's head does not necessarily change one's inner being also.

227.8f. *nominal Christianity:* i.e. those who avoid the Test Act by observing occasional, though merely token, communion in the Anglican church, in order to qualify for offices within the state.

228.8. *Deorum offensa Diis curae:* an inaccurate version of Tacitus, *Annals*, I, 73, 'the gods must look to their own wrongs'.

228.18. *the Allies:* England's allies in the War of the Spanish Succession included Holland, Austria, Savoy, Prussia and Portugal.

228. 36. *Asgill, Tindal, Toland, Coward:* all united by Swift's contempt for rationalist critics of revelation, John Asgill (1670–1722), an eccentric deist and convert from Catholicism; Matthew Tindal (1657–1733), a prominent deist and sometime Catholic, author of the sensational *Rights of the Christian Church Asserted* (1706) and *Christianity as Old as the Creation* (1730); John Toland (1670–1722), deist author of *Christianity Not Mysterious* (1696), which provoked the Deist-Orthodox clash (Toland had also been Catholic); William Coward (c. 1657–1725), physician and deist. All but Coward had their books burnt by the public hangman.

229.6. *Empson and Dudley:* willing instruments of Henry VII's vigorous taxation policies.

229.10. *ten Thousand Parsons:* the Anglican clergy.

230.9. *common Dormitories:* lodging-houses.

231.15f. *Heydukes . . . Mamalukes, Mandarins . . . Potshaws:* exotic (Turkish and Chinese) parallels equivalent to robber, slave, bureaucrat, nobleman, respectively.

231.20. *the Monument:* Wren's memorial commemorating the Great Fire of London (1666).

231.23f. *Margarita . . . Mrs. Tofts . . . Valentini:* singers in the fashionable Italian opera (Valentini was a male soprano).

231.26. *Prasini and Veneti:* Roman factions whose rivalry led to civil war.

233.8f. *Inventions of Politicians:* Swift describes the theory as a 'common Atheistical Notion' in *The Examiner*, no. 43 (1710).

233.28. *Wickets:* small gates.

234.35. *choqued:* shocked.

234.36. *daggled-tail:* slovenly.

236.2. *Jus Divinum:* literally, the divine law which, in a way not easily defined or definable, entitled Anglican bishops to the government of the church.

236.20f. *ingenious Author:* Matthew Tindal (see note above).

237.12. *Sorites:* a term from logic; an abridged way of stating a series of syllogisms, of which the conclusion of each is a premiss of the succeeding.

A VINDICATION OF THE BEGGAR'S OPERA

239.2. *The Beggar's Opera*, by Swift's friend John Gay (1685–1732), was produced, with extraordinary success, in 1728.

240.32f. *the Character that gives Horace the Preference to Juvenal:* This is the traditional differentiation between the two great Latin satirists.

242.7f. *faulty, with Regard to Courtiers and Statesmen:* Gay, a Tory, is in much of his work (including *The Beggar's Opera*) wittily satiric of Walpole and his Whig government.

242.10. *the Duke of Cumberland:* William Augustus (1721–65), second son of George II, the future 'Butcher' Cumberland of Culloden.

A MODEST PROPOSAL

259.31. *Salmanaazor:* George Psalmanayar (1679?–1763), a literary impostor. Born in southern France, he posed as a Formosan and wrote a description of the island. In later years he reformed his ways and became a considerable Hebraic scholar.